THE
BONE SEASON
SAMANTHA SHANNON

Praise for THE BONE SEASON Series

Sunday Times Bestseller

New York Times Bestseller

Asian Age Bestseller

USA Today Bestseller

Indie Bestseller List

Daily Mail Book of the Year

Stylist Book of the Year

Huffington Post Book of the Year

Nominated for a FutureBook Innovation Award

Bookseller Ones to Watch

Today Book Club Pick

GoodReads Choice Awards Fantasy Nominee

Amazon Rising Star

A Note on the Author

SAMANTHA SHANNON was born in west London in 1991. She started writing at the age of fifteen. Between 2010 and 2013 she studied English Language and Literature at St Anne's College, Oxford. In 2013 she published *The Bone Season*, the first in a seven-book series. *The Bone Season* was a *New York Times*, a *Sunday Times* and an *Asian Age* bestseller, was picked as a Book of the Year by the *Daily Mail*, *Stylist* and *Huffington Post* and was named one of Amazon's 2013 Best Books of the Year. It has been translated into twenty-six languages and the film rights have been acquired by the Imaginarium Studios and 20th Century Fox. In 2014, Samantha Shannon was included on the *Evening Standard*'s Power 1000 list.

samanthashannon.co.uk/@say_shannon

By the Same Author

The Mime Order

The Song Rising

On the Merits of Unnaturalness

The Bone Season

Samantha Shannon

B L O O M S B U R Y

LONDON · NEW DELHI · NEW YORK · SYDNEY

For the dreamers

Bloomsbury Paperbacks
An imprint of Bloomsbury Publishing Plc

50 Bedford Square London WC1B 3DP UK
1385 Broadway New York NY 10018 USA
29 Earlsfort Terrace, Dublin 2, Ireland

www.bloomsbury.com

BLOOMSBURY and the Diana logo are trademarks of Bloomsbury Publishing Plc

The Bone Season first published in Great Britain 2013
The Pale Dreamer first published in Great Britain 2016

This paperback edition first published in 2017

The Bone Season © Samantha Shannon-Jones, 2013
The Pale Dreamer © Samantha Shannon-Jones, 2016

Illustrations copyright © by Emily Faccini, 2017

Samantha Shannon-Jones has asserted her right under the Copyright, Designs
and Patents Act, 1988, to be identified as Author of this work.

This is a work of fiction. Names and characters are the product of the author's imagination
and any resemblance to actual persons, living or dead, is entirely coincidental.

Excerpt from the Old Bailey Online, www.oldbaileyonline.org

British Library Cataloguing-in-Publication Data
A catalogue record for this book is available from the British Library.

ISBN: PB: 978-1-4088-8252-8
ePub: 978-1-4088-3644-6

6 8 10 9 7

Typeset by Hewer Text UK Ltd, Edinburgh
Printed and bound in Great Britain by CPI Group (UK) Ltd, Croydon CR0 4YY

MIX
Paper from
responsible sources
FSC® C020471
www.fsc.org

To find out more about our authors and books visit www.bloomsbury.com.
Here you will find extracts, author interviews, details of forthcoming
events and the option to sign up for our newsletters.

Besides this earth, and besides the race of men, there is an invisible world and a kingdom of spirits: that world is round us, for it is everywhere.

Charlotte Brontë

Contents

The Seven Orders of
CLAIRVOYANCE

According to On The Merits of Unnaturalness

I. SOOTHSAYERS

Purple

Require ritual objects (numa) to connect with the æther. Most often used to predict the future.

- Seers
- Common Soothsayers

II. AUGURS

Blue

Use organic matter, or elements, to connect with the æther. Most often used to predict the future.

- Vile Augurs
- Common Augurs

III. MEDIUMS

Green

Connect with the æther through spiritual possession. Subject to some degree of control by spirits.

- Trance Mediums
- Restive Mediums

IV. SENSORS

Yellow

Privy to the æther on a sensory and linguistic level. Can sometimes channel the æther.

- Gustant
- Sniffer
- Polyglot
- Whisperer

V. GUARDIANS

Orange

Have a higher degree of control over spirits than average and can bend ordinary ethereo-spatial limits.

- Binder
- Summoner
- Necromancer
- Exorcist

VI. FURIES

Orange-red

Subject to internal change when connecting with the æther, typically to the dreamscape.

- Sibyl
- Unreadable
- Berserker

VII. JUMPERS

Red

Able to affect the æther outside their own physical limits. Greater than average sensitivity to the æther.

- Dreamwalker
- Oracle

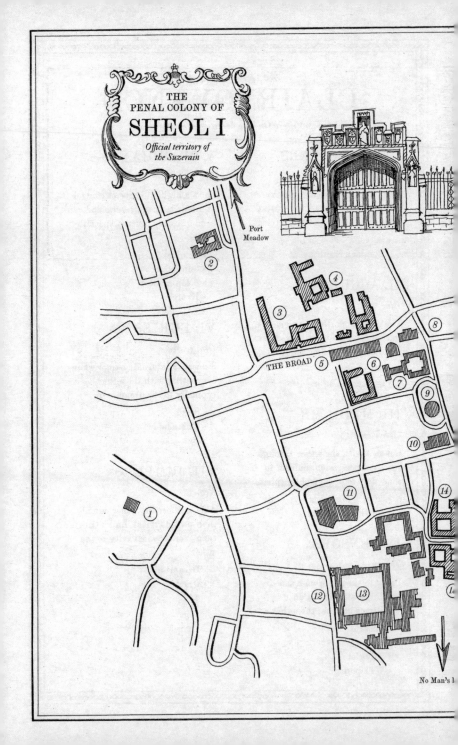

THE
PENAL COLONY OF
SHEOL I

*Official territory of
the Suzerain*

Port
Meadow

THE BROAD

No Man's l

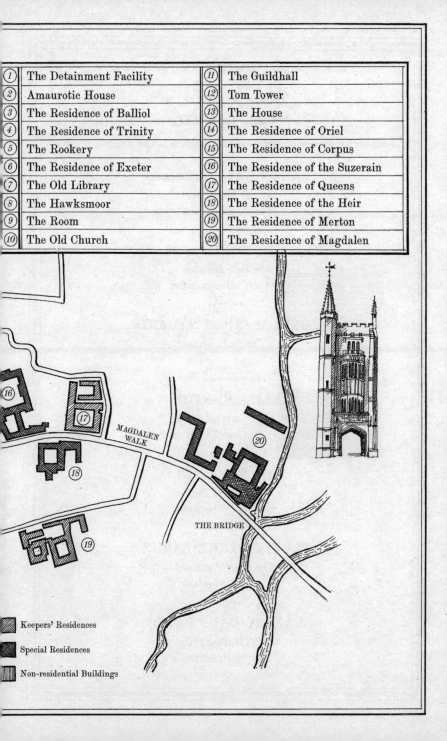

①	The Detainment Facility	⑪	The Guildhall
②	Amaurotic House	⑫	Tom Tower
③	The Residence of Balliol	⑬	The House
④	The Residence of Trinity	⑭	The Residence of Oriel
⑤	The Rookery	⑮	The Residence of Corpus
⑥	The Residence of Exeter	⑯	The Residence of the Suzerain
⑦	The Old Library	⑰	The Residence of Queens
⑧	The Hawksmoor	⑱	The Residence of the Heir
⑨	The Room	⑲	The Residence of Merton
⑩	The Old Church	⑳	The Residence of Magdalen

MAGDALEN WALK

THE BRIDGE

Keepers' Residences

Special Residences

Non-residential Buildings

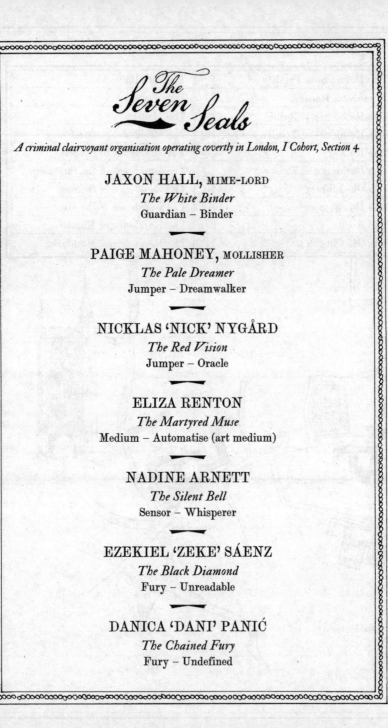

The Seven Seals

A criminal clairvoyant organisation operating covertly in London, I Cohort, Section 4

JAXON HALL, MIME-LORD
The White Binder
Guardian – Binder

———

PAIGE MAHONEY, MOLLISHER
The Pale Dreamer
Jumper – Dreamwalker

———

NICKLAS 'NICK' NYGÅRD
The Red Vision
Jumper – Oracle

———

ELIZA RENTON
The Martyred Muse
Medium – Automatise (art medium)

———

NADINE ARNETT
The Silent Bell
Sensor – Whisperer

———

EZEKIEL 'ZEKE' SÁENZ
The Black Diamond
Fury – Unreadable

———

DANICA 'DANI' PANIĆ
The Chained Fury
Fury – Undefined

The Curse

I like to imagine there were more of us in the beginning. Not many, I suppose. But more than there are now.

We are the minority the world does not accept. Not outside of fantasy, and even that's blacklisted. We look like everyone else. Sometimes we act like everyone else. In many ways, we *are* like everyone else. We are everywhere, on every street. We live in a way you might consider normal, provided you don't look too hard.

Not all of us know what we are. Some of us die without ever knowing. Some of us know, and we never get caught. But we're out there.

Trust me.

I had lived in that part of London that used to be called Islington since I was eight. I attended a private school for girls, leaving at sixteen to work. That was in the year 2056. AS 127, if you use the Scion calendar. It was expected of young men and women to scratch out a living wherever they could, which was usually behind a counter of one sort or another. There were plenty of jobs in the service industry. My father thought I would lead a simple life; that I was bright but unambitious, complacent with whatever work life threw at me.

My father, as usual, was wrong.

From the age of sixteen I had worked in the criminal underworld of Scion London – SciLo, as we called it on the streets. I worked among ruthless gangs of voyants, all willing to floor each other to survive. All part of a citadel-wide syndicate headed by the Underlord. Pushed to the edge of society, we were forced into crime to prosper. And so we became more hated. We made the stories true.

I had my little place in the chaos. I was a mollisher, the protégée of a mime-lord. My boss was a man named Jaxon Hall, the mime-lord responsible for the I-4 area. There were six of us in his direct employ. We called ourselves the Seven Seals.

I couldn't tell my father. He thought I was an assistant at an oxygen bar, a badly paid but legal occupation. It was an easy lie. He wouldn't have understood if I'd told him why I spent my time with criminals. He didn't know that I belonged with them. More than I belonged with him.

I was nineteen years old the day my life changed. Mine was a familiar name on the streets by that time. After a tough week at the black market, I'd planned to spend the weekend with my father. Jax didn't twig why I needed time off – for him, there was nothing worth our salt outside the syndicate – but he didn't have a family like I did. Not a living family, anyway. And although my father and I had never been close, I still felt I should keep in touch. A dinner here, a phone call there, a present at Novembertide. The only hitch was his endless list of questions. What job did I have? Who were my friends? Where was I living?

I couldn't answer. The truth was dangerous. He might have sent me to Tower Hill himself if he'd known what I really did. Maybe I should have told him the truth. Maybe it would have killed him. Either way, I didn't regret joining the syndicate. My line of work was dishonest, but it paid. And as Jax always said, better an outlaw than a stiff.

It was raining that day. My last day at work.

A life-support machine kept my vitals ticking over. I looked dead, and in a way I was: my spirit was detached, in part, from my body. It was a crime for which I could have faced the gallows.

I said I worked in the syndicate. Let me clarify. I was a hacker of sorts. Not a mind *reader*, exactly; more a mind radar, in tune with the workings of the æther. I could sense the nuances of dreamscapes and rogue spirits. Things outside myself. Things the average voyant wouldn't feel.

Jax used me as a surveillance tool. My job was to keep track of ethereal activity in his section. He would often have me check out other voyants, see if they were hiding anything. At first it had just been people in the room – people I could see and hear and touch – but soon he realised I could go further than that. I could sense things happening elsewhere: a voyant walking down the street, a gathering of spirits in the Garden. So long as I had life support, I could pick up on the æther within a mile radius of Seven Dials. So if he needed someone to dish the dirt on what was happening in I-4, you could bet your broads Jaxon would call yours truly. He said I had potential to go further, but Nick refused to let me try. We didn't know what it would do to me.

All clairvoyance was prohibited, of course, but the kind that made money was downright sin. They had a special term for it: *mime-crime*. Communication with the spirit world, especially for financial gain. It was mime-crime that the syndicate was built on.

Cash-in-hand clairvoyance was rife among those who couldn't get into a gang. We called it busking. Scion called it treason. The official method of execution for such crimes was nitrogen asphyxiation, marketed under the brand name NiteKind. I still remember

3

the headlines: PAINLESS PUNISHMENT: SCION'S LATEST MIRACLE. They said it was like going to sleep, like taking a pill. There were still public hangings, and the odd bit of torture for high treason.

I committed high treason just by breathing.

But back to that day. Jaxon had wired me up to life support and sent me out to reconnoitre the section. I'd been closing in on a local mind, a frequent visitor to Section 4. I'd tried my best to see his memories, but something had always stopped me. This dreamscape was unlike anything I'd ever encountered. Even Jax was stumped. From the layering of defence mechanisms I would have said its owner was several thousand years old, but that couldn't be it. This was something different.

Jax was a suspicious man. By rights a new clairvoyant in his section should have announced themselves to him within forty-eight hours. He said another gang must be involved, but none of the I-4 lot had the experience to block my scouting. None of them knew I could do it. It wasn't Didion Waite, who headed the second-largest gang in the area. It wasn't the starving buskers that frequented Dials. It wasn't the territorial mime-lords that specialised in ethereal larceny. This was something else.

Hundreds of minds passed me, flashing silver in the dark. They moved through the streets quickly, like their owners. I didn't recognise these people. I couldn't see their faces; just the barest edges of their minds.

I wasn't in Dials now. My perception was further north, though I couldn't pin down where. I followed the familiar sense of danger. The stranger's mind was close. It drew me through the æther like a glym jack with a lantern, darting over and under the other minds. Moving fast, as if the stranger sensed me. As if he was trying to run.

I shouldn't follow this light. I didn't know where it would lead me, and I'd already gone too far from Seven Dials.

Jaxon told you to find him. The thought was distant. *He'll be angry.* I

4

pressed ahead, moving faster than I ever could in my body. I pulled against the restraints of my physical location. I could make out the rogue mind now. Not silver, like the others: no, this was dark and cold, a mind of ice and stone. I shot towards it. He was so, *so* close . . . I couldn't lose him now . . .

Then the æther trembled around me and, in a heartbeat, he was gone. The stranger's mind was out of reach again.

Someone shook my body.

My silver cord – the link between my body and my spirit – was extremely sensitive. It was what allowed me to sense dreamscapes at a distance. It could also snap me back into my skin. When I opened my eyes, Dani was waving a penlight over my face. 'Pupil response,' she said to herself. 'Good.'

Danica. Our resident genius, second only to Jax in intellect. She was three years older than me and had all the charm and sensitivity of a sucker punch. Nick classified her as a sociopath when she was first employed. Jax said it was just her personality.

'Rise and shine, Dreamer.' She slapped my cheek. 'Welcome back to meatspace.'

The slap stung: a good, if unpleasant sign. I reached up to unfasten my oxygen mask.

The dark glint of the den came into focus. Jax's crib was a secret cave of contraband: forbidden films, music and books, all crammed together on dust-thickened shelves. There was a collection of penny dreadfuls, the kind you could pick up from the Garden on weekends, and a stack of saddle-stapled pamphlets. This was the only place in the world where I could read and watch and do whatever I liked.

'You shouldn't wake me like that,' I said. She knew the rules. 'How long was I there for?'

'Where?'

'Where do you think?'

Dani snapped her fingers. 'Right, of course – the æther. Sorry. Wasn't keeping track.'

Unlikely. Dani never lost track.

I checked the blue Nixie timer on the machine. Dani had made it herself. She called it the Dead Voyant Sustainment System, or DVS². It monitored and controlled my life functions when I sensed the æther at long range. My heart dropped when I saw the digits.

'Fifty-seven minutes.' I rubbed my temples. 'You let me stay in the æther for an hour?'

'Maybe.'

'An entire hour?'

'Orders are orders. Jax said he wanted you to crack this mystery mind by dusk. Have you done it?'

'I tried.'

'Which means you failed. No bonus for you.' She gulped down her espresso. 'Still can't believe you lost Anne Naylor.'

Trust her to bring that up. A few days before I'd been sent to the auction house to reclaim a spirit that rightfully belonged to Jax: Anne Naylor, the famous ghost of Farringdon. I'd been outbid.

'We were never going to get Naylor,' I said. 'Didion wouldn't let that gavel fall, not after last time.'

'Whatever you say. Don't know what Jax would have done with a poltergeist, anyway.' Dani looked at me. 'He says he's given you the weekend off. How'd you swing that?'

'Psychological reasons.'

'What does that mean?'

'It means you and your contraptions are driving me mad.'

She threw her empty cup at me. 'I take care of you, urchin. My contraptions can't run themselves. I could just walk out of here for my lunch break and let your sad excuse for a brain dry up.'

'It *could* have dried up.'

'Cry me a river. You know the drill: Jax gives the orders, we comply, we get our flatches. Go and work for Hector if you don't like it.'

Touché.

With a sniff, Dani handed me my beaten leather boots. I pulled them on. 'Where is everyone?'

'Eliza's asleep. She had an episode.'

We only said *episode* when one of us had a near-fatal encounter, which in Eliza's case was an unsolicited possession. I glanced at the door to her painting room. 'Is she all right?'

'She'll sleep it off.'

'I assume Nick checked on her.'

'I called him. He's still at Chat's with Jax. He said he'd drive you to your dad's at five-thirty.'

Chateline's was one of the few places we could eat out, a classy bar-and-grill in Neal's Yard. The owner made a deal with us: we tipped him well, he didn't tell the Vigiles what we were. His tip cost more than the meal, but it was worth it for a night out.

'So he's late,' I said.

'Must have been held up.'

Dani reached for her phone. 'Don't bother.' I tucked my hair into my hat. 'I'd hate to interrupt their huddle.'

'You can't go by train.'

'I can, actually.'

'Your funeral.'

'I'll be fine. The line hasn't been checked for weeks.' I stood. 'Breakfast on Monday?'

'Maybe. Might owe the beast some overtime.' She glanced at the clock. 'You'd better go. It's nearly six.'

She was right. I had less than ten minutes to reach the station. I grabbed my jacket and ran for the door, calling a quick 'Hi, Pieter' to the spirit in the corner. It glowed in response: a soft, bored glow.

I didn't see that sparkle, but I felt it. Pieter was depressed again. Being dead sometimes got to him.

There was a set way of doing things with spirits, at least in our section. Take Pieter, one of our spirit aides – a muse, if you want to get technical. Eliza would let him possess her, working in slots of about three hours a day, during which time she would paint a masterpiece. When she was done, I'd run down to the Garden and flog it to unwary art collectors. Pieter was temperamental, mind. Sometimes we'd go months without a picture.

A den like ours was no place for ethics. It happens when you force a minority underground. It happens when the world is cruel. There was nothing to do but get on with it. Try and survive, to make a bit of cash. To prosper in the shadow of the Westminster Archon.

My job – my life – was based at Seven Dials. According to Scion's unique urban division system, it lay in I Cohort, Section 4, or I-4. It was built around a pillar on a junction close to Covent Garden's black market. On this pillar there were six sundials.

Each section had its own mime-lord or mime-queen. Together they formed the Unnatural Assembly, which claimed to govern the syndicate, but they all did as they pleased in their own sections. Dials was in the central cohort, where the syndicate was strongest. That's why Jax chose it. That's why we stayed. Nick was the only one with his own crib, further north in Marylebone. We used his place for emergencies only. In the three years I'd worked for Jaxon there had only been one emergency, when the Night Vigilance Division had raided Dials for any hint of clairvoyance. A courier tipped us off about two hours before the raid. We were able to clear out in half that time.

It was wet and cold outside. A typical March evening. I sensed spirits. Dials was a slum in pre-Scion days, and a host of miserable souls still drifted around the pillar, waiting for a new purpose. I called a spool of them to my side. Some protection always came in handy.

Scion was the last word in amaurotic security. Any reference to an afterlife was forbidden. Frank Weaver thought we were unnatural, and like the many Grand Inquisitors before him, he'd taught the rest of London to abhor us. Unless it was essential, we went outside only during safe hours. That was when the NVD slept, and the Sunlight Vigilance Division took control. SVD officers weren't voyant. They weren't permitted to show the same brutality as their nocturnal counterparts. Not in public, anyway.

The NVD were different. Clairvoyants in uniform. Bound to serve for thirty years before being euthanised. A diabolical pact, some said, but it gave them a thirty-year guarantee of a comfortable life. Most voyants weren't that lucky.

London had so much death in its history, it was hard to find a spot without spirits. They formed a safety net. Still, you had to hope the ones you got were good. If you used a frail ghost, it would only stun an assailant for a few seconds. Spirits that lived violent lives were best. That's why certain spirits sold so well on the black market. Jack the Ripper would have gone for millions if anyone could find him. Some still swore the Ripper was Edward VII – the fallen prince, the Bloody King. Scion said he was the very first clairvoyant, but I'd never believed it. I preferred to think we'd always been there.

It was getting dark outside. The sky was sunset gold, the moon a smirk of white. Below it stood the citadel. The Two Brewers, the oxygen bar across the street, was packed with amaurotics. Normal people. They were said by voyants to be afflicted with amaurosis, just as they said we were afflicted with clairvoyance. *Rotties*, they were sometimes called.

I'd never liked that word. It made them sound putrid. A tad hypo-critical, as we were the ones that conversed with the dead.

I buttoned my jacket and tugged the peak of my cap over my eyes. Head down, eyes open. That was the law by which I abided. Not the laws of Scion.

'Fortune for a bob. Just a bob, ma'am! Best oracle in London, ma'am, I promise you. A bit for a poor busker?'

The voice belonged to a thin man, huddled in an equally thin jacket. I hadn't seen a busker for a while. It was rare in the central cohort, where most voyants were part of the syndicate. I read his aura. This one wasn't an oracle at all, but a soothsayer; a very stupid soothsayer – the mime-lords spat on beggars. I made straight for him. 'What the hell do you think you're doing?' I grabbed him by the collar. 'Are you off the cot?'

'Please, miss. I'm starved,' he said, his voice rough with dehydration. He had the facial twitches of an oxygen addict. 'I got no push. Don't tell the Binder, miss. I just wanted—'

'Then get out of here.' I pressed a few notes into his hand. 'I don't care where you go – just get off the street. Get a doss. And if you have to busk tomorrow, do it in VI Cohort. Not here. Got it?'

'Bless you, miss.'

He gathered his meagre possessions, one of which was a glass ball. Cheaper than crystal. I watched him run off, heading for Soho.

Poor man. If he wasted that money in an oxygen bar, he'd be back on the streets in no time. Plenty of people did it: wired themselves up to a cannula and sucked up flavoured air for hours on end. It was the only legal high in the citadel. Whatever he did, that busker was desperate. Maybe he'd been kicked out of the syndicate, or rejected by his family. I wouldn't ask.

No one asked.

Station I-4B was usually busy. Amaurotics didn't mind the trains. They had no auras to give them away. Most voyants avoided public transport, but sometimes it was safer on the trains than on the streets. The NVD were stretched thin across the citadel. Spot checks were uncommon.

There were six sections in each of the six cohorts. If you wanted to leave your section, especially at night, you needed a travel permit and a stroke of good luck. Underguards were deployed after dark. A subdivision of the Night Vigilance Division, they were sighted voyants with the standard life guarantee. They served the state to stay alive.

I'd never considered working for Scion. Voyants could be cruel to each other – I could sympathise a little with those who turned on their own – but I still felt a sense of affinity with them. I could certainly never arrest one. Still, sometimes, when I'd worked hard for two weeks and Jax forgot to pay me, I was tempted.

I scanned my documents with two minutes to spare. Once I was past the barriers, I released my spool. Spirits didn't like to be taken too far from their haunts, and they wouldn't help me if I forced them.

My head was pounding. Whatever medicine Dani had been pumping through my veins was wearing off. An *hour* in the æther . . . Jaxon really was pushing my limits.

On the platform, a luminous green Nixie displayed the train schedule; otherwise there was little light. The pre-recorded voice of Scarlett Burnish drifted through the speakers.

'This train calls all stations within I Cohort, Section 4, northbound. Please have your cards ready for inspection. Observe the safety screens for this evening's bulletins. Thank you, and have a pleasant evening.'

I wasn't having a pleasant evening at all. I hadn't eaten since dawn. Jax only gave me a lunch break if he was in a very good mood, which was about as rare as blue apples.

A new message came to the safety screens. RDT: RADIESTHESIC DETECTION TECHNOLOGY. The other commuters took no notice. This advertisement ran all the time.

'In a citadel as populous as London, it's common to think you might be travelling alongside an unnatural individual.' A dumbshow of silhouettes appeared on the screen, each representing a denizen. One turned red. 'The SciSORS facility is now trialling the RDT

11

Senshield at the Paddington Terminal complex, as well as in the Archon. By 2061, we aim to have Senshield installed in eighty per cent of stations in the central cohort, allowing us to reduce the employment of unnatural police in the Underground. Visit Paddington, or ask an SVD officer for more information.'

The adverts moved on, but it played on my mind. RDT was the biggest threat to voyant society in the citadel. According to Scion, it could detect aura at up to twenty feet. If there wasn't a major delay to their plans, we'd be forced into lockdown by 2061. Typical of the mime-lords, none of them had come up with a solution. They'd just squabbled. And squabbled. And squabbled about their squabbles.

Auras vibrated on the street above me. I was a tuning fork, humming with their energy. For want of a distraction, I thumbed my ID. It bore my picture, name, address, fingerprints, birthplace and occupation. Miss Paige E. Mahoney, naturalised resident of I-5. Born in Ireland in 2040. Moved to London in 2048 under special circumstances. Employed at an oxygen bar in I-4, hence the travel permit. Blonde. Grey eyes. Five foot nine. No distinctive features but dark lips, probably caused by smoking.

I'd never smoked in my life.

A moist hand grabbed my wrist. I started.

'You owe me an apology.'

I glared up at a dark-haired man in a bowler and a dirty white cravat. I should have recognised him just from his stink: Haymarket Hector, one of our less hygienic rivals. He always smelled like a sewer. Sadly, he was also the Underlord, head honcho of the syndicate. They called his turf the Devil's Acre.

'We won the game. Fair and square.' I pulled my arm free. 'Haven't you got something to do, Hector? Cleaning your teeth would be a good start.'

'Perhaps *you* should clean up your game, little macer. And learn some respect for your Underlord.'

'I'm no cheat.'

'Oh, I think you are.' He kept his voice low. 'Whatever airs and graces that mime-lord of yours puts on, all seven of you are nasty cheats and liars. I hear tell you're the downiest on the black market, my dear Dreamer. But you'll disappear.' He touched my cheek with one finger. 'They all disappear in the end.'

'So will you.'

'We'll see. Soon.' He breathed his next words against my ear: 'Have a *very* safe ride home, dollymop.' He vanished into the exit tunnel.

I had to watch my step around Hector. As Underlord he had no real power over the other mime-lords – his only role was to convene meetings – but he had a lot of followers. He'd been sore since my gang had beaten his lackeys at tarocchi, two days before the Naylor auction. Hector's people didn't like it when they lost. Jaxon didn't help, riling them. Most of my gang had avoided being green-lit, largely by staying out of their way, but Jax and I were too defiant. The Pale Dreamer – my name on the streets – was somewhere on their hit list. If they ever cornered me, I was dead.

The train arrived a minute late. I dropped into a vacant seat. There was only one other person in the carriage: a man reading the *Daily Descendant*. He was voyant, a medium. I tensed. Jax was not without enemies, and plenty of voyants knew me as his mollisher. They also knew I sold art that couldn't possibly have been painted by the real Pieter Claesz.

I took out my standard-issue data pad and selected my favourite legal novel. Without a spool to protect me, the only real security I had was to look as normal and amaurotic as possible.

As I flicked through the pages, I kept one eye on the man. I could tell I was on his radar, but neither of us spoke. As he hadn't already grabbed me by the neck and beaten me senseless, I guessed he probably wasn't a freshly duped art enthusiast.

I risked a glance at his copy of the *Descendant*, the only broadsheet still mass-produced on paper. Paper was too easy to misuse; data pads meant we could only download what little media had been approved by the censor. The typical news glowered back at me. Two young men hanged for high treason, a suspicious emporium closed down in Section 3. There was a long article rejecting the 'unnatural' notion that Britain was politically isolated. The journalist called Scion 'an empire in embryo'. They'd been saying that for as long as I could remember. If Scion was still an embryo, I sure as hell didn't want to be there when it burst out of the womb.

Almost two centuries had passed since Scion arrived. It was established in response to a perceived threat to the empire. The *epidemic*, they called it – an epidemic of clairvoyance. The official date was 1901, when they pinned five terrible murders on Edward VII. They claimed the Bloody King had opened a door that could never be shut, that he'd brought the plague of clairvoyance upon the world, and that his followers were everywhere, breeding and killing, drawing their power from a source of great evil.

What followed was Scion, a republic built to destroy the sickness. Over the next fifty years it had become a voyant-hunting machine, with every major policy based around unnaturals. Murders were always committed by unnaturals. Random violence, theft, rape, arson – they all happened because of unnaturals. Over the years, the voyant syndicate had developed in the citadel, formed an organised underworld, and offered a haven for clairvoyants. Since then Scion had worked even harder to root us out.

Once they installed RDT, the syndicate would fall apart and Scion would become all-seeing. We had two years to do something about it, but with Hector as Underlord, I couldn't see that we would. His reign had brought nothing but corruption.

The train went past three stops without incident. I'd just finished the chapter when the lights went out and the train came to a halt. I realised what was happening a split second before the other passenger did. He sat up very straight in his seat.

'They're going to search the train.'

I tried to speak, to confirm his fear, but my tongue felt like a piece of folded cloth.

I switched off my data pad. A door opened in the wall of the tunnel. The Nixie display in the carriage clicked to SECURITY ALERT. I knew what was coming: two Underguards on their rounds. There was always a boss, usually a medium. I'd never experienced a spot check before, but I knew few voyants got away from them.

My heart dashed against my chest. I looked at the other passenger, trying to measure his reaction. He was a medium, though not a particularly powerful one. I could never quite put a finger on how I could tell – my antennae just perked up in a certain way.

'We have to get out of this train.' He rose to his feet. 'What are you, love? An oracle?'

I didn't speak.

'I know you're voyant.' He pulled at the handle of the door. 'Come on, love, don't just sit there. There must be a way out of here.' He wiped his brow with his sleeve. 'Of all the days for a spot check – the *one day*—'

I didn't move. There was no way to get out of this. The windows were toughened, the doors safety-locked – and we were out of time. Two torch beams shone into the carriage.

I held very still. Underguards. They must have detected a certain number of voyants in the carriage, or they wouldn't have killed the lights. I knew they could see our auras, but they'd want to find out exactly what kind of voyants we were.

They were in the carriage. A summoner and a medium. The train carried on moving, but the lights didn't come on. They went to the man first.

'Name?'

He straightened. 'Linwood.'

'Reason for travel?'

'I was visiting my daughter.'

'Visiting your daughter. Sure you're not on your way to a séance, medium?'

These two wanted a fight.

'I have the necessary documents from the hospital. She's very ill,' Linwood said. 'I'm allowed to see her every week.'

'You won't be allowed to see her at all if you open your trap again.' He turned to bark at me: 'You. Where's your card?'

I pulled it from my pocket.

'And your travel permit?'

I handed it over. He paused to read it.

'You work in Section 4.'

'Yes.'

'Who issued this permit?'

'Bill Bunbury, my supervisor.'

'I see. But I need to see something else.' He angled his torch into my eyes. 'Hold still.'

I didn't flinch.

'No spirit sight,' he observed. 'You must be an oracle. Now *that's* something I haven't heard of for a while.'

'I haven't seen an oracle with tits since the forties,' said the other Underguard. 'They're going to love this one.'

His superior smiled. He had one coloboma in each eye, a mark of permanent spirit sight.

'You're about to make me very rich, young lady,' he said to me. 'Just let me double-check those eyes.'

'I'm not an oracle,' I said.

'Of course you're not. Now shut your mouth and open up those shiners.'

Most voyants thought I was an oracle. Easy mistake. The auras were similar – the same colour, in fact.

The guard forced my left eye open with his fingers. As he examined my pupils with a slit light, searching for the missing colobomata, the other passenger made a break for the open door. There was a tremor as he hurled a spirit – his guardian angel – at the Underguards. The back-up shrieked as the angel crunched into him, scrambling his senses like a whisk through soft eggs.

Underguard 1 was too fast. Before anyone could move, he'd summoned a spool of poltergeists.

'Don't move, medium.'

Linwood stared him down. He was a small man in his forties, thin but wiry, with brown hair greying at the temples. I couldn't see the 'geists – or much else, thanks to the slit light – but they were making me too weak to move. I counted three. I'd never seen anyone control *one* poltergeist, let alone three. Cold sweat broke out at the back of my neck.

As the angel pivoted for a second attack, the poltergeists began to circle the Underguard. 'Come with us quietly, medium,' he said, 'and we'll ask our bosses not to torture you.'

'Do your worst, gentlemen.' Linwood raised a hand. 'I fear no man with angels at my side.'

'That's what they all say, Mr Linwood. They tend to forget that when they see the Tower.'

Linwood flung his angel down the carriage. I couldn't see the collision, but it scalded all my senses to the quick. I forced myself to stand. The presence of three poltergeists was sapping my energy. Linwood was a tough talker, but I knew he could feel them; he was struggling to fortify his angel. While the summoner controlled the poltergeists, Underguard 2 was reciting the threnody: a series of words that compelled spirits to die completely, sending them to a realm beyond the reach of voyants. The angel trembled. They'd need to know its full name to banish it, but so long as one of them kept chanting, the angel would be too weak to protect its host.

Blood pounded in my ears. My throat was tight, my fingers numb. If I stood aside, we'd both be detained. I saw myself in the Tower, being tortured, at the gallows . . .

I would *not* die today.

As the poltergeists converged on Linwood, something happened to my vision. I homed in on the Underguards. Their minds throbbed close to mine, two pulsing rings of energy. I heard my body hit the ground.

I only intended to disorientate them, give myself time to get away. I had the element of surprise. They'd overlooked me. Oracles needed a spool to be dangerous.

I didn't.

A black tide of fear overwhelmed me. My spirit flew right out my body, straight into Underguard 1. Before I knew what I was doing, I'd crashed *into* his dreamscape. Not just against it – into it, through it. I hurled his spirit out into the æther, leaving his body empty. Before his crony could draw breath, he met the same fate.

My spirit snapped back into my skin. Pain exploded behind my eyes. I'd never felt pain like it in my life; it was knives through my skull, fire in the very tissue of my brain, so hot I couldn't see or move or think. I was dimly aware of the sticky carriage floor against my cheek. Whatever I'd just done, I wasn't going to do it again in a hurry.

The train rocked. It must be close to the next station. I pushed my weight onto my elbows, my muscles trembling with the effort.

'Mr Linwood?'

No response. I crawled to where he was lying. As the train passed a service light, I caught sight of his face.

Dead. The 'geists had flushed his spirit out. His ID was on the floor. William Linwood, forty-three years old. Two kids, one with cystic fibrosis. Married. Banker. *Medium.*

Did his wife and children know about his secret life? Or were they amaurotic, oblivious to it?

I had to speak the threnody, or he would haunt this carriage for ever. 'William Linwood,' I said, 'be gone into the æther. All is settled. All debts are paid. You need not dwell among the living now.'

Linwood's spirit was drifting nearby. The æther whispered as he and his angel vanished.

The lights came back on. My throat closed.

Two more bodies lay on the floor.

I used a handrail to get back on my feet. My clammy palm could hardly grip it. A few feet away, Underguard 1 was dead, the look of surprise still on his face.

I'd killed him. I'd killed an Underguard.

His companion hadn't been so lucky. He was on his back, his eyes staring at the ceiling, a slithering ribbon of saliva down his chin. He twitched when I came closer. Chills crept down my back and the taste of bile burned my throat. I hadn't pushed his spirit far enough. It was still drifting in the dark parts of his mind: the secret, silent parts in which no spirit should dwell. He'd gone mad. No. I'd *driven* him mad.

I set my jaw. I couldn't just leave him like this – even an Underguard didn't deserve such a fate. I placed my cold hands on his shoulders and steeled myself for a mercy kill. He let out a groan and whispered, 'Kill me.'

I had to do it. I owed it to him.

But I couldn't. I just couldn't kill him.

When the train arrived at Station I-5C, I waited by the door. By the time the next passengers found the bodies, they were too late to catch me. I was already above them on the street, my cap pulled down to hide my face.

The Liar

I slipped into the flat and hung my jacket up. The Golden Crescent complex had a full-time security guard called Vic, but he'd been doing his rounds when I swiped in. He hadn't seen my death-white face, my shaking hands as I reached for my key card.

My father was in the living room. I could see his slippered feet propped up on the ottoman. He was watching ScionEye, the news network that covered all Scion citadels, and on the screen Scarlett Burnish was announcing that the Underground across I Cohort had just been closed.

I could never hear that voice without a shudder. Burnish was only about twenty-five, the youngest ever Grand Raconteur: the assistant of the Grand Inquisitor, the one who pledged their voice and wit to Scion. People called her Weaver's whore, perhaps out of jealousy. She had clear skin and six-seater lips, and she favoured thick red eyeliner. It matched her hair, which she wore in a chic Gibson tuck. Her high-collared dresses always made me think of the gallows.

'*In foreign news, the Grand Inquisitor of the French Republic, Benoît*

Ménard, will be visiting Inquisitor Weaver for Novembertide festivities this year. With eight months to go, the Archon is already making preparations for what looks to be a truly invigorating visit.'

'Paige?'

I pulled off my cap. 'Hi.'

'Come and sit down.'

'Just a minute.'

I headed straight for the bathroom. I was sweating not so much bullets as shotgun shells.

I'd killed someone. I'd actually *killed* someone. Jax had always said I was capable of it – bloodless murder – but I'd never believed him. Now I was a murderer. And worse, I'd left evidence: a survivor. I didn't have my data pad, either, and it was smothered in my fingerprints. I wouldn't just get NiteKind – that would be too easy. Torture and the gallows, for sure.

As soon as I got to the bathroom, I vomited my guts into the toilet. By the time I'd brought up everything but my organs, I was shaking so violently I could hardly stand. I tore off my clothes and stumbled into the shower. Burning water pounded on my skin.

I'd gone too far this time. For the first time ever, I'd *invaded* other dreamscapes. Not just touched them.

Jaxon would be thrilled.

My eyes closed. The scene in the carriage replayed again and again. I hadn't meant to kill them, I'd meant to give them a push – just enough to give them a migraine, maybe make their noses bleed. Cause a distraction.

But something made me panic. Fear of being found. Fear of becoming another anonymous victim of Scion.

I thought of Linwood. Voyants never protected one another, not unless they were in the same gang, but his death still weighed on me. I pulled my knees up to my chin and held my aching head in both hands. If only I'd been faster. Now two people were dead – one insane – and if I wasn't very lucky, I'd be next.

I huddled in the corner of the shower, my knees strapped against my chest. I couldn't hide in here for ever. They always found you in the end.

I had to think. Scion had a containment procedure for these situations. Once they'd cleared the station and detained any possible witnesses, they would call a gallipot – an expert in ethereal drugs – and administer blue aster. That would temporarily restore my victim's memories, allowing them to be seen. When they had the relevant parts recorded, they would euthanise the man and give his body to the morgue in II-6. Then they would flick through his memories, searching for the face of his killer. And then they would find me.

Arrests didn't always happen at night. Sometimes they caught you in the day, when you stepped onto the street. A torch in your eyes, a needle in your neck, and you were gone. Nobody reported you missing.

I couldn't think about the future now. A fresh wave of pain broke through my skull, bringing me back to the present.

I counted my options. I could go back to Dials and lie low in our den for a while, but the Vigiles might be out looking for me. Leading them to Jax wasn't an option. Besides, with the stations closed off there was no way I could get back to Section 4. A buck cab would be hard to find, and the security systems worked ten times harder at night.

I could stay with a friend, but all my friends outside the Dials were amaurotic – girls at school I'd barely kept in touch with. They'd think I'd gone off the cot if I said I was being hunted by the secret police because I'd killed someone with my spirit. They'd almost certainly report me, too.

Wrapped in an old dressing gown, I padded barefoot to the

kitchen and put a pan of milk on the stove. I always did it when I was home; I shouldn't break routine. My father had left my favourite mug out, the big one that said GRAB LIFE BY THE COFFEE. I'd never been a fan of flavoured oxygen, or Floxy®, the Scion alternative to alcohol. Coffee was just about legal. They were researching whether or not caffeine triggered clairvoyance. But, then, GRAB LIFE BY THE FLAVOURED OXYGEN just wouldn't have the same vitality.

Using my spirit had done something to my head. I could hardly keep my eyes open. As I poured the milk, I looked out of the window. My father had impeccable taste when it came to interior design. It helped that he had money enough to afford the high-security places on the exclusive Barbican Estate. The apartment was fresh and spacious, full of light. The hallways smelled of potpourri and linen. There were large square windows in every room. The biggest was in the living room, a vast skylight covering the west-facing wall, next to the elaborate French doors that led out to the balcony. As a child I'd often watched the sun set from that window.

Outside, the citadel whirled on. Above our complex stood the three brutalist columns of the Barbican Estate, where the white-collar Scion workers lived. At the top of the Lauderdale Tower was the I-5 transmission screen. It was from this screen that they projected public hangings on a Sunday evening. At present it bore the Scion system's static insignia – a red symbol resembling an anchor – and a single word in black: SCION, all on a clinical white background. Then there was that awful slogan: NO SAFER PLACE.

More like no *safe* place. Not for us.

I sipped my milk and looked at the symbol for a while, wishing it all the way to hell. Then I washed up my mug, poured a glass of water and headed for my bedroom. I had to call Jaxon.

My father intercepted me in the hallway.

'Paige, wait.'

I stopped.

Irish by birth, with a scalding head of red hair, my father worked in the scientific research division of Scion. When he wasn't doing that, he was scribbling formulae on his data pad and waxing lyrical about clinical biochemistry, one of his two degrees. We looked nothing alike.

'Hi,' I said. 'Sorry I'm so late. I did some extra hours.'

'No need to apologise.' He beckoned me into the living room. 'Let me get you something to eat. You look peaky.'

'I'm fine. Just tired.'

'You know, I was reading about the oxygen circuit today. Horrible case in IV-2. Underpaid staff, dirty oxygen, clients having seizures – very unpleasant.'

'The central bars are fine, honestly. The clients expect quality.' I watched him lay the table. 'How's work?'

'Good.' He looked up at me. 'Paige, about your work in the bar—'

'What about it?' I said.

A daughter working in the lowest echelons of the citadel. Nothing could be more embarrassing for a man in his position. How uncomfortable he must have been when his colleagues asked about his children, expecting him to have sired a doctor or a lawyer. How they must have whispered when they realised I worked *in* a bar, not *at* the Bar. The lie was a small mercy. He could never have coped with the truth: that I was an unnatural, a criminal.

And a murderer. The thought made me sick.

'I know it isn't my place to say this, but I think you should consider reapplying for a place at the University. That job is a dead end. Low money, no prospects. But the University—'

'No.' My voice came out harder than I'd intended. 'I like my job. It was my choice.'

I still remembered the Schoolmistress giving me my final report. 'I'm sorry you chose not to apply for the University, Paige,' she'd said, 'but it might be for the best. You've had far too much time away from school. It's not considered proper for a young lady of quality.' She'd handed me a thin, leather-bound folder bearing the school crest. 'Here is an employment recommendation from your tutors. They note your aptitude for Physical Enrichment, French and Scion History.'

I didn't care. I'd always hated school: the uniform, the dogma. Leaving was the high point of my formative years.

'I could arrange something,' my father said. He'd so wanted an educated daughter. 'You could reapply.'

'Nepotism doesn't work on Scion,' I said. 'You should know.'

'I didn't have the choice, Paige.' A muscle flinched in his cheek. 'I didn't have that luxury.'

I didn't want to have this conversation. I didn't want to think of what we'd left behind.

'Still living with your boyfriend?' he said.

The boyfriend lie had always been a mistake. Ever since I'd invented him, my father had been asking to meet him. 'I broke up with him,' I said. 'It wasn't right. But it's okay. Suzette has a spare place in her apartment – you remember.'

'Suzy from school?'

'Yes.'

As I spoke, a sharp pain lanced through the side of my head. I couldn't wait for him to make dinner. I had to call Jaxon, tell him what had happened. Now.

'Actually, I've got a bit of a headache,' I said. 'Do you mind if I turn in early?'

He came to my side and took my chin in one hand. 'You always have these headaches. You're overtired.' He brushed his thumb over my face, the shadows under my eyes. 'There's a good documentary on, if you're up to it – I'll get you set up on the couch.'

'Maybe tomorrow.' I gently pushed his hand away. 'Do you have any painkillers?'

After a moment, he nodded. 'In the bathroom. I'll do us an Ulster fry in the morning, all right? I want to hear all your news, *seillean*.'

I stared at him. He hadn't made me breakfast since I was about twelve; nor had he called me by that nickname since we'd lived in Ireland. Ten years ago. A lifetime ago.

'Paige?'

'Okay,' I said. 'See you in the morning.'

I pulled away and headed for my room. My father said nothing more. He left the door ajar, as he always did when I was home. He'd never known how to act around me.

The guest room was as warm as ever. My old bedroom. I'd moved to Dials as soon as school was over, but my father had never taken a lodger – he didn't need one. Officially, I still lived here. Easier to leave it on the records. I opened the door to the balcony, which stretched between my room and the kitchen. My skin had gone from cold to burning hot and my eyes had an odd strained feeling, like I'd stared into a light for hours. All I could see was the face of my victim – and the vacuity, the *insanity*, of the one I'd left alive.

That damage had been caused in seconds. My spirit wasn't just a scout – it was a weapon. Jaxon had been waiting for this.

I found my phone and called Jaxon's room in the den. It barely rang before he was off.

'Well, well! I thought you'd left me for the weekend. Where's the fire, honeybee? Have you rethought the holiday? You don't *really* need one, do you? I thought not. I absolutely cannot lose my walker for two days. Have a heart, darling. Excellent. I'm delighted you agree. Did you get your hands on Jane Rochford, by the way? I'll transfer you another few thousand if you need it. Just don't tell me that toffee-nosed bastard Didion nabbed Anne Naylor *and*—'

'I killed someone.'

Silence.

'Who?' Jax sounded odd.

'Underguard. They tried to detain a medium.'

'So you killed the Underguard.'

'I killed one.'

He inhaled sharply. 'And the other?'

'I put him in his hadal zone.'

'Wait, you did it with your—?' When I didn't reply, he began to laugh. I could hear him clapping his hand on his desk. 'At last. At *last*. Paige, you little *thaumaturge*, you did it! You're wasted on séances, really you are. So this man – the Underguard – he's really a vegetable?'

'Yes.' I paused. 'Am I fired?'

'Fired? By the zeitgeist, dolly, of course not! I've been waiting years for you to put your talents to good use. You've bloomed like the ambrosial flower you are, my winsome wunderkind.' I pictured him taking a celebratory puff of his cigar. 'Well, well, my dreamwalker has finally entered another dreamscape. And it only took three years. Now, tell me – were you able to save the voyant?'

'No.'

'No?'

'They had three 'geists.'

'Oh, come now. No medium could control three poltergeists.'

'Well, this medium managed. He thought I was an oracle.'

His laugh was soft. 'Amateurs.'

I looked out of the window at the tower. A new message had appeared: PLEASE BE AWARE OF UNEXPECTED UNDERGROUND DELAYS. 'They've closed the Underground,' I said. 'They're trying to find me.'

'Try not to panic, Paige. It's unbecoming.'

'Well, you'd better have a plan. The whole network's in lockdown. I need to get out of here.'

'Oh, don't worry about *that*. Even if they try and extract his memories, that Underguard's brain is nought but a hashed brown. Are you certain you pushed him all the way to his hadal zone?'

'Yes.'

'Then it will take them at least twelve hours to extract his memories. I'm surprised the hapless chap was still alive.'

'What are you saying?'

'I'm saying you should sit tight before you run headfirst into a manhunt. You're safer with your Scion daddy than you are here.'

'They have this address. I can't sit here and wait to be detained.'

'You won't be detained, O my lovely. Trust in my schmooze. Stay home, sleep away your troubles, and I'll send Nick with the car in the *ante meridiem*. How does that sound?'

'I don't like it.'

'You don't have to like it. Just get your beauty sleep. Not that you need it,' he added. 'By the way, could you do me a favour? Pop into Grub Street tomorrow and pick up those Donne elegies from Minty, will you? I can't *believe* his spirit is back, it's absolutely—'

I hung up.

Jax was a bastard. A genius, yes – but still a sycophantic, tight-fisted, cold-hearted bastard, like all mime-lords. But where else could I turn? I'd be vulnerable alone with a gift like mine. Jax was just the lesser of two evils.

I had to smile at that thought. It said a lot about the world when Jaxon Hall was the lesser of two evils.

I couldn't sleep. I had to prepare. There was a palm pistol in one of the drawers, concealed under a stack of spare clothes. With it was a first edition of one of Jaxon's pamphlets, *On the Merits of Unnaturalness*. It listed every major voyant type, according to his research. My copy was covered in his annotations – new ideas, voyant contact numbers. Once the pistol was loaded, I dragged a backpack out from under the bed. My emergency pack, stored here for two years, ready for the day I'd have to run. I stuffed the pamphlet into the front pocket. They couldn't find it in my father's home.

I lay on my back, fully clothed, my hand resting on the pistol. Somewhere in the distance, in the darkness, there was thunder.

I must have fallen asleep. When I woke, something seemed wrong.

The æther was too open. Voyants in the building, on the stairwell. That wasn't old Mrs Heron upstairs, who used a frame and always took the lift. Those were the boots of a collection unit.

They had come for me.

They had finally come.

I was on my feet at once, throwing a jacket over my shirt and pulling on my shoes and glovelettes, my hands shaking. This was what Nick had trained me for: to run like hell. I could make it to the station if I tried, but this run would test my stamina to the limit. I would have to find and hail a cab to reach Section 4. Buck cabbies would take just about anyone for a few bob, voyant fugitive or not.

I slung on my backpack, tucked the pistol into my jacket pocket, and opened the door to the balcony. The wind had blown it shut. Rain battered my clothes. I crossed the balcony, climbed onto the kitchen windowsill, grabbed the edge of the roof and, with one strong pull, I was up. By the time they reached the apartment, I'd started to run.

Bang. There went the door – no knock, no warning. A moment later, a gunshot split the night. I forced myself to keep running. I couldn't go back. They never killed amaurotics without reason; certainly not Scion employees. The shot had most likely been from a simple tranquilliser, to shut my father up while they detained me. They would need something much, much stronger to bring me down.

The estate was quiet. I looked over the edge of the roof, surveying it. No sign of the security guard, he must be on his rounds again. It didn't take me long to spot the paddy wagon in the car park, the van with blacked-out windows and gleaming white headlights. If anyone had taken the time to look, they would have seen the Scion symbol on its back doors.

I stepped across a gap and climbed onto a ledge. Perilously slick. My shoes and gloves had decent grip, but I'd have to watch my step. I pressed my back to the wall and edged towards an escape ladder, the rain plastering my hair to my face. I climbed up to a wrought-iron balcony on the next floor, where I forced open a small window. I tore through the deserted apartment, down three flights of stairs and out through the front door of the building. I needed to get on to the street, to vanish into a dark alley.

Red lights. The NVD were parked right outside, blocking my escape. I doubled back and slammed the door, activating the security lock. With shaking hands I pulled a fire axe from its case, smashed a ground-floor window and hauled myself into a small courtyard, cutting my arms on the glass. Then I was back in the rain, clambering up the drainpipes and windowsills, barely holding on, until I reached the roof.

My heart stopped when I saw them. The exterior of the building was infested with men in red shirts and black jackets. Several torch beams moved towards me, glaring into my eyes. My chest surged. I'd never seen that uniform in London before – were they from Scion?

'Stop where you are.'

The nearest of them stepped towards me. In his gloved hand was a gun. I backed away, feeling a vivid aura. The leader of these soldiers was an extremely powerful medium. The torchlights revealed a gaunt face, sharp chips of eyes, and a thin, wide mouth.

'Don't run, Paige,' he called across the roof. 'Why don't you come out of the rain?'

I did a quick sweep of my surroundings. The next building was a derelict office block. The jump was wide, maybe twenty feet, and beyond it was a busy road. It was further than I'd ever tried to jump

– but unless I wanted to attack the medium and abandon my body, I would have to try.

'I'll pass,' I said, and took off again.

There was a shout of alarm from the soldiers. I leapt down to a lower stretch of the roof. The medium ran after me. I could hear his feet pounding on the roof, seconds behind mine – he was trained for these pursuits. I couldn't afford to stop, not even for a moment. I was light and slim, narrow enough to slip between rails and under fences, but so was my pursuer. When I fired a shot from the pistol over my shoulder, he ducked it without stopping. His laugh was swept up on the wind, so I couldn't tell how close he was.

I shoved the pistol back into my jacket. There was no point in shooting; I'd only miss. I flexed my fingers, ready to catch the gutter. My muscles were hot, my lungs at bursting point. A flare in my ankle alerted me to an injury, but I had to keep going. Fight or fly. Run or die.

The medium leapt over the ledge, swift and fluid as water. Adrenalin streaked through my veins. My legs pumped and the rain thrashed at my eyes. I leapt over flexi-pipes and ventilation ducts, building up momentum, trying to turn my sixth sense on the medium. His mind was strong, moving as fast as he was. I couldn't pin it down, couldn't even get a picture from it. There was nothing I could do to deter him.

As I built up speed the adrenalin numbed the fire in my ankle. A fifteen-storey drop spread out to meet me. Across the gap there was a gutter, and beyond that was a fire escape. If I could get down it, I could disappear into the throbbing veins of Section 5. I could get away. Yes, I could make it. Nick's voice was in my head, urging me on: *Knees towards your chest. Eyes on your landing spot.* It was now or never. I pushed off my toes and launched myself over the precipice.

My body collided with a solid wall of brick. The impact split my lip, but I was still conscious. My fingers gripped the gutter. My feet kicked at the wall. I used what strength I had left to push myself up, the gutter biting deep into my hands. A loose coin fell from my jacket, into the dark street below.

My victory was short-lived. As I dragged myself onto the edge of the roof, my palms scalding and raw, a bolt of crucifying pain tore up my spine. The shock might have made me let go, but one hand still grasped the roof. I craned my neck to look over my shoulder gasping. A long, thin dart was buried in my lower back.

Flux.

They had *flux*.

The drug swept into my veins. In six seconds my whole bloodstream was compromised. I thought of two things: first that Jax was going to kill me, and second, that it didn't matter – I was going to die anyway. I let go of the roof.

Nothing.

Confined

It lasted a lifetime. I couldn't remember when it started, and I didn't see when it would end.

I remembered movement, a throaty roar, being strapped to a hard surface. Then a needle, and the pain took over.

Reality was warped. I was close to a candle, but the flame kept bursting to the size of an inferno. I was trapped in an oven. Sweat dripped from my pores like wax. I was fire. I burned. I blistered and seared – then I was freezing, desperate for heat, feeling as if I would die. There was no middle ground. Just endless, limitless pain.

AUP Fluxion 14 was developed as a collaborative project between the medical and military divisions of Scion. It produced a crippling effect called phantasmagoria, dubbed 'brain plague' by embittered voyants: a vivid series of hallucinations, caused by distortions to the human dreamscape. I fought my way through vision after vision, crying out when the pain grew too intense to bear in silence. If there is a definition for hell, this was it. It was *hell*.

My hair stuck to my tears as I retched, trying in vain to force the poison from my body. All I wanted was for everything to end.

Whether it was sleep, unconsciousness or death, something had to take me from this nightmare.

'There, now, treasure. We don't want you to die just yet. We've already lost three today.' Cold fingers stroked my forehead. I arched my back, pulled away. If they didn't want me to die, then why do this to me?

Dead flowers skittered past my eyes. The room twisted into a helix, round and round until I had no idea which way was up. I bit a pillow to stop the screams. I tasted blood and knew I'd bitten something else – my lip, my tongue, my cheek, who knew?

Flux didn't just leave your system. No matter how many times you vomited or passed urine, it kept on circulating, borne by your blood, reproduced by your own cells, until you could force the antidote into your veins. I tried to plead, but I couldn't get a note out. The pain washed over me in wave after wave after wave, until I was sure I would die.

A new voice registered.

'Enough. We need this one alive. Get the antidote, or I will see to it that you take twice the dosage she did.'

The antidote! I might yet live. I tried to see past the rippled veil of visions, but I couldn't make out anything but the candle.

It was taking too long. Where was my antidote? It didn't seem to matter. I wanted sleep, the longest sleep of all.

'Let me go,' I said. 'Let me out.'

'She's speaking. Bring water.'

The cold lip of a glass clashed on my teeth. I took deep, thirsty gulps. I looked up and tried to see the face of my saviour.

'Please,' I said.

Two eyes looked back at me. They burst into flame.

And finally, the nightmare stopped. I fell into a deep, black sleep.

When I woke, I lay still.

I could feel enough to get a good mental picture of where I was:

spread on my stomach on a rigid mattress. My throat was roasted. It was such a severe pain that I was forced to come to my senses, if only to seek water. I realised with a start that I was naked.

I pivoted onto my side, resting my weight on my elbow and hip. I could taste dry vomit in the corners of my mouth. As soon as I could focus, I reached for the æther. There were other voyants here, somewhere in this prison.

It took a while for my eyes to adjust to the gloom. I was in a single bed with cold, damp sheets. On the right was a barred window with no glass. The floor and walls were made of stone. A bitter draught sent goose bumps racing all over me. My breath came out in tiny clouds. I pulled the sheets around my shoulders. Who the hell had taken my clothes?

A door was ajar in the corner. I could see light. I stood, testing my strength. When I was sure I wasn't going to fall, I moved towards the light. What I found was a rudimentary bathroom. The light was coming from a single candle. There was an ancient toilet and a rusted tap, the latter of which had been placed high on the wall. The tap was perishing to the touch. When I turned the nearby valve, a deluge of freezing water engulfed me. I tried turning the valve the other way, but the water refused to heat up more than about half a degree. I decided to take turns with my limbs, dipping one after the other under the crude excuse for a shower. There were no towels, so I used the sheets on the bed to dry off, keeping one wrapped around me. When I tried the main door, I found it locked.

My skin prickled. I had no idea where I was, or why I was here, or what these people would do to me. Nobody knew what happened to detainees; none of them had ever come back.

I sat on the bed and took a few deep breaths. I was still weak from hours of phantasmagoria, and I didn't need a mirror to know I looked even more like a corpse than usual.

My shivers weren't just from the cold. I was naked and alone in a dark room, with bars at the window and no sign of an escape route. They must have taken me to the Tower. Taken my backpack, too, and the pamphlet. I huddled against the bedpost and tried my best to conserve my body heat, my heart thumping. A thick knot filled my aching throat.

Would they hurt my father? He was valuable, yes – a commodity – but would he be forgiven for harbouring a voyant? That was misprision of treason. But he was important. They had to spare him.

For a while I lost track of time. I fell into a fitful doze. Finally the door crashed open, and I snapped awake.

'Get up.'

A paraffin lamp swung into the room. Holding it was a woman. She had polished nut-brown skin and an elegant bone structure, and she was taller than me by several inches. Her loosely curled hair was long and black, as was her high-waisted dress, the sleeves of which fell to the tips of her gloved fingers. It was impossible to guess her age: she could have been twenty-five or forty. I clutched the sheet around my body, watching her.

I noticed three odd things about the woman. First, her eyes were yellow. Not the kind of amber you might call yellow in certain lights. These were real yellow, almost chartreuse, and they glowed.

The second thing was her aura. She was voyant, but I'd never encountered this type before. I couldn't pinpoint why exactly it was strange, but it didn't sit well with my senses.

And the third – the one that chilled me – was her dreamscape. Exactly like the one I'd felt in I-4, the one we hadn't been able to identify. The stranger. My instinct was to attack her, but I already knew I wouldn't be able to breach that kind of dreamscape, certainly not in my current state.

'Is this the Tower?' My voice was hoarse.

The woman ignored my question. She moved her lamp close to

my face, scrutinising my eyes. I started to wonder if this was still brain plague.

'Take these,' she said.

I looked at the two pills in her hand.

'Take them.'

'No,' I said.

She hit me. I tasted blood. I wanted to hit back, to fight, but I was so weak I could barely lift my hand. With difficulty, given my freshly burst lip, I took the pills. 'Cover yourself,' my captor said. 'If you disobey me again, I will ensure you never leave this room. Not with flesh on your bones.'

She threw a bundle of clothes at me.

'Pick them up.'

I didn't want to be hit again. I'd fall this time. With my jaw set tight, I picked them up.

'Put them on.'

I looked down at the clothes, dripping blood from my lip. A spot grew on the white tunic in my hands. It had long sleeves and a square neckline. With it was a black sash, matched with trousers, socks and boots, a set of plain underwear and a black gilet stitched with a small white anchor. Scion's symbol. I dressed in rigid strokes, forcing my cold limbs to move. When I was finished, she turned to the door. 'Follow me. Do not speak to anyone.'

It was deathly cold outside the room and the threadbare carpet did little to improve the temperature. It must have been red once, but now it was faded and stained with vomit. My guide led me through a labyrinth of stone corridors, past small barred windows and burning torches. They seemed too bright, too raw, after the cool blue streetlights of London.

Could this be a castle? I didn't know anywhere within a thousand miles of London that had a castle – we hadn't had a monarch since

37

Victoria. Maybe it was one of the old Category D prisons. Unless it was the Tower.

I risked a glance outside. It was night, but I could see a courtyard by the light of several lanterns. I wondered how long I'd been under the influence of flux. Had this woman watched me as I struggled? Did she take orders from the NVD, or did they take orders from her? Maybe she worked for the Archon, but they wouldn't employ a voyant. And whatever else she might be, she was most definitely voyant.

The woman stopped outside a door. A boy was shoved out from inside. He was a skinny, rat-faced creature, with a mop of sandy hair, and had all the symptoms of flux poisoning: glazed eyes, bone-white face, blue lips. The woman looked him up and down.

'Name?'

'Carl,' he rasped.

'I beg your pardon?'

'*Carl.*' You could tell he was in agony.

'Well, congratulations on surviving Fluxion 14, Carl.' She sounded anything but congratulatory. 'That may have been the last sleep you have for a while.'

Carl and I exchanged a glance. I knew I must look as awful as he did.

As we traipsed through the corridors, we collected several more captive voyants. Their auras were strong and distinctive; I could hazard a guess at what they all were. A seer. A chiromancer – palmist – with a pixie cut, dyed electric blue. A tasseographer. An oracle with a shaved head. A slim and thin-lipped brunette, probably a whisperer, who seemed to have a broken arm. None of them looked much older than twenty, or much younger than fifteen. All of them were pale and sick from flux. In the end there were ten of us. The woman turned to face her little flock of freaks.

'I am Pleione Sualocin,' she said. 'I will be your guide for your first day in Sheol I. Tonight you will attend the welcome oration.

There are a number of simple rules you are expected to observe. You will not look any Rephaite in the eye. You will keep your gazes on the floor, where they belong, unless you are invited to look at something else.'

The palmist raised a hand, keeping her eyes on her feet. 'Rephaite?'

'You will find out soon enough.' Pleione paused. 'An additional rule: you will not speak unless a Rephaite addresses you. Is there any confusion on these matters?'

'Yeah, there is.' It was the tasser that spoke. He was not looking at the floor. 'Where are we?'

'You are about to find out.'

'What the hell gives you the right to nib us? I weren't even busking. I ain't no law-breaker. Prove I've got an aura! I'll go straight back to the city and you ain't going to—'

He stopped. Two dark beads of blood seeped from his eyes. He made a soft sound before he collapsed.

The palmist screamed.

Pleione assessed the tasser's form. When she looked up at us, her eyes were gas-flame blue. I swerved my gaze away from them.

'Any other questions?'

The palmist clapped a hand over her mouth.

We were herded into a small room. Wet walls and floor, dark as a crypt. Pleione locked us in and left.

For a minute, nobody dared speak. The palmist heaved out sobs, close to hysteria. Most of the others were still too weak to talk. I sat down in a corner, out of the way. Beneath my sleeves, my skin was stippled with goose flesh.

'Is this still the Tower?' said an augur. 'It looks like the Tower.'

'Shut up,' someone said. 'Just shut up.'

Someone started praying to the zeitgeist, of all things. Like that would help. I rested my chin on my knees. I didn't want to know what they would do to us. I didn't know how strong I'd be if they put me on the waterboard. I'd heard my father talk about it, how they only let you breathe for a few seconds at a time. He said it wasn't torture. It was therapy.

A seer sat down beside me. He was bald and broad-shouldered. I couldn't see much of him in the gloom, but I could see his large, intensely dark eyes. He extended a hand.

'Julian.'

He didn't seem afraid. Just quiet. 'Paige,' I said. Best not to use full names. I cleared my dry throat. 'What's your cohort?'

'IV-6.'

'I-4.'

'That's the White Binder's territory.' I nodded. 'Which part?'

'Soho,' I said. If I said I was in Dials, he'd know I must be one of Jaxon's nearest and dearest.

'I envy you. I'd love to have lived central.'

'Why?'

'Syndicate's strong there. My section doesn't see much action.' He kept his voice low. 'Did you give them a reason to arrest you?'

'Killed an Underguard.' My throat ached. 'You?'

'Minor disagreement with a Vigile. Long story short, the Vigile is no longer with us.'

'But you're a seer.' Most voyants regarded seers – a class of sooth-sayer – with disdain. Like all soothsayers, they communed with spirits through objects; in a seer's case, anything reflective. Jax hated soothsayers with a passion ('*shit*sayers, dolly, call them shitsayers'). And augurs, come to think of it.

Julian seemed to read these thoughts. 'You don't think seers cap-able of murder.'

'Not with spirits. You couldn't control a big enough spool.'

'You do know your voyants.' He rubbed his arms. 'You're right. I shot him. Didn't stop them arresting me.'

I didn't reply. Icy water dripped from the ceiling, onto my hair, and ran down my nose. Most of the other prisoners were silent. One boy was rocking back and forth on his heels.

'You have a strange aura.' Julian looked at me. 'I can't work out what you are. I'd say oracle, but—'

'But?'

'I haven't heard of a woman being an oracle in a long time. And I don't think you're a sibyl.'

'I'm an acultomancer.'

'What'd you do, stab someone with a needle?'

'Something like that.'

There was a crash from outside, and an awful scream. Everyone stopped talking.

'That's a berserker.' The voice was male, afraid. 'They're not going to put a berserker in here, are they?'

'There's no such thing as a berserker,' I said.

'Have you not read *On the Merits*?'

'Yes. It's a hypothetical type.'

He didn't look relieved. The thought of the pamphlet made me colder than ever. It could be anywhere, in anyone's hands – a first edition of the most seditious pamphlet in the citadel, covered in fresh notes and contact details. I could never have got such a thing without knowing the writer.

'They're going to torture us again.' The whisperer was cradling her broken arm. 'They want something. They wouldn't have just let us out.'

'Out of where?' I said.

'The Tower, idiot. Where we've all been for the last two years.'

'Two?' There was a half-hysterical laugh from the corner. 'Try nine. Nine years.' Another laugh, a giggle.

Nine years. From what we knew, detainees were given two choices: join the NVD or be executed. There was no need to *store* people. 'Why nine?' I said.

There was no answer from the corner. After a minute Julian spoke up.

'Anyone else wondering why we're not dead?'

'They killed everyone else.' A new voice. 'I was there for months. The other voyants in my wing all got the noose.' Pause. 'We've been picked for something.'

'SciSORS,' somebody whispered. 'We're gonna be lab rats, aren't we? The doctors want to cut us up.'

'This isn't SciSORS,' I said.

There was a long silence, broken only by the bitter tears of the palmist. She couldn't seem to stop. Finally, Carl addressed the whisperer. 'You said they must want something, hisser. What could they want?'

'Anything. Our sight.'

'They can't take our sight,' I said.

'Please. You're not even sighted. They won't want *disabled* voyants.'

I resisted the urge to break her other arm.

'What did she do to the tasser?' The palmist was shaking. 'His eyes – she didn't even move!'

'Well, I thought we'd be killed for sure,' Carl said, as if he couldn't imagine why the rest of us were so worried. His voice was less hoarse. 'I'd take anything over the noose, wouldn't you?'

'We might still get the noose,' I said.

He fell silent.

Another boy, so pale it looked as if the flux had burned the blood out of his veins, was beginning to hyperventilate. Freckles dusted his nose. I hadn't noticed him before; he had no trace of an aura. 'What is this place?' He could hardly get the words out. 'Who – who are you people?'

Julian glanced at him. 'You're amaurotic,' he said. 'Why have they taken you?'

'Amaurotic?'

'Probably a mistake.' The oracle seemed bored. 'They'll kill him all the same. Tough luck, kid.'

The boy looked as though he might faint. He leapt to his feet and yanked at the bars.

'I'm not meant to be here. I want to go home! I'm not unnatural, I'm not!' He was almost in tears. 'I'm sorry, I'm sorry about the stone!'

I clapped a hand over his mouth. 'Stop it.' A few of the others swore at him. 'You want her to reef you, too?'

He was trembling. I guessed he was about fifteen, but a weak fifteen. I was forcefully reminded of a different time – a time when I was frightened and alone.

'What's your name?' I tried to sound gentle.

'Seb. S-Seb Pearce.' He crossed his arms, trying to make himself smaller. 'Are you – are you all – unnaturals?'

'Yeah, and we'll do unnatural things to your internal organs if you don't shut your rotten trap,' a voice sneered. Seb cringed.

'No, we won't,' I said. 'I'm Paige. This is Julian.'

Julian just nodded. It looked like it was my job to make small talk with the amaurotic. 'Where are you from, Seb?' I said.

'III Cohort.'

'The ring,' Julian said. 'Nice.'

Seb looked away. His lips shook with cold. No doubt he thought we'd chop him up and bathe in his blood in an occult frenzy. The ring was where I'd gone to secondary school, a street name for III Cohort. 'Tell us what happened,' I said.

He glanced at the others. I couldn't find it in myself to blame him for his fear. He'd been told from the second he could talk that clairvoyants were the source of all the world's evils, and here he was in prison with them. 'One of the sixth-formers planted contraband in my satchel,' he said. Probably a shew stone, the most common numen on the black market. 'The Schoolmaster saw me trying to give it back to them in class. He thought I'd got it from one of those beggar types. They called the school Vigiles to check me.'

Definitely a Scion kid. If his school had its own Gillies, he must be from an astronomically rich family.

'It took hours to convince them I'd been framed. I took a short-cut home.' Seb swallowed. 'There were two men in red on the corner. I tried to walk past them, but they heard me. They wore masks. I don't know why, but I ran. I was scared. Then I heard a gunshot, and – and then I think I must have fainted. And then I was sick.'

I wondered about the effects of flux on amaurotics. It made sense that the physical symptoms would appear – vomiting, thirst, inexplicable terror – but not phantasmagoria. 'That's awful,' I said. 'I'm sure this is all a terrible mistake.' And I was sure. There was no way a well-bred amaurotic kid like Seb should be here.

Seb looked encouraged. 'Then they'll let me go home?'

'No,' Julian said.

My ears pricked. Footsteps. Pleione was back. She pulled open the door, grabbed the nearest prisoner and hauled him to his feet with one hand. 'Follow me. Remember the rules.'

We left the building through a set of double doors, the palmist guided by the whisperer. The frigid air hit every inch of exposed skin. I started when we came to the gallows – maybe this *was* the Tower – but Pleione walked past it. I had no idea what she'd done to the tasser, or what the scream had been, but I wasn't about to ask. Head down, eyes open. That would be my rule here, too.

She led us through deserted streets, illumined by gaslight and wet after a night of heavy rain. Julian fell into step beside me. As we walked, the buildings grew larger – but they weren't skyscrapers. They were nowhere near that scale. No metal framework, no electric light. These buildings were old and unfamiliar, built when aesthetic tastes were different. Stone walls, wooden doors, leaded windows glazed with deep red and amethyst. When we rounded the last corner, we were greeted by a sight I would never forget.

The street that stretched in front of us was oddly wide. There wasn't a car in sight: just a long line of ramshackle dwellings, winding drunkenly from one end to the other. Plywood walls propped up slats of corrugated metal. On either side of this little town were larger buildings. They had heavy wooden doors, high windows and crenellation, like the castles of Victoria's days. They reminded me so much of the Tower that I had to look away.

Several feet from the nearest hut, a group of svelte figures stood on an open-air stage. Candles had been placed all around them, illuminating their masked faces. A violin sang below the boards. Voyant music, the sort only a whisperer could perform. Looking up at them was a large audience. Every member of that audience wore a red tunic and a black gilet.

As if they'd been awaiting our arrival, the figures began to dance. They were all clairvoyant; in fact, everyone here was clairvoyant – the dancers, the spectators, *everyone*. Never in my life had I seen so many voyants in one place, standing peacefully together. There must have been a hundred observers clustered around the stage.

This was no secret meeting in an underground tunnel. This wasn't Hector's brutal syndicate. This was different. When Seb reached for my hand, I didn't shake him off.

The show went on for a few minutes. Not all of the spectators were paying attention. Some were talking among themselves, others jeering at the stage. I was sure I heard someone say 'cowards'. After the dance, a girl in a black leotard stepped out onto a higher platform. Her dark hair was slicked back into a bun, and her mask was gold and winged. She stood there for a moment, still as glass – then she jumped from the platform and seized two long red drapes that had been dropped from the rigging. Weaving her legs and arms around them, she climbed up twenty feet before unravelling into a pose. She earned a smattering of applause from the audience.

My brain was still drug-addled. Was this some kind of voyant cult? I'd heard of stranger things. I forced myself to study the street. One thing was certain: this wasn't SciLo. There was no sign of Scion's presence at all. Big old buildings, public performances, gas lamps and a cobbled street – it was like we'd rewound time.

I knew exactly where I was.

Everyone had heard about the lost city of Oxford. It was part of the Scion school curriculum. Fires had destroyed the university in the autumn of 1859. What remained was classified as a Type A Restricted Sector. No one was allowed to set foot there for fear of some indefinable contamination. Scion had just wiped it from the maps. I'd read in Jaxon's records that an intrepid journalist from the *Roaring Boy* had tried to drive there in 2036, threatening to write an exposé, but his car was driven off the road by snipers, never to be seen again. The *Roaring Boy*, a penny paper, disappeared just as quickly. It had tried far too often to uncover Scion's secrets.

Pleione turned to look at us. The darkness made it hard to see her face, but her eyes still burned.

'It is unseemly to stare,' she said. 'You do not want to be late for the oration.'

Yet we couldn't help but stare at the dance. We followed her, but she couldn't stop us looking.

We trooped after Pleione until we reached a pair of enormous wrought-iron gates. They were unlocked by two men, both of whom resembled our guide: same eyes, same satin skin, same auras. Pleione sailed right past them. Seb was starting to go green. I kept hold of his hand as we walked through the grounds of the building. This amaurotic should mean nothing to me, but he seemed too vulnerable to be left alone. The palmist was in tears. Only the oracle, picking at his knuckles, seemed fearless. As we walked, we were joined by several other groups of white-clad newcomers. Most of them looked frightened, but a few seemed exhilarated. My group drew closer together as we joined the ranks.

We were being herded.

We spilled into a long and lofty room. Olive-green shelves stretched from the floor to the ceiling, packed with beautiful old books. Eleven stained glass windows lined one wall. The décor was classical, with a dressed stone floor inlaid in a diagonal pattern. The captives jostled into lines. I stood between Julian and Seb, my senses on red alert. Julian was tense, too. His eyes moved from one white-clad captive to another, sizing them up. It was a real melting pot: a cross-section of voyants, from augurs and soothsayers to mediums and sensors.

Pleione had left us. Now she stood on a plinth with what I guessed were eight of her fellow Rephaite creatures. My sixth sense quaked.

Once we were assembled, a deathly hush swept over the room. A single woman stepped forward. And then she began to speak.

A Lecture upon the Shadow

'Welcome to Sheol I.'

The speaker was about six and a half feet tall. Her features were perfectly symmetrical: a long, straight nose, high cheekbones, deep-set eyes fixed in her face. The candlelight ran through her hair and across her burnished skin. She wore black, like the others, but her sleeves and sides were slashed with gold.

'I am Nashira Sargas.' Her voice was cool and low-pitched. 'I am the blood-sovereign of the Race of Rephaim.'

'Is this a joke?' someone whispered.

'Shh,' hissed another.

'First of all, I must apologise for the harrowing start to your time here, especially if you were housed first in the Tower. The vast majority of clairvoyants are under the impression that they are going to be executed when they are summoned to our fold. We use Fluxion 14 to ensure their transmission to Sheol I is safe and straightforward. After being sedated, you were placed on a train and taken to a detainment facility, where you were monitored. Your clothing and belongings have been confiscated.'

As I listened, I examined the woman, looking into the æther. Her aura was unlike anything I'd ever sensed before. I wished I could see it. It was as if she'd taken several different types of aura and forged them all into one strange field of energy.

There was something else, too. A cold edge. Most auras gave off a soft, warm signal, like I'd walked past a space heater, but this one gave me deep chills.

'I understand that you are surprised to see this city. You may know it as Oxford. Its existence was disavowed by your government two centuries ago, before any of you were born. It was supposedly quarantined after an outbreak of fire. This was a lie. It was closed off so we, the Rephaim, could make it our home.

'We arrived two centuries ago, in 1859. Your world had reached what we call the "ethereal threshold".' She assessed our faces. 'The majority of you are clairvoyant. You understand that sentient spirits exist all around us, too cowardly or stubborn to meet their final death in the heart of the æther. You can commune with them, and in return they will guide and protect you. But that connection has a price. When the corporeal world becomes overpopulated with drifting spirits, they cause deep rifts in the æther. When these rifts become too wide, the ethereal threshold breaks.

'When Earth broke its threshold, it became exposed to a higher dimension called Netherworld, where *we* reside. Now we have come here.' Nashira levelled her gaze on my line of prisoners. 'You humans have made many mistakes. You packed your fertile earth with corpses, burdened it with drifting spirits. Now it belongs to the Rephaim.'

I looked at Julian and saw my exact fear mirrored in his eyes. This woman had to be insane.

Silence filled the room. Nashira Sargas had our attention.

'My people, the Rephaim, are all clairvoyant. There are no amaurotics among us. Since the rip between our worlds occurred, we have been forced to share the Netherworld with a parasitic race called the

Emim. They are mindless, bestial creatures with a taste for human flesh. If not for us, they would have come here from beyond the threshold. They would have come for you.'

Mad. She was mad.

'You were all detained by humans in our employ. They are called red-jackets.' Nashira indicated a line of men and women, all clad in scarlet, at the back of the library. 'Since our arrival, we have taken many clairvoyant humans under our wing. In exchange for protection, we train you to destroy the Emim – to protect the "natural" population – as part of a penal battalion. This city acts as a beacon to the creatures, drawing them away from the rest of the corporeal world. When they breach its walls, red-jackets are summoned to destroy them. Such breaches are announced by a siren. There is a high risk of mutilation.'

There is also, I thought, *a high risk that this is all in my head.*

'We offer you this fate as an alternative to what Scion would offer: death by hanging, or asphyxiation. Or, as some of you have already experienced, a long, dark sentence in the Tower.'

In the row behind me, one girl began to whimper. She was shushed by the people on either side of her.

'Of course, we do not have to work together.' Nashira paced along the front row. 'When we came to this world, we found it vulnerable. Only a fraction of you are clairvoyant, and still less have marginally useful abilities. We might have let the Emim turn on you. We would have been justified in doing so, given what you have done to this world.'

Seb was crushing my hand. I was aware of a faint ringing in my ears.

This was ridiculous. A bad joke. Or brain plague. Yes, it must be brain plague. Scion was trying to make us think we'd gone insane. Maybe we had.

'But we had mercy. We took pity. We negotiated with your rulers, starting on this small island. They gave us this city, which we named

Sheol I, and sent us a certain number of clairvoyants each decade. Our primary source was, and remains, the capital city of London. It was this city that worked for seven decades to develop the Scion security system. Scion has greatly increased the chance of clairvoyants being recognised, relocated and rehabilitated into a new society, away from so-called amaurotics. In exchange for that service, we have vowed not to destroy your world. Instead, we plan to take control of it.'

I wasn't certain that I understood what she was saying, but one thing was clear: if she was telling the truth, Scion was no more than a puppet government. Subordinate. And it had sold us out.

It didn't really come as a surprise.

The girl in the row behind couldn't stand it any longer. With a choked scream, she made a break for the door.

She didn't stand a chance against the bullet.

Screams erupted everywhere. So did the blood. Seb's nails dug into my hand. In the chaos, one of the Rephaim stepped forward.

'SILENCE.'

The noise stopped at once.

Blood flowered under the girl's hair. Her eyes were open. Her expression lingered: distraught, terrified.

The killer was human, wearing red. He holstered his revolver and put his hands behind his back. Two of his companions, both girls, took the body by the arms and dragged it outside. 'Always one yellow-jacket,' one said, loud enough for everyone to hear.

The marble floor was stained. Nashira looked at us with no hint of emotion.

'If any more of you would like to run, now is the time to do so. Be assured, we can make room in the grave.'

Nobody moved.

In the silence that followed, I risked a glance at the plinths. One of the Rephaim was looking at me.

He must have been examining me for some time. His gaze cleaved straight to mine, as if he'd been waiting for me to look, watching for a flicker of dissent. His skin was a dark honey gold, setting off two heavy-lidded yellow eyes. He was the tallest of the five males, with coarse brown hair, clothed in embroidered black. Wrapped around him was a strange, soft aura, overshadowed by the others in the room. He was the single most beautiful and terrible thing I'd ever laid eyes on.

A spasm tore through my insides. I snapped my gaze back to the floor. Would they shoot me just for looking?

Nashira was still speaking, pacing up and down the rows. 'Clairvoyants have developed great strength over the years. You are used to survival. The mere fact that you are standing here, having evaded capture for so long, is a testimony to your collective ability to adapt. Your gifts have proven invaluable in keeping the Emim at bay. This is why, over ten years, we collect as many of you as possible, keeping you in the Tower to await your transition from Scion. We call these decadal harvests Bone Seasons. This is Bone Season XX.

'You will be given identification numbers in due course. Those of you who are clairvoyant will now be assigned a Rephaite keeper.' She indicated her companions. 'Your keeper is your master in all things. He or she will test your abilities and assess your value. If any of you show cowardice, you will be given the yellow tunic: that of a coward. Those of you who are amaurotic – that is, the few of you who have no idea what I am talking about,' she added, 'will be put to work in our residences. To serve us.'

Seb didn't appear to be breathing.

'If you do not pass your first test, or if you earn the yellow tunic twice, you will be placed under the care of the Overseer, who will mould you into a performer. Performers are there for our entertainment, and the entertainment of those in our employ.'

I wondered at the choice: circus freak or conscription. My lips shook, and my free hand balled into a fist. I had imagined many reasons for voyants being taken, but nothing like this.

Human trafficking. No, *voyant* trafficking. Scion had sent us into slavery.

A few people were weeping now; others stood in rapt horror. Nashira didn't seem to notice. She hadn't even blinked when the girl died. She hadn't blinked at all.

'Rephaim do not forgive. Those of you who adapt to this system will be rewarded. Those who do not will be punished. None of us want that to happen, but should you show us disrespect, you will suffer. This is your life now.'

Seb fainted. Julian and I propped him up between us, but he was still a dead weight.

The nine Rephaim stepped down from their plinths. I kept my head down.

'These Rephaim have offered their services as keepers,' Nashira informed us. 'They will decide which of you they wish to take.'

Seven of the nine began to walk around the room, between the rows. The last one – the one I'd looked at – stayed with Nashira. I didn't dare look at Julian, but I said in a whisper, 'It can't be true.'

'Look at them.' He barely moved his lips. Our proximity on either side of Seb was all that allowed me to hear him. 'They're not human. They're from somewhere else.'

'You mean this "Netherworld"?' I shut my mouth when a Reph passed, then continued: 'The only other dimension is the æther. That's *it*.'

'The æther exists alongside meatspace – around us, not outside of us. This is something more.'

A frantic laugh bubbled up inside me. 'Scion's gone mad.'

Julian didn't answer. Across the room, a Rephaite took Carl by the elbow. 'XX-59-1,' she said, 'I lay claim to you.' Carl swallowed as he was led to a plinth, but he kept up his brave face. Once he was deposited, the Rephaim returned to their circling, like flimps sizing up a wealthy target.

I wondered how they were choosing us. Was it bad for Carl to have been chosen so soon?

Minutes ticked by. The rows dwindled. The whisperer, now XX-59-2, joined Carl. The oracle went with Pleione, seemingly uninterested by the procedure. A cruel-faced male dragged the palmist to his plinth. She started to cry, gasping 'please' over and over, to no avail. Soon Julian was taken. XX-59-26. He shot me a look, nodded, and went with his new keeper to the plinths.

Twelve more names were changed to numbers. They got to 38. Finally there were eight of us left: the six amaurotics, a julker, and me.

Someone had to choose me. Several of the Rephaim had examined me, paying close attention to my body and my eyes, but none had claimed me. What would happen if I wasn't chosen?

The julker, a small boy with cornrows, was led away by Pleione. 39. Now I was the only voyant left.

The Rephaim looked to Nashira. She looked at those of us who remained. My spine pulled tight as rope.

Then the one that had watched me stepped forwards. He didn't speak, but he drew closer to Nashira, and his head tilted towards me. Her eyes flicked to my face. She raised a hand and crooked a long finger. Like Pleione, she wore black gloves. All of them did.

Seb was still unconscious. I tried to let him slide to the floor, but he clung. Noticing my predicament, one of the amaurotic men took him from my arms.

Every eye was on me as I walked across the marble floor and stopped in front of the pair. Nashira seemed much taller up close, and the male stood a clear foot above me.

'Your name?'

'Paige Mahoney.'

'Where are you from?'

'I Cohort.'

'Not originally.'

They must have seen my records. 'Ireland,' I said. A tremor passed through the room.

'Scion Belfast?'

'No, the free part of Ireland.' Somebody gasped.

'I see. A free spirit, then.' Her eyes seemed bioluminescent. 'We are intrigued by your aura. Tell me: what are you?'

'A cipher,' I said.

I turned cold under her stare.

'I have good news for you, Paige Mahoney.' Nashira placed her hand on her companion's arm. 'You have attracted the attention of the blood-consort: Arcturus, Warden of the Mesarthim. He has decided to be your keeper.'

The Rephaim looked at each other. They didn't speak, but their auras seemed to ripple.

'It is rare that he takes interest in a human,' Nashira said, her voice as quiet as if she were entrusting me with some closely guarded secret. 'You are very, very fortunate.'

I didn't feel fortunate. I was sickened.

The blood-consort leaned down to my level. A long way down. I didn't look away.

'XX-59-40.' His voice was deep and soft. 'I lay claim to you.'

So this man was to be my master. I looked right into his eyes, even though I shouldn't. I wanted to know the face of my enemy.

The last of the voyants had been taken from the floor. Nashira raised her voice to the six amaurotics. 'You six will wait here. An escort will be sent to lead you to the barracks. The rest of you will go with your keepers to the residences. Good luck to you all, and remember: the choices you make here are yours alone. I only hope you make the right ones.'

With that, she turned and walked away. Two red-jackets followed her. I was left to stand with my new keeper, numb.

Arcturus moved towards the door. He made a motion with his hand, beckoning me to follow. When I didn't come at once, he stopped and waited.

Everyone was looking at me. My head spun. I saw red, then white. I walked out after him.

The first stain of dawn had touched the spires. The voyants came out after their keepers, three or four to each group. I was the only one with an individual keeper.

Arcturus came to stand beside me. Too close. My back stiffened.

'You should know that we sleep by day here.'

I said nothing.

'You should also know that it is not my custom to take tenants.' What a nice word for *prisoners*. 'If you pass your tests, you will live with me on a permanent basis. If you do not, I will be forced to evict you. And the streets here are not kind.'

I still said nothing. I knew that streets weren't kind. They couldn't be much worse than they were in London.

'You are not mute,' he said. 'Speak.'

'I didn't know I was allowed to speak without permission.'

'I will allow you that privilege.'

'There's nothing to say.'

Arcturus examined me. His eyes held a dead heat.

'We are stationed at the Residence of Magdalen.' He turned his back from the dawn. 'I take it you are strong enough to walk, girl?'

'I can walk,' I said.

'Good.'

So we walked. We walked out of the building and onto the street, where the sinister performance had come to an end. I spotted the contortionist near the stage, feeding her silks into a bag. She met my eyes, then looked away. She had the delicate aura of a cartomancer. And the bruises of a prisoner.

Magdalen was a magnificent building. It was from a different age, a different world. It had a chapel and bell towers and high glass windows that burned with the ferocious light of torches. A bell clanged out five chimes as we approached and went through a small door. A boy in a red tunic bowed when we passed a series of cloisters. I followed Arcturus into the gloom. He went up a winding stone staircase and stopped before a heavy door, which he unlocked with a small brass key. 'In here,' he said to me. 'This will be your new home. The Founder's Tower.'

I looked into my prison.

Behind the door was a large rectangular room. The furnishings were nothing short of opulent. The walls were white, devoid of clutter. All that hung on them was a crest, topped with three flowers, with a black-and-white pattern beneath them. A slanted chessboard. Heavy red curtains fell on either side of the windows, which looked out over courtyards. Two armchairs faced a magnificent wood-burning fireplace, and a red daybed sat in the corner, piled with silk cushions. Beside it, a grandfather clock stood against the wall. A gramophone played 'Gloomy Sunday' from a dark wood writing table, and there was an elegant nightstand beside the lavish four-poster bed. Beneath my feet was a richly patterned carpet.

Arcturus locked the door. I watched him tuck the key away. 'I have little knowledge of humans. You may have to remind me of your needs.' He tapped his finger on the table. 'In here are medicinal substances. You are to take one of each pill every night.'

I didn't speak, but I skimmed his dreamscape. Ancient and strange, indurated by time. A magic lantern in the æther.

The stranger in I-4 had most definitely been one of them.

I sensed his eyes reading beyond my face. Studying my aura, trying to work out what he'd saddled himself with. Or what buried treasure he'd uncovered. The thought brought on another surge of hatred.

'Look at me.'

It was an order. I raised my chin, met his gaze. I'd be damned if I let him see the fear he stirred in me.

'You do not have the spirit sight,' he observed. 'That will be a disadvantage here. Unless you have some means of compensating, of course. Perhaps a stronger sixth sense.'

I didn't answer. It had always been my dream to be at least half-sighted, but I remained spirit-blind. I couldn't see the æther's little lights; I could only ever sense them. Jaxon had never thought it a weakness.

'Do you have any questions?' His unpitying eyes searched every inch of my face.

'Where do I sleep?'

'I will have a room prepared for you. For now you will sleep here.' He indicated the daybed. 'Anything else?'

'No.'

'I will be away tomorrow. You may acquaint yourself with the city in my absence. You will be back by dawn every day. You will return to this room at once if you hear the siren. If you steal or touch or otherwise meddle with anything, I will know.'

'Yes, sir.'

The *sir* just slipped out.

'Take this.' He held out a capsule. 'Take a second tomorrow night, along with the others.'

I didn't take it. Arcturus poured a glass of water from a decanter, not looking at me. He handed me the glass and the capsule. I wet my lips.

'What if I don't take it?'

There was a long silence.

'It was an order,' he said. 'Not a request.'

My heart palpitated. I rolled it between my fingers. It was olive in colour, tinged with grey. I swallowed it. It tasted bitter.

He took the glass.

'One more thing.' Arcturus grasped the back of my head in his free hand, turning it to face him. A cold tremor rolled down my spine. 'You will address me only by my ceremonial title: Warden. Is that understood?'

'Yes.'

I forced myself to say it. He looked right into my eyes, burning his message into my skull, before he loosened his hand. 'We will begin your training upon my return.' He made for the door. 'Sleep well.'

I couldn't help it. I laughed a low, bitter laugh.

He half-turned his head. I watched his eyes empty. Without another word, he left. The key turned in the lock.

The Indifferent

A red sun glinted through the window. The light roused me from a deep sleep. There was a bad taste in my mouth. For a moment I thought I was back in my bedroom in I-5, away from Jax, away from work.

Then I remembered. Bone Seasons. Rephaim. A gunshot and a body.

I was definitely not in I-5.

The cushions lay on the floor, cast off in the night. I sat up to assess my surroundings, rubbing my stiff neck. The small of my back ached, and my head pounded. One of my 'hangovers', as Nick called them. Arcturus – Warden – was nowhere to be seen.

The gramophone was still sorrowing away. I recognised Saint-Saëns' 'Danse Macabre' immediately, and with alarm: Jax listened to it when he was particularly cantankerous, usually over a glass of vintage wine. It had always given me the creeps. I switched it off, pushed the drapes from the window and looked down at the east-facing courtyard. There was a Rephaite guard positioned by a pair of giant oak doors.

A fresh uniform had been laid out on the bed. I found a note on the pillow, written in a bold black cursive.

Wait for the bell.

I thought back to the oration. Nobody had mentioned a bell. I scrunched the note into my hand and tossed it into the hearth, where other scraps were waiting to be burned.

I spent a few minutes scouring the room, checking every corner. There were no bars on these windows, but they couldn't be opened. The walls hid no secret seams or sliding panels. There were two more doors, one of which was hidden behind thick red drapes – and locked. The other led to a large bathroom. Finding no light switch, I took one of the oil lamps inside. The bath was the same black marble as the library floor, surrounded by diaphanous curtains. A gilded mirror took up most of one wall. I approached this first, curious to see if the mutilation of my life showed on my face.

It didn't. Save for the cut lip, I looked just the same as I had before they caught me. I sat in the darkness, thinking.

The Rephaim had struck their deal in 1859, exactly two centuries ago. That was Lord Palmerston's time in office, if I remembered my classes correctly. It was long before the end of the monarchy in 1901, when a new Republic of England took power and declared war on unnaturalness. That republic had taken the country through nearly three decades of indoctrination and propaganda before it was named Scion in 1929. That was when the First Inquisitor was chosen, and London became the first Scion citadel. All this suggested to me that somehow, the Rephaim's arrival had *triggered* Scion. All that bullshit about unnaturalness, just to sate these creatures that had come from nowhere.

I took a deep breath. There must be more to this, there must be. Somehow I would understand. My first priority was to get out of here. Until I could do that, I would search this place for answers. I couldn't just walk away, not now I knew where voyants were being sent. I couldn't forget all I'd heard and seen.

First I would find Seb. His amaurosis made him ignorant and scared, but he was only a kid. He didn't deserve this. Once I'd located him, I'd find Julian and the other detainees from Bone Season XX. I wanted to know more about the Emim, and until my keeper got back, they were my only source of information.

A bell rang in the tower outside, echoed by another, louder chime in the distance. *Wait for the bell.* There must be a curfew.

I placed the lamp on the edge of the bath. As I splashed my face with cold water, I considered my options. It was best to play along with the Rephaim for now. If I survived long enough I would try and contact Jax. Jax would come for me. He never left a voyant behind. Not a voyant he employed, anyway. I'd seen him leave buskers to die more than once.

It was getting darker in the chamber. I pulled open the middle drawer of the writing table. Inside were three blister packs of pills. I didn't want to take them, but I had a feeling he might count them to make sure I did. Unless I just threw them away.

I popped out one from each packet. Red, white and green. None of them were labelled.

The city was full of non-humans, full of things I didn't yet understand. These pills might be there to protect me from something: toxins, radiation – the contamination Scion had warned us about. Maybe it wasn't a lie. Maybe I should take them. I would have to in the end, when he came back.

But he wasn't here now. He couldn't see me. I washed all three pills down the sink. He could take his medicine and choke.

When I tried the door, I found it unlocked. I descended the stone steps, back into the cloisters. This residence was enormous. At the door to the street, a bony girl with a pink nose and dirty blonde hair had replaced the boy in the red. She looked up from a counter when I approached.

'Hello,' she said. 'You must be new.'

'Yes.'

'Well, you've started your journey in a great place. Welcome to Magdalen, the best residence in Sheol I. I'm XIX-49-33, the night porter. How can I help you?'

'You can let me go outside.'

'Do you have permission?'

'I don't know.' I didn't care, either.

'Okay. I'll check for you.' Her smile was getting tense. 'Can I take your number?'

'XX-59-40.'

The girl consulted her ledger. When she found the right page, she looked up at me with wide eyes. 'You're the one the Warden took in.'

Well, *took in* was one way of putting it.

'He's never taken a human tenant before,' she continued. 'Not many of them do at Magdalen. Mostly it's just Rephs with a few human assistants. You're very lucky to be lodging with him, you know.'

'So I've been told,' I said. 'I have a few questions about this place, if you don't mind.'

'Go ahead.'

'Where do I get food?'

'The Warden left a note about that.' She poured a handful of blunted needles, cheap tin rings and thimbles into my palm. 'Here. They're numa. The harlies always need them. You can exchange them for food in the stalls outside – there's a sort of squatter settlement, you know – but it's not very good. I'd wait for your keeper to feed you.'

'Is he likely to do that?'

'Maybe.'

Well, now that was cleared up. 'Where is the settlement?' I said.

'On the Broad. Take the first right out of Magdalen, then the first left. You'll see it.' She turned to a new page in her ledger. 'Remember, you mustn't sit down in public areas without permission, or enter any of the residences. Don't wear anything apart from your uniform, either. Oh, and you absolutely *must* be back here by dawn.'

'Why?'

'Well, the Rephs sleep by day. I assume you know that spirits are easier to see when the sun goes down.'

'And that makes training easier.'

'Exactly.'

I really didn't like this girl. 'Do you have a keeper?'

'Yes, I do. He's away at the moment, you know.'

'Away where?'

'I don't know. But I'm sure it's for something important.'

'I see. Thanks.'

'You're welcome. Have a nice night! And remember,' she added, 'don't go beyond the bridge.'

Well, someone was brainwashed. I smiled and took my leave.

As I left the residence, my breath already clouding, I began to wonder what I'd got myself into. *The Warden.* His name was whispered like a prayer, like a promise. Why was this one different from the others? What did *blood-consort* mean? I promised myself I would look into it later. For now I would eat. Then I would find Seb. At least I had somewhere to sleep when I returned. He might not have been so lucky.

A thin fog had descended. There seemed to be no electricity in the city. To my left was a stone bridge, set on both sides with gas lamps. This must be the bridge I couldn't cross. A line of red-clad guards blocked the route between the city and the outside world. When I didn't move, all ten of them pointed their guns at me. Scion weapons. Military grade. With all ten sights trained on my back, I set off to find the little town.

The street ran alongside Magdalen's grounds, separated from the residence by a high wall. I passed three heavy wooden doors, each guarded by a human in a red tunic. The wall was topped with iron spikes. I kept my head down and followed 33's directions. The next street was just as deserted as the first, with no gas lamps to light my way. When I emerged from the darkness, my hands raw with cold, I found myself in something like a city centre. Two large buildings towered on the left. The nearest had pillars and a decorated pediment, like the Grand Museum in I Cohort. I walked past it, onto the Broad. Tealights shone on every step and ledge. The sound of human life strained through the night.

Rickety stalls and food booths had been constructed down the centre of the street, lit by dirty lanterns. They were skeletal and gloomy. On either side of them were rows of rudimentary huts, shacks and tents, made of corrugated metal and plywood and plastic – a shantytown in the centre of a city.

And the siren. An old mechanical model with a single, gaping horn. Not like the hive-like electrical clusters on NVD outposts, designed for use in a national emergency. I hoped I never heard the sound that swelled up from its rotors. The last thing I needed was some flesh-eating killing machine on my tail.

The smell of roasting meat drew me towards the shantytown. My stomach was tight with hunger. I walked into a dark, close tunnel, following my nose. The shacks seemed to be linked by a series of plywood tunnels, patched up with bits of scrap metal and cloth. They had few windows; instead they were lit by candles and paraffin lamps. I was the only person in a white tunic. These people all wore filthy clothes. The colours did little for their sallow complexions, their lifeless bloodshot eyes. None of them looked healthy. These must be the performers: humans who had failed their tests and been condemned to amuse the Rephaim for the rest of their lives, and probably their afterlives. Most were soothsayers or augurs, the most common kinds of voyant. A few people glanced at me, but they soon moved on. It was like they didn't want to look for too long.

The source of the smell was a large square room with a hole cut into the corrugated metal roof to let out smoke and steam. I stood in a dark corner, trying not to draw attention to myself. The meat was being served in wafer-thin slices, still pink and tender in the middle. The performers passed around plates of meat and vegetables and scooped cream from silver tureens. People were fighting over the food, stuffing it into their mouths, licking the hot juices from their fingers. Before I could ask, a voyant pressed a plate into my hands. He was scrawny, dressed in little more than rags. His thick glasses were scratched all over.

'Is Mayfield still in the Starch?'

I raised an eyebrow. 'Mayfield?'

'Yes, Abel Mayfield.' He sounded it out in syllables. 'Is he still in the Archon? Is he still Grand Inquisitor?'

'Mayfield died years ago.'

'Who is it now?'

'Frank Weaver.'

'Oh, right. You haven't got a copy of the *Descendant*, have you?'

'They confiscated everything.' I glanced around for somewhere to sit down. 'Did you really think Mayfield was still the Inquisitor?' It was impossible not to know the Inquisitor's identity. Scarlett Burnish excluded, Weaver was the heart and soul of Scion.

'All right, don't get on your high horse. How was I supposed to know? We only get news once a decade.' He grabbed my arm, leading me to a corner. 'Did they ever bring back the *Roaring Boy*?'

'No.' I tried to free my arm, but he clung.

'Is Sinatra still blacklisted?'

'Yes.'

'Shame. What about the Fleapit? Did they ever find it?'

'Cyril, she's just arrived. I think she'd like something to eat.'

Someone had noticed my predicament. Cyril rounded on the speaker, a young woman with her arms crossed and her chin tipped up. 'You are an absolute stinking bloody curmudgeon, Rymore. Did you pick up ten of swords again today?'

'Yeah, when I was thinking about you.'

With a glower, Cyril snatched the plate and scarpered. I made a grab for his shirt, but he was faster than a flimp. The girl shook her head. She had small, quick features, framed by matted black ringlets. Her red lipstick stood out like a fresh wound against her skin.

'You had your oration last night, little sister.' Her voice carried a burr. 'Your stomach wouldn't have taken it.'

'I ate yesterday morning,' I said. I wasn't sure whether to laugh at being called *little sister* by this tiny girl.

'Trust me, it's the flux. It's janxed your brain.' She glanced around the room. 'Quick. Come with me.'

'Where?'

'I have a crib. We can talk.'

I didn't much like the idea of following a stranger, but I had to talk to someone. I went after her.

My guide seemed to know everyone. She touched hands with various people, always keeping an eye on me to make sure I was still behind her. Her clothes appeared to be in better condition than those of the other performers: a flimsy bell-sleeved shirt, trousers too short for her legs. She must be freezing. She drew back a ragged curtain. 'Quick,' she said again. 'They'll see.'

It was dim beyond the curtain, but a paraffin stove kept the shadows at bay. I sat down. A pile of stained sheets and a cushion made a rudimentary bed. 'Do you always take in strays?'

'Sometimes. I know how it is when you arrive.' The girl sat down by the stove. 'Welcome to the Family.'

'I'm part of a family?'

'You are now, sister. And it's not the cult kind of family, if that's what you're thinking. Just a family formed for protection.' Her fingers worked at the stove. 'I'm guessing you came from the syndicate.'

'Maybe.'

'I didn't. The centrals didn't need my sort.' A faint smile touched her lips. 'I came here during the last Bone Season.'

'How long ago was that?'

'Ten years. I was thirteen.' She extended a callused hand. After a moment, I shook it. 'Liss Rymore.'

'Paige.'

'XX-59-40?'

'Yes.'

Liss caught my expression. 'Sorry,' she said. 'Force of habit. Or maybe I'm brainwashed.'

I shrugged. 'What number are you?'

'XIX-49-1.'

'How do you know mine?'

She poured a little methylated spirit into the stove. 'News travels fast in a city this small. We can't get any word from outside. They don't like us to know what's going on out there in the free world. If you call Scion "free".' A blue flame leapt up. 'Your number is on everyone's lips.'

'Why?'

'Didn't you hear? Arcturus Mesarthim has never taken a human to his residence. He's never shown interest in humans at *all*, in fact. It's big news here, sad to say. Happens when you can't get the penny papers.'

'Do you know why he chose me?'

'My best guess is that Nashira has got her lamps on you. He's the blood-consort – her fiancé. We stay out of his way. Not that he ever leaves that tower.' She attached a billycan onto the stove. 'Let me get you something to eat before we talk. Sorry. It's been years since we've eaten at tables, us harlies.'

'Harlies?'

'It's what jackets call the performers. They don't like us much.'

She heated up some broth and poured it into a bowl. I offered her a few rings, but she shook her head. 'On the house.'

I took a sip of the broth. It was odourless and translucent, and it tasted vile, but it was warm. Liss watched as I scraped the bowl clean.

'Here.' She passed me a hunk of stale bread. 'Skilly and toke. You'll get used to it. Most of the keepers conveniently forget that we need to eat on a regular basis.'

'There's meat in there.' I gestured to the central room.

'That's just to celebrate Bone Season XX. I made this skilly from the juices earlier.' She poured herself a bowl. 'We rely on the rotties to keep us from starving. This junk is all from the kitchens,' she said, nodding to the stove and billycan. 'They're only meant to cook for red-jackets, but they sneak us food when they can. Having said that, they've been less willing to help us since one of the girls was caught.'

'What happened?'

'The rottie got beaten. The voyant she was feeding got four days of sleep dep. He was raving by the time they let him out.'

Sleep deprivation. It was a novel punishment. Voyant minds functioned on two levels: life and death. It was tiring. Being kept awake for four days would drive a voyant mad. 'Who brings the food into the city?'

'No idea. Maybe the train. It runs from London to Sheol I. Nobody knows where the entrances to the tunnel are, obviously.' She shifted her feet closer to the stove. 'How long did you think the brain plague lasted?'

'For ever.'

'It was five days. They let the rookies go through hell for five days before they give them the antidote.'

'Why?'

'So they learn their place as quickly as possible. You're no more than a number here unless you earn your colours.' Liss helped herself to a bowl of broth. 'So you're at Magdalen.'

'Yes.'

'You're probably sick of hearing this, but consider yourself lucky. Magdalen is one of the safest residences for a human.'

'How many are there?'

'Humans?'

'Residences.'

'Oh, right. Well, each residence is a small district. There are seven for humans: Balliol, Corpus, Exeter, Merton, Oriel, Queens and Trinity. Nashira lives at the Residence of the Suzerain, where you had your oration. Then there's the House, a little way south, and the Castle – the Detainment Facility – and this dump, the Rookery. The street is called the Broad. The street that runs parallel is Magdalen Walk.'

'And beyond that?'

'Deserted countryside. We call it No Man's Land. It's rigged with mines and trap-pits.'

'Has anyone ever tried to cross it?'

'Yes.'

Her shoulders were tense. I took another sip of skilly.

'How was the Tower?'

I looked up at her. 'I didn't go to the Tower.'

'Were you born on a boon or something?' When I frowned, Liss shook her head. 'They collect voyants for each Bone Season over ten years. Some of them are in the Tower for a decade before they get posted here.'

'You're kidding.' That explained the poor sap that had been there for nine years.

'Nope. They're pretty cokum when it comes to keeping us tame. They know all our weak points, how to break us. Ten years in the Tower would break anyone.'

'What are they?'

'No idea, except they're not human.' She dabbed some bread in the skilly. 'They act like gods. That's how they like to be treated.'

'And we're their worshippers.'

'Not just their worshippers. We owe them our lives. They never let us forget they're protecting us from the Buzzers, and that slavery is "for our own good". We'd rather be slaves than dead, they say. Or victimised outside by the Inquisitor.'

'Buzzers?'

'The Emim. That's what we call them.'

'Why?'

'We've always called them that. Think the red-jackets came up with it. They're the ones that have to fight them off.'

'How often?'

'Depends on the time of year. They attack a lot more in winter. Listen out for the siren. A single blast summons the red-jackets. If the tone starts to change, get inside. It means they're coming.'

'I still don't understand what they are.' I tore up some bread. 'Are they anything like the Rephaim?'

'I've heard stories. The red-jackets like scaring us.' The firelight played across her face. 'They say the Emim take on different forms. Just being near them can kill you. Some say they can rip your spirit straight out of your body. Some call them rotting giants, whatever that means. Others say they're walking bones that need skin to cover themselves. I don't know how much of it is true, but they definitely eat human flesh. They're addicted to it. Don't be surprised if you see a few missing limbs out there.'

I should have been sickened; instead I was numb. It just didn't seem real. Liss reached over to adjust the curtain, concealing us from the people outside. A stack of coloured silk caught my eye.

'You're the contortionist,' I said.

'Did you think I was good?'

'Very good.'

'That's how I earn my flatches here. Lucky for me I picked it up quickly – used to busk near the penny gaff.' She licked her lips clean. 'I saw you with Pleione last night. Your aura was a talking point.'

I didn't say anything. It was dangerous to talk about my aura, especially when I'd only just met this girl.

Liss studied me. 'Are you sighted?'

'No.' That was true.

'What were you arrested for?'

'I killed someone. An Underguard.' True.

'How?'

'Knife,' I said. 'Heat of the moment.' False.

Liss looked at me for a long time. She was full-sighted, typical of soothsayers. She could see my red aura as clearly as my face. If she'd read up on the subject, she'd know which category I fell into.

'I don't think so.' Her fingers drummed on the floor. 'You've never spilled that much blood.'

She was good, for a soothsayer.

'You're not an oracle,' she stated, more to herself than to me. 'I've seen oracles. You're too calm to be a fury, and you're definitely not a medium. So you must be' – recognition dawned in her eyes – 'a dreamwalker.' Her gaze returned to mine. 'Are you?'

I held her eye contact. Liss sat back on her heels.

'Well, that solves it.'

'What?'

'Why Arcturus took you on. Nashira has never found a walker, and she *really* wants one. She'll want to make sure you're protected. Nobody will touch you if you're his human. If she thinks there's the slightest chance that you might be a walker, she'll do you right down.'

'How so?'

'You won't like this.'

I doubted anything could surprise me now.

'Nashira has a gift,' Liss said. 'Did you notice that weird aura coming off her?' I nodded. 'She doesn't just have one ability. She walks several different paths to the æther.'

'That's impossible. We all have one gift.'

'You know reality? Forget it. Sheol I has its own rules. Accept that now and everything will be easier.' She pulled her battered knees up to her chin. 'Nashira has five guardian angels. Somehow she gets them to stay with her.'

'Is she a binder?'

'We don't know. She must have been a binder once, but her aura's been corrupted.'

'By what?'

'By the angels.' When I frowned, she sighed. 'This is just a theory. We *think* she can use the gifts they had when they were alive.'

'Not even binders can do that.'

'Exactly.' She glanced at me. 'If you want my advice, you'll keep your head down. Give no inkling of what you are. If she finds out you're a walker, you're bones.'

I kept my expression neutral. Three years in the syndicate had inured me to danger, but this place was different. I would have to learn to duck new threats. 'How do I stop her finding out?'

'It'll be hard. They'll test you to expose your gift. That's what the tunics mean. Pink after your first test, red after the second.'

'But you failed your tests.'

'Luckily. Now I answer to the Overseer.'

'Who was your keeper?'

Liss looked back at the stove. 'Gomeisa Sargas.'

'Who is he?'

'The other blood-sovereign. There are always two, a male and a female.'

'But Arcturus is—'

'Betrothed to Nashira, yes. But he's not of "the blood",' she said, with a note of disgust. 'Only the Sargas family can take the crown. The blood-sovereigns can't be a mated pair – that would be incestuous. Arcturus is from a different family.'

'So he's the prince consort.'

'Blood-consort. Same thing. More skilly?'

'I'm fine. Thanks.' I watched her drop the bowl into a tub of greasy water. 'How did you fail your tests?'

'I stayed human.' She offered a small smile. 'Rephs aren't human. No matter how much they look like us, they're not like us. They've got nothing *here*.' Her finger tapped her chest. 'If they want us to work with them, they have to get rid of our souls.'

'How?'

Before she could answer, the curtain was torn back. A lean male Rephaite stood in the doorway.

'You,' he snarled at Liss. Her hands flew to her head. 'Get up. Get dressed. Lazy filth. And with a *guest*? Are you a queen?'

Liss stood. All her strength was gone, leaving her small and fragile. Her left hand shook. 'I'm sorry, Suhail,' she said. '40 is new here. I wanted to explain the rules of Sheol I.'

'40 should already know the rules of Sheol I.'

'Forgive me.'

He raised his gloved hand as if to strike her. 'Get onto the silks.'

'I didn't think I was performing tonight.' She backed into the corner of the shack. 'Have you talked to the Overseer?'

I took a good look at her interrogator. He was tall and golden, like the other Rephaim, but he didn't have that blank stare the others favoured. Every crease of his face was loaded with hatred.

'I do not need to speak with the Overseer, little pull-string puppet. 15 remains indisposed. The red-jackets expect their favourite fool to replace him.' His lips drew back over his teeth. 'Unless you wish to join him in the Detainment Facility, you will perform in ten minutes.'

Liss flinched. Her shoulders pulled towards her chest, and she looked away. 'I understand,' she said.

'There's a good slave.'

He ripped the curtain down on his way out. I helped Liss gather it up. She was shaking, physically shaking.

'Who was that?'

'Suhail Chertan. The Overseer's always a bit tense under all that greasepaint – he answers to Suhail if we do something wrong.' She dabbed her eyes with her sleeve. '15 is the one that got sleep dep. Jordan. He's the other contortionist.'

I took the curtain from her hands. Her sleeve was dark with blood. 'You cut yourself?'

'It's nothing.'

'No, it's not.' Blood was never nothing.

'It's okay.' She wiped her face, leaving red smears below her eyes. 'He just took a bit of my glow.'

'He what?'

'He fed on me.'

I was sure I'd misheard her. 'He *fed* on you,' I repeated.

Liss smiled. 'Did they forget to mention that Rephs feed on aura? That always slips their mind.'

Her face was streaked with blood. My stomach clenched. 'That's impossible. Aura doesn't sustain life,' I said. 'It sustains voyance. Not—'

'It sustains *their* life.'

'But that would mean they weren't just clairvoyant. They would have to be the æther incarnate.'

'Maybe they are.' Liss pulled a threadbare blanket around her shoulders. 'That's what we harlies are here for. We're just aura machines. Reph fodder. But you jackets – you don't get fed on. That's your privilege.' She looked at the stove. 'Unless you fail your tests.'

I was silent for a while. The idea that the Rephaim fed on *aura* just didn't compute. It was a link to the æther, unique to each voyant. I couldn't imagine how they could use it for survival.

But the news was like a light on Sheol I. That was why they took voyants into their fold. That was why the performers weren't bumped off if they couldn't fight the Emim. They didn't just want them to dance – why should they? Those were asinine distractions, to stop them getting bored with all their power. We weren't only their slaves; we were their food source. That was why we were paying for human error, not the amaurotics.

And to think I'd been in London a few days before this, living my life in Seven Dials, not knowing that this colony existed.

'Someone has to stop them,' I said. 'This is insane.'

'They've been here for two hundred years. Don't you think someone would have stopped them by now?'

I turned away, my head pounding.

'I'm sorry.' Liss glanced at me. 'I don't want to scare you, but I've been here ten years. I've seen people fight, people who wanted to go back to their old lives, and they've all wound up dead. In the end you'll just stop trying.'

'Are you a seer?' I knew she wasn't, but I wondered if she'd lie.

'Broadsider.' It was an old word for a cartomancer, street slang of a decade past. 'The very first time I read the cards, they knew.'

'What did you see?'

For a minute I thought she hadn't heard me. Then she crossed the shack and knelt beside a small wooden box. She took out a deck of tarot cards, tied with a red ribbon, and handed one to me. The Fool.

'I always knew I was destined to be the bottom of the pile,' she said. 'I was right.'

'Can you read mine?'

'Another time. You have to go.' Liss took a cake of rosin from the chest. 'Come and see me again soon, sister. I can't protect you, but

I've been here a decade. I might be able to stop you getting yourself killed.' She gave me a tired smile. 'Welcome to Sheol I.'

Liss gave me directions to Amaurotic House, where Seb had been taken by the Grey Keeper – the Reph that kept the small number of amaurotic workers in check. His name was Graffias Sheratan. She gave me some bread and meat to slip to Seb. 'Don't let Graffias see you,' she said.

I'd learned a lot in the space of forty minutes. The most troubling revelation was that I was on Nashira's radar, and I wasn't too keen on being her spirit slave for time everlasting. Not going straight to the heart of the æther, the place where all things die, was something I'd always feared. I hated the thought of being a restless spirit, a clip of spare ammo, for voyants to abuse and trade. Still, that had never stopped me summoning spools of spirits to protect myself, or bidding on Jax's behalf for a very angry Anne Naylor, who'd been a young girl when she was murdered.

And Liss's warning unnerved me. *In the end you'll just stop trying.*

She was wrong.

Amaurotic House was outside the main network of residences. I had to go through several abandoned streets to reach it. I'd seen maps of the city in an old copy of the *Roaring Boy* – yet another bit of memorabilia Jax had swindled from Didion Waite – and I knew at least roughly where most of its landmarks were. I headed north up the main road. A few red-jackets were stationed outside buildings, but they only gave me passing glances. There must be some kind of barrier to stop us escaping, that and the mines in No Man's Land. How many voyants had died trying to cross it?

I found the building within a few minutes. It was discreet and austere, with a small iron lunette over the gates. Whatever words had been there had been replaced with AMAUROTIC HOUSE. There was a phrase in Latin underneath: DOMUS STULTORUM. I didn't want to know what that meant. I peered between the bars – and locked gazes with a Rephaite guard. He had dark, curling hair that spilled over his shoulders, and his lower lip was full and petulant. This must be Graffias.

'I hope you have good reason to be near Amaurotic House,' he said, his deep voice thick with scorn.

All reason faded from my mind. The proximity of this creature made me cold to the bone.

'No,' I said, 'but I have these.'

I held out my numa – rings, thimbles, needles. Graffias gave me a look of such hatred, such disgust, that I flinched. I almost preferred their callous stares. 'I do not take *bribes*. Nor do I require worthless human trinkets to access the æther.'

I slipped the worthless human trinkets back into my pocket. Stupid idea. Of course they didn't use the damn things. It was a beggar's currency.

'Sorry,' I said.

'Get back to your residence, white-jacket, or I will summon your keeper to discipline you.'

He drew a spool of spirits. I turned and walked away from the gate, out of his line of sight, not looking back. Just as I was about to hightail it to Magdalen, a quiet voice came from somewhere above my head.

'Paige, wait!'

A hand reached through the bars of a second-floor window. My shoulders sagged in relief. Seb.

'Are you okay?'

'No.' He sounded choked. 'Please, Paige – please get me out of here. I have to get out of here. I'm – I'm sorry I called you unnatural, I'm sorry—'

I glanced over my shoulder. No one was looking my way. I climbed up the side of the building, reached into my tunic, and slipped Seb the food package. 'I'll let you off the hook.' I squeezed his icy hand through the bars. 'I'll try my best to get you out, but you have to give me time.'

'They'll kill me.' He unwrapped the package with shaking fingers. 'I'll be dead before you get me out.'

'What do they do?'

'They made me scrub the floors until my hands bled, and then I had to sort through broken glass, looking for clean pieces for their ornaments.' I noticed his hands, cut all over. Deep, dirty cuts. 'Tomorrow I'm supposed to start work in the residences.'

'What sort of work?'

'I don't know yet. I don't want to know. Do they think I'm an – I'm one of you?' His voice was hoarse. 'Why do they want me?'

'I don't know.' His right eye was swollen and bloodshot. 'What happened there?'

'One of them hit me. I didn't do anything, Paige, really. He said I was human scum. He said—'

He hung his head, and his lip shook. This was only his first day, and already they'd used him as a punchbag. How would he survive a week, or a month? Or a decade, like Liss?

'Eat that.' I clasped his hands around the food package. 'Try and come to Magdalen tomorrow.'

'Is that where you live?'

'Yes. My keeper probably won't be there. You can take a bath, maybe get some food. Okay?'

Seb nodded. He seemed delirious; no doubt he was concussed. He needed a hospital, a proper doctor. But there was no doctor here. Nobody cared about Seb.

There was nothing more I could do for him tonight. I gave his arm a gentle squeeze before I dropped from the window, landed on my feet, and headed back towards the inner city.

Community

I was back at the residence by dawn. The red-clad day porter gave me a spare key to the Warden's chamber. 'Leave it on his desk,' he said. 'Don't even think about keeping it.'

I didn't answer. I went up the dark staircase, avoiding the two guards. It chilled me how their eyes shone in the passages, natural searchlights in the dark. This was supposed to be a safe residence. I couldn't imagine what the others must be like.

The bells chimed from the tower, calling the humans back to their prisons. Once I was in the chamber, I locked the door and left the key on the desk. No sign of the Warden. I found a box of matches in a drawer and used them to light a few candles. There were three identical pairs of black leather gloves in the same drawer, and a broad silver ring, set with a red jewel.

A curio cabinet stood against the wall, made of dark rosewood. When I opened the glass-fronted doors my sixth sense twinged. A collection of instruments sat inside. Some I recognised from the black market. Some were numa. Most were just bric-à-brac: a plan-chette, some chalk, a spirit slate – useless bits of séance equipment, the sort of thing amaurotics hysterically associated with clairvoyance. Others, like the crystal ball, could be used to scry by seers. I wasn't a soothsayer; none of the objects were useful to me. Like Graffias, I didn't need objects to touch the æther.

What I needed was life support. Until I could find some oxygen apparatus, I'd have to be careful how often I detached my spirit. That was how I widened my perception of the æther: I could push my spirit from its natural place, to the farthest edges of my dreamscape. Problem was that if I did it for too long, my breathing reflex stopped dead.

Something caught my eye. A small case, rectangular, with a stylised heartwood flower engraved in the lid. Eight petals. I flipped the clasp and opened it. Inside were four crimp vials, each containing a viscous liquid, such a dark red it was almost black. I closed it. I didn't want to know.

A dull pain stabbed at my eye. I couldn't see any nightclothes. Why I'd expected them, I had no idea. He didn't care what I wore or how well I slept. His only concern was that I drew breath.

I kicked off my boots and lay on the daybed. The room was cold as stone without a fire, but I didn't dare touch the sheets on his bed. I set my cheek against the velvet bolster.

The flux attack had left me weak and tired. As I drifted on the verge of sleep, my spirit wandered in and out of the æther. I brushed past dreamscapes, catching waves of memory. Blood and pain were common denominators. There were other Rephs in this residence, but their minds were as impenetrable as ever. The humans were more open, their defences thinned by fear. Their dreamscapes gave off a harsh, tainted light – a signal of distress. Eventually I slept.

I woke to the sound of floorboards creaking. I opened my eyes to see the Warden come through the doorway. Aside from the two remaining candles, his eyes were the only light. He walked across the room towards my corner. I feigned sleep. Finally, after what seemed like aeons, he left. This time his footsteps were less cautious, and I could tell from their pattern that he was sporting a heavy limp. The bathroom door slammed shut behind him.

What could injure such a creature as a Rephaite?

He was gone for a few minutes. In that time I could count every heartbeat. When the lock turned in the door, I dropped my head back into my arms. Warden stepped out, naked as sin. I closed my eyes.

I kept up my act as he moved towards the four-poster, knocking a glass orb to the floor. Ripples flickered through the æther. He wrenched the drapes around the bed, concealing him from view. Only when his mind quietened did I open my eyes and sit up. No movement.

Barefoot, I approached the bed and I slid my fingers between the drapes, opening them just enough to see him. He lay on his side, covered by the sheets, his skin glistening in the half-light. His hair was snarled over his face. As I watched, a dim light spread through the bedding, close to where his right arm lay.

I brushed his dreamscape. Something was different. I couldn't get much from it, but it wasn't quite as it should be. Every dreamscape had a kind of invisible light: an inner glow, imperceptible to amaurotic senses. Now his vital light was going out.

He was still as the grave. When I looked down at the sheets, I found them spotted with a softly luminous, yellow-green liquid. It had a thin, metallic scent. My sixth sense felt as if it was being plucked, as if I was inhaling the æther. I rolled the heavy bedclothes down.

A bite oozed on the inside of his arm. I swallowed. I could see the faint imprints of teeth, skin ripped in a vicious frenzy. The wound wept beads of light. Blood.

It was his *blood*.

He must have told the other Rephaim he was going somewhere.

They would have known he was doing something dangerous. There was no way they could find the evidence to blame me if he died.

Then I remembered what Liss had said to me in the shack. *Rephs aren't human. No matter how much they look like us, they're not like us.*

Like they would care if there was no evidence. They could fabricate evidence. They could say whatever they liked. If he died on this bed, they could easily claim I'd smothered him. It would give Nashira an excuse to kill me early.

Maybe I should do it. This was my chance to get rid of him. I'd killed before. I could do it again.

I had three options. I could sit here and watch him die, kill him, or try and stop it. I'd rather watch him die, but I sensed it might be better to save him. I was reasonably safe in Magdalen. The last thing I wanted to do at this stage was move.

He hadn't hurt me yet, but he would. To own me he would have to subjugate me, torture me, make me obey by any means necessary. If I killed him now, I might save myself. My hand reached for a pillow. I could do it, I could suffocate him. *Yes, come on, kill him.* I flexed my fingers, grasped the cotton. *Kill him!*

I couldn't. He'd wake up. He'd wake up and break my neck. Even if he didn't, I wouldn't be able to escape. The guards outside would string me up for murder.

I had to save him.

Something told me not to touch the sheets. I didn't trust that liquid. The glow said *radioactive*, and I couldn't forget Scion's warnings of contamination. I went to the drawer and pulled on a pair of his gloves. They were massive, made for Rephaite hands. My fingers lacked dexterity. I ripped up one of the cleaner sheets. Flimsy things, useless for warmth. Once I had a few long strips, I took them to the bathroom and soaked them in hot water. This might not work, but it might just buy him a few hours to wake up and seek treatment from the other Rephaim. If he was lucky.

Back in the chamber, I steeled my nerves. Warden looked and felt like death. The cold seeped through the gloves. His skin had a grey tinge. I wrung out the sheet and set to work on the wound. At first I was cautious, but he didn't stir. He wasn't going to wake.

Outside, through the windows, the play of sunlight began to change. I squeezed water on the wound, cleaned away the blood, mangled coaxed grit from the flesh. After what seemed like hours, I'd finally made a dent in the mess. I could see the rise and fall of his chest, the soft surge in his throat. I used another sheet to pad the wound, secured the makeshift wadding with the sash of my tunic, then pulled the bedding over his arm. It was up to him to survive now.

I woke a few hours later.

I could tell from the silence that the room was unoccupied. The bed was made. The sheets had been replaced. The drapes were tied with embroidered sashes, waxing the walls in the light of the moon.

Warden was gone.

The windows dripped with condensation. I went to sit by the fire. I couldn't have imagined the whole encounter; not unless I was still having flux flashes – but I had taken the antidote. My blood was clean. So that meant Warden, for whatever reason, had left again.

There was a fresh uniform laid out on the bed, along with a second note. Written in the same bold hand, it simply read:

Tomorrow.

So he hadn't passed away in his sleep. And my training was delayed for yet another day.

The gloves were gone. He must have taken them. I went to the bathroom and scrubbed my hands with hot water. I changed into my uniform, popped the three pills from their packets, and washed them down the sink. I would find out more today. I didn't care what Liss said – we couldn't just accept this. I didn't care if the Rephs had been here for two hundred years or two million: I would not let them abuse my clairvoyance. I wasn't their soldier, and she wasn't their lunch.

The night porter signed me out of the residence. I headed into the Rookery and bought a bowl of porridge. It tasted as bad as it looked – like cement – but I forced myself to eat it. The performer whispered that Suhail was on the prowl; I couldn't sit down to eat. Instead I asked her whether she knew where I might find Julian, describing him in as much detail as I could. She told me to check at the central residences, giving me their names and locations before she returned to her paraffin stove.

I stood in a dark corner. As I ate, I watched the people milling around me. They all had the same dead eyes. Their bright clothes were almost offensive, like graffiti on a headstone.

'Makes you sick, doesn't it?'

I looked up. It was the whisperer who was detained with me that first night. She wore a filthy bandage on her arm. Looking bored, she sat down beside me.

'Tilda.'

'Paige,' I said.

'I know. I hear you ended up at Magdalen.' She had a roll of paper in her hand. Smoke wafted thickly from the end, smelling of spice and perfume. I recognised the bouquet of purple aster. 'Here.'

'I don't, thanks.'

'Come on, it's just a bit of regal. Better than tincto.'

Tincto – laudanum – was the favoured vice for those amaurotics willing to risk altering their mental state. Not all of them liked Floxy.

Occasionally an amaurotic would be arrested on suspicion of unnaturalness, only for the NVD to discover they'd been poisoning themselves with tincto. It didn't do much for voyants; it wasn't strong enough to dent our dreamscapes. Tilda must use for the sake of it.

'Where did you get it?' I said. I couldn't imagine the Rephs allowing the use of ethereal drugs.

'There's a gallipot in here who sells it by the donop. Says he's been here since Bone Season XVI.'

'He's been here forty years?'

'Since he was twenty-one. I got talking to him earlier. He seems all right.' She offered her roll. 'Sure you don't want a smoulder?'

'I'll pass.' I paused to watch her smoke. Tilda had the dab hand of an aster junkie, or courtier, as they called themselves; only they would call a pound a donop. She might be able to help me. 'Why aren't you training?'

'Keeper's gone somewhere. Why aren't *you* training?'

'Same reason. Who's your keeper?'

'Terebell Sheratan. She seems like a bit of a bitch, but she hasn't tried to slate me yet.'

'Right.' I watched her smoke. 'Do you know what's in the pills they give us?'

Tilda nodded. 'The little white one is a standard contraceptive. Surprised you haven't seen it before.'

'Contraceptive? What for?'

'To stop us breeding, obviously. And bleeding. I mean, would *you* want to punch out a sprog in this place?'

She had a point. 'The red one?'

'Iron supplement.'

'And the green one?'

'What?'

'The third pill.'

'There's no third pill.'

'It's a capsule,' I pressed. 'Sort of olive green. Tastes bitter.'

Tilda shook her head. 'No idea, sorry. If you bring me one I can take a look at it.'

My gut clenched. 'I will,' I said. She was about to take a mouthful of fumes when I interrupted: 'You went with Carl, didn't you? At the oration.'

'I don't associate with that turncoat.' I raised an eyebrow. Tilda exhaled lilac smoke. 'Didn't you hear? He's turned nose. That palmist, Ivy – the one with blue hair – he caught her sneaking food from a rottie. Blew to her keeper. You should see what they did to her.'

'Go on.'

'Beat her. Shaved her head. I don't want to talk about it.' Her hand shook, just a little. 'If that's what you have to do to survive in this place, then send me to the æther. I'll go quietly.'

Silence stretched between us. Tilda tossed away her roll of aster.

'Do you know which residence Julian is at?' I said after a while. '26.'

'The bald guy? Trinity, I think. You can have a look through the gates at the back; that's where the rookies have been training, on the lawns. Just don't let any of *them* see you.'

I left her to light another roll.

Aster was a killer. Possibly the most abused plant on the streets. Addiction was rife in places like Jacob's Island. Its flowers came in white, blue, pink and purple, each of which had a different effect on the dreamscape. Eliza was addicted to white aster for years; she'd told me all about it. In comparison with blue, which restored memories, white aster produced an effect we called whitewashing, or partial memory loss. For a while she'd forgotten her own last name. Later she got hooked on purple, saying it helped with her art. She'd made me swear never to touch any ethereal drug, and I saw no reason to break that promise.

It chilled me to discover that I had an extra pill. Unless Tilda was unusual to have two. I'd have to ask someone else.

The Residence of Trinity was guarded on the street side. I skirted round the edges of the shantytown, using my limited knowledge of the city to work out where the back of the residence would be. I ended up outside the palisade that enclosed its massive grounds. Tilda had been right: there was a group of white-jackets on the lawn, directed by a female Reph. Julian was among them. They were using flanged batons to push spirits through the air, working by the light of green gas lamps. At first I thought they were numa: objects through which the æther could flow, from which soothsayers drew their power, but I'd never seen objects being used to *control* spirits.

I let my sixth sense take over. The dreamscapes of the humans were all clustered together in the æther, with the Reph acting as a sort of linchpin. They were drawn to her like insects to a hanging lantern.

The Reph chose that moment to pick on Julian. She swiped her baton, sending an angry spirit hurtling towards him. He crashed to the ground on his back, stunned.

'On your feet, 26.'

Julian didn't move.

'Stand up.'

He couldn't do it. Of course he couldn't – he'd just been hit in the face by a furious spirit. No voyant could just *stand up* after that.

His keeper delivered a hard kick to the side of his head. The white-jackets all stumbled back, as if she might turn on them next. She gave them a cold look before she swept away to the residence, her black dress billowing behind her. The humans exchanged glances before they followed. Not one of them stayed to help Julian. He lay on the grass, curled into the foetal position. I tried to push the gates open, but they caught on a heavy chain.

'Julian,' I called.

He twitched, then raised his head. When he saw me, he pushed himself back up and walked to the gates. His face glistened with sweat. Behind him, the lanterns went out.

'She likes me really,' he said. His mouth tweaked in a half-smile. 'I'm her star pupil.'

'What kind of spirit was it?'

'Just an old ghost.' He rubbed his raw eyes. 'Sorry, still seeing things.'

'What do you see?'

'Horses. Books. Fire.'

The ghost had left an impression of its death. It was an unpleasant aspect of spirit combat.

'Which Reph was that?' I said.

'Her name's Aludra Chertan. I don't know why she volunteered to be a keeper. She hates us.'

'They all hate us.' I looked at the lawn. Aludra hadn't returned. 'Can you come outside?'

'I can try.' He raised a hand to his head, grimacing. 'Has your keeper fed on you yet?'

'I've barely seen him.' Something told me not to mention what had happened the night before.

'Aludra fed on Felix yesterday. He couldn't stop shaking when he came round. She still made him train.'

'Was he okay?'

'Terrified. Couldn't feel the æther for two hours.'

'They're insane to do that to a voyant.' I looked over my shoulder, checking for guards. 'I won't let them feed on me.'

'You may not have a choice.' He unhooked a lantern from the gate. 'Your keeper has quite the reputation. You say you've barely seen him?'

'He always leaves.'

'Why?'

'No idea.'

Julian looked at me for a long time. This close, I saw that he was full-sighted, like Liss. Half-sighted people could switch their spirit sight on and off, but Julian was forced to see the little threads of energy all the time.

'Let me come outside,' he said. 'I haven't eaten since yesterday morning. Evening. Whatever.'

'Can you get permission?'

'I can ask for it.'

I watched his shadow disappear into the residence. It occurred to me that he might never come out.

I waited for him near the Rookery. I was about to give up when a flash of white tunic caught my eye. Julian emerged through a small doorway, his hand over his face. I beckoned him.

'What happened?'

'The inevitable.' He sounded congested. 'She said I could have food, but I wouldn't be able to smell it. Or taste it.'

He took his hand away from his face. I drew in a sharp breath. Thick, dark blood seeped down his chin. Bruises were beginning to form under his eyes. His nose was red and swollen, shot with broken vessels. 'You need ice.' I pulled him behind a plywood wall. 'Come on. The performers will have something to treat it.'

'I'm all right. I don't think it's broken.' He touched the bridge of his nose. 'We need to talk.'

'We'll talk with food.'

As I made my way through the Rookery with Julian, I searched for any sign of a weapon. Even something crude would do: a sharp hairpin, a shard of glass or metal. Nothing jumped out at me. If the performers really were unarmed, they had no way to defend themselves if the Emim were to breach the city. The Rephs and the red-jackets were their only protection.

Inside the food shack, I forced Julian to eat a bowl of skilly and some toke, then slipped my remaining numa to a soothsayer in exchange for a stolen pack of acetaminophen. He wouldn't tell me who he'd stolen it from, or how he'd done it, and he vanished into the crowd as soon as the needles were in his hand. He must be a real acultomancer. I moved Julian to a dark corner.

'Take these,' I said. 'Don't let anyone see.'

Julian didn't say anything. He popped two capsules and washed them down. I found a cloth and some water in an empty shack. He used it to mop up the drying blood.

'So,' he said, a little thickly, 'what do we know about the Emim?'

'Nothing on my end.'

'I've been finding out a bit about how this place works, if you're interested.'

'Of course I'm interested.'

'The white-jackets go through the basics for a few days. Mostly spirit combat – showing you can make spools, that kind of thing. Then you get your first test. That's when you have to verify your gift.'

'Verify it?'

'Prove it's useful. Soothsayers have to make a prediction. Mediums have to incite a possession. You get the picture.'

'What do they count as useful?'

'You have to do something to prove your loyalty. I spoke to the porter at Trinity about it. He didn't want to say much, but he said his prediction got somebody else brought into Sheol I. You have to show them what they want to see, even if it puts another human in danger.'

My throat tightened. 'And the second test?'

'Something to do with the Emim. I guess you get to be a red-jacket if you live.'

My gaze wandered across the shack. There were one or two yellow tunics among the performers. 'Look,' Julian said, keeping his voice low. 'The one in the corner. Her fingers.'

I followed his line of sight. A young woman was scooping up her skilly, talking to a sickly-looking man. Three of her fingers were stumps. When I looked around the room again, I noticed other injuries: a missing hand, bite marks, claw-like scars on arms and legs.

'Guess they do have a taste for human flesh,' I said. Liss hadn't lied.

'Looks like.' Julian offered me his bowl. 'You want to finish this?'

'No, thanks.'

We sat in silence for a while. I didn't look, but I couldn't stop thinking about the injuries these people had sustained. They'd been gnawed on like chicken bones, then thrown out with the rubbish. They were always at risk in this miserable, unprotected slum.

I didn't want the Rephaim to know what I was. To pass the first test, I'd have to show them.

Did I *want* to pass these tests? I ran my fingers through my hair, thinking. I'd have to wait and see what the Warden expected me to do when he returned. He had so much control over my fate.

After a few minutes of watching the performers, I spied a familiar face: Carl. There was a hush. The performers cleared a path for him, their gazes cast down. I craned over their heads and saw what they were looking at: his pink tunic. What was he was doing in the Rookery?

'Tilda told me he passed his first test,' I said to Julian. 'What do you think he had to do? Just dob Ivy in?'

'He's a soothsayer. He probably just had to find his dead aunt in a teacup,' he said.

'That's augury. And aren't *you* a soothsayer?'

'I never actually said I was a soothsayer.' He gave me a faint smile. 'You're not the only one with a deceptive aura.'

That gave me pause for thought. Soothsayers were considered the lowest class of voyants; certainly the commonest – he might find the label insulting. Or maybe I wasn't as good at identifying voyants as Jax had claimed I was.

Jax. I wondered what he was doing. Whether or not he was worried about me. But of course he was worried about me – I was his dreamwalker, his mollisher. How he would find me, I didn't know. Maybe Dani or Nick could work it out. They had Scion careers. There must be a database of prisoners somewhere, hidden by the Archon.

'They're trying to bribe him.' Julian watched two performers. They were holding out numa to Carl, talking to him. 'They must think he has sway over the Rephs now.'

It did look that way. Carl waved them off, and they retreated.

'Julian,' I said, 'how many pills do you get?'

'One.'

'What does it look like?'

'Round and red. Think it's iron.' He swallowed his skilly. 'Why, how many do you get?'

Of course. Scion did produce an injection for male contraception, but it made no sense to sterilise both sexes. I was saved from answering the question by Carl.

'So then I looked into the stone,' he was saying to a white-jacket, watched by several harlies, 'and I decided to scry for her *desires*. Turns out she's very keen on finding this White Binder, and of course, as soon as I saw his face, I knew precisely where he was. Apparently he's the mime-lord of I-4.'

A deathly cold swept over me. That was Jaxon.

'Paige?' Julian said.

'I'm fine. Won't be a second.'

Before I knew it, I was walking straight towards Carl. His eyes popped when I grabbed his tunic and dragged him into a corner.

'What did you see?'

My voice came out as a hiss. Carl stared at me as if I'd grown a second head. 'What?'

'What did you tell her about the White Binder, Carl?'

'It's XX-59-1.'

'I don't care. Tell me what you saw.'

'I don't see what business it is of yours.' He eyed my white tunic. 'You don't seem to have progressed as quickly as everyone thought you would. Did you disappoint your special keeper?'

I moved my face so it was about two inches away from his. He looked even more like a rat at this proximity.

'I'm not playing games, Carl,' I said, my voice low. 'And I don't like turncoats. Tell me what you saw.'

The nearest lanterns flickered. Nobody seemed to notice – the performers had already turned their attention to other things – but Carl did. There was a glint of fear in his eyes. 'I didn't see exactly where he was,' he admitted, 'but I did see a sundial.'

'You scried it?'

'Yes.'

'What does she want with the Binder?' My grip on his tunic tightened.

'I don't know. I just did what she said.' He pulled away from me. 'Why are you asking all this?'

Blood roared in my ears. 'No reason.' I let go of his tunic. 'I'm sorry. I'm just nervous about the tests.'

Carl softened, flattered. 'That's understandable. I'm sure you'll get your next colour soon.'

'And what happens after that?'

'After pink? We join the battalion, of course! I can't wait to get my hands on those filthy Buzzer bastards. I'll be red in no time.'

He was already under their spell. Already a soldier, a killer in the making. I forced a smile and left.

Carl had reason to be proud. He was a good seer. He had used Nashira to call a subject into focus, to see it in the gleaming surface of whichever numen he favoured. That was the gift of soothsayers, as well as some augurs. They could dovetail their gifts with the desires of another person – the querent – in order to read their future. Cartomancers and palmists did it all the time. And no matter what Jaxon said, it often came in handy. The æther was like the Scionet: a network of dreamscapes, each containing information that could be accessed at the click of a button. The querent provided a kind of search engine, a way to see through the eyes of drifting spirits.

Carl had found the perfect querent in Nashira. Not only had he seen Jax, but he had also seen a clue as to his location. One of the six sundials on the pillar.

I had to warn him. Soon. I didn't know what she wanted with Jax, but I wasn't going to let her bring him here.

Julian followed me outside. 'Paige?' He caught my sleeve. 'What did he say to you?'

'Nothing.'

'You look pale.'

'I'm fine.' It was only when I caught sight of the toke in his hand that I remembered Seb. 'Are you going to eat that?'

'No. You want it?'

'Not for me. Seb.'

'Where did you find him?'

'Amaurotic House.'

'Right. So they lock up voyants in London and amaurotics here?'

'Maybe it makes sense to them.' I pocketed the toke. 'I'll see you tomorrow. Dusk?'

'Dusk.' He paused. 'If I can get out.'

Amaurotic House was dark when I arrived. Even the lamps outside had been extinguished. I knew better than to try and talk my way past Graffias; instead I climbed straight up the drainpipe.

'Seb?'

There was no light in the room. I could smell the dank, cold air inside it. Seb didn't reply.

I grasped the bars and crouched on the ledge. 'Seb,' I hissed. 'Are you in there?'

But he wasn't. There were no dreamscapes in this room. Even amaurotics had dreamscapes, albeit colourless ones. No emotional nuances, no spiritual activity. Seb had vanished.

Maybe they'd taken him to a residence to work. Maybe he'd be back.

Or maybe this was a trap.

I pulled the toke from my sleeve, stuck it between the bars and climbed down the drainpipe. Only once I was back on solid ground did I feel safe.

The feeling didn't last. As I turned back towards the inner city, my arm was caught in what felt like a vice. Two scalding eyes, hot and hard, locked on mine.

The Bait

He was standing very still. He wore a black shirt with a high collar, edged with gold. Its sleeves concealed the arm I'd bandaged in the day.

He gazed down at me with no expression. I wet my lips, trying to think of an excuse.

'So,' he said, drawing me closer, 'you bandage wounds *and* feed the amaurotic slaves. How quaint.'

Revulsion made me jerk my arm away. He let me do it. I could fight him if I wasn't cornered – but then I saw the others. Four Rephs, two male and two female. All four had those ironclad dreamscapes. When I took up a defensive stance they laughed at me.

'Don't be a fool, 40.'

'All we want to do is speak to you.'

'Speak to me now,' I said.

My voice was nothing like my own.

Warden had never taken his eyes off my face. In the light of a nearby gas lamp, those eyes boiled with a new colour. He hadn't laughed along with the others.

I was a hunted animal, surrounded. Trying to get out of this situation wouldn't just be stupid – it would be suicidal.

'I'll go,' I said.

Warden nodded.

'Terebell,' he said, 'go to the blood-sovereign. Tell her we have XX-59-40 in custody.'

In *custody*? I glanced at the female. This must be Tilda and Carl's keeper, Terebell Sheratan. She looked back at me with steady yellow eyes. Her hair was dark and glossy; it curved around her face like a hood. 'Yes, blood-consort,' she said.

She went ahead of the escort party. I kept my eyes on my boots. 'Come,' Warden said. 'The blood-sovereign is waiting.'

We walked towards the city centre. The guards dropped back, keeping a respectful distance from Warden. His eyes really were a different colour: orange. He caught me looking.

'If you have a question,' he said, 'you may ask.'

'Where are we going?'

'To your first test. Anything else?'

'What bit you?'

He looked straight ahead. Then he said, 'I rescind your invitation to speak.'

I almost bit my tongue in two. Bastard. I'd spent hours cleaning his wounds. I could have killed him. I *should* have killed him.

Warden knew the city well. He led us down several different streets until we reached the back of another residence, the residence where we'd had our oration. A plaque outside read THE RESIDENCE OF THE SUZERAIN. The guards bowed when he passed them, pressing their fists to their chests. Warden didn't acknowledge either of them.

The gates closed behind us. The clang of the locks drew my muscles into bars. My eyes roved from wall to wall, from nook to cranny, seeking purchase for my hands and feet. Climbing plants grew thick and wild on the buildings, fragrant honeysuckle and ivy and wisteria, but only to a few feet above ground level. After that they were replaced by windows. We walked around a sand-coloured path encircling an oval of grass, where a single lamppost stood. Its light shone through panes of red glass.

At the end of the path was a door. Warden didn't look at me, but he stopped.

'Do not speak of the wounds,' he said, almost too quietly to hear, 'or you will have cause to regret saving my life.'

He motioned to his entourage. Two of them went to stand on either side of the door; the other, a curly-haired male with an arresting stare, came to stand on my other side. Flanked by the guards, I was pushed through the door and into the cool interior of the building.

The room I entered was narrow and ornate, with walls of ivory stone. The left wall was scattered with warm colours, light refracted by the stained glass windows, which seemed to drink in the glow of the moon. I could make out five memorial plaques, but I didn't have time to stop and read them – I was being led to where light shone from an archway. Warden led me up three black marble steps, then dropped to one knee and bowed his head. I did the same when the guard stared at me.

'Arcturus.'

A gloved hand lifted his chin. I risked a glance.

Nashira had appeared. Tonight she wore a black dress that covered her from the neck down, rippling like water under the candlelight. She pressed her lips to Warden's forehead, and he placed his hand against her abdomen.

'I see you have brought our little prodigy,' Nashira said, eyes on me. 'Good evening, XX-40.'

She looked me up and down, and I had the sense that she was trying to read my aura. I threw up some precautionary barriers. Warden didn't move. I couldn't see his face.

A line of Rephaim stood behind the pair, all hooded and cloaked. Their auras seemed to fill the chapel, jostling mine. I was the only human present. 'I suppose you know why you are here,' Nashira said.

I kept my mouth shut. I knew I was in trouble for taking food to Seb, but I could be in trouble for a host of other things: bandaging Warden, sneaking around, being human. Most likely Carl had reported my interest in his vision.

Or maybe they knew what I was.

'We found her outside Amaurotic House,' the guard declared. He was the spitting image of Pleione, right down to the shape of his eyes. 'Sneaking around in the dark like a sewer rat.'

'Thank you, Alsafi.' Nashira looked down at me, but didn't invite me to stand. 'I understand you have been sneaking food to one of the amaurotic hands, 40. Is there a reason for that?'

'Because you're starving him and beating him like an animal. He needs a doctor, a hospital.'

My voice echoed around the dark chapel. The hooded Rephaim were silent. 'I am sorry you feel that way,' Nashira said, 'but in Rephaite eyes – the eyes that now preside over your country – the human and the beast exist on the same level. We do not provide doctors for beasts.'

I could feel myself turning white with anger, but I bit back my next words. I'd only get Seb killed.

Nashira turned away. Warden stood; so did I.

'You might remember from the oration, 40, that we like to test those humans we assemble during the Bone Seasons. You see, we send our red-jackets after humans with an aura, but we cannot always identify what abilities that aura carries. I confess we have made mistakes in the past. A promising case might turn out to be no more exciting than an errant cartomancer, but no doubt you will be far more entertaining than that. Your aura precedes you.' She beckoned. 'Come, show us your talents.'

Warden and Alsafi stepped away from me. Nashira and I were now facing each other across the room.

My muscles tautened. Surely they didn't want me to *fight* her? I would lose. She and her angels would shatter my dreamscape. I could sense them circling her, waiting to defend their host.

But then I remembered what Liss had told me: that Nashira wanted a dreamwalker. I thought fast. Maybe there was something I could do that she had no power to deter, some advantage I could use against her.

I thought of the train. Without a dreamwalker or an oracle in her entourage, Nashira couldn't affect the æther. And unless she'd somehow consumed the spirit of an unreadable, I could still let my spirit loose in her mind.

I could kill her.

Plan A crumbled when Alsafi returned. He bore a frail figure in his arms, a figure with a black bag over its head. The prisoner was lowered into a chair and handcuffed there. My fingers turned numb. Was it one of the others? Had they found the Dials, found my gang?

But I sensed no aura. This was an amaurotic. I thought of my father and felt sick – but the figure was too small, too thin.

'I believe you two know one another,' Nashira said.

They ripped off the bag. My blood ran cold.

Seb. They'd got him. His eyes were swollen to the size of small plums, his hair hung in bloodied strings around his face and his lips were cracked and bleeding. The rest of his face was caked in dry blood. I'd seen serious beatings before, when Hector's victims came crawling to the Dials for aid from Nick, but never anything like this. I'd never seen a victim so young.

The guard whacked another bruise onto his cheek. Seb was barely conscious, but he managed to look up at me.

'Paige.'

His broken voice made blood burn in my eyes. I rounded on Nashira. 'What have you done to him?'

'Nothing,' she said, 'but *you* will.'

'What?'

'It is time for you to earn your next tunic, XX-40.'

'What the hell are you talking about?'

Alsafi gave me such a blow on the head it damn-near knocked me down. He grabbed me by the hair and yanked me around to face him. 'You will *not* use vulgarities in the presence of the blood-sovereign. Hold your tongue or I will stitch your mouth.'

'Patience, Alsafi. Let her be angry.' Nashira raised a hand. 'After all, she was angry on the train.'

My ears were ringing. Two faces burst out from my memory. Two bodies on the carriage floor. One dead, one insane. My victims. My kills.

That was my test. To earn my new colours, I had to kill an amaurotic.

I had to kill Seb.

Nashira must have guessed what I was. She had guessed that my spirit was capable of leaving its natural place in my body. That I was capable of swift, bloodless murder. She wanted to see it happen. She wanted me to dance. She wanted to know if this was a gift worth stealing.

'No,' I said.

Nashira was very still.

'No?' When I was silent, she continued: 'Refusal is not an option. You will obey, or we will be forced to dispose of you. No doubt the Grand Inquisitor would be pleased to correct your insolence.'

'Kill me, then,' I said. 'Why wait?'

The thirteen judges said nothing. Nor did Nashira. She just looked at me, into me. Trying to work out if I was bluffing.

Alsafi didn't beat about the bush. He grabbed my wrist and

dragged me towards the chair. As I kicked and struggled, he wrapped a muscled arm around my neck. 'Do it,' he snarled against my ear, 'or I will crush your ribs and drown you in your own blood.' He shook me so hard my vision wobbled. 'Kill the boy. Do it now.'

'No,' I said.

'Obey.'

'*No.*'

Alsafi squeezed harder. I dug my nails into his sleeve. My fingers scraped down his side – and found the knife at his belt. A paper knife, for cutting envelopes, but it would do. One stab was all it took to make him drop me. I staggered into a pew, the knife still in my hand.

'Stay away,' I warned.

Nashira laughed. The judges echoed her. To them, after all, I was just another breed of performer. Another flimsy human with a head full of confetti and fireworks.

But Warden didn't laugh. His gaze was soldered to my face. I thrust the point of the knife at him.

Nashira walked towards me. 'Impressive,' she remarked. 'I like you, XX-40. You have spirit.'

My hand shook.

Alsafi glanced at the cut on his arm. Luminous fluid seeped from his skin. When I looked down at the knife, I saw the same stuff coated all over the blade.

Seb was crying. I tightened my grip on the blade, but my hands were clammy. I couldn't use a paper knife against all these Rephaim. Besides, I could barely use irons, let alone throw a knife with precision.

Save the five angels around Nashira, there were no spirits to make a spool. I would have to get much closer to cut Seb loose. After that, I would have to work out how to get us both out of here alive.

'Arcturus, Aludra – disarm her,' Nashira said. 'Without spirits.'

One of the judges removed her hood. 'With pleasure.'

I sized her up. It was Julian's keeper. She was a sly-looking creature, all sleek blonde hair and feline eyes. Warden stayed behind her. I measured their auras.

Aludra was a feral thing. She might have appeared civilised, but I sensed she was only just stopping herself from slavering. She was spoiling for a fight, excited by Seb's weakness, and starving for my aura. She wanted some glow, and she wanted it now. Warden was darker, colder, his intentions obscure – but that made him more lethal. If I couldn't read his aura, I couldn't predict what he might do.

I had a sudden thought. Warden's blood had made me feel closer to the æther. Maybe it would work again. I inhaled, holding the blade close to my face. The cold scent knocked my senses into overdrive. The æther wrapped around me like cold water, submerging me. With a flick of my wrist, I threw the knife at Aludra's face, aiming right between the eyes. She only just ducked. My accuracy had improved. A lot.

Aludra seized a heavy candelabrum and whirled on me. 'Come, child,' she said. 'Dance with me.'

I backed away. I was no use to Seb if my skull was in pieces.

Aludra charged. Her mission: to do me down and feed on what was left. Without my heightened senses, she probably would have succeeded. I rolled to avoid her, and instead of crushing me, the candelabrum struck off the head of a statue. I was on my feet again at once, vaulting over the altar and sprinting across the chapel, past the hooded Rephs in the pews.

Aludra recovered her weapon. I heard the whistle of air as she hurled it across the chapel. Seb screamed my name as it soared over his head.

I'd been making for the open doors, but my escape was cut short.

A guard slammed them closed from outside, locking me into the chapel with my audience. With no time to slow down, I ran straight into the doors. The impact struck the breath from my lungs. I lost my footing. My head hit solid marble. A split second later, the candelabrum smashed into the doors. I barely had time to move before it went crashing to the floor where my legs had been. The noise rang through the chapel like a stricken bell.

There was a dull pain in the back of my skull, but I had no time to rest. Aludra had caught up with me. While her leather-clad fingers gripped my neck, her thumbs pressed against my throat. I choked. My eyes filled with blood, blinding me. She was taking my aura, *my* aura. Her eyes brightened to sweltering red.

'Aludra, stop.'

She didn't seem to hear. I tasted metal.

The knife lay beside me. My fingers inched towards it, but Aludra pinned my wrist. 'My turn now.'

I had one chance to live. As she held the knife to my cheek I pushed my spirit into the æther.

In spirit form, I saw through new eyes, on a new plane. Here, I was sighted. The æther appeared as a silent void, studded with starlike orbs, each orb a dreamscape. Aludra was physically close to me; her 'orb', consequently, wasn't too far away. It would be suicidal to try and break into her mind – it was very old, very strong – but her lust for glow had weakened her defences. It was now or never. I flew into her mind.

She wasn't ready, and I was fast. I reached her midnight zone before she realised what had happened. When she did, I was thrown out with the force of a bullet. I was back in my body before I knew it, staring at the ceiling of the chapel. Aludra was on her knees, clutching her head.

'Get her out, get her out,' she screeched. 'She walks!' I scrambled to my feet, gasping for air, only to lurch into Warden, who caught me by the shoulders. His gloved fingers dug into my skin. He wasn't trying to hurt me – just to hold me, to restrain me – but my spirit was like a flytrap: it reacted to danger. Almost against my will, I tried the same attack.

This time I didn't even reach the æther. I couldn't move.

Warden. It was him. This time it was he who was sucking the energy out of me, leeching my aura. I could only watch in shock as I was drawn towards him like a flower to the sun.

Then he stopped. It was as if a wire between us had snapped. And his eyes were bright red, like blood.

I stared into them. He stepped back and looked at Nashira.

Silence reigned. Then the hooded Rephaim applauded. I sat on the floor, stunned.

Nashira knelt beside me and placed a gloved hand on my head. 'Beautiful. My little dreamwalker.'

I tasted blood. She knew.

Nashira stood and turned towards Seb, who had watched with as much fear as his injuries would allow. Now his barely open eye came to rest on her as she walked to the back of the chair.

'Thank you for your services. We are grateful.' She placed her hands on either side of his head. 'Goodbye.'

'No, please, don't – *please*! I don't want to die. Paige—!'

She jerked his head to the side. His eyes widened, and a gurgle came from his between his lips.

She'd just killed him.

'No!' The word ripped from my throat. I could hardly process it. I couldn't take my eyes off her. 'You – you just—'

'Too late.' Nashira let go of his head. It flopped. 'You could have done it, 40. Painlessly. If only you'd done as I asked.'

It was her smile that did it. She was *smiling*. I ran at her, raw heat writhing in my blood. Warden and Alsafi grabbed my arms, hauling me back. I kicked and thrashed and struggled until my hair was lank with sweat. 'You bitch,' I screamed. 'You *bitch*, you evil bitch! He wasn't even voyant!'

'True. He was not.' Nashira walked around behind the chair. 'But amaurotic spirits make the best servants. Don't you think?'

Alsafi was about to dislocate my shoulder. I clawed at Warden's arm, the bad one, the one I'd treated. He stiffened. I didn't care. 'I'll kill you,' I said, and I aimed it at all of them. I could hardly breathe, but I said it. 'I'll kill you. I swear I'll kill you.'

'No need to swear, 40. Let us swear for you.'

Alsafi threw me to the floor. My skull cracked against hard marble. My vision flashed. I tried to move, but something pinned me down. A knee on my back. My fingers dragged on the marble floor. Then a blinding pain in my shoulder, the most agonising pain I'd ever felt. Hot, too hot. The smell of roasted meat. I couldn't help but scream.

'We swear your undying allegiance to the Rephaim.' Nashira never took her eyes off me. 'We swear it with the mark of fire. XX-59-40, you are bound for ever to the Warden of the Mesarthim. You will renounce your true name, as long as you shall live. Your life is ours.'

The fire was in my skin. I couldn't think of anything but the pain. This was it. They'd killed Seb, and now they were killing me. A needle caught the light.

Of my Name

There was too much flux in my blood.

I ran in circles through my dreamscape. Flux had deformed it, made the shapes and the colours rupture. I heard my heart pounding, the air burning up my throat, through my nose.

They're killing me. I thought this as I fought against my mind, watching it crumble like wood in a furnace. This was it. Nashira knew what I was. She'd poisoned me and now I was dying. It wouldn't be long, after all, a dreamscape couldn't keep its shape in a dead body. Then the thought unravelled and slipped away, and I was left wandering through the dark parts of my head.

Then I found it. My sunlit zone, where beauty lived. Safety. Warmth. I ran towards it, but it was like running through wet sand. The dark clouds clung to me, hauling me back into cloud and shadow. I struggled against the flux, kicking and twisting myself free of its hold, and tumbled like a seed into the sunlight, into the field of flowers.

Everyone in the world had a dreamscape, the beautiful mirage inside their mind. In dreams, even amaurotics saw their sunlit zone

– just not very clearly. Voyants could see into their own minds, live in there until they starved to death. My sunlit zone was a field of red flowers, a field that rippled and changed depending on my mood. I saw flashes of the world outside my body, felt the roll in the earth as I emptied my stomach of my tiny meal. But in my mind I was calm, watching as flux wreaked havoc around me. I lay down in the flowers and waited for the end.

I was back in the room at Magdalen. The gramophone was warbling nearby. Another of Jaxon's blacklisted favourites, 'Did You Ever See a Dream Walking?' I was lying on my stomach on the daybed, naked from the waist up. My hair had been twisted into a knot.

My hand went to my face. Skin. Cold, clammy skin. I was alive. In pain, yes – but alive. They hadn't killed me.

I was too sore to lie still. I tried to sit up, but the weight of my head kept me from rising more than a few inches. The back of my right shoulder burned with a ferocious heat. A dull throb in my groin told me where I'd been injected – but this time the damage was deeper.

Flux was one of the few drugs that worked better in an artery than it did in veins. My thigh was hot and swollen. My chest heaved. I was burning up. Whichever Reph had done this had not only been very clumsy, but very cruel. I had a vague memory of Suhail leering at me before the lights went out.

Maybe they *had* tried to kill me. Maybe I was dying.

I turned my head to the side. A fire had been lit in the hearth. And someone was in the room: my keeper.

He was sitting in his chair, staring at the flames. I gazed across the room, hating him. I could still feel his hands on me, holding me back, stopping me from saving Seb. Did he harbour any guilt for that pointless killing? Did he care about the helpless slaves at Amaurotic House? I wondered if he cared about anything at all. Even his interactions with Nashira seemed mechanical. Did anything make this creature tick?

He must have sensed my gaze, because he stood. I held still, scared to move. Too many parts of me hurt. Warden knelt beside the daybed. When he raised his hand, I flinched. He laid the backs of his fingers against my scorching cheek. His eyes had returned to neutral apple-gold.

My throat was sore, full of fever. 'His spirit,' I forced out. It was agony to speak. 'Did it leave?'

'No.'

It took all my strength to mask my pain. If no one had said the threnody, Seb would be forced to linger. He was still afraid, still alone, and worst of all, still a prisoner.

'Why didn't she kill me?' The words chafed my throat. 'Why didn't she just get it over with?'

Warden ignored the question. After examining my shoulder, he took a chalice from the nightstand. It brimmed with dark liquid. I watched him. He lifted the chalice to my lips, taking the back of my head in one hand. I pulled against him. A soft growl escaped his throat. 'It will ease the swelling in your leg,' he said. 'Drink.'

I jerked my head away. Warden took the cup from my lips.

'Do you not wish to heal?'

I stared him out.

It must have been an accident that I'd survived. There was no reason for them not to have killed me.

'You were branded,' he said. 'You must allow me to treat the wound for a few days, or it will become infected.'

I twisted to look at my shoulder, covering my breasts with the sheets. 'Branded with – with what?' My fingers shook as I traced the taut skin. XX-59-40. *No, no!* 'Oh – you *bastard*, you sick bastard – I'll kill you. Just wait – when you're asleep—'

My throat was too sore. I stopped, heaving. Warden flicked his gaze over my face, like he was trying to read a foreign language.

He wasn't stupid. Why was he looking at me like that? They'd branded me like some kind of animal. Lower than an animal. A number.

The silence was broken only by my gasping breaths. Warden placed a gloved hand over my knee. I pulled my leg from his grip, sending a bolt of pain down to my toes. 'Don't touch me.'

'The brand will stop hurting, in time,' he said, 'but your femoral artery is a different matter.'

He slid his hand lower, pulling the sheets away from my leg. When I saw my bare thigh, I thought I would chuck up again. Swollen past its normal size, it was stained with bruises that had spread almost to my knee. The area around my groin was black and bloodshot. Warden applied just the slightest bit of pressure to my leg, barely enough to spring a hair-trigger. I choked.

'This injury will not repair itself. No wound caused by flux can heal without a second, stronger antidote.'

I thought I would die if he pressed any harder.

'Go to hell,' I gasped out.

'There is no hell. There is only æther.'

I clenched my teeth, shaking with the effort of not sobbing. Warden removed his hand from my leg and turned away.

I couldn't tell how long I lay there, weak and delirious. All I could think was how much he must love this, seeing our natural roles restored. It was him with power over me this time, power to watch me suffer and sweat. And this time it was him with the remedy.

Dawn broke. The clock ticked. Warden just sat in his chair, stoking the fire. I had no idea what he was waiting for. If he wanted me to change my mind about the remedy, he was going to be there a long, long time. Maybe he had just been told to watch me, to make sure I didn't top myself. I can't say I wouldn't have tried. The pain was excruciating. My leg was rigid, and it only moved in spasms. The swollen skin strained and glistened, like a blister on the edge of bursting.

As the hours crept past, Warden moved from place to place: the window, the armchair, the bathroom, the desk, back to the armchair. Like I wasn't there. Once he left the room and came back with some warm bread, but I pushed it away. I wanted to make him think I was on hunger strike. I wanted my power back. I wanted to make him feel as small as I felt.

The pain in my thigh refused to ease; if anything it got worse. I pressed the blackened skin. I kept on pressing, harder and harder, until stars burst in my eyes. I had hoped it would make me lose consciousness, just so I could have a few hours of relief, but all it made me do was throw up yet again. Warden watched as I choked acidic bile into a basin. His gaze was empty. He was waiting for me to give in, to beg.

I looked at the basin through blurred eyes. I was starting to bring up blood, thick clots of it. My head rolled against the cushions.

I must have fallen unconscious. It was getting dark again when I woke. Julian must be wondering where I was, assuming he'd been able to leave his residence. Probably not. My brain could only focus on these things because all my pain, inexplicably, had gone.

So had the sensation in my leg.

Fear chilled my spine. I tried to move my toes, to rotate my ankle, but nothing happened.

Warden was at my side.

'I should mention,' he said, 'that if the infection is not treated, you are very likely to lose your leg. Or your life.'

I would have spat at him, but the vomiting had dehydrated me. I shook my head. My vision was fading.

'Don't be a fool.' He grasped my head, made me look at him. 'You need your legs.'

He had me in a bind. He was right: I couldn't lose my leg. I needed to run. This time, when he took the back of my head in his hand, I opened my mouth and drank from the goblet. It tasted rank, like earth and metal. Warden nodded. 'Good.'

I mustered a look of loathing, but the effect was dampened by relief as my leg tingled. I drank the foul liquid to the dregs, and wiped my lips with a steady hand.

Warden lifted the sheets again. My thigh was already returning to its normal dimensions.

'We're even now,' I whispered. My throat scorched. 'No more. I healed you, you healed me.'

'You have never healed me.'

I faltered. 'What?'

'I have never been injured.'

'You don't remember?'

'It never happened.'

I didn't believe for a moment that I'd imagined the whole encounter. He was still wearing sleeves, so I could hardly point it out to him, but it had happened. His denial wouldn't make a shade of difference.

'Then I must have made a mistake,' I said.

Warden never took his eyes off me. He was looking at me with interest. A cold, dispassionate interest.

'Yes,' he said. 'You did make a mistake.'

And that was my warning.

The bell chimed in the tower. Warden glanced out of the window.

'You may go. You are in no fit state to begin training tonight, but you should find something to eat.' He indicated the urn on the mantelpiece. 'There are more numa in there. Take as many as you need.'

'I don't have any clothes.'

'That is because you were due a new uniform.' He held up a pink tunic. 'Congratulations, Paige. You have been promoted.'

That was the first time he used my name.

Variety

I had to get out of this place. That was my first thought when I stepped into the bitter cold. Sheol I looked just the same as it did before, just as if Seb had never walked its streets – but I looked different. Instead of white, I wore a pale pink tunic. On my new gilet, the anchor was the same sickly pink. I was stained.

I couldn't take another test. I couldn't. If they'd killed a child in the first, what would they do to me in the second? How much blood would be spilled before I was a red-jacket? I had to leave. There had to be some way out, even if I had to dance around landmines. Anything was better than this nightmare.

As I found a path through the Rookery, my right leg weak and heavy, an unfamiliar cold spread through my gut. Each time a performer looked at me, their expression changed. Their features went blank. Their heads went down. My tunic was a warning: turncoat, traitor. Stay away. I am a killer.

I *wasn't* a killer. Nashira had killed Seb, not me – but the performers didn't know that. They must despise anyone who wasn't a white-jacket. I should have just stayed at Magdalen for the night. But then I would have had to be with Warden, and I couldn't bear to spend another moment in his company. I limped through the claustrophobic passages. I had to find Liss. She could help me out of this nightmare. There had to be a way.

'Paige?'

I stopped, my leg shaking. The effort of walking was exhausting. Liss was looking out of her room. She took one glance at my pink tunic and stiffened. 'Liss,' I started.

'You passed.'

Her face was dark. 'Yes,' I said, 'but—'

'Who did you get arrested?'

'No one.' When she looked disbelieving, I realised I had to tell her. 'They tried to make me kill – Seb. The amaurotic.' I looked down. 'And now he's dead.'

She flinched.

'Right,' she said. 'See you later, then.'

'Liss,' I said. 'Please listen. You don't—'

She yanked the curtain across her door, cutting me off. I slid down the wall, drained. I wasn't one of them.

Seb. I said his name in my head, trying to coax his spirit from wherever they'd hidden it, but there was nothing from the æther. Not even a twinge. Even with his surname, there was nothing; I had to be missing a name. The boy that had been so dependent on me, so certain that I would save him, was still a stranger to me in death.

The curtain seemed to glare at me. Liss must think I was pure scum. I closed my eyes, trying to ignore the dull ache in my thigh. Maybe I could find another pink-jacket to exchange information with – but I didn't want to do that. I couldn't trust them. Most of them *were* murderers. Most of them *had* turned somebody in. If I wanted to talk to someone who wasn't a turncoat, I had to prove to Liss that she could trust me. With an effort that left me coated in sweat, I pulled myself up and headed for the food shack. I might find Julian there. Not that he'd want to talk to me, either, but he might give me a chance.

A light caught my eye. A stove. A group of performers were smoking in a tiny lean-to, slumped on their sides, snatching at the air. Aster again. Tilda was among them, her head propped on a cushion, her white tunic filthy and crumpled, like a used tissue. I groped in my gilet for the green capsule I'd taken. Minding my leg, I knelt beside her.

'Tilda?'

Her eyes cracked open. 'What s'matter?'

'I brought the pill.'

'Hold on. Still reigning. Give me a minute, doll. Maybe two. Or five.' She rolled onto her stomach, racked with silent laughter. 'Dreamscape's gone all purple. Are you real?'

I waited for the aster to wear off. Tilda spent a solid minute laughing, flushed to the roots of her hair. I could sense the wildness in her aura, the way it jerked and shifted with the drug. The other voyants showed no sign of wanting to wake up. With shaking hands, Tilda rubbed her face and nodded.

'Okay, I'm dethroned. Where's the pill?'

I handed it to her. She looked at it from every angle. Ran her finger over it, testing the texture. Split it in half. Crushed one half between her fingers. Smelled the residue, tasted it.

'Your keeper's out again,' I said.

'She's out a lot.' She handed me the remnants of the pill. 'It's herbal. Couldn't tell you which herb.'

'Do you know anyone who could tell me?'

'There's a jerryshop in here. The guy that sold me the aster might be able to tell you. Password's *specchio*.'

'I'll see him.' I stood. 'I'll leave you to your aster.'

'Thanks. S'later.'

She collapsed back onto the cushion. I wondered what Suhail would do if he found them.

It took me a while to find the jerryshop. The Rookery had many rooms, most of which were occupied by groups of two or three. They spent their days in cramped shacks, huddled around a paraffin stove, and slept on sheets that reeked of damp and urine. They ate what they could find. If they found nothing, they starved. They stayed together for two reasons: because there was no room for them to do otherwise, and because of the bitter cold in the city. There were no hygiene facilities and no medical supplies, except for what they obtained through theft. This was where you came to die.

The jerryshop was hidden behind a series of thick curtains. You had to know where to look; I only found it after interrogating a harlie for its whereabouts. She seemed reluctant to tell me, warning me of blackmail and high prices, but pointed me in the right direction.

Guarding the shop was the julker boy I'd seen at the oration. He sat on a cushion, playing with dice. No sign of his white tunic. He must have failed his test. What use did the Rephaim have for a julker?

'Hello,' I said.

'Hi.' A pure, sweet note. A julker voice.

'Can I see the pawnbroker?'

'What's the password?'

'*Specchio.*'

The boy stood. His right eye was thick with paste. Infected. He pulled the curtains aside, and I went through.

London jerryshops were usually small, unlicensed places in the bad parts of the central cohort. There were lots in the Chapel too, over in II-6. This was no different. The pawnbroker had set up shop in a kind of tent, made from the sort of drapes Liss used in her performances. Lit by a single paraffin lamp, half the space had been turned into a house of mirrors. The pawnbroker sat on a battered leather armchair, staring into the spotted glass. He was a grey-haired man with too much of a full stomach to be a performer. The mirrors betrayed his speciality: catoptromancy.

When I entered, he raised a monocle to one eye and looked at my reflection. He had the misty eyes of a seer that had seen too much.

'I don't believe I've seen you before. In my mirrors *or* my shop.'

'Bone Season XX,' I said.

'I see. Who owns you?'

'Arcturus Mesarthim.'

I was sick of that name: hearing it, saying it.

'My, my.' He patted his stomach. 'So *you're* his tenant.'

'What's your name?'

'XVI-19-16.'

'Your real name.'

'I no longer remember it, but the performers call me Duckett. If you prefer to use *real* names.'

'I do.'

I bent to look at his stock. Most of the items were numa: cracked hand mirrors, glass bottles of water, bowls and cups, pearls, bags of animal bones, cards and shew stones. Then there were the plants. Aster, briar, sage, thyme, other burning herbs. There were more practical items, too, essential for survival. I looked through the pile. Sheets, limp cushions, matches, a pair of tweezers, rubbing alcohol, aspirin and oxytetracycline, cans of Sterno, a dripper bottle of fusidic acid, bandages and disinfectants. I picked up an old tinder-box. 'Where did you get all this?'

'Here and there.'

'I presume the Rephs don't know about it.' He smiled, just slightly. 'So how does this illegal shop work?'

'Well, say you were an osteomancer. You would require bones

to supplement your clairvoyance. If the bones were confiscated, you would have to find more.' He indicated a bag marked COMMON RAT. 'I would give you a task to do. I might ask you to bring more supplies, or to carry a message for me – the more valuable the item you needed, the more dangerous the task. If you managed it, I would give you the bones to keep. For a limited loan, you would have to bring me a certain number of numa, which I would return to you when you returned the item. A simple, but effective system.'

It didn't sound like a conventional jerryshop, which loaned money in exchange for pawned items. 'What do you charge for information?'

'That depends on the information you seek.'

I put the remaining half of the pill in front of him. 'What's this?'

He peered at it. He dropped his monocle, picked it up. His thick fingers were shaking. 'For this,' he said, 'I will give you anything you like from the shop. Free of charge.'

I frowned. 'You want to keep it?'

'Oh, yes. This is *very* valuable.' He placed the half in his palm. 'Where did you get this?'

'Information costs, Mr Duckett.'

'If you bring me more of these, I will never charge you anything. Take whatever you like. One item per pill.'

'Tell me what it is or no deal.'

'Two items.'

'No.'

'Information is dangerous. One can't put a price on it.' He held the pill near the paraffin lamp. 'I can tell you is that it is a herbal capsule, and that it is harmless. Is that enough?'

Two items in exchange for the pills. Items like these could save lives in the Rookery.

'Three,' I said, 'and we've got a deal.'

'Excellent. You are a shrewd businesswoman.' He steepled his fingers. 'What else are you?'

'A cultomancer.'

It was my standard lie. A test of competence, in a way. I liked to see whether or not they'd believe me. Duckett chuckled. 'You're not a soothsayer. If I were sighted, I think you'd be on the other end of the spectrum. Yours is a hot aura. Like embers.' He tapped his fingers on a mirror. 'We might have another interesting season this year.'

I tensed. 'What?'

'Nothing, nothing. Just talking to myself. Best way to keep one's sanity after forty years.' A smile tempted his mouth. 'Tell me – what do you think of the Warden?'

I put the tinderbox back on the table.

'I'd have thought it was obvious,' I said.

'Not at all. There are a variety of opinions here.' Duckett ran his thumb over the lens of his monocle. 'The blood-consort is considered by many to be the most attractive of the Rephaim.'

'Maybe you think so. I find him repulsive.' I held his gaze. 'I'll take my items.'

He sat back in his seat. I picked out a Sterno can, a few aspirin and the fusidic acid. 'Nice doing business with you,' he said, 'Miss—?'

'Mahoney. Paige Mahoney.' I turned my back on him. 'If you prefer to use real names.'

I walked out of the den. His eyes stung my back.

Those questions had felt like an interrogation. I hadn't said anything wrong, I was sure. I'd said exactly what I thought about Warden. Why Duckett wanted me to say anything otherwise, I had no idea.

On my way out, I tossed the fusidic acid to the julker. He looked up at me with a tilted head.

'For your eye,' I said.

He blinked. I kept on walking.

When I reached the right shack, I rapped my knuckles on the wall outside. 'Liss?' No reply. I knocked again. 'Liss, it's Paige.'

The curtain was pulled back. Liss was carrying a small lantern. 'Leave me alone,' she said, her voice thick and embittered. 'Please. I don't talk to pinks or reds. I'm sorry, I just don't. You'll have to find other jackets, okay?'

'I didn't kill Seb.' I offered the Sterno and the aspirin. 'Look, I got these from Duckett. Can I just talk to you?'

She looked from the items to my face. Her forehead creased, and her lips pursed. 'Well,' she said, 'you'd better come in.'

I didn't cry when I told her about the test. I couldn't. Jax hated tears. (*'You're a ruthless street trasseno, darling. Do act like one, there's a good dolly.'*) Even here, where he could never get to me, I felt that he watched my every move. Still, the thought of Seb's broken neck made me sick. I couldn't forget the shock in his eyes, the scream of my name. I sat in silence once I'd told the story, keeping my stiff leg stretched out in front of me.

Liss handed me a steaming glass.

'Drink this. You're going to have to keep your strength up if you want to avoid Nashira.' She sat back. 'She knows what you are now.'

I sipped. It tasted of mint.

My eyes were hot and my throat still ached, but I wouldn't cry for Seb. It felt disrespectful to cry with Liss sitting next to me. Her face was swollen, her neck bruised by fingers and her shoulder dislocated – yet she'd still put my welfare above hers. 'You're part of the Family now, sister,' she'd said, and treated my brand one-handed with a warm poultice. The raw burn in my skin was easing, but she said it would definitely scar. That was the point. To remind me, every day, whom I belonged to.

Julian was asleep under a discoloured sheet. His keeper had gone to meet with her family, the Chertan. I'd given him some aspirin before he drifted off. His nose looked a bit better. He'd come looking for me after my no-show at dawn, and Liss had taken him in. The two of them had patched up the shack as best they could, but the place was like an icebox. Still, Liss had invited me to stay for the whole night, and I had every intention of doing just that. I needed to get away from Magdalen.

Liss cracked open the Sterno with an old tin-opener.

'Thanks for getting this. Haven't seen canned heat for a while.' She took out a match and lit the jellied alcohol. A clean blue flame appeared. 'You got this from Duckett?'

'For a price.'

'What did you give him?'

'One of my pills.'

Liss raised an eyebrow. 'Why would he want one of those?'

'Because I get a pill that no one else gets. No idea what it is.'

'If you can use them to bribe Duckett, they're worth keeping. His tasks are risky. He makes people go into the residences and steal for him. More often than not, they get caught.'

She winced and reached for her shoulder. I took the Sterno from her hand and placed it between us. 'Gomeisa did this,' I said.

'He gets bored of the cards after a while. Doesn't always like what they show him.' She lay on her back, pulling the pillow under her neck. 'It doesn't matter. I don't see him very much. I don't think he's even in the city most of the time.'

'Were you his only human?'

'Mm. That's why he hates me. I was in exactly the same situation as you, taken in by a Reph that had never chosen a human before. He thought I had potential, thought I could be one of the best bone-grubbers in Sheol I.'

'Bone-grubbers?'

'It's what we call the red-jackets. He thought I'd earn that colour. I disappointed him.'

'How?'

'He asked me to do a reading for one of the harlies. They thought he was a traitor, that he'd tried to run. I knew it was true. The reading would have incriminated him. I refused to do it.'

'I didn't want to do it. She still saw what I was.' I rubbed my temple. 'And now Seb's dead, too.'

'Amaurotics die all the time here. He would have been bones whatever you did.' She sat up again. 'Come on. Let's eat.'

She reached over to her wooden chest. I stared at what was inside: a packet of coffee granules, cans of beans, four eggs. 'How did you get those?'

'I found them.'

'Where?'

'One of the amaurotics hid them near his residence. Leftovers from the Bone Season supplies.' Liss took out an iron pot and filled it with water from a bottle. 'There. We'll eat like queens.' She pushed the pot over the Sterno. 'How are you holding up, Jules?'

Our voices must have woken him. He pushed off the sheet and sat cross-legged. 'Better.' He pressed his nose with his fingers. 'Thanks for the meds, Paige.'

I nodded. 'When do you take your test?'

'No idea. Aludra's supposed to be teaching us about subliming, but she spends most of her time kicking us around.'

'Subliming?'

'Turning normal objects into numa. Those batons we were using the other night, when you came to see me – they were sublimed. Anyone can use them, not just soothsayers.'

'What do they do?'

'They exert some control over the nearest spirits, but they can't be used to see the æther.'

'So they're not really numa.'

'Still dangerous,' Liss said. 'Rotties can use them. The last thing we need is an ethereal weapon Scion can use.'

Julian shook his head. 'Scion would never use numa. They're repulsed by clairvoyance.'

'Not by the Rephaim.'

'I doubt they like the Rephs,' I said. 'They're clairvoyant. They just don't have a choice but to obey, with the Emim at their doorstep.'

The water boiled and steamed. Liss poured it into three paper cups and mixed it with coffee. I hadn't smelled coffee in days, or weeks. How long had I been in this place?

'Here.' She handed one cup to me, one to Julian. 'Where does Aludra keep you, Jules?'

'A room with no lights. I think it used to be a wine cellar. We sleep on the floor. Felix is claustrophobic, and Ella misses her family. They spend half the day crying, so I don't sleep.'

'Just get evicted. It's harsh out here, but not as harsh as it is to have a keeper. We only get fed on if we're in the wrong place at the wrong time.' Liss sipped from her cup. 'Some people can't take it. I had a friend who stayed in here with me, but she begged her keeper for another chance. She's a bone-grubber now.'

We drank our coffee in silence. Liss boiled the eggs, and we ate them straight out of the shell.

'I was thinking,' Julian said. 'Can the Rephs actually go back to wherever they came from?'

Liss shrugged. 'I guess so.'

'I just don't understand why they stay. I mean, they weren't always here. What did they do for aura before they found us?'

'It might be about the Buzzers,' I said. 'Nashira said they were a "parasitic race", didn't she?'

Julian nodded. 'Think the Buzzers took something from them?'

'Their sanity?'

He snorted. 'Yeah. Or maybe they used to be nice until the Buzzers sucked it all out of them.'

Liss didn't laugh. 'It could be the ethereal threshold,' I said. 'Nashira did say they appeared when it broke.'

'I don't think we'll ever know.' Liss sounded tense. 'It's not like they're going to broadcast it.'

'Why not? If they're so powerful and we're so feeble, where's the need for secrecy?'

'Knowledge is power,' Julian said. 'They have it. We don't.'

'You're wrong, brother. Knowledge is dangerous.' Liss pulled her knees up to her chin. It was just what Duckett had implied. 'Once you know something, you can't get rid of it. You have to carry it. Always.'

Julian and I exchanged a glance. Liss had been here for a long time; maybe we should just take her advice. Or maybe we shouldn't. Maybe her advice would kill us.

'Liss,' I said, 'do you ever think about fighting back?'

'Every day.'

'But you don't do it.'

'I think about gouging out Suhail's eyes with my bare hands.' She said it through gritted teeth. 'I think about shooting Nashira a hundred times, in every part of her body. I think about stabbing Gomeisa in the gullet, but I know they'd kill me first, so I don't do it.'

'But if you think like that, you'll be stuck here for ever,' Julian said gently. 'Do you want that?'

'Of course I don't want that. I want to go home. Whatever that means.' Liss turned her face away. 'I know what you must think of me. You think I've got no backbone.'

'Liss,' I said, 'we didn't mean—'

'Yes, you did. I don't blame you. But let me tell you something, if you want knowledge so much. There was a rebellion here during Bone Season XVIII, back in 2039. The whole human population of Sheol I rose up against the Rephs.' The pain in her eyes aged her by decades. 'They all died – amaurotics, voyants, the whole lot. Without the red-jackets to fight them, the Emim got in and killed them all. And the Rephs just let them do it.'

I looked at Julian. He didn't take his eyes off Liss.

'They said they deserved it. For their disobedience. It was the first thing they told us when we arrived.' She ran her cards between her fingers. 'I know you're both fighters, but I don't want to see you die here. Not like that.'

Her words silenced me. Julian rubbed a hand over his head, looking at the stove.

We didn't go back to the subject of rebellion. We ate the beans, scraping the cans clean. Liss kept her deck on her lap. After a minute, Julian cleared his throat.

'Where did you live, Liss? Before this.'

'Cradlehall. It's near Inverness.'

'What's Scion like up there?'

'Same as down here, really. The big cities are all under the same system, but with a smaller security force than London. They're still bound by Inquisitorial legislation, like the citadel.'

'Why did you come south?' I said. 'Surely the Highlands were safer for voyants.'

'Why does anyone go to SciLo? Work. Money. We need to eat just as much as amaurotics.' Liss drew a sheet around her shoulders. 'My parents were too afraid to live in central Inverness. Voyants aren't organised there, not like the syndicate. Dad thought we should try our luck in the citadel. We spent our savings to get to London. We approached some mime-lords, but none of them needed soothsayers. Once the money ran out, we had to busk just to get a doss at night.'

'And you were caught.'

'Dad got too ill to go out. He was in his sixties, giving himself all sorts of bugs on the streets. I took his usual stake. A woman approached me and asked for a reading.' She ran her thumb over the tops of her cards. 'I was nine. I didn't realise she was NVD.'

Julian shook his head. 'How long were you in the Tower?'

'Four years. They put me on the waterboard a few times, tried to make me tell them where my parents were. I said I didn't know.'

This couldn't be making her feel better. 'What about you, Julian?' I said.

'Morden. IV-6.'

'That's the smallest section, isn't it?'

'Yeah, that's why the syndicate doesn't bother with it. I had a little group, but we didn't do mime-crime. Just the odd séance.'

I felt a bitter pang of loss. I wanted *my* group.

Julian soon succumbed to his exhaustion. The fuel ran lower and lower on the Sterno. Liss watched it to the end. I pretended to sleep, but all I could think about was Bone Season XVIII. So many people must have died. Their families would never have been told. There would have been no trials, no appeals. The injustice of it made me sick. No wonder Liss was so afraid to fight.

That was when the siren sounded.

Julian jerked awake. The noise cranked and creaked, working itself up like heaving bellows, before it let out a scream. My body reacted at once: a prickling at my legs, a thumping heart.

Footsteps thundered through the passages. Julian peeled back the rag door. Three red-jackets ran past, one carrying a powerful torch. Liss opened her eyes, perfectly still.

'They have knives,' Julian said.

Liss pushed herself into the corner of the shack. She picked up her deck of cards, scooped an arm around her knees, and put her head down. 'You have to go,' she said. 'Now.'

'Come with us,' I said. 'Just sneak into one of the residences. You're not safe in—'

'Do you *want* to get a slating from Aludra? Or the Warden?' She glared up at us. 'I've been doing this for ten years. Get out of here.'

We exchanged glances. We were already late. I didn't know what Warden would do to me, but we both knew how violent Aludra Chertan was. She might just kill him this time. We ducked out of the shack and ran like hell.

10

The Message

The sirens were still howling when I got back to the residence. XIX-49-33 only opened the door when I'd knocked for the umpteenth time and shouted my number over the noise. Once she'd established I was human, she hauled me through the door and slammed it behind me, swearing she'd never let me in again if I was that bloody slow to follow basic orders. I left her drawing bolts across the door in agitation, her fingers trembling.

The sirens stopped as I reached the cloisters. The Emim had not breached the city this time. I scraped back my hair, trying to slow my breathing. After a minute, I made myself look at the doorway, at the winding stone steps. I had to do it. I took another moment to compose myself, then walked up those steps to the tower, his tower. My skin crawled at the thought of sleeping in the same room as him; of sharing his space, his heat, his air.

The key was in the door when I arrived. I turned it and stepped quietly onto the flagstones.

Not quietly enough. The second I crossed the threshold, my keeper was on his feet. His eyes blazed.

'Where have you been?'

I kept a tenuous mental guard up. 'Outside.'

'You were told to return here if the siren sounded.'

'I thought you meant to Magdalen, not this exact room. You should be more specific.'

I could hear the insolence in my voice. His eyes darkened, and his lips pressed into a hard line.

'You will speak to me with the proper respect,' he said, 'or you will not be allowed outside this room at all.'

'You've done nothing to earn my respect.' I stared him down. He stared right back at me. When I didn't move or break his gaze, he stalked past me and slammed the door. I didn't flinch.

'When you hear that siren,' he said, 'you stop what you are doing and return to this room. Do you understand me?'

I just looked at him. He leaned down so his face was at my level.

'Do I need to repeat myself?'

'I'd rather you didn't,' I said.

I was sure he'd hit me. Nobody, *nobody* could speak to a Reph like that. All he did was straighten to his full height.

'We begin your instruction tomorrow,' he said. 'I expect you to be ready when the night-bell rings.'

'Instruction for what?'

'For your next jacket.'

'I don't want it,' I said.

'Then you will have to become a performer. You will have to spend the rest of your life being mocked and spat upon by the red-jackets.' He looked me over. 'Do you wish to be a jester? A fool?'

'No.'

'Then you had better do as I say.'

My throat closed up. Much as I hated this creature, I had good reason to fear him. I recalled his merciless face in the dark chapel, when he'd stood over me and drawn on my aura. Auras were as vital to voyants as blood or water. Without one, I would go into spirit shock and end up dead or insane, wandering around with no connection to the æther.

He approached the drapes and pulled them back, revealing the little door beyond them was ajar. 'The amaurotics have cleared the upper floor for you. Unless I say otherwise, you are to keep to it at all times.' He paused. 'You should also know it is forbidden for the two of us to make direct physical contact, except in training. Even with gloves.'

'So if you were to come into this room injured,' I said, 'I would leave you to die?'

'Yes.'

Liar. I didn't bite the next words off my tongue quite fast enough: 'That's one order I'm happy to obey.'

Warden just looked at me. It almost made me angry, how little notice he took of my disrespect. He had to have a pressure point. All he did was reach into the drawer and hold out my pills.

'Take them.'

I knew there was no point in arguing. I took the pills.

'Drink this.' He handed me a glass. 'Go to your quarters. You will need to be well rested for tomorrow.'

My right hand drew into a fist. I was sick of his orders. I should have left him to bleed out. Why the hell had I bandaged his wound? What kind of criminal was I, patching up my enemies? Jax would have laughed himself stupid if he'd seen me. *Honeybee*, he would have said, *you just don't have the sting in you.* And maybe I didn't. Yet.

I was careful to avoid any contact with Warden when I passed him. I caught his gaze before I stepped into the dark passage. He locked the door behind me.

Another winding staircase took me to the upper floor of the tower. I looked at my new abode: a large, bare room. It reminded me of the Detainment Facility, with a damp floor and barred windows. A paraffin lamp burned on the windowsill, giving little light and even less heat. Beside it was a bed, the type with rails and a lumpy mattress. The sheets were prudish in comparison to the luscious velvet mantles of Warden's four-poster; in fact, the whole room smacked of human inferiority – but anything was better than sharing.

I checked every corner and crevice of the room, as I had with the lower floor. No way out, of course, but there was a bathroom. In it was a toilet, a sink and a few hygiene supplies.

I thought of Julian in his dark cellar and thought of Liss, shivering in her shack. She didn't have a bed. She didn't have anything. It wasn't nice in here, but it was far warmer and cleaner than the Rookery. And safer. I had stone walls to protect me from the Emim. All she had were tattered curtains.

As I hadn't been given nightclothes, I stripped to my underwear. There was no mirror, but I could see I was losing weight. Stress, flux poisoning and a lack of nutritious food were already taking their toll. I dimmed the lamp and slid between the sheets.

I hadn't felt tired before, but I found myself dozing. And thinking. Thinking of the past, of the strange days that had led me to this place. I thought back to the very first time I met Nick. It was Nick who put Jaxon and me in contact. Nick, the man who saved my life.

When I was nine, shortly after I came to England, my father and I left London and went south for what he called a 'business trip'. He had to put our names on a waiting list in order for us to leave the citadel. After months of waiting, we were finally allowed to visit my father's old friend Giselle. She lived on a slanted, cobbled hill, in a sugar-pink house with a roof that hung over the windows. The surrounding land reminded me of Ireland: open, sumptuous beauty, wild and untamed nature, everything that Scion had destroyed. At sunset, when my father wasn't looking, I would climb up to the roof and tuck myself against the tall brick chimney. I would stare out at the hills, at the reams of trees under the sky, and I would remember my cousin Finn and the other ghosts of Ireland, and I would miss my grandparents so terribly it hurt. I had never understood why they didn't come with us.

But what I wanted was open water. The sea, the wondrous sea, the glittering road that stretched to the free lands. It was over the sea that Ireland waited to bring me home – back to the ashen meadow, to the cloven tree of the rebels' song. My father promised we would see it, but he was too busy with Giselle. They always talked deep into the night.

I was too young to understand what the village was really like. Voyants might have been in danger in the citadel, but they couldn't escape to these idylls in the countryside. Far from the Archon, small-town amaurotics grew nervous. Suspicions about unnaturalness pervaded those close-knit communities. They made a habit of watching one another, eyes peeled for a crystal ball or shew stone, waiting to call the nearest Scion outpost – or take justice into their own hands. A real clairvoyant wouldn't last a day. Even if they did, there was no work. The land needed tending, but not by many hands. They had machines to farm the fields. It was only in the citadel that voyants could make decent money.

I didn't like to go far from the house, not without my father. The people talked too much, looked too much, and Giselle talked and looked straight back at them. She was a stern woman, thin and hard-faced, with a ring on every finger and long, string-like veins that bulged from her arms and neck. I didn't like her. But one day, from the rooftop, I spotted a haven: a poppy field, a pool of red beneath the iron sky.

Every day, when my father thought I was playing upstairs, I would walk to that field and read on my new data pad for hours, watching the poppies nod their heads around me. It was in that field that I had my first true encounter with the spirit world. The æther. At the time I had no idea I was clairvoyant. Unnaturalness was still a story to a child of nine, a boogeyman with no clear features. I had yet to understand this place. I only knew what Finn had told me: that the bad people over the sea didn't like little girls like me. I was no longer safe.

That day, I found out what he'd meant. When I walked onto the field, I sensed the angry presence of the woman. I didn't see her. I *felt* her. I felt her in the poppies, in the wind. I felt her in the earth and in the air. I stretched my hand out, hoping somehow to work out what it was.

And then I was on the ground. And bleeding. It was my first encounter with a poltergeist, an angry spirit that could breach the corporeal world.

My saviour soon came. A young man, tall and sturdy, with ice-blond hair and a face that seemed kind. He asked my name. I stammered it. When he saw my tattered arm, he wrapped me in his overcoat and took me to his car. SCIONAID was stitched on his shirt. My little body flooded with terror when he took out a needle. 'My name's Nick,' he said. 'You're safe, Paige.'

The needle went into my skin. It stung, but I didn't cry. The world gradually turned too dark to see.

In the dark, I dreamed. I dreamed of poppies struggling from dust. I'd never seen colours when I slept, but now all I could see was the red flowers and the evening sun. They sheltered me, shedding their petals, blanketing my fevered body. When I woke, I was propped up in a bed with white sheets. My arm was bandaged. The pain was gone.

The blond man was beside me. I remember his smile; just a small smile – but it made me smile back. He looked like a prince.

'Hello, Paige,' he said.

I asked where I was.

'You're in hospital. I'm your doctor.'

'You don't look old enough to be a doctor,' I said. Or scary enough. 'How old are you?'

'I'm eighteen. Still learning.'

'You didn't sew my arm funny, did you?'

He laughed. 'Well, I tried my best. You'll have to let me know what you think.'

He'd told my father where I was, he said, and he was on his way to see me. I said I felt sick. He said that was normal, but I'd have to rest to make it go away. I couldn't eat just yet, but he'd get me something nice for dinner. He sat with me for the rest of the day, only leaving me to bring sandwiches and a bottle of apple juice from the hospital canteen. My father had told me never to talk to strangers, but I wasn't afraid of this kind, soft-spoken boy.

Dr Nicklas Nygård, a transfer from the Scion Citadel of Stockholm, kept me alive that night. He saw me through the shock of becoming fully clairvoyant. If not for him, it might have been too much for me to stand.

My father drove me home a few days later. He knew Nick from a medical conference. Nick was training in the town before he took a permanent position at SciSORS. He never said what he'd been doing in the poppy field. While my father waited for me in the car, Nick knelt in front of me and took my hands. I remember thinking how handsome he was, and how perfectly his eyebrows arched over his lovely winter-green eyes.

'Paige,' he said, very quietly, 'listen to me. This is very important. I've told your father you were attacked by a dog.'

'But it was a lady.'

'Yes – but that lady was invisible, *sötnos*. Some grown-ups don't know about invisible things.'

'But *you* do,' I said, confident in his wisdom.

'I do. But I don't want other grown-ups to laugh at me, so I don't tell them.' He touched my cheek. 'You must never, ever tell anyone about her, Paige. Let's make it our secret. Promise?'

I nodded. I would have promised him the world. He had saved

my life. I watched him through the window as my father drove me back to the citadel. He raised a hand and waved at me. I watched until we turned a corner.

I still had scars from the attack. They formed a cluster in the middle of my left palm. The spirit left other cuts, all the way to my elbow – but the ones on my hand were the ones that stayed.

I made good on my promise. For seven years I never said a word. I kept his secret close to my heart, like a night-blooming flower, only thinking of it when I was alone. Nick knew the truth. Nick held the key. For all that time I wondered where the days had taken him, and if he ever thought of that little Irish girl he'd carried from the poppy field. And after seven long years, I had my reward: he found me again. If only he could find me now.

There was no sound from the lower floor. As the hours ticked away, I listened for a footstep, or the echoing melody of the gramophone. All I could hear was the same thick silence.

I fell into a light sleep for the rest of the daylight hours. Fever burned through me, a remnant of the latest flux attack. I jerked awake every so often, my eyes bursting with pictures of the past. Had I ever worn anything but these tunics, these boots? Had I ever known a world in which there were no spirits, no wandering dead? No Emim, no Rephaim?

A knock woke me. I barely had time to grab a sheet before Warden entered the room.

'There is not long before the bell.' He placed a fresh uniform on the end of the bed. 'Get dressed.'

I looked at him in silence. His gaze lingered for a moment before he left, closing the door behind him. There was nothing for it. I got up, smoothed my curls into a knot and washed myself with icy water. I pulled on my uniform and zipped the gilet to my chin. My leg seemed to have healed.

Warden was leafing through a dusty novel when I came into the chamber. *Frankenstein.* Scion didn't allow that kind of fantastical literature. Nothing with monsters or ghosts. Nothing unnatural. My fingers twitched, aching to reach out and turn its pages. I'd seen it on Jaxon's bookshelf, but never found time to read it. Warden put the book aside and stood.

'Are you ready?'

'Yes,' I said.

'Good.' He paused, then asked: 'Tell me, Paige – what does your dreamscape look like?'

The directness of the question took me by surprise. It was considered rude among voyants to ask. 'A field of red flowers.'

'What kind of flowers?'

'Poppies.'

No response. He reached for his gloves, pulled them on, and led me from the room. The night-bell hadn't chimed, but the porter let us pass without question. Nobody questioned Arcturus Mesarthim.

Sunlight. I hadn't seen it for a while. The sun was just setting, softening the edges of the buildings. Sheol I glowed in a dwindling haze. I'd thought we would be training indoors, but Warden led me north, past Amaurotic House and into unknown territory.

The buildings in the furthest reaches of the city had all been abandoned. They were dilapidated, with windows broken; some of the walls and roofs looked scorched. Maybe there really had been fires here once. We passed a tight-packed street of houses. It was a ghost town. No living people whatsoever. I could sense spirits nearby, bitter spirits that wanted their lost homes back. Some were weak poltergeists. I was wary, but Warden didn't seem afraid. None of them came near him.

We reached the very edge of the city. My breath smoked from between my lips. A meadow stretched as far as I could see. The grass was long since dead, and the ground glistened with frost. Strange, for early spring. A fence had been put up around it, at least thirty feet high, topped with coils of barbed wire. Behind the fence were trees, needled with soft rime. They grew around the edges of the meadow, blocking my view of the world beyond. A rusted notice read PORT MEADOW. FOR TRAINING PURPOSES ONLY. USE OF DEADLY FORCE IS AUTHORISED. Standing at the gate was the deadly force itself: a Reph male.

He wore his golden hair in a tight ponytail. Beside him stood a thin, dirty figure with a shaved head: Ivy, the palmist. She wore a yellow tunic, the mark of a coward. It was torn from the neck, exposing her bony shoulder to the cold. I caught sight of her brand. XX-59-24. Warden stepped forward, and I followed. Seeing us, Ivy's keeper swept into a bow.

'Behold the royal concubine,' he said. 'What brings you to Port Meadow?'

At first I thought he was talking to me. I'd never heard Rephs speak to each other with such disgust. Then I realised he was glaring at my keeper.

'I am here to instruct my human.' Warden was looking at the meadow. 'Open the gate, Thuban.'

'Patience, concubine. Is it armed?'

He meant me. The human. 'No,' Warden said. 'She is not.'

'Number?'

'XX-59-40.'

'Age?'

He glanced at me. 'Nineteen,' I said.

'Is it sighted?'

'These questions are irrelevant, Thuban. I do not appreciate being treated like a child – especially not *by* a child.'

Thuban just looked at him. He was in his late twenties, by my reckoning, certainly not a child. Neither of their faces showed any hint of anger; their words were enough.

'You have three hours before Pleione brings her herd.' He shoved the gate open. 'If 40 tries to escape, it will be shot on sight.'

'And if you ever disrespect your elders in that manner again, you will be sequestered on sight.'

'The blood-sovereign would not allow it.'

'She would not have to know. Such an accident is not too hard to conceal.' Warden towered over him. 'I do not fear your Sargas name. I am the blood-consort, and I will exercise the power that befits my station. Do I make myself clear, Thuban?'

Thuban looked up at him, his eyes roaring blue. 'Yes,' he said, in a whisper, 'blood-*consort.*'

Warden walked past him. I had no idea what to make of their exchange, but it was fairly satisfying to see a Sargas get a verbal slating. As I followed Warden through the gate, Thuban struck Ivy across the face. Her head snapped around. Her eyes were dry, but her face was swollen and discoloured, and she was thinner than before. Blood and dirt streaked her arms. She was being kept in her own filth. I remembered Seb looking at me that way, like all the hope in the world had crumbled.

For Seb, for Ivy, for the ones who would follow, I would make this training session count.

Port Meadow was vast. Warden took long strides, too long for me to keep up. I trudged behind him, trying to work out the dimensions of the meadow. It was difficult in the waning light, but I could see the ugly fences on either side, dividing the beaten ground into several large arenas. They were strung with thin wires, lined with icicles. The posts were curved towards the top; some bore heavy brackets, each dripping a lantern. A watchtower stood on the western side, and I could just see a human – or Reph – inside it.

We walked past a shallow pool of water. Its frozen surface was smooth as a mirror, perfect for scrying. Come to think of it, everything about this meadow was perfect for spirit combat. The ground was solid, the air clear and fresh – and there were spirits. I could sense them everywhere, all around me. I wondered what kind of fence enclosed this meadow. Could they have worked out a way to *trap* spirits?

No. Spirits might sometimes breach meatspace, but they were not subject to physical restrictions. Only binders could trap them. Their order – the fifth order – could bend the limits between meatspace and æther.

'The fences are not charged with electricity' – Warden saw where I was looking – 'but with ethereal energy.'

'How is that possible?'

'Ethereal batteries. A fusion of Rephaite and human expertise, pioneered in 2045. Your scientists have been working on hybrid technology since the early twentieth century. We simply replace the chemical energy in a battery with a captive poltergeist, a spirit that can interact with the corporeal world. It creates a field of repulsion.'

'But poltergeists can escape their bindings,' I said. 'How could you capture one?'

'Use a willing poltergeist, of course.'

I stared at his back. The words *willing* and *poltergeist* were as opposite as war and peace.

'Our counsel also led to the invention of Fluxion 14 and Radiesthesic Detection Technology,' he said, 'the latter of which remains experimental. From our last reports, we hear Scion is close to perfecting it.'

I clenched my fist. Of course the Rephaim were responsible for RDT. Dani had always wondered how they'd managed it.

After a while Warden stopped. We had come to a concrete oval, ten foot across. A gas lamp flared to life nearby.

'Let us begin,' he said.

I waited.

With no warning, he aimed a mock punch at my face. I ducked. When he jabbed his other fist, I blocked it with my arm.

'Again.'

He was faster this time, trying to make me defend myself quickly, from all angles. I kept my hands open and blocked each hit.

'You learned to fight on the streets.'

'Maybe,' I said.

'Once more. Try and stop me.'

This time he made as if to grab my neck, placing both hands high on my décolletage. A flimp had tried this on me once. I twisted my body to the left and thrust my right arm in the same direction, cutting his hands away from my throat. I could feel the strength in those hands, but he let go. I brought my elbow against his cheek, a move that had knocked the flimp right into the gutter. He was letting me win.

'Excellent.' Warden stepped back. 'Few humans come here prepared to be part of a penal battalion. You are several steps ahead of most, but you will not be able to engage in that sort of scrap with an Emite. Your most important asset is your ability to affect the æther.'

I spied the silver glint. There was a blade in his hand. My muscles tensed rigid. 'From what I have seen, your gift is triggered by danger.' He levelled the blade at my chest. 'Demonstrate.'

My heart pounded at the tip of his blade. 'I don't know how.'

'I see.'

With a flick of his wrist, he brought the blade against my throat. My body hummed with adrenalin. Warden leaned in very close to me.

'This blade has been used to draw human blood,' he said, very softly. 'Blood like that of your friend Sebastian.'

I trembled.

'It calls for more.' The blade slid along my neck. 'It has never tasted the blood of a dreamer.'

'I'm not afraid of you.' The tremor in my voice betrayed the lie. 'Don't touch me.'

But he did. The blade traced my throat, trailed up to my chin and touched my lips. I jerked my fist up, shoved his hand away. He dropped the blade, took my wrists in one hand and pinned them to the concrete. His strength was incredible: I couldn't move a muscle.

'I wonder.' He used the knife to tip my chin up. 'If I cut your throat, how long will it take for you to die?'

'You wouldn't,' I said, daring him.

'Oh, but I would.'

I tried to wrench my knee into his groin, but he grabbed my thigh, forcing my leg down. That leg was still weak; it was easy. He was making me look feeble. When I pulled a hand free, he twisted my arm behind my back. Not hard enough to hurt, but enough to immobilise me.

'You will always lose that way,' he said against my ear. 'Play to your strengths.'

Was there no weak spot on this creature? I thought of all the vulnerable places on a human: eyes, kidneys, solar plexus, nose, groin – nothing within my reach. I would have to move and run. I pushed my weight backwards, straight between his legs, and rolled back to my feet in one movement. In the instant he took to stand, I tore into a sprint across the meadow. If he wanted me, he could damn well come and get me.

There was nowhere to run. He was gaining on me. Thinking back to my training sessions with Nick, I changed direction. Then I was running again, into the darkness, away from the watchtower. There had to be a weak point in a fence like this, somewhere I could squeeze between the wires. Then I had to deal with Thuban. But I had my spirit. I could do it. I *could* do it.

For someone with excellent visual acuity, I could be incredibly short-sighted. Within a minute I was lost. Away from the concrete oval and the lamps, I was left to stumble through the vastness of the meadow. And Warden was out there, hunting me. I ran towards a gas lamp. My sixth sense quivered as I drew nearer to the fence. By the time I was six feet away I was nauseous, my limbs limp and heavy.

But I had to try. I grabbed the frozen wire.

I can't fully describe the sensation that seized my body. My vision turned black, then white, then red. Goose bumps broke out all over me. A hundred memories flashed before my eyes, memories of a scream in a poppy field; and new memories, too – the 'geist's memories. It was a murder victim. A deafening *bang* shook my every bone. My stomach gave an almighty heave. I hit the ground and retched.

I must have stayed there for a minute, racked by pictures of blood on a cream carpet. This person had been killed with a shotgun. His skull had burst open, spraying brain and shattered bone. My ears rang. When I came to my senses, my body felt uncoordinated. I dragged myself along the ground, blinking away bloody visions. A silver-white burn slashed across my palm. The mark of a poltergeist.

Something shot past my ear. I looked up to see another watch-tower, and the guard standing inside it.

Flux dart.

A second dart fired in my direction. I scrambled to my feet, turned east and ran – but soon enough I came to another watch-tower, and another gun had me running south. It was only when I saw the oval that I realised I was being driven back to Warden.

The next dart hit me in the shoulder. The pain was instant and excruciating. I reached up and tore the thing out. Blood flowed from the wound, and a wave of disorientating nausea swept over me. I was fast enough to stop the drug – it took about five seconds to self-inject – but the message was clear: get back on the oval, or get shot. Warden was waiting for me.

'Welcome back.'

I swiped the sweat from my forehead. 'So I'm not allowed to run.'

'No. Unless you would like me to present you with a yellow tunic, which we give only to cowards.'

I ran at him, blinded by anger, and drove my shoulder into his abdomen. Given his size, nothing happened. He just took me by the tunic and tossed me away. I landed hard on the same shoulder.

'You cannot fight me with your bare hands.' He prowled the edge of the oval. 'Nor can you run from an Emite. You are a *dreamwalker*, girl. You have the power to live and die as you decree. Lay waste to my dreamscape. Drive me mad!'

A part of me tore away. My spirit flew across the space between us. It slashed through the outer ring of his mind, like a knife through taut silk. I broke through the darkest part of his dreamscape, straining against impossibly powerful barriers, aiming for the distant patch of light that was his sunlit zone, but it wasn't as easy as it had been on the train. The centre of his dreamscape was so far away, and my spirit was already being driven out. Like an elastic band stretched too far, I snapped back into my own mind. The weight of my own spirit knocking me off my feet. My head rapped against the concrete.

The gas lamps swam back into focus. I pushed myself up on my elbows, my temples throbbing. Warden was still standing. I hadn't brought him to his knees, as I had with Aludra, but I had tampered with his perception. He ran a hand over his face and shook his head.

'Good,' he said. 'Very good.'

I stood. My legs shook.

'You're trying to make me angry,' I said. 'Why?'

'It seems to work.' He pointed the blade. 'Again.'

I looked up at him, trying to catch my breath. 'Again?'

'You can do better than that. You barely touched my defences. I want you to make a dent.'

'I can't do it again.' Black spotted my vision. 'It doesn't work like that.'

'Why not?'

'Because it stops me breathing.'

'Have you never gone swimming?'

'What?'

'The average human can hold their breath for at least thirty seconds without causing lasting damage. That is more than enough time for you to attack another mind and return to your body.'

I'd never thought of it like that. Nick had always ensured I used life support when I sensed the æther at a distance.

'Think of your spirit as a muscle, tearing from its natural place,' Warden said. 'The more you use it, the stronger and faster it will become, and the better your body will cope with the repercussions. You will be able to jump quickly between dreamscapes – before your body hits the ground.'

'You don't know anything,' I said.

'Nor do you. I suspect the incident on the train was the first time you ever walked in another dreamscape.' He didn't move the blade. 'Walk in mine. I challenge you.'

I searched his face. He was inviting me to come into his mind, to wound his sanity.

'You don't really care. You're just training me,' I said. We circled each other. 'Nashira asked you to choose me. I know what she wants.'

'No. I chose you. I laid claim to your instruction. And the last thing I want' – he stepped towards me – 'is for you to embarrass me with your incompetence.' His eyes were hard as flint. 'Attack me again. And do it properly this time.'

'No.' I'd call his bluff. Let him be embarrassed. Let him be as mortified by me as my father. 'I'm not going to kill myself just so you can get a gold star from Nashira.'

'You want to hurt me,' he said, softer now. 'You loathe me. You resent me.' He lifted the knife. 'Destroy me.'

At first I did nothing. Then I remembered the hours I'd spent cleaning his arm, and how he'd threatened me. I remembered how he'd stood aside and watched Seb die. I flung my spirit back at him.

In the time we spent on that meadow, I barely fractured his dreamscape. Even when he dropped most of his defences, I couldn't get any further than his hadal zone – his mind was just too strong. He goaded me the whole time. He told me I was weak, that I was pathetic, that I was a disgrace to all clairvoyants. That it was no wonder humans were good for nothing but slavery. Did I want to live in a cage, like an animal? He was happy to oblige. At first the provocation did its job, but the more the night wore on, the less his insults roused me. In the end they were just frustrating, not enough to force my spirit out.

That was when he threw a blade. He aimed well away from me, but the sight of the flying knife was enough to set my spirit loose. Each time I did it, my body fell. If my foot so much as slipped off the oval, a flux dart came whistling in my direction. I soon learned to premeditate the sound, and to duck before the needle could hit home.

I managed five or six jumps out of my body. Each time was like having my head ripped open. Finally I could take no more. My vision went double and a migraine swelled above my left eye. I bent at the waist, hungry for air. *Don't show weakness. Don't show weakness.* My knees were going to give.

Warden knelt in front of me and wrapped an arm around my waist. I tried to push him away, but my arms were like string.

'Stop,' he said. 'Stop resisting.'

He lifted me into his arms. I'd never experienced this quick-fire jumping; I didn't know if my brain would stand it. The backs of my eyes throbbed. I couldn't look at the lantern.

'You did well.' Warden looked down at me. 'But you could do much better.'

I couldn't reply.

'Paige?'

'I'm fine.' My voice was slurred.

He seemed to take my word for it. Still holding me, he made his way towards the gate.

Warden set me on my feet again after a while. We walked in silence back to the entrance where Thuban had left his post. Ivy was sitting against the fence, her face in her hands, her shoulders shaking. When we approached the sally port, she stood and undid the bolt. Warden glanced at her as we passed. 'Thank you, Ivy.'

She looked up. There were tears in her eyes. When was the last time she'd been called by her real name?

Warden kept his silence as we walked through the ghost town. I was only half-awake. Nick would have made me rest in bed for hours if I'd been with him, and scolded me for good measure.

It was only when we walked past Amaurotic House that Warden spoke again: 'Do you often try to sense the æther at a distance?'

'None of your business,' I said.

'Your eyes hold death. Death and ice.' He turned to face me. 'Strange, when they burn so hot in your anger.'

I met his gaze. 'Your eyes change, too.'

'Why do you think that might be?'

'I don't know. I don't know anything about you.'

'That is true enough.' Warden looked me up and down. 'Show me your hand.'

After a moment, I showed him my right hand. The burn had

taken on an ugly, nacreous appearance. He took out a tiny vial of liquid from his pocket, tipped it against his gloved finger and spread its contents over the mark. Before my eyes, it melted away, leaving no trace. I pulled my hand back.

'How did you do that?'

'It is called amaranth.' He put the vial away, then looked back at me. 'Tell me, Paige – are you afraid of the æther?'

'No,' I said. My palm tingled.

'Why not?'

It was a lie. I *was* afraid of the æther. When I pushed my sixth sense too far, I ran the risk of death, or at least brain injury. Jax had told me from the beginning that if I worked for him, I was likely to cut my lifespan by about thirty years, maybe more. It all rested on luck.

'Because the æther is perfect,' I said. 'There's no war. There's no death, because everything there is already dead. And there's no sound. Just silence. And safety.'

'Nothing is safe in the æther. And even the æther is not exempt from war and death.'

I studied his profile as he looked at the black sky. His breath didn't cloud in the cold, not like mine. But for a moment – just the briefest moment – there was something human in his face. Something pensive, almost bitter. Then he turned to face me again, and it was gone.

Something was amiss outside the Rookery. A group of red-jackets were crouched on the cobblestones, watched by silent harlies, talking in quick, hushed voices. I glanced up at Warden to see if he was concerned. If he was, he didn't show it. He walked towards the group, causing most of the harlies to shrink back into their shacks.

'What is it?'

One of the red-jackets looked up, saw who had spoken, and flicked his gaze back down. His tunic was caked in mud. 'We were in the woods,' he said, his voice hoarse. 'We got lost. The Emim – they—'

Warden's hand strayed to his forearm.

The red-jackets were gathered around a boy of perhaps sixteen. His entire right hand was missing, and it wasn't just his tunic that was red. My mouth clenched up. His hand had been ripped and twisted from his arm, as if it had been caught in a machine. Warden analysed the scene with no hint of emotion.

'You say you were lost,' he said. 'Which keeper was with you?'

'The blood-heir.'

Warden levelled his gaze on the street. 'I should have known.'

My eyes burned on his back. He was just *standing* there. The red-jacket was trembling uncontrollably, his face shining with sweat. He was going to die if someone didn't bandage the stump, or at least get a blanket over him.

'Take him to Oriel.' Warden turned away from the group. 'Terebell will deal with him. The rest of you, get back to your residences. The amaurotics will tend to your wounds.'

I looked at his hard-bitten features, searching for a hint of something warm. I found nothing. He didn't care. I didn't know why I kept looking.

The red-jackets lifted their friend and staggered towards an alley-way, leaving spots of blood in their wake. 'He needs a hospital.' I made myself say it. 'You've got no idea how to—'

'He will be dealt with.'

He was silent then, and his eyes grew hard. I guessed that meant I'd overstepped the line.

But I was starting to wonder where exactly the line had been drawn. Warden never beat me. He let me sleep. He used my real name when we were alone. He had even let me attack his mind, made himself vulnerable to my spirit – a spirit that could break his very sanity apart. I couldn't understand why he would take the risk. Even Nick was wary of my gift. ('Call it a healthy respect, *sötnos*.')

As we headed towards the residence, I let my hair down from its knot. I almost jumped out of my body again when someone else's hands took over, pulling my damp curls around my shoulders.

'Ah, XX-40. A pleasure to see you again.' The voice was tinged with amusement. High-pitched for a man. 'I must congratulate you, Warden. She looks even more ravishing in a tunic.'

I turned to face the man behind me. It took effort not to recoil.

It was the medium, the one that had chased me across the rooftops of I-5, but he wasn't carrying a flux gun tonight. He wore a strange uniform in the colours of Scion. Even his face matched the colour code: red mouth, black eyebrows, face dusted with zinc oxide. He was probably in his late thirties, and he carried a heavy leather whip. I was sure I could see blood on it. This must be the Overseer, the man who kept the harlies in check. Behind him was the oracle from the first night. He looked at me with disconcerting eyes: one dark and piercing, one a clear hazel. His tunic was the same colour as mine.

Warden looked down at them. 'What do you want, Overseer?'

'Pardon my intrusion. I merely wanted to see the dreamer again. I have watched her progress with great interest.'

'She is not a performer. Her progress is not for watching.'

'Indeed. But what a charming sight she is.' He flashed me a smile. 'Allow me to welcome you personally to Sheol I. I am Beltrame, the Overseer. I hope my flux dart didn't scar your back.'

I reacted. I couldn't help it. 'If you hurt my father—'

'I did not give you permission to speak, XX-40.'

Warden stared me down. The Overseer laughed, patted my cheek. I jerked away from him. 'There, now. Your father is safe and well.' He made a sign on his chest. 'Cross my heart.'

I should have been relieved, but all I could feel was anger at his nerve. Warden looked at the younger man. 'Who is this?'

'This is XX-59-12.' The Overseer placed a hand on his shoulder. 'He is a *very* loyal servant to Pleione. He has done exceptionally well in his studies over the last few weeks.'

'I see.' Warden's eyes flicked over him, assessing his aura. 'You are an oracle, boy?'

'Yes, Warden.' 12 bowed.

'The blood-sovereign must be pleased with your progress. We have had no oracles since Bone Season XVI.'

'I hope to be among those in her service soon, Warden.' There were traces of the north in his accent.

'As you will be, 12. You'll do very well against your Emite, I think. 12 is about to take his second test,' the Overseer said. 'We were just on our way back to Merton to join the rest of his battalion. Pleione and Alsafi will lead them.'

'Are the Sualocin aware of the injured red-jacket?' Warden said.

'Yes. They hunt the same Emite that bit him.'

Warden's expression flickered.

'The best of luck to you in that endeavour, 12,' he said.

12 bowed again.

'But I do have another reason to interrupt, before we leave,' the Overseer added. 'I am here to extend an invitation to the dreamwalker. If I may.'

Warden turned to face him. The Overseer took his silence as permission to continue.

'We are putting on a very special celebration in honour of this Bone Season, XX-40. The *twentieth* Bone Season.' He swept a hand towards the Rookery. 'Our finest performers. A feast for the senses. A saturnalia of music and dancing to show off all our boys and girls.'

'You refer to the Bicentenary,' Warden said.

It was the first time I'd heard the word.

'Precisely.' The Overseer smiled. 'The ceremony during which the Great Territorial Act will be signed.'

That didn't sound good. Before I could hear any more, I was blinded by a vision.

As an oracle, Nick could send soundless images through the æther. He called them *khrēsmoi*, a Greek word. I could never pronounce it, so I just called them his 'snapshots'. 12 had the same gift. I saw a clock, both hands pointing towards twelve, followed by four pillars and a flight of steps. A moment later, I blinked, and the images were gone. I opened my eyes to see him looking at me.

It had all happened in a second. 'I am aware of the Act,' Warden was saying. 'Get to the point, Overseer. 40 is exhausted.'

The Overseer didn't baulk at Warden's tone. He must be used to being despised. Instead he offered me a smile, soft as oil.

'I would like to invite 40 to perform with us on the day of the Bicentenary. I was impressed with her strength and agility on the night I captured her. It gives me great pleasure to invite her to be my principal performer, along with XIX-49-1 and XIX-49-8.'

I was about to refuse, in such a way as to earn myself a severe punishment, when Warden spoke.

'As her keeper,' he said, 'I forbid it.'

I looked up at him.

'She is not a performer, and unless she fails her tests before the Bicentenary, she remains in my keeping.' Warden stared directly at the Overseer. '40 is a dreamwalker. The dreamwalker *you* were assigned to bring to this colony. I will not allow her to be paraded in front of the Scion emissaries like a common seer. That is an assignment for your humans. Not mine.'

The Overseer wasn't smiling now.

'Very good.' He bowed, not looking at me. 'Come, 12. Your challenge awaits.'

12 slid me a look, one eyebrow raised in question. I nodded. He

turned and followed the Overseer back to the Rookery, walking with an easy stride. He didn't seem afraid of what he was about to face.

Warden's eyes scorched on my face. 'Do you know the oracle?'

'No.'

'He never took his eyes off you.'

'Forgive me, *master*,' I said, 'but am I not permitted to speak with other humans?'

He didn't take his eyes off me. I wondered whether the Rephs understood sarcasm.

'Yes,' he said. 'You are permitted.'

He swept past me without another word.

Of Weeping

I didn't sleep well. My head hurt too much, a pain that throbbed at my left temple. I lay between the sheets and watched the candle burn to nothing.

Warden had not sent me to my room at once. He'd offered me a little food and water, which I'd accepted out of sheer dehydration. Then he'd sat by the fire, gazing into the flames. It had taken me a good ten minutes to ask if I could retire for the day, a question he'd answered with a curt affirmative.

The upper floor was cold. The windows were like paper, and there was a leak. I wrapped myself in the thin sheets, shivering. After a while, I dozed off. Warden's words trembled in my ears — that my eyes held death and ice. XX-12's images flashed up every few minutes, still imprinted on my dreamscape. I'd seen a few oracular images before. Nick had once shown me a snapshot of me falling off a low roof and breaking my ankle, which had happened the next week. I never questioned his weather predictions again.

XX-12 had summoned me to meet him at midnight. I saw no reason not to go.

When I woke up, the clock was striking eleven. I washed and dressed before I went down to Warden's chamber. It was silent. The curtains had been left open, admitting the light of the moon. For the first time in several days, I found one of his notes on the desk.

Find out what you can about the Emim.

A cold shiver ran under my skin. If I had to research the Buzzers, that must mean I was destined to face them. It also meant I was free to see 12. In a way, I'd be following orders. 12 had just faced his second test. I wondered what he'd seen during the night so far. Finally I'd have some solid facts about the Emim, provided 12 hadn't been eaten, of course.

Just before midnight I made my way down the steps, closing the door behind me. Time to do my homework.

I passed the night porter. She didn't greet me. When I requested more numa she handed them over, but she kept her nose turned up. Still sore over the siren incident.

It was cool outside, the air misted with rain. I walked to the Rookery and picked up breakfast – skilly in a paper cup. In exchange, I parted with a few needles and rings. Once I'd forced myself to take a sip or two, I headed for the building the harlies called the Hawksmoor, the great stone sentinel of the library and its courtyard.

12 was waiting behind one of the pillars, wearing a clean red tunic. There was a cut across his cheek. When he spotted my cup, he lifted an eyebrow.

'You *eat* that?'

I sipped from it. 'Why, what do you eat?'

'What my keeper gives me.'

'We're not all bone-grubbers. Congratulations, by the way.'

He held out a hand, and I shook it. 'David.'

'Paige.'

'Paige.' His dark eye itself fixed on my face. The other seemed less focused. 'If you haven't got anything better to do with your time, I thought I'd take you for a little walk.'

'Like a dog?'

He laughed without moving his lips.

'This way,' he said. 'If anyone asks, I'm bringing you in for questioning about an incident.'

We walked together down a narrow street, towards the Residence of the Suzerain. David was about two inches taller than me, long in the arms and thick in the torso. He wasn't starving, like the harlies.

'Bit risky, isn't it?' I said.

'What?'

'Talking to me. You're a red-jacket now.'

He smiled. 'I didn't think you'd be easy meat. You're already falling into their trap, aren't you?'

'What do you mean?'

'Segregation, 40. You see I'm a red-jacket and think I shouldn't talk to you. Did your keeper tell you that?'

'No. That's just how it is.'

'There you have it. That's the whole point of this place: to brainwash us. To make us feel inferior. Why do you think they leave people in the Tower for years on end?' When I didn't reply, he shook his head. 'Come on, 40. Waterboarding, isolation, days without food. After that, even somewhere like this seems like a slice of heaven.' He had a point. 'You should hear the Overseer. He thinks the Rephs should lead us, that they should be our new monarchy.'

'Why would he think that?'

'Because he's indoctrinated.'

'How long has he been here?'

'Only since Bone Season XIX, from what I can gather, but he's loyal as a dog. He's been trying to root out good voyants from the syndicate.'

'So he's a procurer.'

'He's not very good. Nashira wants a new one. Someone who can sense the æther on a higher level.'

I was about to ask more when I stopped. Through the thin grey haze, I could see a circular building with a vast dome. It squatted in a deserted square, massive and cumbersome, opposite the Residence of the Suzerain. Dim amber light filtered through its windows.

'What is that?' I looked up at it.

'The harlies call it the Room. Been trying to find out what it's for, but nobody seems to like talking about it. No humans allowed.'

He walked ahead without even glancing at it. I jogged to catch up with him. 'You said he's been trying to get voyants from the syndicate,' I prompted. 'Why?'

'Don't ask too many questions, 40.'

'I thought that was the point of this rendezvous.'

'Maybe. Or maybe I just liked the look of you. Here's our stop.'

Our destination was an ancient church. It must once have been magnificent, but now it was falling apart. The windows had no glass, the steeple was skeletal and wooden slats blocked the south porch. I raised an eyebrow.

'Is this a good idea?'

'I've done it before. Besides' – he ducked under a slat – 'from what the Overseer tells me, you're accustomed to unsafe structures.' He looked over my shoulder. 'Quick. Grey Keeper.'

I slid between the boards. Just in time: Graffias passed by the entrance, leading three undernourished amaurotics. I followed David through the church. A large portion of the ceiling had fallen into the chapel. Wooden beams and concrete had flattened the pews, and glass lay in fragments across the floor. I picked my way through the rubble. 'What happened here?'

David didn't answer the question. 'One hundred and twenty-four stairs to the top,' he said. 'Up for it?'

He was gone before I could answer. I followed him to the staircase.

I was used to climbing. I'd climbed hundreds of buildings in I Cohort. Most of the steps were still intact, it seemed like no time before we reached the top. A high wind caught my hair, whipping it back from my face. The scent of fire was strong and thick. David rested his arms on a stone balustrade.

'I like this place.' He pulled a roll of white paper from his sleeve and used a match to light it. 'Higher ground.'

We stood on a balcony, right below the crumbling steeple. Part of the balustrade was missing, and another sign warned of the unstable structure. I looked up at the stars. 'You passed your second test,' I said. 'If you want to talk, tell me about the Emim.'

Eyes closed, he exhaled the smoke. His fingers were stained. 'What exactly do you want to know?'

'What they are.'

'No idea.'

'You must have seen one.'

'Not much. The woods are dark. I know it looked like a human – had a head and arms and legs, in any case – but it moved like an animal. It also stank like a cesspit. And sounded like one.'

'How can you sound like a cesspit?'

'Like flies, 40. Bzzzz.'

Buzzer.

'What about its aura?' I pressed. 'Did it have one?'

'Not that I could see. It made the æther seem like it was collapsing,' he said. 'Like there was a black hole around its dreamscape.'

This didn't sound like the sort of thing I wanted to face. I looked down at the city. 'Did you kill it?'

'I tried.' When he saw my face, he tapped his roll. 'They put a bunch of us in there, all pink-jackets. Two groups. Two reds came with us, 30 and 25. They gave us all a knife each and told us to track the Buzzer with whatever we could find. 30 said straight out that the knives were just there to make us feel better. The best way to track the thing was to use the æther.

'One of the pinks was a rhabdomancer, so we made some lots from twigs. 30 gave us a bottle of blood from some guy that got his hand bitten off – that way we could use him as a querent. We smeared the blood on the twigs and the rhabdomancer cast them. They pointed west. We kept casting lots and changing direction. Of course, the Buzzer was moving as well, so we didn't get anywhere. 21 suggested that we bring it to us. We made a fire and did a séance, calling the spirits from the woods.'

'Are there many?'

'Yep. All the idiots that tried to escape through the minefield, according to the reds.'

I suppressed a shiver.

'We sat there for a few minutes. The spirits vanished. We heard noises. Flies started coming out of the woods, crawling over my arms. Then this thing came out of nowhere – this giant, bloated *thing*. Two seconds later it's got 19's hair in its mouth. Nearly takes her skin with it, too,' he added. 'She's screaming, the thing gets confused. It rips out some of her hair and goes after 1.'

'Carl?'

'Don't know their names. Anyway, he squeals like a piglet and tries to stab it. Nothing happens.' He examined the burning end of his roll. 'The fire was going out, but I could still see it. I tried using an image on it. I thought of white light and tried to stick it in the Buzzer's dreamscape to blind it. Next thing I know, my head feels like it's being run over and it's like there's been an oil spill in the æther. Everything's dark and dead. All the spirits in the area are trying to get away from the mess. 20 and 14 both run for it. 30 shouts after them that they're yellow-jackets, but they're too scared to come back. 10 throws a knife and hits 5. He falls. The Buzzer's on him in two seconds flat. The fire goes out. It's pitch black. 5 starts screaming for help.

'Everyone's blind now. I use the æther to work out where the thing is. 5's getting eaten. He's already dead. I grab the thing's neck and pull it off him. All this wet dead skin's coming away in my hands. It turns on me. I can see these white eyes in the dark, just staring at me. Next thing I know I'm flying through the air, bleeding like a stuck pig.'

He pulled down the neck of his tunic and peeled back a bandage. Below it were four deep gouges. The skin surrounding them was a milky, bloodshot grey. 'They look like poltergeist wounds,' I said.

'Wouldn't know.' He secured the bandage over the wounds. 'I can't move. The thing's coming towards me, dripping blood on me. 10's been trying to help 5, but now he gets up. He's got a guardian angel, the only spirit that hasn't flown the coop. He throws it at the Buzzer. I send another image into its dreamscape at the same time. It screams. Really screams. Starts crawling away, making this awful noise, dragging a chunk of 5 with it. By this point 21 has set fire to a branch. He throws it after the Buzzer. I smell burning flesh. After that I passed out. Woke up in Oriel, covered in bandages.'

'And they gave you all red tunics.'

'Not 20 and 14. They got yellow. And had to pick up what was left of 5.'

We stood in silence for a few minutes. All I could think of was 5, eaten alive in the woods. I didn't know his real name, but I hoped someone had said the threnody. What a horrific way to go.

I cast my gaze further afield. In the distance I could make out a spot of light, little more than a candle flame from here.

'What is that?'

'Bonfire.'

'What for?'

'Buzzer corpses. Or human corpses, depending who won.' He tossed away his roll. 'I'm thinking they use the bones for some kind of augury.'

Ash drifted past my eyes as he said it. I caught a flake on my finger. Augurs touched the æther through signs of the natural world: the body, wildlife, the elements. One of the lower orders, in Jaxon's eyes. 'Maybe the fire attracts them,' I said. 'They did say this city was a beacon.'

'It's an *ethereal* beacon, 40. Lots of voyants and spirits and Rephs together. Think about how the æther works.'

'How the hell do you know so much about it?' I turned to face him. 'You're not from the syndicate. So who are you?'

'A cipher. Just like you.'

I fell silent, grinding my lower jaw.

'You've got more questions,' he said, after a brief silence. 'Sure you want to ask them?'

'Don't you start.'

'Start what?'

'Telling me what I want to know. I want answers.' The words came fast and hot. 'I want to know everything about the place I'm supposed to be living in for the rest of my life. Can't you understand that?'

Looking over the balustrade, we gazed down at the Room. For fear that it might crumble under my touch, I tried not to put too much weight on the stone.

'So,' I said, 'Can I ask those questions?'

'This isn't a parlour game, 40. I'm not here to play Twenty Questions. I brought you here to see if you really were a dreamwalker.'

'In the flesh,' I said.

'Not always, from the sound of it. Sometimes you jump out of that flesh.' He looked me up and down. 'They got you from the central cohort. From the inner sanctum of the syndicate. You must have been careless.'

'Not careless. Unlucky.' I stared him out. 'What's their concern with the syndicate?'

'It's keeping all the good voyants for itself. It's hiding all the binders and dreamwalkers and oracles – all the higher orders, the ones Nashira wants in her colony. That's their concern with the syndicate, 40. That's why they're going to sign this new Act.'

'What does it say?'

'Nashira's been struggling to get hold of decent voyants. They're all protected by gangs. Until they figure out how to disband the mime-lords in London, they have no choice but to expand to get better ones. The Act promises that a Sheol II will be established within two years, with Scion Paris as its harvest citadel.' He traced the wounds on his chest. 'And who's going to stop them, with the Emim there to kill us if we try?'

A strange, cold feeling came over me.

Nashira considered the syndicate a threat. That was news to me. I knew the mime-lords as a band of backbiting, self-seeking egoists – at least, that was what the central ones were like. The Unnatural Assembly hadn't met for years; the mime-lords had been allowed to do as they liked in their own areas, seeing as Hector was too busy whoring and gambling to manage them. Yet far away in Sheol I, the blood-sovereign of the Rephaim feared the lawless rabble.

'You're one of her loyal followers now.' I glanced at his red tunic. 'Are you going to help them?'

'I'm not loyal, 40. That's just what I tell them.' He looked at me. 'Have you ever seen a Reph bleed?'

I didn't know what to say.

'Their blood is called ectoplasm. Duckett's ultimate obsession.

Rephs are something like the æther in flesh. Their blood is the æther liquefied. You see ectoplasm; you see the æther. You drink it; you become the æther. Like them.'

'Wouldn't that mean amaurotics could use the æther? All they'd have to do is touch a bit of ectoplasm.'

'Right. For rotties, in theory, ecto would act as a kind of substitute aura. Short-term, of course. The side-effects only last about fifteen minutes. Still, if we did some science and smoothed out the rough edges, I'm willing to bet we could sell an "instant clairvoyance" pill within a few years.' He gazed out down at the city. 'It'll happen one day, 40. We'll be the ones experimenting on these bastards, not the other way around.'

The Rephs had been foolish to make this man a red-jacket. It was clear that he despised them.

'One more question,' David said.

'Fine.' I paused, then thought of Liss. 'What do you know about Bone Season XVIII?'

'I wondered if you'd ask about that.' He moved another slat aside, exposing a broken window. 'Come on. I'll show you.' I followed him through it.

There were spirits in this room. I wished I could see how many there were; I guessed about eight or nine. The air was mildewed, tinged with the sickly smell of dying flowers. A shrine had been assembled in the corner. A roughly cut oval of metal, surrounded by humble offerings: candle stubs, broken sticks of incense, a wilted sprig of thyme, labels with names. In the centre of it all was a small bouquet of buttercups and lilies. It was the lilies that were giving off the smell. They were fresh. David pulled a torch out of his pocket.

'Take a look at the ruins of hope.'

I looked closer. Words were scored onto the metal.

'2039,' I said. 'Bone Season XVIII.'

One year before I was born.

'There was a rebellion that day, on Novembertide.' David kept the torch on the shrine. 'A group of Rephs rose up against the Sargas. They got most of the humans on their side. Tried to kill Nashira and evacuate the humans to London.'

'Which Rephs?'

'No one knows.'

'What happened?'

'A human betrayed them. XVIII-39-7. One weak link in the foundation and the whole thing came crashing down. Nashira tortured the Reph perpetrators. Scarred them. The humans were all slaughtered by the Emim. Rumour has it there were only two survivors, apart from Duckett: the traitor and the kid.'

'Kid?'

'Duckett told me everything. He was spared because he was too much of a yellow-jacket to rebel. He begged on his knees for them to spare him. He told me there was a kid brought here that year – four, maybe five years old. XVIII-39-0.'

'Why the hell would they bring a child here?' Ice settled in my stomach. 'Children can't fight Buzzers.'

'No idea. He thinks they were trying to see if she'd survive.'

'Of course she wouldn't survive. A four-year-old couldn't live in that slum.'

'Exactly.'

My insides started to twist. 'She died.'

'Duckett swears her body wasn't found. He had to clear up the corpses,' David said. 'Part of the exchange for his survival. He says he never found the little girl, but this says otherwise.'

He shone his torch at one of the offerings. A filthy teddy bear with button eyes. Around its neck was a note. I held it up to David's light.

XVIII-39-0
No life lived is lost

Silence fell, broken by a distant chime. I laid the bear back among the flowers.

'Who did all this?' My voice hurt. 'Who made this shrine?'

'The harlies. And the scarred ones. The mysterious Rephs that rose up against Nashira.'

'Are they still alive?'

'No one knows. But I'm willing to bet they're not. Why would Nashira let them walk around the city, knowing they're traitors?'

My fingers shook. I hid them under my sleeves.

'I've seen enough,' I said.

David walked me back to Magdalen. It was still a few hours until dawn, but I didn't want to see anyone else. Not tonight.

When the tower was in sight, I turned to face David. 'I don't know why you spoke to me,' I said, 'but thank you.'

'For what?'

'Showing me the shrine.'

'You're welcome.' His face was cast in shadow. 'I'll give you one more question. Provided I can answer it in less than a minute.'

I thought about it. I still had so many questions, but one had bothered me for a few days.

'Why are they called Bone Seasons?'

He smiled.

'Don't know if you know, but *bone* used to mean "good", or "prosperous". From the French, *bonne*. You might still hear it on the streets. That's why they named it: the Good Season, the Season of Prospect. They see it as collecting their reward, the great condition of their bargain with Scion. Of course, the humans see it differently. To them, *bone* just means that: bones. Starvation. Death. That's why they call us *bone-grubbers*. Because we help lead people to their deaths.'

By now my whole body was cold. Part of me had wanted to stay out here. Now I wanted to leave.

'How *do* you know all this?' I said. 'The Rephs can't have told you.'

'No more questions, I'm afraid. I've already said too much.'

'You could be lying.'

'I'm not.'

'I could tell the Rephs about you.' I stood my ground. 'I could tell them what you know.'

'Then you'd have to tell them that you know, too.' He smiled at me, and I knew I'd lost. 'You can owe me a favour for the information. Unless you want to pay me back now.'

'How?'

My answer came when he touched my face. His hand pressed against my hip. I tensed.

'Not that,' I said.

'Come on.' His hand stroked up and down my waist, and his face came closer to mine. 'You hock up your pill?'

'What, you want some sort of payment?' I pushed him away, hard. 'Go to hell, red-jacket.'

David never took his eyes off me.

'Do me a favour,' he said. 'Found this in Merton. See if you can make anything of it. You're smarter than I thought.' He pressed something into my hand. An envelope. 'Sweet dreaming, 40.'

He walked away. I stood there for a moment, stiff and cold, before I leaned against the wall. I shouldn't have gone to that place with him. I knew better than to walk with strangers on dark streets. Where were my instincts?

I'd learned too much in one night. Liss had never mentioned that Rephs – *Rephs* – had been partially responsible for the uprising of Bone Season XVIII. Perhaps she didn't know.

The scarred ones. I should look for them, for the ones that had helped us. Or perhaps I should keep my head down and get on with my new life. That was safe. That was easy.

I wanted Nick. I wanted Jax. I wanted my old life back. Yes, I'd been a criminal, but I had also been among friends. I'd chosen to be with them. My position as a mollisher had protected me from people like David. Nobody had dared touch me in my own territory.

But this wasn't my territory. Here I had no power. For the first time I wanted the protection that lay inside the stone walls of Magdalen. I wanted the protection Warden's presence guaranteed, even if I hated it. I pocketed the paper and headed for the door.

When I got back to the Founder's Tower, I expected to find an empty room. What I found was blood.

Reph blood.

A Fever

The room was in disarray. Glass shattered, instruments broken, a curtain half-torn from its rail, and spots of glowing chartreuse on the flagstones, soaked into the fibres of the rug. I stepped over the glass. The candle on the desk had been snuffed out; so had the paraffin lamps. It was deathly cold. I could feel the æther everywhere. I kept my guard up, ready to sling my spirit at a potential attacker.

The drapes were drawn around the bed. Another dreamscape was behind it. *Reph*, I thought.

I stepped towards the bed. Once I was within reach of the drapes, I tried to think rationally about what I was about to do. I knew Warden was behind them, but I had no idea of what sort of state he would be in. He might be injured, sleeping, dead. I wasn't sure I wanted to know which one it was.

I steeled my nerves. My fingers flexed before they grasped the heavy fabric. I pulled the drape aside.

He was slumped on the bed, still as a corpse. I climbed onto the covers and shook him. 'Warden?'

Nothing.

I sat back on the bed. He'd told me explicitly that I wasn't allowed to touch him, that I wasn't supposed to help him if this happened, but this time the damage looked much, much worse. His shirt was drenched. I tried to turn him over, but he was a dead weight. I was checking his breathing when his hand snatched out and caught my wrist.

'You.' His voice was thick and raw. 'What are you doing in here?'

'I was—'

'Who saw you come in?'

I held very still. 'The night porter.'

'Anyone else?'

'No.'

Warden pushed his weight onto his elbow. His hand – still gloved – went straight to his shoulder. 'Since you are here,' he said, 'you may as well stay and watch me die. You will enjoy that.'

He was shaking all over. I tried to think of something spiteful to say, but what came out was quite different: 'What happened to you?'

He didn't answer. Slowly, I reached for his shirt. His grip on my wrist tightened. 'You need to air the wounds,' I said.

'I am aware of that.'

'So do it.'

'Do *not* tell me what to do. I may be dying, but I am not subject to your orders. You are subject to mine.'

'What are your orders?'

'To let me die in peace.'

But the order lacked force. I shoved his gloved hand from his shoulder, revealing a mess of chewed flesh.

Buzzer.

His eyes flared up as if some volatile chemical had reacted inside them. For a moment I thought he would kill me. My spirit strained against my mind, bursting to attack.

Then his fingers loosened around my wrist. I scanned his face. 'Get me water.' His voice was barely audible. 'And – and salt. Look in the cabinet.'

I didn't have much choice but to do it. With his eyes on my back, I unlocked the curio cabinet and pulled open the doors. I took out a heartwood salt cellar, a golden bowl and a flagon of water, along with a stack of linen. Warden tore open the ties at the top of his shirt. His chest was slick with sweat.

'There is a pair of gloves in the drawer,' he said, nodding to the writing table. 'Put them on.'

'Why?'

'Just do it.'

I clenched my jaw, but I did as he said.

In the drawer, beside the gloves, his black-handled blade lay sheathed and clean. The sight of it gave me pause. I turned my back to him and pulled on the gloves. I wouldn't even leave a fingerprint. I used my thumb to push the blade from its sheath.

'I would not try it.'

The sound of his voice made me stop.

'Cold steel cannot kill a Rephaite,' he said softly. 'If you buried that blade in my heart, it would not stop beating.'

The silence thickened. 'I don't believe you,' I said. 'I could gut you. You're too weak to run.'

'If you wish to take the risk, then be my guest. But ask yourself this: why do we allow red-jackets to carry weapons? If your weapons could kill us, why would we be so foolish as to arm our prisoners?' His eyes scalded my back. 'Many have tried. They are not here now.'

A cold tingling started along the back of my arm. I returned the knife to the drawer. 'I don't see why I should help you,' I said. 'You weren't exactly grateful last time.'

'I will forget that you were going to kill me.'

The grandfather clock ticked with my pulse. Finally, I looked over my shoulder. He looked back at me, the light ebbing from his eyes.

I crossed the room, slowly, and placed the items on the nightstand. 'What did this?' I said.

'You know.' Warden pressed his back against the headboard, his jaw rigid. 'You did the research.'

'Emite.'

'Yes.'

The confirmation chilled my blood. Working in silence, I mixed the salt and water in the bowl. Warden watched me. Once I'd soaked and wrung out a square of linen, I leaned across to his right shoulder. The sight and smell of the wound made me jerk back.

'This is necrotic,' I said.

The wound had darkened to a rotten, oozing grey. His skin was hot as coal. I guessed his temperature was probably around twice what it should be in humans, so hot I could feel it through the gloves. The flesh around the bite was beginning to die. What I needed was an antipyretic. I didn't have any quinine, which was what Nick usually used to crank down our temperatures. It was easy to sneak out of oxygen bars – they used it for fluorescence – but I doubted I could find it here. Saline and good luck would have to do.

I squeezed some water into the wound. The muscles in his arm hardened, and the tendons of his hand pushed out.

'Sorry,' I said, then wished I hadn't. He wasn't sorry when he watched me get branded, or when Seb died. He wasn't sorry for anything.

'Speak,' he said.

I looked at him. 'What?'

'I am in pain. Some idle distraction would be helpful.'

'Like you're interested in anything I say.' The words came out before I could stop them.

'I am,' he said. He was pretty damn calm, considering his

171

condition. 'I am interested to know about the person with whom I share quarters. I know you are a murderer' – I tensed – 'but there must be more to you than that. If not, I have made a very poor choice in claiming you.'

'I never asked you to claim me.'

'Yet I did.'

I kept sluicing away at the wound, pressing a little too hard. I saw no reason to be gentle with him.

'I was born in Ireland,' I said, 'in a town called Clonmel. My mother was English. She ran away from Scion.'

He nodded, barely. I continued: 'I lived with my father and grandparents in the Golden Vale, in the southern dairy-farming district. It was beautiful there. Not like Scion citadels.' I wrung out the linen, soaked it again. 'But then Abel Mayfield got greedy. He wanted Dublin. That was when the Molly Riots started. Mayfield's Massacre.'

'Mayfield,' Warden said, looking at the window. 'Yes, I remember him. An unpleasant character.'

'You met him?'

'I have met every Scion leader since 1859.'

'But that would make you at least two hundred years old.'

'Yes.'

I tried not to falter in my work.

'We thought we were safe,' I said, 'but in the end, the violence spread south. We had to leave.'

'What happened to your mother?' Warden kept his eyes on mine. 'Was she left behind?'

'She died. Placental abruption.' I sat back. 'Where's the next bite?'

He pulled open his shirt. The wound ripped down his chest. I couldn't tell if it was teeth or claws or something else that had made it. His muscles locked when I dabbed water on the torn skin. 'Continue,' he said.

So I wasn't such a boring human. 'We moved to London when I was eight,' I said.

'Out of choice?'

'No. My father was conscripted by SciSORS that year.' I took his silence to mean that he didn't know the shorthand. 'Scion: Special Organisation for Research and Science.'

'I know it. Why was he conscripted?'

'He was a forensic pathologist. Used to do lots of work for the Gardaí. Scion told him to find a scientific explanation for why people become clairvoyant, and why spirits linger after death.' I sounded bitter, even to my own ears. 'He thinks it's an illness. He thinks it can be cured.'

'Then he cannot sense your clairvoyance.'

'He's amaurotic. How could he?'

He didn't comment. 'Did you have your gift from birth?'

'Not fully. I could sense auras and spirits from when I was very small. Then I was touched by a poltergeist.' I sat back to wipe my brow. 'How long do you have left?'

'I am uncertain of that. Salt staves off the inevitable, but not for long.' He was quite blasé about this. 'When did you develop the ability to dislocate your spirit?'

The talking was keeping me calm. I decided to be truthful, if only because he probably knew everything about me. Nashira had known I was from Ireland; they must have all sorts of records. He might be testing me, seeing if I'd lie to him.

'After the poltergeist touched me, I started having the same dream – at least, I thought it was a dream.' I emptied some water over his shoulder. 'I dreamed of a field of flowers. The further I ran through the field, the darker it became. Every night I would go a little further, until one day I was at the very edge and I jumped, and then I was falling.' I set to work on the wound. 'I was falling into the æther, falling out of my body. I woke up in the ambulance. My father said

I'd sleepwalked into the living room, then just stopped breathing. They said I must have fallen into a coma.'

'But you survived.'

'Yes. And I wasn't brain damaged. Brain hypoxia is a risk of my . . . condition,' I said. I didn't like telling him about myself, but I supposed it was better that he knew. If he forced me into the æther for too long without life support, my brain would end up damaged beyond repair. 'I was lucky.'

Warden watched as I cleaned his shoulder wound. 'That would suggest to me that you do not enter the æther very often, for safety,' he said, 'but you seem familiar with it.'

'Instinct.' I looked away from his eyes. 'Your fever won't break without medicine.'

In a sense I wasn't lying. My gift *was* instinctive, but I wasn't about to tell him that I'd been nurtured and trained by a mime-lord, who'd kept me wired on life support.

'The poltergeist,' he said. 'Did it leave scars?'

I took off one glove and held out my left hand. He looked down at the marks. I let him. It was unusual for a developing voyant to be so violently exposed to the æther.

'I guess there was already a break in me, something that let the æther in,' I said. 'The 'geist just . . . flayed me open.'

'Is that how you see it?' he said. 'The æther invading you?'

'How do you see it?'

'I make no comment on my own opinion. But many clairvoyants see themselves as invading the æther, not the other way around. They see it as disturbing the dead.' He didn't wait for an answer. 'I have seen this happen before. Children are vulnerable to sudden changes in their clairvoyance. If they are exposed to the æther before their aura has properly developed, it can become unstable.'

I pulled my hand back. 'I'm not unstable.'

'Your gift is.'

I couldn't argue. I'd already killed with my spirit. If that wasn't unstable, I didn't know what was.

'There is a type of necrosis in my wounds,' Warden stated, 'but it only affects Rephaim. The human body is able to fight it.' I waited for the point. 'Rephaite necrosis can be destroyed by human blood. Provided their bloodstream is not compromised, a human can survive a bite.' He indicated my wrist. 'Around a pint of your blood would save my life.'

My throat tightened. 'You want to drink my blood.'

'Yes.'

'What are you, a vampire?'

'I would never have thought a Scion denizen would have read about vampires.'

I tensed. Shoot. Only a high-up syndicate member would have access to literature that included vampires, or any other supernatural creature. In my case it was a penny dreadful, *The Vamps of Vauxhall*, written by an anonymous medium from Grub Street. He spun all sorts of stories to make up for the lack of interesting literature available from Scion, using folk tales from the world beyond. His tales had such titles as *Tea With a Tasser* and *The Fay Fiasco*. The same writer had knocked out a few decent potboilers about voyants, like *The Mysteries of Jacob's Island*. Now I wished I'd never read them.

Warden seemed to take my silence as a symptom of disquiet. 'I am not a vampire, nor anything else you might have read about,' he said. 'I do not feed on flesh or blood. It gives me no pleasure to ask for it. But I am dying, and it so happens that your blood – on this occasion, given the nature of my wounds – can restore me.'

'You don't look or sound like you're dying.'

'Trust me. I am.'

I didn't want to know how they'd found out that human blood could combat this infection. I didn't even know if it was true.

'Why should I trust you?' I said.

'Because I saved you the humiliation of having to perform in the Overseer's troupe of fools. If you require one reason.'

'What if I need two?'

'I will owe you a favour.'

'Any favour?'

'Anything but your freedom.'

The word died on my lips. He'd anticipated my request. I should have known freedom was too much to ask – but a favour from him might be invaluable.

I picked up a shard of glass from the floor, part of a vial, and I sliced across my wrist. When I offered it, he narrowed his eyes.

'Take it,' I said. 'Before I change my mind.'

Warden looked at me for a long time, assessing my face. Then he took my wrist and pulled it against his mouth.

His tongue skimmed over the open wound. There was a slight pressure as his lips closed over it, as he squeezed my arm to force out blood. His throat throbbed as he drank. He settled into a steady cadence. There was no sudden bloodlust, no frenzy. He was treating this as a medical procedure: clinical, detached, nothing more or less.

When he let go of my wrist, I sat back on the bed. Too fast. Warden guided me to the pillows. 'Slowly.'

He walked to the bathroom, strong again already. When he returned, he was carrying a glass of cold water. He slid an arm under my back and lifted me into a sitting position, holding me in the crook of his elbow. I drank. It had been sweetened.

'Does Nashira know about this?' I said.

His expression darkened.

'She may question you about my absences. And my injuries,' he said.

'So she doesn't know.'

No reply. He propped me up on some heavy velvet cushions,

making sure my head was supported. The nausea was passing, but my wrist still dripped blood. Seeing it, Warden reached for the nightstand and procured a roll of gauze. My gauze. I recognised the band I'd secured it with. He must have taken it from my backpack. It made me cold to think of it in his hands. It reminded me of the missing pamphlet. Did he have it? He took my wrist. His massive, gloved hands were gentle, covering the cut in sterile white. His way of thanking me, I supposed. Once the blood had stopped seeping through the gauze, he fixed the dressing with a pin and laid my arm across my chest. I kept my eyes on his face.

'It seems we are at a stalemate,' he said. 'You have a talent for finding me in delicate situations. I would expect you to take pleasure in my times of weakness, yet you give me your blood. You clean my wounds. What is your motive?'

'I might need a favour. And I don't like to watch things die. I'm not like you.'

'You judge too easily.'

'You watched while she killed him.' I should have been afraid to say these words, but I didn't give a damn. 'You *watched*. You must have known what she was going to do.'

Warden was unresponsive. I turned away from him.

'Perhaps I am a whited sepulchre,' he started.

'A what?'

'A hypocrite. I rather like the turn of phrase,' he said. 'Perhaps you think me evil, but I do keep my word. Do you keep yours?'

'What are you getting at?'

'Tonight's events must never leave this room. I wish to know if you will keep them secret.'

'Why should I?'

'Because it would not help you to tell it.'

'It would get rid of you.'

I thought his eyes changed.

'Yes. It would get rid of me,' he said, 'but your life would not improve. If you were not thrown onto the streets, you might be given another keeper, and not all of them are as liberal as I am. By rights I should have beaten you to death for some of the things you have said to me over the past few days. But I understand your value. Others will not.'

I opened my mouth to retort, but the words fizzled out. It was true, I didn't want another keeper, not if they were all like Thuban.

'So you want me to keep your secret.' I rubbed my wrist. 'And in exchange?'

'I will try to keep you safe. There are an infinite number of ways you could die here, and you do not help yourself avoid them.'

'I have to die eventually. I know what Nashira wants with me. You can't protect me.'

'Perhaps not, in the end, but I presume you would like to survive your tests.'

'What's the point?'

'You can prove to her how strong you are. You are no yellow-jacket. You can learn to fight.'

'I don't want to fight.'

'Yes, you do. It is in your nature to fight.'

The clock in the corner chimed.

Having a Reph ally was wrong. At the same time, it would significantly increase my chances of survival. He could help me get supplies, help me survive. Maybe for long enough to escape this place.

'Fine,' I said. 'I won't tell anyone. But you still owe me a favour.' I held up my wrist. 'For the blood.'

Just as I said it, the door burst open. A Reph woman swept into the room: Pleione Sualocin. She looked first at the state of the room, then at me, and finally at Warden. Without a word, she tossed him a Vacutainer. Warden caught it in one hand. I looked at it.

Blood. Human blood. It was labelled with a small grey triangle. And a number: AXIV. Amaurotic 14.

Seb.

I looked at Warden. He inclined his head, like we'd shared a little secret. A visceral revulsion overwhelmed me. I stood up, still weak from blood loss, and lurched up the stairs to my prison.

His Picture

I first met Nick Nygård when I was nine years old. When I saw him next, I was sixteen.

It was the summer term of 2056 and at the III-5 School for Girls of Quality, we Year Elevens had entered the most important period of our lives. We could stay at school for another two years, during which we would be doing University prep, or leave and find a job. In an effort to convert the undecided, the Schoolmistress had organised a series of lectures from inspirational speakers: SVD agents, media raconteurs – even an Archon politician, the Minister of Migration. That day was geared towards medical science. All two hundred of us were herded into the lecture hall, dressed in our black suits, red ribbons and white blouses. Miss Briskin, the chemistry mistress, stepped up to the lectern.

'Good morning, girls,' she said. 'Good to see you all so bright and early. Many of you have expressed an interest in scientific research as a career path' – I hadn't – 'so this should be one of our most thought-provoking lectures.' A smattering of applause. 'Our speaker has already had a terribly exciting career.' I wasn't convinced. 'He transferred from the University of Scion Stockholm in 2046, completed his studies in London, and now works for SciSORS, the largest research facility in the central cohort. We're truly honoured to have him here today.' There was a shiver of excitement from the front. 'Please put your hands together and welcome our speaker – Dr Nicklas Nygård.'

My head snapped up. It was him.

Nick.

He hadn't changed a bit. He was exactly as I remembered him: tall, soft-featured, handsome. Still young, though his eyes bore the burden of a hectic adult life. He wore a black suit and a red tie, like all Scion officials. His hair was smoothed back with pomade, a style popular in Stockholm. When he smiled, the prefects sat up straighter.

'Good morning, ladies.'

'Good morning, Dr Nygård.'

'Thank you for having me here today.' He shuffled his papers with the same hands that had stitched my injured arm when I was nine. He looked right at me, and he smiled. Behind my ribs, my heart flickered. 'I hope this talk is enlightening, but I won't take offence if you fall asleep.'

Laughter. Most officials weren't so jocular. I couldn't take my eyes off him. Seven years of wondering where he might be, and he'd walked into my school. A picture from my memory. He talked about his research into the causes of unnaturalness, and about his experiences as a student in two different Scion citadels. He made jokes and encouraged audience participation, asking questions as often as he answered them. He even had the Schoolmistress smiling. When the bell rang, I was first out of the lecture hall, heading for the corridor at the back of the lecture theatre.

I had to find him. For seven years I'd tried to understand what had happened in the poppy field. There had been no dog. He was the only one who could tell me what had left the cold scars on my hand. The only one who could give me answers.

I headed down the corridor, buffeting past chattering Year Eights. There he was, outside the staff room, shaking the hand of the Schoolmistress. When he saw me, his eyes brightened.

'Hello,' he said.

'Dr Nygård—' I could hardly get the words out. 'Your speech was – very inspiring.'

'Thank you.' He smiled again, and his eyes pierced mine. He knew. He remembered. 'What's your name?'

Yes, he knew. My palms tingled.

'This is Paige Mahoney,' the Schoolmistress said, putting emphasis on my surname. My very Irish surname. She looked me up and down, taking in my loose bow and unbuttoned blazer. 'You ought to get to class, Paige. Miss Anville has been very disappointed with your attendance of late.'

Warmth rose to my cheeks.

'I'm sure Miss Anville can spare Paige for a few minutes.' Nick gave her a winning smile. 'I'd love to spend some time with her.'

'That's very kind of you, Dr Nygård, but Paige has been with the nurse a great deal recently. She needs to attend *all* her classes.' She turned to him, lowering her voice. 'Irish girl. These brogues often make up their own minds as to how much work is necessary.'

My vision tunnelled. A pressure pushed at the inside of my skull, as if it were about to explode. A trail of blood crept from the Schoolmistress's nose.

'You're bleeding, Miss,' I said.

'What?' When she looked down, blood dripped onto her shirt. 'Oh, for – now look what I've done.' She covered her nose. 'Don't just stand there *gawking*, Paige. Get me a handkerchief.'

My head gave a throb. A grey web pulled across my eyes, tightening my vision. Nick stared at me as he handed her a packet of tissues. 'Perhaps you should sit down, Schoolmistress.' He placed a hand on her back. 'I'll join you in a moment.'

As soon as the Schoolmistress was gone, Nick turned to face me.

'Do people often have nosebleeds around you?'

His voice was quiet. After a moment, I nodded.

'Have they noticed?'

'I've never been called unnatural yet.' I sought his gaze. 'Do you know why it happens?'

He glanced over his shoulder. 'I might,' he said.

'Tell me. Please.'

'Dr Nygård?' Miss Briskin put her head around the staff room door. 'The governors would like to speak to you.'

'On my way.' As soon as she was gone, Nick said against my ear, 'I'll come back in a few days. Do *not* sign up for the University, Paige. Not yet. Trust me.'

He squeezed my hand. Then, just as quickly as he'd come, he was gone. I was left to cradle my books to my pounding heart, my cheeks hot and my hands clammy. A day hadn't gone by when I hadn't thought of Nick, and now he had returned. I gathered my composure and walked to my class, still struggling to see or think. He'd remembered my name. He knew I was that little girl he'd saved.

I didn't think he'd come back. I couldn't be that important to him, not now he'd made his fortune in the world. But two days later, he was waiting for me outside the school gates. Something strange had happened that morning: I'd daydreamed about a silver car. The picture had come to me during French, leaving me nauseated. Now the same car was outside, and Nick was in the driver's seat, wearing sunglasses. I sleepwalked to the window, away from the other girls. He leaned out of it.

'Paige?'

'I didn't think you'd come back,' I said.

'Because of the nosebleed.'

'Yes.'

'That's why I'm here.' He pushed his shades to the end of his nose, so I could see his tired eyes. 'If you want to know more, I can tell you, but it can't be here. Will you come with me?'

I glanced over my shoulder. None of the students were paying attention. 'All right,' I said.

'Thank you.'

Nick took me away from the school. As he drove towards the central cohort, he shot me little glances. I stayed quiet. When I caught sight of myself in the side-mirror, I realised I was flushed. I wanted so much to talk to him, but I couldn't wrap my tongue around a coherent sentence. After a few minutes, Nick spoke: 'Did you ever tell your father what happened in the field?'

'No.'

'Why?'

'You told me not to.'

'Good. That's a start.' His hands tightened on the wheel. 'I'm going to tell you a lot of things you won't understand, Paige. You're not like you were before that day, and you need to know why.'

I kept my eyes on the road. He didn't have to tell me. I'd known I was different well before the poppy field, even as a child I'd been sensitive to people. Sometimes I'd felt tremors when they passed me, like my fingers had brushed a live wire. But things had changed since that day. Now I couldn't just sense people – I could hurt them. I could make people bleed, make their heads ache and their eyes blur. I would fall asleep in class, only to wake up with my skin drenched in cold sweat. The nurse knew me better than anyone else at the school.

Something was emerging from inside me, pushing out into the world. In the end, the world was going to see it.

'I can help you control it,' he said. 'I can keep you safe.'

He'd kept me safe once before. 'Can I still trust you?' I watched his face, the face I'd never forgotten. Nick looked at me.

'Always,' he said.

We went to a greasy spoon in Silk Street and sipped coffee. It was the first time I'd ever tried it, and I secretly thought it tasted like mud. We talked for a while about my life. I told him about school, about my father's job, but that wasn't why we were there, and we both knew it.

'Paige,' he said, 'you've heard about unnaturalness. I don't want to frighten you, but you're showing signs of it.'

My throat closed. He did work for Scion.

'Don't worry.' He placed his hand over mine. My pulse warmed. 'I'm not going to turn you in. I'm going to help you.'

'How?'

'I'd like you to come and talk to a friend of mine.'

'Who is it?'

'Someone I trust. Someone who's very interested in you.'

'Is he——?'

'Yes. So am I.' He squeezed my hand. 'You had a daydream earlier. You saw my car.' I stared at him, perplexed. 'That's my gift, Paige. I can send pictures. I can make people see things.'

'I——' My mouth was dry. 'I'll see him.'

I left a message with my father's secretary, telling him I would be home late. Nick drove me to a small French restaurant in Vauxhall. Waiting for us was a tall, fine-boned man, probably in his late thirties. His eyes were alive with a sort of agitated intelligence. He had candle-white skin and a head of rich, dark hair, and his lips were pale and petulant. You could have sharpened pencils on his cheekbones. He wore a gold cravat and a black embroidered waistcoat with a pocket watch.

'You must be Paige,' he said, in a deep, slightly amused voice. 'Jaxon Hall.'

He offered a bony hand. I took it.

'Hello,' I said.

His grip was cold and firm. I sat down. Nick sat beside me.

When the waitron came, Jaxon Hall ordered no food; just a glass of mecks, or non-alcoholic wine. Expensive stuff. He had fine tastes.

'I have a proposition for you, Miss Mahoney.' Jaxon Hall swilled his mecks. 'Dr Nygård came to speak to me yesterday. He informed me that you can inflict certain . . . medical abnormalities on other people. Is that correct?'

I glanced at Nick.

'Go on.' He gave me a smile. 'He's not from Scion.'

'Don't insult me.' Jaxon took a sip of mecks. 'Further from the Archon than the cradle from the grave. Not that those two states are all that far apart, but you understand my meaning.'

I wasn't sure I did. He certainly didn't *act* like a Scion official.

'You mean the nosebleeds,' I said.

'Yes, the nosebleeds. Fascinating.' His hands were clasped on the table. 'Anything else?'

'Headaches. Sometimes migraines.'

'And how do *you* feel when it happens?'

'Tired. Sick.'

'I see.' His eyes roved over my face. They were cool and analytical, and they seemed to see beyond me. 'How old are you?'

'Sixteen,' I said.

'Almost time for you to leave school. Unless,' he added, 'you are asked to attend the University.'

'Not likely.'

'Excellent. But young people do struggle to find work in the citadel.' His fingers drummed on the table. 'I'd like to offer you a job for life.'

I frowned. 'What kind of job?'

'The sort that pays well. The sort that will protect you.' Jaxon examined me. 'Do you have any idea what clairvoyance means?'

Clairvoyance. The forbidden word. I glanced around the restaurant, but nobody was looking. Or listening, it seemed.

'Unnaturalness,' I said.

Jaxon smiled thinly. 'So the Archon calls it. But do you know what the *word* means? From the French.'

'Clear vision. A kind of extrasensory perception. Knowing things that are hidden.'

'And where are they hidden?'

I hesitated. 'In the subconscious?'

'Sometimes, yes. Or sometimes' – he blew out the candle in the middle of the table – 'in the æther.'

I looked into the smoke, drawn to it. A chill spread through my chest. 'What's the æther?'

'The infinite. We come from it, we live within it, and when we die, we pass back into it. But not all of us are willing to part ways with the physical world.'

'Jax,' Nick said, keeping his voice low, 'this is meant to be an introduction, not a lecture series. She's sixteen.'

'I want to know,' I pressed.

'Paige—'

'Please.' I *had* to know.

His expression softened. He sat back in his seat and sipped his water. 'Your choice.'

Jaxon, who was looking at us with raised eyebrows, pursed his lips before continuing. 'The æther is a higher plane of existence,' he said. 'It exists alongside the corporeal plane. Clairvoyants – people like us – have the ability to draw on the æther.'

I was sitting in a restaurant with two unnaturals. 'How?' I said.

'Oh, there are an infinite number of ways. I've spent fifteen years trying to categorise them.'

'But what does it *mean* to "draw on the æther"?' Asking questions about clairvoyance gave me a sinful little thrill.

'It means you can commune with spirits,' Nick clarified. 'The dead. Different voyants can do it in different ways.'

'So the æther is like the afterlife?'

'Purgatory,' Jaxon said.

'Afterlife,' Nick said.

'Excuse Dr Nygård – he's trying to be delicate.' Jaxon sipped his mecks. 'Unfortunately, death is not delicate. I would like to educate you about what clairvoyance truly is, in preference to Scion's sadly warped perspective of the condition. It is a miracle, not a perversion. You must understand that, my dear, or they will snuff that lovely glow out.'

They both fell silent when the waitron brought my salad. I looked back at Jax.

'Tell me more.'

Jaxon smiled.

'The æther is the "source" of which Scion occasionally deems to speak,' he said. 'The realm of the restless dead. The source which the Bloody King supposedly accessed during a séance, causing him to commit five ghastly murders and bring an epidemic of clairvoyance upon the world. All utter tosh, of course. The æther is simply the spiritual plane, and clairvoyants are those with the ability to access it. There was no epidemic. We have always been there. Some of us are good; others are evil, if there is any such thing as evil – but whatever we are, we are not a disease.'

'So Scion lied.'

'Yes. Harden yourself to the idea.' Jaxon lit a cigar. 'Edward might well have been Jack the Ripper, but I highly doubt he was clairvoyant at all. Far too clumsy.'

'We have no idea why they pinned it all on clairvoyance,' Nick said. 'It's a mystery only the Archon understands.'

'How does it work?' My skin was prickling and hot. I could be unnatural. I could be one of *them*.

'Not all spirits go peacefully into the heart of the æther, where we think some kind of final death is found,' Jaxon said. He was relishing this, I could tell. 'Instead they linger, roving between the corporeal and spiritual planes. When they're in this state, we call them drifters. They still have personality, and most can be contacted. They only have a certain degree of freedom, and are usually happy to assist voyants.'

'You're talking about real, dead *people*,' I said. 'You can just pull their strings, and they'll dance?'

'Correct.'

'Why would any of them want that?'

'Because it means they can stay with their loved ones.' He sniffed, like he didn't understand the concept. 'Or with people they'd like to haunt. They sacrifice free will in exchange for a kind of immortality.'

I took a mouthful of salad and chewed. It was like chewing a wad of wet cotton.

'Of course, they don't start off as spirits.' Jaxon tapped the back of my hand. 'You have a flesh body. You can walk on the corporeal plane. But you also have a private connection to the æther. We call it the dreamscape. The scenery of the human mind.'

'Wait, wait. You keep saying "we",' I said. 'Who are *we*, exactly? Clairvoyants?'

'Yes. It's a very vibrant community.' Nick gave me a warm smile. 'But a very secret one.'

'You can identify voyants by their aura. That's how Nick recognised you,' Jaxon said. My growing interest seemed to animate him. 'Everyone has a dreamscape, you see. An illusion of safety, a kind of *locus amoenus*. You understand.' I wasn't sure I did. 'Voyants have coloured dreamscapes. The rest have black-and-white ones. They see their dreamscapes when they dream. Amaurotics, consequently, dream in monochrome. Voyants, conversely—'

'—dream in colour?'

'Voyants don't *dream*, my dear girl. Not in the same way that amaurotics do. That idle pleasure is for them alone. But the colour of a clairvoyant dreamscape shines through his or her corporeal form, creating an aura. People of the same voyant type tend to have very similar auras. You'll learn to group them.'

'Can I see auras?'

They exchanged glances. Nick reached up and peeled two filmy lenses from his eyes. Chills ran down my back.

'Look at my eyes, Paige.'

He didn't need to tell me twice. I remembered those eyes as clearly as if it had been yesterday. That exquisite grey-green, those delicate lines radiating through the iris. What I hadn't noticed was the small, keyhole-shaped defect in his right pupil.

'Some voyants have a kind of third eye.' He sat back. 'They can see auras; they can also see drifters. You can be half-sighted, like me – with just one coloboma – or full-sighted, like Jax.'

Jaxon pulled his eyelids wide open for me. He had the defect in both eyes.

'I don't have that,' I said. 'So I'm clairvoyant, but I don't have a third eye?'

'Unsightedness is quite common in the higher orders. Your gift doesn't require you to see spirits.' Jaxon gave me a pleased look. 'You can feel auras and drifters, but you don't perceive them visually.'

'It's not really a disadvantage.' Nick patted my hand. 'Your sixth sense will be much more attuned without the visual aid.'

Though the restaurant was warm, the cold was spreading all over my body. I looked between the two men, their different faces. 'What kind of clairvoyant am I?'

'That's what we want to find out. Over the years I've classified seven orders of clairvoyance. I believe you, my dear girl, are of the very highest order, making you one of the rarest clairvoyants in the modern world. If I am proved correct' – he pulled a folder out of his expensive leather satchel – 'I'd like you to sign a job contract.'

His eyes rested on mine. 'I could write an infinite variety of numbers on this cheque, Paige. What will it take me to keep you?'

My heart thumped at my ribs. 'A drink, for starters.'

Jaxon sat back.

'Nick,' he said, 'get the young lady some mecks. She's a keeper.'

The Sun Rising

For the next few nights, Warden and I did not speak; nor did we train. Every night I would leave as soon as the bell rang, not looking at him as I passed. He would watch, but he would never stop me. I almost wished he would, just so I could let the anger out.

One night I tried going to see Liss. It was raining outside, and I longed for the warmth of her stove. But I couldn't. Not after what had happened with Warden. After I'd helped the enemy, again, I couldn't have looked her in the eye.

I soon found a new refuge, a place to call my own: an enclosed archway on the steps of the Hawksmoor. It must once have been a majestic structure, but now its grandeur made it tragic: it was cold and heavy, crumbling at the edges, waiting for an age that might never come again. That place became my bolthole. I went there every night. Sometimes, provided there were no bone-grubbers on duty, I would steal into the abandoned library and take a stack of books back to the archway. They had so many illegal novels in there, I started to wonder if this was where Scion sent them all. Jax would have sold his soul to get his mitts on them. If he had a soul to sell.

Four nights had passed since the bloodletting. I still didn't understand why I'd helped him. What sort of dirty trick was he playing? The thought of my blood inside him made me sick. I couldn't stand to think of what I'd done.

The window was ajar. I'd hear them if they came for me. I wouldn't let them sneak up on me, like they had in I-5. I'd discovered a book called *The Turn of the Screw*, hidden among the bookshelves. The rain was heavy; I had elected to stay indoors, in the library. I lay prone under a desk and lit a little oil lamp to see the pages.

Outside, the Broad was quiet. Most of the harlies were starting to practise for the bicentennial celebration. Rumour had it that the Grand Inquisitor himself was due to attend. He had to be impressed by how we were spending our new lives, or he might not allow the *special arrangement* to continue. Not that he had much choice. Still, we had to show that we were useful, if only for entertainment. That we were worth a little more than it would cost to give us NiteKind.

I took out the envelope David had given me. Inside was a fragment of text from a notebook, torn and yellowed. I'd studied it several times. It looked as if a candle had fallen on it: the corners were hard with wax, and a large hole had been burned right through the middle. There was a blurred sketch in the corner of the page, something that must once have been a face, but now looked faded and disfigured. I could only make out the occasional word.

Rephaim are – – creatures. In the – – called – – within – – boundaries of –
– able – – limitless periods of time, but – – new form, that – – hunger,
uncontrollable and – – energy surrounding the purported – – red flower, the –
– sole method – – nature of the – – and only then can – –

I tried yet again to thread the words together, to find some kind of pattern. It wasn't difficult to link the fragments about hunger and energy, but I couldn't think of what *red flower* could mean.

There was something else in the envelope, too. A faded daguerreotype. The date 1842 had been scrawled on the corner. I looked at it for a long time, but I couldn't make anything out but white smears on black. I tucked the envelope back into my tunic and nibbled on a bit of stale toke. When my eyes grew tired, I blew out the oil lamp and wrapped myself into the foetal position.

My mind was a tangle of loose ends. Warden and his injuries. Pleione bringing him Seb's blood. David and his interest in my welfare. And Nashira, with her all-seeing eyes.

I forced myself to think only of Warden. I still tasted bile when I thought of Seb's blood, bottled and labelled, ready for consumption. I hoped they'd taken it when he was still alive, not from his dead body. Then there was Pleione. She'd brought him the blood; she must have known he was going to contract necrosis, or at least that he *might* have contracted it. She must have arranged to bring him human blood before it was too late. When she'd been delayed, he'd drunk my blood instead. Whatever he was doing, he was doing it in her confidence.

Warden had a secret. So did I. I was hiding my link to the underworld, one that Nashira no doubt wanted to root out. I could live with his silence if he could live with mine.

I traced my bandaged arm. Still the wound refused to heal. To me it was as ugly as the brand. If it scarred, I would never forget the shame and fear I'd felt when I did it. So much like the fear I felt the first time I encountered the spirit world. Fear of what I was. What I could be.

I must have drifted off. A sharp pain in my cheek brought me back to reality.

'Paige!'

Liss was shaking me. My eyes were raw and puffy.

'Paige, what the hell are you *doing* in here? It's past dawn. There are bone-grubbers out looking for you.'

I looked up, groggy. 'Why?'

'Because the Warden *told* them to look for you. You were supposed to be at Magdalen an hour ago.'

She was right: the sky was turning gold. Liss pulled me to my feet. 'You're lucky they didn't find you in here. It's forbidden.'

'How did you find me?'

'I used to come in here myself.' She grasped my shoulders, looked me dead in the eyes. 'You have to beg the Warden's forgiveness. If you beg, he might not punish you.'

I almost laughed. 'Beg?'

'It's the only way.'

'I won't beg him for anything.'

'He'll beat you.'

'I still won't beg. They'll have to take me to him.' I glanced out of the window. 'Will you get in trouble if they find me in your crib?'

'Better that than they find you in here.' She grabbed my wrist. 'Come on. They'll search in here soon.'

I kicked the oil lamp and the book under a shelf, hiding the evidence. We ran down the dark stone staircase, back into the open. The air smelled crisp, like rain.

Liss held me back until the coast was clear. We slipped through the courtyard, under the damp archway, and back onto the Broad. The sun shone over the buildings. Liss forced two loose plywood panels apart, and we ducked into the Rookery. She steered me past huddles of performers. Their scavenged possessions littered the passages, as if their shacks had been overturned. One boy was propped against the wall, bleeding from the eyes. They whispered in our wake.

I ducked into the crib. Julian was waiting, a bowl of skilly balanced on his knee. He looked up when we ducked into the shack.

'Morning.'

I sat. 'Glad to see me?'

'I s'pose.' He gave me a smile. 'If only to remind me how urgently I need to find an alarm clock.'

'Shouldn't *you* be inside?'

'I was just about to go, but now you're here I'd feel like I was missing the party.'

'You two!' Liss glared at us. 'They take the curfew very seriously, Jules. You're both going to get a right slating.'

I ran my fingers through my damp hair. 'How long until they find us?'

'Not long. They'll check the rooms again soon.' She sat down. 'Why don't you just go?'

Every muscle in her body was locked. 'It's fine, Liss,' I said. 'I'll take the heat.'

'The bone-grubbers are brutal. They won't listen. And I'm telling you now, the Warden will kill you if you—'

'I don't care about him.' Liss rested her head in her hand. I looked back at Julian. His novice's outfit was gone, replaced by a pink tunic. 'What did you have to do?'

'Nashira asked me what I was,' he said. 'I said I was a palmist, but it was obvious I couldn't make anything of her hands. She brought an amaurotic into the room, a girl, and had her tied to a chair. I remembered Seb and asked if she'd let me use water as a scrying pool.'

'You're a hydromancer?'

'No, but I don't want her to know what I am. It was just the first thing that came into my head.' He rubbed his head. 'She filled a golden bowl and told me to look for somebody named Antoinette Carter.'

I frowned. Antoinette Carter had been an Irish celebrity in the early forties. I recalled her as middle-aged and thin, as frail as she was enigmatic. She had a TV show, *Toni's Truths*, which broadcast every Thursday night. She would touch people's hands and claim to see their futures, sounding them out in her deep, measured voice. The show was cancelled after the Incursion of 2046, when Scion had taken Ireland, and Carter had gone into hiding. She still ran an illegal pamphlet, *Stingy Jack*, which spoke out against Scion's atrocities.

For reasons unknown to us, Jaxon had asked a screever called Leon – an expert in sending messages outside Scion – to make contact with her. I'd never heard the outcome. Leon was a good screever, but it took time to bypass Scion's security systems.

'She's a fugitive,' I said. 'She used to live in Ireland.'

'Well, she's not in Ireland now.'

'What did you see?' I didn't like the look on his face. 'What did you tell her?'

'You're not going to be happy.' When he saw my expression, he sighed. 'I said I'd seen the sundials. I remembered Carl said he'd scried them, and I thought it was believable if I repeated what he'd said.'

I looked away. Nashira was searching for Jaxon. Sooner or later she'd work out where those dials were.

'I'm sorry. I could have kicked myself.' Julian rubbed his forehead. 'Why are the sundials so important?'

'I can't tell you. I'm sorry. But whatever happens' – I glanced at the entrance to the shack – 'Nashira must never hear of those sundials again. It will put some friends of mine in danger.'

Liss pulled a blanket around her shoulders. 'Paige,' she said, 'I think your friends have been trying to contact you.'

'What do you mean?'

'Gomeisa took me to the Castle for a while.' Her expression grew stiff. 'I was in my cell, sorting through my deck for his reading, when I was drawn towards the Hanged Man. When I picked it up, it was inverted. I saw the æther. The face of a man. He reminded me of snow.'

Nick. Soothsayers always said that about Nick when they saw him, that he was like snow. 'What did he send?'

'A picture of a phone. I think he's trying to find out where you are.'

A phone. Of course – he didn't know where I was. The gang didn't know I'd been taken by Scion, though they must have smelled a rat by now. Nick wanted me to call him, to tell him I was all right.

It must have taken him days to find the right path through the æther. If he tried again, with a séance, he might be able to send me a message. I couldn't work out why he'd sent it to Liss. He knew my aura; it should have been far easier to find. Maybe it was the pills, or some kind of interference from the Rephs – but it didn't matter. He'd tried to reach me. He wouldn't give up.

Julian's voice broke through my thoughts: 'You really know other jumpers, Paige?' When I looked at him, he shrugged. 'I thought the seventh order was the rarest.'

Jumpers. A loaded word. An order of voyants, like soothsayers and augurs. It was the category into which I fell: those voyants that could affect or enter the æther. Jax had started the great separation of voyants in the thirties, when he was about my age. It started with *On the Merits of Unnaturalness*, which had spread like a plague through the voyant underworld. In it, he'd identified seven orders of clairvoyance: soothsayers, augurs, mediums, sensors, furies, guardians and jumpers. The latter three, he'd written, were vastly superior to the others. It was a novel way of looking at clairvoyance, which had never previously been categorised – but the 'lower' orders hadn't reacted well to it. The resulting gang wars had lasted two bloody years. Jax's publishers had finally withdrawn the pamphlet, but the grudges lingered.

'Yes,' I said. 'Just one. He's an oracle.'

'You must be pretty high up in the syndicate.'

'Quite high up.'

Liss ladled a bowl of skilly for me. If she had an opinion on the pamphlet, she didn't voice it. 'Jules,' she said, 'could I have a few minutes with Paige?'

'Of course,' Julian said. 'I'll keep an eye out for the reds.'

He left the shack. Liss looked at the stove. 'What's wrong?' I said. She drew the blanket closer.

'Paige,' she said, 'I'm scared for you.'

'Why?'

'I just have a bad feeling about the celebration – you know, the Bicentenary. I may not be an oracle, but I see things.' She took out her deck. 'Will you let me do your reading? I get the urge to read certain people.'

I hesitated. I'd only ever used cards for tarocchi. 'If you want.'

'Thanks.' She placed the deck between us. 'Have you had your signs read before? By a soothsayer or an augur?'

'No.' I'd been asked many times if I wanted a reading, but I'd never been convinced that peeking into the future was a good idea. Nick sometimes gave me hints, but I usually didn't let him elaborate.

'Okay. Give me your hand.'

I held out my right hand. Liss grasped it. An expression of intense concentration took over her face as her fingers dipped into the deck. She removed seven cards and placed them face-down on the floor.

'I use the ellipse spread. I read your aura, then pick out seven cards and interpret them. Not all broadsiders will give you the same interpretation of a particular card, so don't be too pissed off if you hear something you don't like.' She released my hand. 'The first one will indicate your past. I'll see part of your memories.'

'You *see* memories?'

Liss allowed herself a faint smile. This was something she still took pride in. 'Card-readers may use objects, but we don't really fit

199

into any category. Even *On the Merits* acknowledged it. I see that as a good thing.'

She turned over the first card. 'Five of Cups,' she said. Her eyes closed. 'You lost something when you were very small. There's a man with auburn hair. It's his cups that are spilled.'

'My father,' I said.

'Yes. You're standing behind him, speaking to him. He doesn't answer. He stares at a picture.' Without opening her eyes, Liss flipped the next card. It was upside-down. 'This is the present,' she said. 'King of Wands, inverted.' Her red lips pursed. 'He controls you. Even now, you can't escape his hold.'

'Warden?'

'I don't think so. Still, he has power. His expectations of you are too high. You're afraid of him.'

Jaxon.

'Next is the future.' Liss turned the card. She drew in a sharp breath. 'The Devil. This card represents a force of hopelessness, restriction, fear – but you've given into it yourself. There's a shadow that the Devil represents, but I can't see its face. Whatever power this person will have over you, you *will* be able to escape it. They'll make you think you're tied to them for ever, but you won't be. You'll just think you are.'

'Do you mean a partner?' My chest was cold. 'A boyfriend? Or is *that* Warden?'

'It could be. I don't know.' She forced a smile. 'Don't worry. The next card will tell you what to do when the time comes.'

I looked down at the fourth card.

'The Lovers?'

'Yes.' Her voice had dropped to a monotone. 'I can't see much. There's tension between spirit and flesh. Too much.' Her fingers crept towards the next card. 'External influences.'

I didn't know if I could take much more. So far only one thing had been positive, and even then it was going to be painful. I certainly hadn't expected The Lovers.

'Death, inverted. Death is a normal card for voyants. Usually it appears in the past or present positions. But here, inverted – I'm not sure.' Her eyes flickered beneath their lids. 'This far ahead, my sight gets hazy. Things are vague. I know the world will change around you, and you'll do everything in your power to resist it. Death itself will work in different ways. By delaying the change, you'll prolong your own suffering.'

'The sixth card. Your hopes and fears.' She picked it up, ran her thumb over it. 'Eight of swords.'

The card showed a woman, bound in a circle of upturned swords. She wore a blindfold. Liss's skin glowed with sweat. 'I can see you. You're afraid.' Her voice trembled. 'I can see your face. You can't move in any direction. You can stay in one place, trapped, or feel the pain of the swords.'

This had to be the most negative spread of cards she'd ever seen. I couldn't stand to see the last card.

'And the final outcome.' Liss reached for the last card in the spread. 'The conclusion of the others.'

I closed my eyes. The æther trembled.

I never saw the card. Three people burst into the shack, startling Liss. The bone-grubbers had found me.

'Well, well, well! Looks like we've sniffed out the fugitive. And her abetter.' One of them seized Liss by the wrist, yanking her to her feet. 'Card-reading for your guest?'

'I was just—'

'You were *just* using the æther. Privately.' This voice was female, spiteful. 'You only read for your keeper, 1.'

I stood. 'I think I'm the one you want.'

All three of them turned to face me. The girl looked a little older than me, with long, ragged hair and a prominent brow.

The two young men looked so similar they could only be brothers.

'True. You *are* the one we want.' The taller of the boys pushed Liss away. 'You going to come quietly, 40?'

'Depends where you want to take me,' I said.

'Magdalen, you bleached mort. It's past dawn.'

'I'll walk.'

'We're escorting you. It's orders.' The girl gave me a really foul look. 'You've broken the rules.'

'Are you going to stop me?'

Liss shook her head, but I ignored her. I stared the girl out. Her teeth clenched together.

'Do the honours, 16.'

16 was the shorter of the two men, but he was burly. He reached out and grabbed my wrist. Quick as a flash, I twisted my arm to the right. His fingers and thumb slipped apart. I jabbed my fist into the hollow of his throat, pushing him into his brother.

'I said I'll walk.'

16 clutched his throat. The other man lunged at me. I ducked his arm, swung my leg up, kicked his exposed stomach. My boot sank into soft fat, winding him. The girl took me by surprise: she grabbed a handful of my hair and pulled. My head crashed into the metal wall. 16 wheezed with laughter as his brother pinned me to the ground.

'I think you need to learn some respect,' he said. He clapped a hand over my mouth, panting. 'Your keeper won't mind if I give you a quick lesson. It's not like he's ever around.'

His free hand groped my chest. He was counting on easy prey, a helpless girl. Not on a mollisher. I cracked my forehead straight into his nose. He cursed. The girl grabbed my arms. I bit her wrist, and she shrieked. 'You little haybag!'

'Get off her, Kathryn!' Liss grabbed her by the tunic, hauling her off me. 'What *happened* to you? Has Kraz made you that cruel?'

'I grew up. I don't want to be like you, living in my own filth.' Kathryn spat at her. 'You're pathetic. Pathetic harlie scum.'

My assailant was sporting an impressive nosebleed, but he wasn't giving up. His blood dripped onto my face. He yanked my tunic, bursting a seam. I shoved at his chest, my spirit close to bursting point. I fought the urge to attack, fought so hard my eyes watered.

Then Julian was there. His eye was bloodshot, his cheek freshly cut. They must have reefed him just to reach the shack. His arm wrapped around the boy's neck. 'That how you grubbers get your kicks?' It was the first time I'd ever seen him angry. 'You only like 'em when they struggle?'

'You're bones, 26,' my assailant choked out. 'Wait until your keeper hears about this.'

'Tell her. I dare you.'

I pulled down my tunic, hands shaking. The red raised his arms to protect himself. With a single, brutal uppercut, Julian socked him in the jaw. Blood spattered the boy's tunic, staining it a shade darker. A chip of tooth slipped from his mouth.

Kathryn lashed out. The back of her hand caught Liss's cheek, jolting a cry from her lips. The cry startled me. It was Seb's cry, all over again – but this time, it wasn't too late. I pushed myself off the floor, intending to tackle Kathryn, but 16 took me down at the waist. He was a medium, but he wasn't using spirits. He wanted blood.

'Suhail,' he roared.

The commotion had attracted a group of harlies. A white-jacket stood among them. I recognised him: the boy with cornrows, the julker. 'Get Suhail, you little tooler,' Kathryn burst out. She had Liss by the hair. 'Get him, *now*!'

The boy stood still. He had large, dark eyes with long lashes. Neither of them were infected now. I shook my head at him.

'No,' he said.

16 let out a bellow. 'Traitor!'

Some of the performers fled from the word. As I shoved at 16, my skin ran with sweat under my tunic. There was a glow on the edge of my vision.

The stove. I stared at the flames creeping along the boards.

Liss struggled free from Kathryn's grasp. She pushed at 16. Julian dragged him away from us.

A thin haze of smoke filled the shack. Liss started to gather her cards, her fingers scraping the deck back together. Kathryn pushed her head down, keeping her still. A muffled scream escaped her.

'Hey, look.' Kathryn held out a card to me. 'I think this one's for you, XX-40.'

The image showed a man lying on his front, staked by ten swords. Liss tried to take it back. 'No! That *wasn't* the—'

'Shut your trap!' Kathryn pinned her down. I struggled against 16, but he had me in a headlock. 'Useless shitsayer bitch. You think you've got a hard life? You think it's so *hard* to dance for them while we're out there getting eaten alive by the Buzzers?'

'You didn't have to go back, Kathy—'

'Shut up!' Kathryn slammed her head into the floor. She was too angry to care about the fire. 'Every night I'm out in the woods watching people get their arms torn off, all to stop the Emim getting in here and ripping your worthless throat out. All so you can sit on your nancy and play with cards and ribbons. I'll never be like you again, you hear me? The Rephs saw MORE in me!'

Julian hauled 16 outside. I made a grab for the cards, but Kathryn got there first. 'Good idea, 40,' she said, almost hysterical with anger. 'Let's teach this yellow-jacket scum a lesson.'

She threw the whole deck onto the fire.

The outcome was instant. Liss let out an awful, gut-wrenching scream. I'd never heard a human being make such a sound. My hair stood on end. The cards burned up like dry leaves. She tried to grab one but I caught her wrist. 'It's too late, Liss!'

But she wouldn't listen. She plunged her fingers into the fire, choking 'no, no', over and over.

With little fuel but the spilled paraffin, the fire soon went out. Liss was left on her knees, with shiny red hands, staring at the scorched remains. Her face was tinged with grey, her lips with purple. She choked out broken-hearted sobs, rocking on her heels. I cradled her against me, staring numbly at the fire. Her small body heaved.

Without her cards, Liss could no longer connect with the æther. She would have to be strong to survive the shock.

Kathryn grabbed my shoulder. 'That wouldn't have happened if you'd come with us.' She wiped her bloody nose. 'Get up.'

I looked at Kathryn and pushed the barest edge of my spirit against her mind. She cringed away from me.

'Stay back,' I said.

The smoke burned my eyes, but I didn't look away. Kathryn tried to laugh, but her nose was starting to bleed. 'You're a freak. What are you, some sort of fury?'

'Furies can't affect the æther.'

She stopped laughing.

A muffled scream came from outside. Suhail shoved his way into the shack, past the terrified performers. He took it all in: the smoke, the disarray. Kathryn dropped to one knee and bowed her head.

I stood very still. Suhail reached out a hand, grabbed me by the hair, and wrenched my face against his. 'You', he said, 'are going to die today.'

His eyes turned red.

That's when I knew he meant it.

Fall of a Wall

The day porter stared as Suhail passed, dragging me by the wrist. My throat was raw, my cheeks streaked with blood. He pulled me up the stairs and banged on Warden's door. 'Arcturus!'

A muffled ringing came to my attention. Liss had said Warden would kill me for missing the dawn. What would he make of resisting arrest?

The door opened. Warden was there, a massive silhouette against the dim chamber. His eyes were two pinpricks of light. I was rooted to the spot. Having my aura sapped had brought on a kind of fit. I couldn't feel the æther. Nothing. If he tried to kill me now, I couldn't do a thing to stop him.

'We found her.' Suhail pulled me forward. 'Hiding in the Rookery. The seditious runt tried to start a fire.'

Warden looked at each of us in turn. The evidence was clear as glass: Suhail's eyes, my blood-streaked cheeks.

'You fed on her,' he said.

'It is my *right* to feed on humans.'

'Not on this one. You took far too much. The blood-sovereign will not be pleased with your lack of restraint.'

I couldn't see Suhail's face, but I imagined him sneering.

In the silence that followed, I coughed: a dry, hacking cough. I was shivering all over. Warden's gaze moved to the rip in my tunic.

'Who did this?'

I was silent. Warden leaned down to my level. 'Who did this?' His voice sent a cold chill through my chest. 'A red-jacket?'

I nodded, just the barest movement of my head. Warden looked up at Suhail. 'You allow the red-jackets to violate other humans at will, on your watch?'

'I care not for their methods.'

'We do not want them *breeding*, Suhail. We have neither the time nor the means to deal with a pregnancy.'

'The pills sterilise them. Besides, their fornication is for the Overseer to manage.'

'You will do as I command.'

'No doubt.' Suhail looked down at me with those chilling red eyes. 'But back to business. Ask your master for forgiveness, 40.'

'No,' I said.

He cuffed me. I lurched to the side, caught the wall. A prisoner's cinema staggered past my eyes. 'Ask your master for *forgiveness*, XX-59-40.'

'You'll have to hit me a lot harder than that.'

He raised his hand to oblige. Before he could strike, Warden blocked his arm. 'I will deal with her in private,' he said. 'It is not for you to punish her. Wake the Overseer and deal with the commotion. I will not have the sun-hours disturbed by this turn of events.'

They stared at each other. Suhail let out a soft snarl, turned, and was gone. Warden looked after him. After a moment, he took me by the shoulder and steered me into the chamber.

His home was the same as it always was: drapes drawn, fire in the hearth. Gramophone chirping out 'Mr Sandman'. The bed looked so warm. I wanted to lie down, but I had to stay on my feet. Warden locked the door and sat in his armchair. I waited, still unsteady from the blow.

'Come here.'

I had no choice. Warden looked up at me; only a short distance – even sitting down, he was almost my height. His eyes were dim and clear, like chartreuse liqueur.

'Do you have a death wish, Paige?'

I didn't answer.

'I do not care what you think of me, but there are certain rules you must obey in this city. One of them is the curfew.'

I still didn't speak. He wouldn't have the satisfaction of scaring me.

'The red-jacket,' he said. 'What did he look like?'

'Dark-blond hair. In his twenties.' My voice was rough. 'There was a boy that looked a bit like him – 16. And a girl, Kathryn.'

A cold spasm racked my stomach as I spoke. Snitching to a Reph felt criminal. Then I pictured Liss's face, her grief, and my resolve strengthened.

'I know them.' Warden looked into the fire. 'The two men are brothers, both mediums. XIX-49-16 and 17. They have been here since they were considerably younger than you.' He clasped his hands. 'I will ensure that they are never allowed to harm you again.'

I ought to have thanked him, but I didn't.

'Sit down,' he said. 'Your aura will renew itself.'

I sank into the opposite armchair. My ribs were beginning to ache, and my legs hurt. Warden watched me.

'Are you thirsty?'

'No,' I said.

'Hungry?'

'No.'

'You must be hungry. The gruel the performers make does far more harm than good.'

'I'm not hungry.'

It wasn't true. Skilly was little more than water, and my stomach yearned for something thick and warm. 'A pity.' Warden motioned to the nightstand. 'I had something prepared for you.'

I'd seen it the second I came in. I'd assumed the plate was for him, but then I remembered what he lived on. Of course the meal wasn't for him.

When I didn't move, Warden did. He set the plate across my lap, along with heavy silver cutlery. I looked down at the meal. The sight made my head spin and my throat ache. Soft-boiled eggs, split open to squeeze out a hot gold yolk. A glass dish of pearl barley, tossed with pine nuts and fat black beans that shone like drops of onyx. A skinned pear, soaked in brandy. A sprig of plump red grapes. Wholegrain bread with butter.

'Take it.'

I clenched my fists.

'You have to eat, Paige.'

I wanted so much to defy him, to throw the plate right back at him, but my head was light and my mouth was furred with thirst and all I wanted was to eat the damned food. I picked up the spoon and took a mouthful of the barley. The beans were warm, the nuts brittle and sweet. Relief flooded my body, and the pain in my abdomen began to subside.

Warden returned to his seat. He watched in silence as I picked my way through the meal. I felt the weight of his gaze, piercing and alight. When I was finished, I put the plate on the floor. The afterburn of brandy lingered on my tongue.

'Thank you,' I said.

I didn't want to say it, but I had to say something. His fingers tapped the arm of his chair.

'I wish to continue your training tomorrow night,' he said. 'Do you have any objections?'

'I have no choice.'

'What if you did?'

'I don't,' I said, 'so it doesn't matter.'

'I am speaking hypothetically. But if you had a choice, if you could control your own fate – would you continue your training with me, rather than take your next test cold?'

My lips were forming a harsh answer when I bit down on my tongue, stopping it. 'I don't know,' I said.

Warden stoked the fire. 'It must be a dilemma. Your morals say "no", but your survival instinct says "yes".'

'I already know how to fight. I'm stronger than I look.'

'Yes, you are. Your flight from the Overseer was a testimony to your strength. And of course, your gift is a great asset – even Rephaim will not expect a second spirit to invade their dreamscape. You have the element of surprise on your side.' The fire danced in his eyes. 'But first you must overcome your limits. There is a reason you find it so difficult to leave your body. Your every move is controlled. Your muscles are constantly locked, ready to run, as if you sense danger in the very air you breathe. It is painful to watch, worse than watching a deer being hunted. A deer, at least, can flee to its herd.' He leaned forward. 'Where is your herd, Paige Mahoney?'

I had no idea how to answer. I understood what he meant – but my herd, my pack, was Jax and the rest of the gang. And I couldn't breathe a word of their existence. 'I don't need one,' I said. 'Lone wolf.'

He wasn't fooled. 'Who trained you to climb buildings? Who taught you to fire a gun? Who helped you see farther into the æther, to move your spirit from its natural place?'

'I taught myself.'

'Liar.'

He reached under his chair. My chest tightened. My emergency backpack. One of the straps hung by a thread.

'You could have died the night you ran from the Overseer. The only reason you did not is because when you lost consciousness, this bag caught on a clothesline, breaking your fall. When I heard of this, I took a personal interest in you.'

He unzipped the pack. My jaw hardened. Those were *my* possessions in there, not his.

'Quinine,' Warden listed, sifting through the contents. 'Adrenalin, Dexedrine and caffeine. Basic medical supplies. Sleep aids. Even a firearm.' He held up my pistol. 'You were remarkably well resourced on that night, Paige. None of the others were.'

A shiver ran behind my ribs. No sign of the pamphlet. Either he'd hidden it somewhere, or it had fallen into other hands.

'Your ID states that you work as an ossista, a waitron in an oxygen bar. From what the Overseer tells me of Scion citadels, payment for that class of job is low. That leads me to believe that you did not purchase these supplies yourself.' He paused. 'So who did?'

'None of your damn business.'

'Did you steal them from your father?'

'I'm not telling you anything more. My life before this place is not yours.'

Warden seemed to consider this before levelling his gaze on me.

'You are right,' he said, 'but your life is mine now.'

My nails dug into the chair.

'If you are open to the general concept of survival, we will begin training again tomorrow. But there will be a second aspect to your instruction.' He nodded to my seat. 'Every night, you will spend at least one hour in that chair, and you will talk to me.'

The words leapt to my tongue: 'I'd sooner die.'

'Oh, you are quite welcome to die. I understand that if you smoke too much purple aster, you will be locked into your dreamscape and your body will shrivel from lack of water.' He nodded to the door. 'Go now, if you choose. Die. Never look upon me again. I see no reason to prolong your suffering.'

'Won't the blood-sovereign be angry?'

'Perhaps.'

'Do you care?'

'Nashira is my betrothed, not my keeper. She has no influence over how I treat my human charges.'

'And how do you plan to treat me?'

'As my student. Not my slave.'

I turned my head away, my jaw set. I didn't want to be his student. I didn't want to become like him – to turn on my kind, to play on his field.

I was starting to feel the æther again. A faint pricking at my senses. 'If you treat me as your student,' I said, 'then I want to treat you as my mentor, not my master.'

'A fair bargain. But mentors should be shown respect. I expect that from you. And I expect you to stay with me, in polite company, for one hour every night.'

'Why?'

'You have the potential to walk between the æther and the corporeal world at your pleasure,' he said. 'But if you do not learn to be still, even in the presence of your enemies, you will find it difficult. And in this city, you will not live very long.'

'And you don't want that.'

'No. I think it a terrible waste of such a singular life. You have great potential, but you do require a mentor.'

His words twisted around my stomach. I *had* a mentor. I had Jaxon Hall.

'I'd like to sleep on it,' I said.

'Of course.' He stood, and I realised again how tall he was. I didn't even reach his shoulder. 'Bear in mind that you do have choices. But I advise you, as a mentor, to think of whoever gave you this.' With a swing of his wrist, he tossed me the heavy backpack. 'Would they want you to die for nothing, or would they want to see you fight?'

Hailstones crashed on the roof of the tower. I rubbed my hands over the paraffin lamp, my lips and fingers numb with cold.

I had to consider Warden's offer. I didn't want to work with him, but I had to learn to survive in this place – at least long enough for me to work out how to get back to London. Back to Nick, back to Jax. Back to ducking Gillies, back to mime-crime. Back to swindling spirits from Didion Waite, taunting Hector and his boys. That was what I wanted. Learning about my gift might just help me get out of this place.

Jaxon had always said that there was more to being a dreamwalker than a heightened sixth sense. I had the potential to walk anywhere, even in other dreamscapes. I'd proven it by killing those two Underguards. Warden might be able to show me even more – but I didn't want him as a teacher. He and I were natural enemies; there was no point in pretending otherwise. And yet he had observed so much about me: the way I held myself, my tension, my vigilance. Jax was for ever telling me to loosen up, to let myself float. But that didn't mean I could trust the man that kept me locked in this cold, dark room.

In the dim light of the lamp, I emptied the backpack. Most of my belongings were still there: the syringes, the equipment, even my gun. No ammo, of course, and the syringes were all empty. My phone had been confiscated. Only one other thing was missing: *On the Merits of Unnaturalness.*

A cold tingle went through all my muscles. If he'd given it to Nashira, she would have summoned me for questioning by now. The Rephaim must have come across the pamphlet before, but they'd never seen my copy.

I lay back on the mattress, minding my bruises and pulled the sheets up to my neck. Broken springs dug into my shoulders. I'd taken three hits to the head in as many minutes, and I was tired. I looked through the bars to the outside world, wishing the answer could shine through it – but of course, nothing came. Only the inevitable dusk.

The night-bell tolled when the sun went down. It seemed normal now, like an alarm clock. By the time I'd dressed, I'd come to a delicate decision. I would try to train with him again, if I could stomach it. There was an hour of talking to put up with, but I could handle that. I could fill that hour with lies.

Warden was waiting for me at the door. He looked me up and down.

'Have you come to a decision?'

I kept my distance. 'Yes,' I said. 'I'll train with you. If we agree that you're not my master.'

'You are wiser than I anticipated.' He handed me a black jacket with pink bands on the sleeves. 'Wear this. You will need it for your next test.'

I shrugged it on and buckled it. The lining was thick and warm. Warden held out a hand. In his palm were the three pills. I didn't take them. 'What's the green one for?'

'That is not your concern.'

'I want to know what it's for. Nobody else gets it.'

'That is because you are different from them.' He didn't retract his hand. 'I know you have not been taking your pills. I have no qualms about force-feeding you.'

'I'd like to see you try.'

His eyes searched my face. My skin prickled. 'I do not want it to come to that,' he said.

I was going to lose this fight. Call it criminal instinct. This was Didion and Anne Naylor all over again – another day at the black market. There were some things on which Warden would relent; this was not one of them. I told myself I'd take tomorrow's green pill to Duckett.

I washed down the pills with a glass of water. Warden took my chin in his gloved hand.

'There are reasons.'

I pulled my chin away. He looked at me for a moment, then opened the door. I followed him down the winding steps, into the cloisters. Grotesque stone figures watched over the courtyard. The temperature had fallen, coating them in a fine layer of frost. I crossed my arms to preserve some warmth. Warden led me out of the residence – but not onto the street. Instead he led me to the other side of Magdalen, through a wrought-iron gate and across a footbridge, which passed over a viridian river. The sharp glint of the moon shone on its surface. The hail had stopped, leaving the ground covered in ice.

As we walked down a dirt path, Warden rolled up the sleeve of his shirt. The wound from the first time was weeping. It was beginning to form a scar, but it still hadn't fully healed.

'Are they poisonous?' I said. 'Buzzers.'

'The Emim carry an infection called the half-urge, which causes madness and death if left untreated. They eat any kind of flesh, fresh or rotted.'

Even as I watched, the wound was starting to heal. 'How are you doing that?' I asked, forgetting myself in my curiosity. 'It's healing.'

'I am using your aura.'

I stiffened. 'What?'

'You must know by now that Rephaim feed on aura. It is easier for me to feed when my host is unaware of it.'

'You just fed on me?'

'Yes.' He studied my face. 'You seem angry.'

'It's not yours to take.' I moved away from him, disgusted. 'You already took my freedom. You have no right to my aura.'

'I did not take enough to damage your gift. I feed on humans in small doses, allowing time for regeneration. Others are not so courteous. And mark my words' – he pulled down his sleeve – 'you do not want me to contract half-urge in your presence.'

I looked at his face. He was still, accepting my scrutiny.

'Your eyes.' I looked right into them, mesmerised and repelled at once. 'That's why they change.'

He didn't deny it. His eyes were no longer yellow, but a dark, softly glowing red. The colour of my aura. 'I meant no offence,' he said, 'but it must be this way.'

'Why? Because you said so?'

Without responding, he walked on. I followed. It made me sick that he could feed on me.

After several minutes of walking, Warden stopped. A thin, blue-tinged mist hung around us. I turned up my collar. 'You feel it,' Warden said. 'The cold. Have you ever wondered why there is frost here, in early spring?'

'It's England. It's cold.'

'Not this cold. Feel it.' He took my hand and peeled off one of my gloves. My fingers burned in the bitter air. 'There is a cold spot nearby.'

I took my glove back. 'Cold spot?'

'Yes. They form when a spirit has dwelled in one place for a long time, creating an opening between the æther and the corporeal world. Have you never noticed how cold it becomes when spirits are near?'

'I suppose.' Spirits did chill me, but I'd never given it much thought.

'Spirits are not supposed to dwell between the worlds. They draw on heat energy to sustain themselves. Sheol I is surrounded by cold spots – ethereal activity here is much higher than it is in the citadel. That is why the Emim are attracted towards us, rather than the amaurotic population in London.' Warden indicated the stretch of hard earth in front of us. 'How do you think you might find the epicentre of a cold spot?'

'Most voyants could see the spirit,' I said. 'They have the third eye.'

'But you do not.'

'No.'

'There are ways for the unsighted to do it. Have you heard of rhabdomancy?'

'I hear it's useless,' I said. Jax had told me so, many times. 'Rhabdomancers say they can find their way back from anywhere. They say they can make numa fall when they get lost, and that spirits will point them in the right direction. Doesn't work.'

'That may be true, but it is not "useless". No type of clairvoyance is useless.'

Warmth rose in my cheeks. I didn't really believe rhabdomancers were useless, but Jax had always told me that they were. You couldn't work for Jaxon Hall and not share his opinions on such things.

'Why is it useful, then?' I asked. Warden looked at me. 'You're supposed to be teaching me. Teach me.'

'Very well. If you wish to learn.' Warden started to walk. 'Most rhabdomancers think that when their numa fall, they are pointing towards home, towards buried treasure – towards whatever they seek to find. In the end it makes them mad. Because what their numa point towards is not gold, but the epicentre of the nearest cold spot. Sometimes they walk for miles, and they do not find what they seek. But they do find a something: a secret door. What they do not know is how to open it.'

He stopped. I was shivering. The air was thin and cold. I breathed deeper, harder. 'It is hard for the living to bear a cold spot,' he said. 'Here.'

He handed me a silver canteen with a screw cap. I looked down at it.

'It is only water, Paige.'

I drank. I was too thirsty to refuse. He took the canteen back and tucked it away. The water cleared my head.

The ground we stood beside was frozen solid, as if it were deep winter. I clenched my chattering teeth together. The spirit responsible for the cold spot was drifting nearby. When it didn't approach us, Warden crouched at the edge of the ice, took out a knife and held it against his arm. I stepped forward. 'What are you doing?'

'Opening the door.'

He cut into his wrist. Three drops of ectoplasm fell onto the ice. The cold spot cracked down the middle and the air turned white. Shapes gathered around me. Voices. *Dreamer, dreamer.* I put my hands over my ears, but it didn't block them. *Dreamer, do not go beyond. Turn back.* Then I looked up, and the darkness surrounded me again.

'Paige?'

'What happened?' My head was light and sore.

'I opened the cold spot.'

'With your blood.'

'Yes.'

His wrist had stopped dripping already. Red lingered in his eyes. My aura was still working on his wounds. 'So you can "open" a cold spot?' I said.

'You can't. I can.'

'Because cold spots lead to the æther.' I paused. 'Can you use them to reach the Netherworld?'

'Yes. That is how we got here. Imagine there are two veils standing between the æther and your world – the world of life. Between those veils is the Netherworld, a medial state between life and death. When rhabdomancers find a cold spot, they find the means to move between the veils. To enter my home, the realm of the Rephaim.'

'Can humans go there?'

'Try.'

I looked up at him. When he nodded to the cold spot, I took a step onto the ice. Nothing happened.

'No corporeal matter can survive beyond the veil,' Warden said. 'Your body cannot pass beyond the gate.'

'What about rhabdomancers?'

'They are still flesh.'

'Why open it now, then?'

The sun had disappeared. 'Because the time is right,' he said, 'for you to face the Netherworld. You will not go in. But you will see.'

Sweat began to bead across my forehead. I stepped off the ice. I was starting to sense spirits everywhere.

'Night is the time of spirits.' Warden looked up at the moon. 'The veils are at their thinnest now. Think of cold spots as rips in the fabric.'

I watched the cold spot. Something about it rattled my spirit.

'Paige, you will have two tasks tonight,' he said, turning to face me. 'Both will test the limits of your sanity. Will you believe me if I tell you they will help you?'

'Not likely,' I said, 'but let's get on with it.'

The Undertaking

Warden didn't tell me where we were going. He led me down another footpath, into the open grounds of Magdalen. I could feel spirits everywhere: in the air, in the water – spirits of the dead that had once walked here. I couldn't hear them, but with a cold spot open within a mile radius, I could feel them as strongly as if they were living presences.

I kept close to Warden in spite of myself. If any of these spirits were malevolent, I sensed he'd be able to repel them more efficiently than I could.

The darkness grew deeper as we made our way through the grounds, away from the lanterns of Magdalen. Warden remained silent as we crossed a wet meadow where the lawns had been replaced by knee-deep weeds and grass. 'Where are we going?' I asked. My boots and socks were already sodden.

Warden didn't reply.

'You said I was your student, not your slave,' I said. 'I want to know where we're going.'

'Into the grounds.'

'Why?'

No reply again.

The night was getting colder, unnaturally cold. After what seemed like hours, Warden stopped and pointed.

'There.'

At first I didn't see it. When my eyes adjusted, the outline of the animal appeared in the dim moonlight. The creature was four-legged, with a silken coat. Its throat was snow-white and its long face narrow, with dark eyes and a small black nose. I wondered which of us looked more astonished.

A deer. I hadn't seen one since I'd lived in Ireland, when my grandparents had taken me to the Galtees. A wave of childish excitement swept over me.

'She's beautiful,' I said.

Warden stepped towards the deer. She was tethered to a post. 'Her name is Nuala.'

'That's an Irish name.'

'Yes, short for Fionnuala. It means *white shoulders*, or *fair shoulders*.'

I looked again. There were two large white spots on either side of her neck. 'Who named her?' In Scion it was risky to give Irish names to pets or children. You might be suspected of sympathising with the Molly rioters.

'I did.'

He released the collar from around her neck. Nuala butted him with her nose. I waited for her to run, but she just stood there, gazing up at Warden. He spoke to her in a strange language, stroking her throat, and she seemed to really listen. She was mesmerised. 'Would you like to feed her?' Warden slid a red apple from his sleeve. 'She has quite a penchant for these.'

He tossed me the apple. Nuala turned her gaze on me, nose twitching. 'Gently,' Warden said. 'She is easily startled with a cold spot open nearby.'

I didn't want to startle her – but if Warden didn't how could I? I held out my hand, presenting the apple. The doe sniffed at the fruit. Warden said something else, and she snatched it.

'Forgive her. She's very hungry.' He patted her neck and gave her another apple. 'I rarely have the chance to see her.'

'But she lives in Magdalen.'

'Yes, but I must be careful. Animals are not permitted within the limits of the city.'

'So why keep her?'

'For company. And for you.'

'For me,' I repeated.

'She's been waiting for you.' He sat down on a flat rock, letting Nuala wander off towards the trees. 'You are a dreamwalker. What does that mean to you?'

He hadn't brought me out here to feed a baby deer.

'I'm attuned to the æther,' I said.

'Say more.'

'I can sense other dreamscapes at a distance. And ethereal activity in general.'

'Precisely. That is your nascent gift, the bottom line: a heightened sensitivity to the æther, an awareness that most other clairvoyants do not possess. It comes from your silver cord, which is flexible. It allows you to dislocate your spirit from the centre of your dreamscape – to widen your perception of the world. It would drive most clairvoyants mad to do that. But when we trained on the meadow, I encouraged you to push your spirit against my dreamscape. To attack it.' His eyes smouldered in the gloom. 'You have the potential to do more than merely sense the æther. You can affect it. You can affect other people.'

I didn't answer.

'Perhaps, when you were younger, you could hurt people. Perhaps you could put pressure on their dreamscapes. Perhaps they noticed things: nosebleeds, distorted vision—'

'Yes.'

He already knew. No point in denying it.

'Something changed on the train,' he continued. 'Your life was endangered. You feared detainment. And for the first time in your life, that power inside you – that power emerged.'

'How did you find out?'

'A report came through that an Underguard had been killed – killed without blood, without weapons, without a single mark on his body. Nashira knew at once that it was the work of a dreamwalker.'

'It could have been a poltergeist.'

'Poltergeists always leave a mark. You should know.'

The scars on my hand seemed to drop a few degrees.

'Nashira wanted you alive,' Warden said. 'The NVD makes clumsy, violent arrests, as do many of our red-jackets. Around half of those arrests end in death. That could not happen with you. You had to be unspoiled. That was why Nashira sent the Overseer, her specialist procurer of clairvoyants.'

'Why?'

'Because she wants to learn your secret.'

'There is no secret. It's what I am.'

'It is also what Nashira wants to be. She longs for rare gifts, including yours.'

'Why doesn't she take it, then? She could have killed me when she murdered Seb. Why the wait?'

'Because she wants to understand the full extent of your abilities. But she will not wait for ever.'

'I won't perform for you,' I said. 'I'm not a harlie yet.'

'I did not ask you to perform for me. Where is the need? I saw your ability in the chapel. You forced your spirit into Aludra's mind. I saw it on the meadow, when you broke into mine. But tell me' – he leaned towards me, his red eyes hot in the dark – 'could you have *possessed* either of us?'

There was a tense silence, broken only by the reedy screech of an owl. The sound made me look up. I looked at the moon, cradled in a smoking cup of cloud. For a brief moment, I was taken back to Jax's office, the first time we'd broached the subject of possession.

'My dear girl,' he'd said, 'you've been a star. Nay, a luminary. You are absolutely and indubitably a keeper, a Seal fit to burst – but now I would like to give you a new task. A task that will test you, but also *fulfil* you.' He'd asked me to force my mind into his, to see if I could take control of his body. The idea had shaken me. I'd given it a half-hearted try, but the complexity of his mind had been too much to fathom. 'Ah well,' he'd said, with a puff of his cigar. 'It was worth a try, O my lovely. Away with you, now. There are broads to spread, and games to play.'

Maybe I could have done it. Maybe if I'd really wanted to, I could have seized Jax's body and stubbed out that bloody cigar, but it was that very ability that frightened me. To control someone was a serious responsibility, too serious for me. Even with the promise of a pay rise. I would wander through the mind of London, but I would never seize control of it. Not for all the money in the world.

'Paige?'

I surfaced from my memories. 'No,' I said. 'I couldn't have possessed Aludra. Or you.'

'Why not?'

'I can't possess people. And I definitely can't possess Rephs.'

'Would you like to?'

'No. You can't make me do it.'

'I do not intend to force you. I am merely presenting you with an opportunity to "broaden your horizons", as you say.'

'By causing pain.'

'If possession is performed well, it should not cause any pain. I do not expect you to possess a human. Certainly not tonight.'

'Then what do you want?'

He looked across the field. I followed his line of sight. The doe was scuffing her hoof against some flowers, watching them bob their heads. 'Nuala,' I said.

'Yes.'

I watched the doe bend her head and snuffle at a patch of grass. I'd never considered practising possession on animals. Animal minds were very different to human minds – less complex, less conscious – but that might make it harder. It might not even be possible for me to fit my human spirit into an animal body. Would I think like a human when I had an animal dreamscape? And then there were other concerns: would it hurt the deer? Would she struggle against my infiltration, or let me straight in?

'I don't know,' I said. 'She's too big. I might not be able to control her.'

'I will find something smaller.'

'What exactly do you want out of this?' When he said nothing, I continued: 'You're pretty pushy for someone who claims to be giving me an *opportunity*.'

'I want you to take this opportunity. I do not deny it.'

'Why?'

'Because I want you to survive.'

I held his gaze for a moment, trying to read him. I couldn't. There was something about Rephaite faces that discouraged emotional guesswork. 'Fine,' I said. 'A smaller animal. An insect, a rodent, maybe a bird. Something with limited sentience.'

'Very well.'

He was about to turn away when he stopped. With a glance in my direction, he removed something from his pocket: a pendant on a thin chain. 'Wear this,' he said.

'Why?'

But he was gone. I sat down on the edge of a small boulder,

fighting a shiver of anticipation. Jax would be nodding his approval, but I wasn't sure Nick would be doing the same.

I looked down at the pendant. It was about as long as my thumb, woven into the shape of wings. As I brushed my finger over it, there was a tiny tremor in the æther. It must have been sublimed. I pulled the chain over my head.

Nuala returned after a while, having grown bored of the grass. I was huddled against the boulder, my hands deep in the pockets of my jacket. It was extraordinarily cold now, and my breath came in white clouds. 'Hello,' I said. Nuala sniffed at my hair, like she was trying to work out what it was, then bent her legs and huddled next to me. She laid her head in my lap and made a sort of contented huff. I pulled off my gloves and stroked her ears. Her coat smelled of musk. I could feel her heartbeat, thick and strong. I'd never been this close to a wild animal. I tried to imagine what it must be like to *be* this little doe: to stand on four legs, to live wild in the woods.

But I wasn't wild. I'd lived in a Scion citadel for over a decade. All the wildness had gone out of me. That was why I'd joined Jax, I supposed. To cling to what was left of my old self.

After a moment, I decided to test the water. I closed my eyes and let my spirit drift. Nuala had a permeable dreamscape, thin and frail as a bubble. Humans built up layers of resistance over the years, but animals didn't have all that emotional armour. In theory, I could control her. I gave her dreamscape the lightest of nudges.

Nuala let out a snort of alarm. I stroked her ears, shushing her. 'Sorry,' I said. 'I won't do it again.' After a moment, she laid her head back on my lap, but she was quivering. She didn't know it was me that had hurt her. I ran my fingers under her chin, scratching gently.

By the time Warden returned I was half-asleep. He roused me with a tap on the cheek. Nuala looked up, but Warden soothed her with a word, and she soon dozed off again.

'Come,' he said. 'I have found you a new body.'

He sat on the boulder. I was struck by how he looked under the moon: perfectly outlined, strong-featured, with a radiance to his skin. 'What is it?' I said.

'See for yourself.'

His hands were caged, fingertips just touching. I looked down at a fragile insect: a butterfly, or a moth. Hard to tell in the darkness.

'It was quiescent when I found it,' he said. 'It is still lethargic. I thought it would make it easier.'

A butterfly, then. It was twitching in his hands.

'Cold spots frighten animals.' His voice was a soft rumble. 'They can sense an open conduit to the Netherworld.'

'Why *did* you open it?'

'You will see.' He raised his gaze to meet mine. 'Are you willing to attempt a possession?'

'I'll try,' I said.

His eyes glowed hotter, like coals.

'You probably already know this,' I said, 'but my body's going to fall when I leave it. I'd appreciate it if you could catch me.'

I had to choke the words out. I hated asking him for a favour, even something so small and obvious.

'Of course,' Warden said.

I broke the eye contact first.

After a deep breath, I dislodged my spirit. At once my senses blurred, and I could see my dreamscape. I could already feel the æther. It grew stronger as I walked towards the edge of the poppy field, where it was dark. The æther was there, waiting for me.

I jumped.

I could see my silver cord, unravelling from my dreamscape, giving me a way to return. Warden's dreamscape was close. The butterfly was only a dot beside it, a grain of sand beside a marble. I slid into its mind. There was no reactive jerk, no sudden panic from my host.

I found myself in a world of dreams. A world of colour, washed in ochre light. The butterfly spent its days feeding on flowers, and their opulent colours made up all its memories. Ambrosial scents wafted from everywhere, lavender and grass and roses. I paced through the dewy dreamscape, heading for the brightest part. Pollen swirled from the flower-laden trees, catching in my hair. I'd never felt so free. There was no resistance; not even the faintest flinch of a defence mechanism. It was so painless, so easy and beautiful, like I'd stepped out of a heavy set of shackles. It felt *natural*. This was what my spirit longed to do, to wander in strange lands. It couldn't stand being trapped in one body all the time. It had wanderlust.

When I came to the sunlit zone, I spied it: the lightest pink wisp of a spirit. I pursed my lips and blew, and it skittered away to the darker parts.

Now for the real test. If I'd worked this out correctly – and if Jax had been right when he explained it – stepping into the sunlit zone would allow me to take control of my new body.

As soon as I stepped into the circle, bright light flooded the whole dreamscape: golden light, rolling over me, filling my eyes and my skin and my blood. It blinded me. The world became a shattered diamond, an asterisk of luminous colour.

For a while, there was nothing. My body vanished, and I couldn't feel a thing. And then I woke up.

Panic registered first. Where were my arms, my legs? Why couldn't I see? Wait, I *could* see – just – but everything was washed in vivid purple, and the green of the grass was too bright for my eyes. A spasm racked my flimsy limbs. It was like brain plague, but so much worse. I was crushed, suffocated, screaming with no lips or voice. And what were these things stuck on either side of me? I tried to move, and they gave a shudder, as if I was in my death throes.

Before I knew it, I'd thrown myself out of the butterfly and back into my body. I was shaking all over, gasping for air. I slid down off the rock and hit the ground on all fours.

'Paige?'

I retched. A vile, acidic taste filled my mouth, but nothing came out. 'N-never doing that again,' I said.

'What happened?'

'Nothing. It was – it was so *easy*, b-but then—' I unzipped my jacket, my chest heaving. 'I can't do it.'

Warden was silent. He watched as I dabbed the sweat from my brow, trying not to hyperventilate. 'You did do it,' he said. 'Even though it was painful, you did it. Its wings moved.'

'I felt like I was *dying* when I did that.'

'But you did it.'

I leaned against the rock. 'How long did I last?'

'Perhaps half a minute.'

Better than I expected, but still pitiful. Jaxon would have cracked a rib laughing. 'Sorry to disappoint you,' I said. 'Maybe I'm not as good as other dreamwalkers.'

His face was hard. 'Yes,' he said, 'you are. But if you do not believe it, you will not achieve your full potential.'

He opened his hand, and the butterfly flew off into the dark. Still alive. I hadn't killed it.

'You're angry,' I said.

'No.'

'Then why do you look like that?'

'Like what?' His eyes were cold.

'Nothing,' I said.

He picked up a bundle of dry wood that had been propped against the boulder. I watched as he struck two rocks together, lighting a small fire, using the wood as kindling. I turned away. Let him simmer. I wasn't there to puppeteer the fauna.

'We will rest here for a few hours.' Warden didn't look at me. 'You need sleep before the next part of your test.'

'Does that mean I passed this half?'

'Of course you passed. You possessed the butterfly. That was all I asked of you.' He watched the flames. 'No more.'

He opened the knapsack and spread out a simple black sleeping bag. 'Here,' he said. 'There is something I must do. You will be safe here for a while.'

'Are you going back to the city?'

'Yes.'

I didn't have much choice but to comply, though I didn't like the thought of sleeping out here – not with this many spirits in the air. There were more of them now, and it was getting colder. I stripped off my wet boots and socks, put them out to dry beside the flames, and zipped myself into the sleeping bag. It wasn't warm, even with my jacket and gilet, but it was better than nothing.

Warden tapped his fingers on his knee, staring into the darkness. His eyes were two live coals, alert for danger. I turned over and looked up at the moon. How dark the world looked. How dark, and how cold.

The Will

'Hurry up, Pip. Come on.'

My cousin Finn pulled harder on my arm. I was six years old and we were in the congested heart of Dublin, surrounded by shouting people. 'Finn, I can't keep up,' I said, but he ignored me. It was the first time ever that my cousin hadn't listened to me.

We were supposed to be at the cinema that day: a crisp February morning in 2046, when the winter sun spilled white gold on the Liffey. I was staying with Aunt Sandra for the mid-term break. She'd told Finn to look after me while she was at work, seeing as he had no classes. I'd wanted to see a film and have lunch in Temple Bar, but Finn said we had to do something else: see the Molly Malone statue. It was important, he said. Too important to miss. A very special day. 'We're going to make history, Pip,' he'd said, squeezing my small, mitten-bound hand.

I'd wrinkled my nose a bit when he told me. History was for school. I loved Finn – he was tall and funny and clever, and he bought me sweets when he had spare change – but I'd seen Molly hundreds of times. I knew all the words of her song off by heart, too.

Everyone was singing it as we approached the statue. I looked up at all the red-faced people, half scared and half excited. Finn was shouting the song with them and I joined in, even though I didn't understand why we were all singing. Maybe it was a street party.

I held Finn's hand as he talked to his friends from Trinity College. They all wore green and waved big signs. I could read enough to work out most of the words, but there was one I didn't know: SCION. It was all over the signs. They flashed past me, high in the air, Irish and English mixed together. DOWN WITH MAYFIELD! ÉIRE GO BRÁCH! DUBLIN SAYS NO! I tugged Finn's sleeve.

'Finn, what's happening?'

'Nothing, Paige, be quiet for a minute – SCION OUT! SCION DOWN! SCION OUT OF DUBLIN TOWN!'

We were near the statue now, jostled by the crowd. I'd always liked Molly. I thought she had a kind face. But she looked different today. Someone had pulled a bag over her head and a rope around her neck. Tears jerked into my eyes.

'Finn, I don't like it.'

'SCION OUT! SCION DOWN! SCION OUT OF DUBLIN TOWN!'

'I want to go home.'

Finn's girlfriend frowned down at me. Kay. I'd always liked her. She had beautiful hair, a dark auburn that shone like copper and curled like springs, and her arms were pale and freckled. Finn had given her a Claddagh ring, which she wore with the heart pointing towards her body. She was dressed all in black, and her cheeks were painted green and white and orange.

'Finn, this could get violent,' she said. 'Shouldn't you take her home?' When he didn't reply, she hit him. 'Finn!'

'What?'

'Take Paige back to the house! Cleary has pipe bombs in his car, for Christ's sake—'

'No way. I'm not missing this for the world. If these bastards get in, we'll never get them out.'

'She's six years old. She shouldn't see this.' Kay grabbed my hand. 'I'll take her home if you won't. Your ma would be ashamed of you.'

'No. I want her to see it.'

He knelt down in front of me and pulled off his cap. His hair was tousled. Finn looked like my father, but his face was warm and open, and his eyes were blue as the summer sky. He put his hands on my shoulders.

'Paige Eva,' he said, in a very serious voice, 'do you know what's happening?'

I shook my head.

'Bad people are coming from over the sea. They're going to lock us up in our city and never let us leave, and turn this place into a prison city like theirs. We won't be allowed to sing our songs any more, or visit people outside Ireland. And people like you, Pip – they don't like you.'

I looked into Finn's eyes, and I understood what he meant. Finn had always known that I could see things. I knew where all the ghosts of Dublin lived. Did that make me bad? 'But why does Molly have a bag over her head, Finn?' I said.

'Because the bad people do that when they don't like other people. They put bags over their heads and ropes around their necks.'

'Why?'

'To kill them. Even little girls, like you.'

Now I was shaking. My eyes hurt. A bubble filled my throat, but I didn't cry. I was brave. I was brave, like Finn.

'Finn,' Kay said, 'I see them!'

'SCION OUT! SCION DOWN!'

My heart was too fast. Finn wiped my tears and put his cap on my head.

233

'They're coming, Paige, and we have to stop them.' He grasped my shoulders. 'Are you going to help me stop them?'

I nodded.

'Finn, oh God, Finn, they've got tanks!'

And then my world exploded. The bad people had raised their guns and aimed their darts of fire into the crowd.

I woke with the sound of guns in my ears.

My skin was slick and cold, but inside I was scalding. The memory had burned through my whole body. I could still see Finn, his face tight with hatred – Finn, who used to call me Pip.

I kicked off the sleeping bag. I could still hear the gunshots, thirteen years later. I could still see Kay, her eyes open, gripped wide in the shock of death. The blood on her shirt. One shot to the heart. That was what made Finn run towards the soldiers, leaving me behind, crouched under Molly's wheelbarrow. I screamed and screamed for him, but he never came back.

I never saw him again.

I didn't remember much after that. I know someone got me home. I know I sobbed for Finn until my throat hurt. And I know my father never let Aunt Sandra see me again, not until the memorial service. After that I didn't cry. Tears couldn't bring people back. I wiped the sweat from my face with my shirt. I must still be in the grounds of Magdalen. I turned on my side, so cold I couldn't feel my feet, and curled into a ball.

The fire must have gone out. It was raining, but I wasn't wet. I reached up. My fingers brushed some kind of canvas sheeting, a temporary shelter from the elements. I pulled up the hood of my jacket and inched out from under it.

'Warden?'

There was no sign of him. Or the deer. Or the fire.

I'd been shivering from cold, but now my shivers worsened. Where had he gone? Surely he couldn't still be in Sheol I. We hadn't even left Sheol I. Magdalen and its grounds were part of the residence system. We'd only strayed about a mile from the cold spot, if that.

The wind was rising. I huddled under my shelter. There was no reason for him to have left me alone, no reason whatsoever. Maybe I just hadn't been asleep for very long. I pulled on my socks and boots and double-checked the sleeping bag. To my surprise, I found a few supplies: a pair of gloves, a hypodermic needle of adrenalin, and a slim silver torch tucked into the lining, along with a manila envelope. My name was written on the front. I recognised his handwriting and tore it open.

Welcome to No Man's Land. Your test is simple: return to Sheol I in as little time as possible. You have no food, no water and no map. Use your gift. Trust your instincts.

And do me this honour: survive the night. I'm sure you would rather not be rescued.

Good luck.

I held the note for a moment, then tore it into strips.

I'd show him. I'd show him right now. He was trying to scare me, and I wouldn't have it. 'Survive the night'? What was that supposed to mean? He must think I was pretty feeble if I couldn't cope with a bit of wind and rain. If I could deal with the sordid streets of SciLo, I could deal with a dark forest. As for food supplies, why would I need them? It wasn't like he'd dumped me in the middle of nowhere. Was it?

When I looked outside the tent, I found a case marked with the symbol of ScionIde, the military arm of the government: two lines at a right angle, like gallows, with three shorter lines scored across the vertical mark. Inside the case was another note.

Be careful with the darts. If they break, the acid inside will send you into cardiac arrest. Use the flare in an emergency. It will summon a squad of red-jackets.

Do not go south.

I shone my torch at the contents of the case: a pistol with a long barrel, a flare gun, an old Zippo lighter, a hunting knife and three pressurised silver darts. The symbols for toxicity and corrosivity were printed across the side, along with the words HYDROFLUORIC ACID (HF).

A tranquilliser gun and a handful of acid darts. Why couldn't he have just given me my pistol? Well, I had to start somewhere, unless I wanted to stay in this clearing all night. I rolled up the sleeping bag, compacting it into a small sack, but left the shelter where it was. I could use it as a marker to make sure I wasn't running in circles.

There was something surrounding the camp. A ring of tiny white crystals. I knelt and dipped my fingers in them, then flicked out the tip of my tongue to taste them.

Salt.

The camp had been made in a circle of salt.

I held very still. There were rumours among voyants that salt could repel spirits – they called it halomancy – but it wasn't true. It certainly didn't stop poltergeists. Was he just trying to scare me, leaving it all over the place?

With my hood pulled up and my jacket zipped to the chin, I packed my limited supplies. I put the darts and pistol in the sack, padding them with the sleeping bag, and tucked the flare gun into my waistband. The knife went into my boot, the syringe into my jacket. I pulled on the gloves.

I couldn't wait to get back and face him, the scurf. I could picture him now, watching the clock, counting the minutes until I got back. Sitting by his nice warm fire.

I'd show him. I would not be overlooked. I was the Pale Dreamer, and he was going to see why. He was going to see why Jax had chosen me: because against all odds, *I had survived*.

I closed my eyes, trying to pick up on ethereal activity, but there was nothing. No dreamscapes. I was alone. When I opened my eyes, the sky caught my attention. It was lucky I'd woken when I did: the stars were about to be swallowed up by cloud, and with the sun gone, I had no other means of navigation. With no sign of Sirius, I searched for Orion's Belt. I knew from Nick's passionate speeches on astronomy that wherever the Belt was, north was roughly in the other direction. I also knew where it was in relation to Sheol I. I located the three stars and turned slowly to face my path. What lay in front of me was a dense stretch of woodland, as dark as it was thick and overgrown.

My heart pounded. I'd never been scared of the dark, but it would force me to rely on my sixth sense to detect any unrest. Which was probably the point. To test me.

I looked over my shoulder. The woodland was just as dark on the other side of the clearing. That path would lead me south, away from the colony.

Do not go south.

I knew his game. He was relying on me to obey, like a good human. Why should I go north, when north would lead me back to slavery – back to Warden, who had put me here in the first place? I didn't need to prove myself to him. I turned to face the Belt. I was going south. I was leaving this hellhole.

Wind rushed through the leaves, chilling my wet skin. It was now or never. By the time I'd finished thinking about what might or might not be lurking in there, I wouldn't have the courage to move. I clenched my jaw and headed into the woods.

It was black. Blind. The rain had softened the earth, leaving it spongy and damp. My feet made no sound as I trekked through the oak trees, walking quickly, sometimes breaking into a jog, using my hands to feel my way past branches. In the thin beam of my torch, I could make out a hazy mist that wreathed the tree trunks and hung in a thin blanket over the ground, obscuring my boots. There was no natural light. I prayed my torch wouldn't expire. It was scored with the Scion symbol, probably a borrowed piece of NVD equipment. It was a small relief: Scion-made items didn't often stop working.

It occurred to me that I must be outside the normal boundaries of Sheol I. This place was called No Man's Land for a reason: it belonged to no one. Maybe Scion owned it; maybe not. I had no idea where this route would lead me, but I did know that Oxford was north of London. I was heading in the right direction. My jacket and trousers were dark enough to hide me from watchful eyes, and my sixth sense was as finely tuned as ever. I could make it past any Reph guards. I could scale a fence just as easily as I could slip under it. And if anyone attacked me, I could use my gift. I'd sense them in advance.

But then I remembered what Liss had said about this place when I'd first arrived: *Deserted countryside. We call it No Man's Land.*' That might have encouraged me if not for what she'd said afterwards, when I'd asked if anyone had ever tried to escape via the southern route. '*Yes*,' was all she'd said. Just *yes*. Barefaced confirmation that there was danger on this path. Other voyants had come this way and died. Maybe they'd been tested like this, too. Was the test simply to resist the temptation to escape? I broke a sweat at the thought. Landmines, booby traps – they had them in here. I imagined cameras in the trees, watching my every move, waiting for me to step on a mine. The thought made me slow down.

No, no. I had to carry on. I could get out of here. They were relying on me to think like that, to think on the safe side. I almost turned north, but determination drove me on. Against my will, I pictured Warden, David and the Overseer by the fire, clinking their glasses as they watched me run into a mine. 'Well, gentlemen, here's to the dreamwalker,' the Overseer would say. 'The biggest idiot we ever brought to Sheol I.' And what would they put on my gravestone? Would they carve in PAIGE MAHONEY, or would it just be XX-59-40? Assuming there was enough of me left to scrape into a grave, of course.

I stopped and leaned against a tree. This was insane. Why was I imagining these things? Warden couldn't stand the Overseer. I squeezed my eyes shut and pictured another group: Jaxon, Nick and Eliza. They were in the citadel, waiting for me, searching for me. If I could just get out of these woods, I could work my way back to them.

After a moment, I opened my eyes. And stared at what was crumpled on the ground.

Bones. Human bones. A skeleton in a ragged white tunic, legs missing from the knee. I backed away, almost falling over my own feet. Something crunched underfoot. A skull.

There was a bag next to the carcass. Its hand still gripped the strap. With a crunch of dry bone, I prised it free. Flies crawled on the remaining flesh: giant, black-haired flies, swollen with dead tissue. They flew up when I snatched the bag from its owner. My torch gleamed on the contents: a hunk of rotten bread and a dry bottle.

My skin turned cold and damp. I turned the torch to my right. A few feet away, a crater yawned among the leaves, half-flooded by the rain. Shards of bone and mine casing scattered the ground.

There really was a minefield.

I pressed my back against the trunk of an oak. I couldn't navigate a minefield in the dark. I edged away from the tree, stepping over the skeleton. *You're fine, Paige.* Legs shaking, I turned north and picked my way back along the path. I hadn't gone far from the clearing. I could make it. After moving several feet from the bones, I tripped over a root and hit the ground. I tensed rigid, my heart lurching, but no explosion followed.

Resting my weight on my elbows, I dug into my jacket, took out the Zippo and flicked it open with my thumb. A clean flame rose. A route to the æther. I wasn't an augur – fire was no friend to me – but I could use it to perform a miniature séance. 'I need a guide,' I whispered. 'If anyone is out there, come to the flame.'

For a long time, there was nothing. The flame flinched and guttered. Then my sixth sense jolted to life, and a young spirit emerged from the trees. I pulled myself to my feet. 'I need to reach my camp.' I held the lighter out to it. 'Will you guide me?'

I couldn't hear it speak, but it started to move back the way I'd come. I sensed it was the spirit of the dead white-jacket and I broke into a run. It had no reason to mislead me.

The circle of salt soon came into sight. The rain blew out the lighter, but the spirit stayed close to me. I took a few minutes to compose myself. It was bitter to concede, but I had no choice but to go north. I checked my belongings were still there, then set off into the trees again, the torch in one hand and the Zippo in the other, the spirit close behind.

After about half an hour of walking, the spirit trailing around my shoulders like a rope, I stopped to check that Orion's Belt was behind me. I adjusted my course a little before I delved into the darkness again. My ears and nose were smarting, and my sixth sense sent tremors through my skin. I could barely feel my toes. I stopped and gripped my knees, taking deep breaths to steady my nerves. As soon as I inhaled, I smelled something. I recognised that smell: death.

My torch beam was unsteady. The stench of putrid flesh was getting stronger. I walked for another minute before I found the source. Another body.

It must once have been a fox. Tufts of auburn fur, matted with dry blood, eye sockets brimful of maggots. I buried my nose and mouth in my sleeve. The smell was atrocious.

Whatever had done this was out here in the woods with me.

Move, Paige. Move. The torch sputtered. I'd just started to leave when a twig snapped.

Had I imagined that? No, of course I hadn't. My hearing worked fine. I could hear the blood beating at my ears. I pressed my back against a tree, trying not to breathe too loudly.

A guard. A red-jacket on night patrol. But then I heard heavy footsteps, too heavy for a human. I turned off the torch, slid it into my pocket. There was no point having it in my hands: turning it on would give away my position.

The silence pressed against my ears. I couldn't see a thing, but I could hear another footstep, closer. Then the sounds of teeth working away at a carcass. Something had found the fox.

Or come back for it.

I cupped a hand around the lighter. My heart was doing strange things. I wasn't sure if it had sped up to a single hum, or if it just wasn't beating any more. Behind me, the spirit shivered.

The minutes ticked away. I waited. I had to move at some point, but I knew, I *knew* there was something in the vicinity.

Three guttural clicks.

Every muscle in my body tensed. I breathed through my nose, keeping my lips clamped together. I didn't know what that sound was, but there was no way a human had made it. I'd heard the Rephs make some strange noises, but never such an ugly, visceral sound.

A sudden wind blew the lighter out. My spirit guide fled.

For a minute, cold fear stilled my fingers. Then I remembered the pistol, tucked into my pack. It would be a fool's game to shoot my stalker, but I could distract it. Give myself some time to move. I thought about climbing a tree, then dismissed the idea. Trees were not my forte. I'd be better off finding a new place to hide. Still, finding higher ground seemed like a sensible idea. If I got to a safe place, I could shine my torch on this creature and see what it was. I tucked the lighter away and dug into my pack.

Once the pistol was in my hand, I set about extracting a dart. Every move I made seemed noisy: every exhalation, every rustle of my jacket. Finally I could feel the cold, smooth cylinder of a dart against my fingers. I knew how to load an ordinary gun, but it took me a few minutes to equip the unfamiliar weapon in the dark, with clammy hands, trying my utmost not to make a sound. Once it was ready, I lifted my arms, aimed, fired.

When the dart hit home it sizzled like hot fat in a pan. The creature ran towards the source of the sound. It carried a sound of its own. A buzzing. Flies.

This wasn't an animal.

Nausea surged through me. I'd heard so much about the Emim, but I'd never really pictured facing one of their number. Even after what I'd heard at the oration, even after the red-jacket had lost his hand, I'd almost started to believe they didn't exist. Until now.

It was all I could do to keep myself standing. My hands shook and my lips trembled. I couldn't breathe, couldn't think. Could it hear my pulse? Could it smell my fear? Was it slavering over my flesh yet, or did I have to get closer before it could detect me?

I loaded another dart into the gun. The Buzzer sniffed at the place I'd shot. I closed my eyes and reached for the æther.

Something was wrong. Very wrong. All the local spirits had fled, like they were afraid, but why would spirits fear any creature of the physical world? It wasn't as if they could die again. Whatever the cause, there was nothing to spool.

I became aware that I couldn't hear the Buzzer any more. My hands were sweat-slick. I could hardly grip the gun. I could be dead at any moment. Dead meat.

The whole thing must have been a set-up. Nashira had never wanted me to earn my colours. She just wanted me to die.

Not today, I thought. *Not today, Nashira.*

I ran out from behind the tree. My boots pounded, my heart thrashed at my chest. Where was it? Had it seen me yet?

Something struck me between the shoulder blades. I was weightless for a moment, suspended in darkness. Then I hit the ground. My wrist bent back and snapped. I bit back a scream half a second too late.

The gun was gone. There was no chance of finding it now. I could hear the thing – it was near me, it was *on* me. With my uninjured hand, I reached into my boot and found the hunting knife.

I forgot about my spirit. I stabbed into soft mush. Wet ran down my wrist. Buzz. Another stab, two stabs. Buzz. Buzz. Things kept hitting my face: small, round things. I blinked them from my eyes, coughed them from my mouth. Fingers clawed at my neck, and hot breath stank against my cheek. Stab, stab. Buzz. Teeth clashed near my ear. I stabbed up, back into the flesh, and pulled down. The blade tore through muscle and gristle.

Then it was gone. I was free. My hands were coated to the wrist in a syrupy, foul-smelling liquid. Bile surged into my throat, burning my mouth and nose.

The torch lay about ten feet away. I crawled towards it, my broken wrist cradled to my chest. I'd broken it before: it was throbbing like a bitch. I dragged myself along on one arm, holding the knife between my teeth, drenched in sour sweat. The smell of corpse wrenched at my stomach, sending painful spasms up my throat.

I grabbed the torch and swung it behind me. I could see dark shapes between the trees. More footsteps. More Buzzers. *No.*

My head was pounding. My vision blurred. *I don't want to die.* Possessing the butterfly had weakened me much more than I'd anticipated. *Run.* I dug into my jacket, pulled out the syringe. My last resort. The flare gun was not a resort. I wouldn't fire. I would not lose this game.

ScionAid Auto-Inject Adrenalin. Much stronger than the diluted cocktail of drugs Jax used to keep me awake. I punched the needle through my trousers, straight into my thigh.

Sharp pain. I cursed, but kept the needle in. A spring-loaded jolt of adrenalin shot into the muscle. Scion adrenalin was designed to wake up your whole body; not just to help it function, but to wipe out pain and make you stronger. Gillies were wired on the stuff constantly. My muscles became supple. My legs grew stronger. I launched myself off the ground and broke into a sprint. The adrenalin had no effect on my sixth sense, but it made it easier to concentrate on the æther.

The Buzzer had a dark, cavernous dreamscape, a black hole in the æther. I wouldn't get far if I tried to break into it. I still tried, not quite leaving my body.

A black cloud engulfed me. My dreamscape darkened, and the edges of my vision clustered together. I needed to repel it. A quick-fire jump should drive it away. My spirit flew from my body, fracturing the edge of its dreamscape. The creature let out an awful scream. Its footsteps stopped. At the same time, a blinding pain shocked me back into my dreamscape. My palms hit the ground. I scrambled back up, heaving.

The woods gave way to open grassland. I could see the spires of the House. The city. The *city*.

The adrenalin surged through my veins, racing through my muscles, pushing me faster. My wrist dangled at my side as I ran like a penitent sinner towards my prison. Better a jailbird than a stiff.

The Buzzer screamed. Its cry echoed through every cell in my body. I vaulted over a chain-link fence and hit the ground running.

There was a watchtower at the top of the House. There would be a red-jacket with a gun. They could subdue the Buzzer, kill it. Sweat drenched my clothes. Not far now. I couldn't feel the pain yet, but I knew I'd torn a muscle. I passed a rusted sign reading USE OF DEADLY

FORCE IS AUTHORISED. Good. I'd never needed deadly force more. I could see the watchtower now. I was about to scream for help, to pull out the flare gun, when I found myself immobilised.

A net. It was all over me: a thick wire net. I shrieked 'no, no, kill it' at the top of my lungs. I struggled like bait on a line. Why had they caught me? I wasn't the enemy! *Of course you are*, said a voice in my head, but I wasn't listening any more. I had to get out of this net. The Buzzer was coming. It would rip me up, just like it ripped up the fox.

A tearing sound. A voice saying my name: 'Paige, calm down, it's all right, you're safe now' – but I didn't trust that voice. That was the voice I feared. I clawed my way out of the net and tried to run again. That was when someone grabbed me, threw me backwards. 'Paige, concentrate! Use your fear, *use* it!' I couldn't focus. I was feral with fear. My heart was too fast, I couldn't keep up. My vision blinked in and out. My mouth was dry. Was I still standing?

'Paige, to your right! Attack it!'

I looked to my right. I couldn't see what it was, but it wasn't human. My fear reached its absolute peak. I flew into the æther. Into nothing. And then into something.

The last thing I saw was my body crumpling to the ground. But not through my eyes. Through the eyes of a deer.

The Good Morrow

There are certain things in life that you never forget. Things that dig deep, things that nest in the hadal zone. I slept like a top, waiting for my brain to block the terror of the woods.

Real sleep was my salvation, the quiet interval between waking and walking. Jax and the others had never understood it, why I loved to sleep so much. When I wanted to rest after hours in the æther, Nadine would always laugh. '*You're crazy, Mahoney,*' she would say. '*You've been snoring away for hours, and now you want more sleep? Not a dog's chance in the Island. Not for the money you're on.*'

Nadine Arnett, the essence of sympathy. She was the only member of the gang I didn't miss.

When I came round, it was night. My wrist was clamped with a spider-like metal frame. Above me was a velvet canopy.

I was in Warden's bed. Why was I in his bed?

The thoughts dragged. I couldn't quite remember what had happened before this. I felt just like I had when Jaxon had let me try real wine. I glanced down at my hand. The frame prevented me from moving my wrist. I wanted to get up – to get out of this bed – but I was too warm and heavy to move. *Sedative*, I thought. And that was fine. It was all fine.

When my eyes opened again, I was more alert. I could hear a familiar voice. Warden had returned – and he had company. I crept towards the drapes and parted them.

A fire roared in the hearth. Warden stood with his back to me, speaking in an unfamiliar language. The words were a low-pitched glissade, resonant as music in a hall. Standing in front of him was Terebell Sheratan. She held a chalice in one hand. She kept motioning towards the bed – towards me. Warden shook his head.

What *was* that language?

I tuned into the nearest spirits, ghosts that had once lived here. They were almost dancing to the beat of Warden and Terebell's conversation. It was exactly what happened when Nadine played the piano, or when a julker sang a lay on the streets. Julkers – polyglots, to use the proper word – could speak and understand a language known only to spirits, but Warden and Terebell weren't julkers. Neither of them had a polyglot aura.

They put their heads together, examining something. When I looked closer, I froze.

My phone.

Terebell turned it over in her hand, ran her thumb over the keys. The battery was long since dead.

If they had my phone and the backpack, they must have the pamphlet. Were they trying to see whose numbers I had? They must suspect I knew the pamphlet's author. If they found Jaxon's number, they could track him back to Seven Dials – and suddenly, Carl's vision would make sense.

I had to get that phone.

Terebell stowed it in her shirt. Warden said something to her. She touched her forehead to his before she exited the room, locking the heavy door behind her. Warden remained where he was for a moment, looking at the window, before his attention shifted to the bed. To me.

He pulled back the drapes and sat on the edge of the covers. 'How are you feeling?' he asked.

'Fuck you.'

His eyes burned. 'Better, I take it.'

'Why does Terebell have my phone?'

'So that Nashira does not find it. Her red-jackets would be able to extract contact information for your friends in the syndicate.'

'I don't have friends in the syndicate.'

'Try not to lie to me, Paige.'

'I'm not lying.'

'Another lie.'

'Because you're always so truthful.' I stared him out. 'You left me with that thing. You left me alone, in the dark, with a Buzzer.'

'You knew it would be coming. You knew you would have to face an Emite. In any case, I did warn you.'

'How the hell did you warn me?'

'Cold spots, Paige. That is how they travel.'

'So you let one out?'

'You were in no danger. I know you were frightened, but I needed you to possess that deer.'

He fixed his eyes on mine. My mouth turned dry.

'You did all that just so I'd be able to possess Nuala.' I wet my lips. 'You set the whole thing up when you opened the cold spot.' He nodded. 'You released the Buzzer.' He nodded again. 'And you made me so scared I—'

'Yes.' He wasn't ashamed of it. 'I suspected your gift was activated by strong emotions: anger, loathing, sadness – and fear. Fear is your real trigger. By forcing you to the absolute limit of mental terror, I forced you to possess Nuala, making you think she was the Buzzer that had stalked you through the woods. But I would never have endangered your life.'

'It could have killed me.'

'I took certain precautions. I repeat: you were never in any immediate danger.'

'That's a flam. If you think a circle of *salt* is a precaution, you're off the cot.' I was slipping into street slang, but I didn't care. 'You must have loved that – seeing me dance—'

'No, Paige. I am trying to help you.'

'Go to hell.'

'I already exist on a level of hell.'

'Exist on one that isn't near mine.'

'No. You and I made a deal, and I do not break deals.' He held my gaze. 'I expect you in ten minutes. You owe me an hour of pleasant conversation.'

I could have spat at him, but the line had been drawn. I left the room and went up to the second floor.

I would not tell him anything more about myself. He already knew too much about my personal life – and he could discover nothing about my involvement with Jax. Nashira was already looking for the gang. If she found out I was one of his closest allies, she'd probably make me arrest him myself. I'd just pretend to be traumatised by the Buzzer, pretend I could hardly talk.

I could hear it again, the breath sawing its throat. I closed my eyes. The memory subsided.

A thin robe hung over my filthy clothes. They smelled of sweat and death. I went through to the bathroom and tore them off. A fresh pink uniform was waiting. I scrubbed at my skin with soap and steaming water. I wanted to remove even the faintest memory of that smell.

When I glanced into the mirror, I realised I was still wearing the pendant. I pulled it off. A fat lot of good it had done me.

When I returned to the chamber, Warden was sitting in his favoured armchair. He gestured towards the opposite seat. 'Please.'

I sat. The chair seemed enormous. 'Did you sedate me?'

'You had a kind of seizure after the possession.' He watched me. 'Did you try to possess the Emite?'

'I wanted to see its dreamscape.'

'I see.' He reached for his goblet. 'A drink?'

I was tempted to ask for something illegal – real wine, perhaps – but I didn't have the energy to keep pushing him. 'Coffee,' I said.

He tugged on a scarlet tassel. It was connected to an old-fashioned bell pull. 'Someone will bring it shortly,' he said.

'An amaurotic?'

'Yes.'

'So you treat them as your butlers.'

'Slaves, Paige. Let us not be delicate.'

'But their blood is valuable.'

He took a sip from his goblet. I sat with my arms crossed, waiting for him to start the conversation.

The gramophone was on again. I recognised the song – 'I Don't Stand a Ghost of a Chance (With You)', the Sinatra version. It was on the Scion blacklist simply because it had the word *ghost* in its title, even though it had little or nothing to do with ghosts. Oh, how I'd missed Ol' Blue Eyes.

'Do all the blacklisted records come to you?' I asked, making a supreme effort to sound casual.

'No, they go to the House. I go there occasionally and take one or two for my gramophone.'

'Do you like our music?'

'Some. Mostly from the twentieth century. I find your languages interesting, but I dislike most modern music productions.'

'Blame the censor. If not for you, there wouldn't be one.'

He raised his goblet. 'Touché.'

I had to ask. 'What is that?'

'Essence of the amaranth flower, mixed with red wine.'

'I haven't heard of amaranth.'

'This variety does not grow on Earth. It heals most spiritual injuries. Had you taken amaranth after your encounter with the poltergeist, the wound might not have scarred so deeply. It would also heal some of the damage done to your brain, should you use your spirit too often without life support.'

Well, well. A cure for my brain. Jaxon would never let me sleep again if he got wind of amaranth. 'Why do you drink it?'

'Old wounds. Amaranth eases the pain.'

There was a brief silence. My turn to speak. 'This is yours.' I held out the pendant.

'Keep it.'

'I don't want it.'

'I insist. It may not repel the Emim, but it could save your life against a poltergeist.'

I placed it on the arm of the chair. Warden glanced at it, then flicked his gaze up to catch mine.

There was a light knock on the door. A boy came in, about my age, maybe older. He wore a grey tunic, and his eyes were bloodshot. Despite that, he was beautiful, like something out of a painting. His hair was a fine gold, cut around his chiselled face, and his lips and cheeks were pink as petals. Past the redness, his eyes were a clear, liquid blue. I thought I could detect the shaky traces of an aura around him.

'Coffee, please, Michael,' Warden said to him. 'Do you take sugar, Paige?'

'No, thank you,' I said. Michael bowed and left. 'So he's your *personal* slave, is he?'

'Michael was a gift from the blood-sovereign.'

'How romantic.'

'Not particularly.' Warden glanced at the windows. 'There is little to be done with Nashira when she wants something. Or someone.'

'I can imagine.'

'Can you?'

'I know she has five angels.'

'Yes, she does. But they are as much her weakness as her strength.' He took another sip of his drink. 'The blood-sovereign suffers under the influence of her so-called angels.'

'I'm sure the angels are sorry.'

'They despise her.'

'You don't say.'

'I do.' He was clearly amused by my disdain. 'We have only been speaking for two minutes, Paige. Try not to waste all your sarcasm in one breath.'

I wanted to kill him. As it happened, I couldn't.

The boy returned with a pot of coffee. He placed the tray on the table with a generous plate of baked chestnuts, dusted with cinnamon. Their sweet smell made my mouth water. There was a vendor near the Blackfriars bridge that sold them in the winter months. These ones looked even better than his, with cracked brown shells and velvety white insides. There was fruit, too: segments of pear, glossy cherries, soft smiles of red apple.

Michael made a sign, and Warden shook his head. 'Thank you, Michael. That will be all.'

He bowed again before he left. I found myself wanting to scream at him. He was so *submissive*.

'When you say "so-called" angels,' I said, forcing myself to be calm, 'what exactly do you mean?'

Warden paused.

'Eat,' he said. 'Please.'

I plucked a chestnut from the plate, still hot from the oven. It tasted like warmth and winter.

'I am sure you know what an angel is: a soul that returns to this plane to protect the person they died to save,' he said. 'We know of angels and archangels, and I assume the voyants of the street do too.' I nodded. 'Nashira can command a third level of angel.'

'Oh?'

'She can trap certain kinds of spirits.'

'So she's a binder.'

'More than merely a binder, Paige. If she chooses to kill a clairvoyant, she can not only trap its spirit, but use it. So long as that spirit is bound to her, its presence affects her aura. Is it that corruption that allows her to have several gifts at once.'

My coffee slopped into my lap. 'She has to kill them herself?'

'Yes. We call them "fallen angels".' He watched me. 'And they are bound to stay for ever with their murderer.'

I stood.

'You're evil.' The cup smashed at my feet. 'How do you ever expect me to talk to you, to treat you like you're human, when your fiancée can do something like that? When you can look her in the face?'

'Did I say I had ever summoned a fallen angel myself?'

'But you've killed people.'

'So have you.'

'That's not the point.'

Warden's expression had changed. Now there was no trace of mockery.

'I do not know what I can do for this world,' he said, 'but I will not let any harm come to you.'

'I don't need you to protect me. Just get rid of me. Palm me off on someone else. I don't want to be your student any more. I want to switch keepers. I want to be with Thuban. Send me to Thuban.'

'You do not want a Sargas keeper, Paige.'

'Don't tell me what I want. I want—'

'You want to feel safe again.' He stood, keeping the coffee table between us. 'You want me to treat you as Thuban and the others treat their humans, because then you would feel that you had every right to hate the Rephaim. But because I do not harm you, and because I try to understand you, you run away. I know why, of course. You do not understand my motives. You ask yourself time and time again why I want to help you, and you come to no conclusions. But that does not mean there *is* no conclusion, Paige. It means you have yet to discover it.'

I sank back into the armchair. The scalding coffee had soaked straight through my trousers. Seeing it, he said, 'I will find you something else.'

He walked to the armoire. My eyes were hot with anger. I could almost hear Jax scolding me. *You really are a silly thing. Look at you, with dewdrops in your shiners. Raise your head, O my lovely! What do you want — sympathy? Pity? You won't find that from him, just like you didn't find it from me. The world is an abattoir, my mollisher. Raise those barking irons, now. Let me see you give him hell.*

Warden presented me with a long black tunic. 'I hope this fits.' He handed it to me. 'It seems a little too large, but it should keep you warm.'

I nodded. Warden turned his back. I pulled the tunic over my head. He was right: it came to my knees. 'Done,' I said.

'Will you sit down?'

'Like I have a choice.'

'I am giving you the choice.'

'I don't know what you want me to say.'

'Ideally, I would like you to tell me who has been so cruel to you in the past as to make you think that you can trust nobody.' Warden returned to his seat. 'But I know you will not tell me that. You want to protect these friends of yours.'

'I don't know what you're talking about.'

'Of course not.'

I cracked. 'Fine, yes, I have voyant friends. Doesn't every voyant have voyant friends?'

'No. The London syndicate has grown stronger over the years. The ones we capture are mostly outsiders – those that live alone, or on the streets, because they are unable to control their powers. Or their families have evicted them. That is why so many of them are happy to serve us: they have been mistreated by their own kind. And while the Rephaim treat them as second-class citizens, they still give them the chance to indulge in the æther. We put them in groups, make them belong to a social structure again.' He motioned to the door. 'Michael was a polyglot – I think your people call them "julkers". His parents were so frightened of his locution that they tried to exorcise him. His dreamscape collapsed. After that he could hardly speak.'

My voice was gone. I had heard of dreamscapes collapsing; it was what had happened to one of the boys in the gang, Zeke. That was how you became unreadable. The dreamscape would grow back with layer upon layer of armour, preventing all spiritual attack.

'The red-jackets picked him up two years ago. He was living rough on the streets of Southwark – an unreadable with no money or food. They put him in the Tower as a suspected unnatural, but I had him brought here prematurely. Though he is treated as an amaurotic, he still has an aura. I taught him how to speak again. I hope that he will find the æther one day, and that he can sing in the way he once did. With the voices of the dead.'

'Wait,' I said. 'You taught him?'

'Yes.'

'Why?'

Silence filled every crevice of the room. Warden reached for his goblet.

'Who *are* you?' I said. He glanced up at me. 'You're the

blood-consort of a Sargas sovereign. You've been puppeteering a government since 1859. You've supported voyant trafficking, watched a whole system develop around it. You've helped them spread lies and hatred and fear. Why are you helping humans?'

'That, I cannot tell you. Just as you will not tell me who your friends are, I will not tell you my ulterior motives.'

'Would you tell me if you found out who my friends were?'

'Perhaps.'

'Have you told Michael?'

'A little. Michael has great loyalty towards me, but I cannot fully trust him in his fragile mental state.'

'Do you think the same about me?'

'I know too little about you to trust you, Paige. But that does not mean you cannot *earn* my trust. In fact' – he sat back in his chair – 'the opportunity will present itself today.'

'What do you mean?'

'You will see.'

'Let me guess. You killed a soothsayer and stole his power, and now you think you can see my future.'

'I am no thief of gifts. But I do know Nashira very well, well enough to guess her moves. I know when she likes to strike.'

The grandfather clock chimed once. Warden glanced at it. 'Well, that is one hour,' he said. 'You are free to go. Perhaps you should visit your friend, the cartomancer.'

'Liss is in spirit shock,' I said.

He glanced up.

'The red-jackets chucked her cards on the fire.' My throat was tight. 'I haven't seen her since.'

Ask for his help. I struggled with myself. *Ask him if he can replace her cards. He'll do it. He helped Michael.*

'A pity,' he said. 'She is a gifted performer.'

I forced out the words: 'Will you help her?'

'I have no cards. She must have her link to the æther.' He met my eyes. 'Amaranth would also be necessary.'

I stayed where I was, watching as he reached for a small box on the coffee table. It looked like an old-fashioned snuff box, made with mother-of-pearl and slivers of gold. In the centre of the lid was the eight-petalled flower, like the one on his box of vials. He flipped it open and withdrew a tiny bottle of oil, tinged with blue dye.

'That's aster extract,' I said.

'Very good.'

'Why do you have it?'

'I use small doses of the star-flower to assist Michael. It helps him remember his dreamscape.'

'Star-flower?'

'It is the Rephaite name for aster. A literal translation from our language – Glossolalia, or Gloss.'

'Is that what julkers speak?'

'Yes. The ancient language of the æther. Michael can no longer speak it, but he understands. So do whisperers.'

So julkers could eavesdrop on the Rephaim. Interesting. 'Are you planning to give him aster . . . now?'

'No. I simply wished to organise my collection of requisitioned drugs,' he said. I had no idea if he was being funny or not. Probably not. 'Some of them, such as the poppy anemone, can be used to harm us.' He took a single red flower from the box. 'Certain poisons must be kept out of human hands.' His eyes were fixed on mine. 'We would not want them used to, say, infiltrate the House. That would put our most secret supplies in jeopardy.'

Red flower. I remembered David's note. *The sole method.*

The sole method of killing Rephaim?

'No,' I said. 'We wouldn't want that.'

It was quiet in the Rookery, I hadn't seen Liss since Suhail had escorted me to Magdalen; I'd had no chance to check on her, to see if she'd survived the loss of her deck.

She was conscious, but not present. Her lips were pale, and her eyes wandered, unfocused. She was in the throes of spirit shock.

Julian and the bespectacled performer from the first day – Cyril – had made it their mission to look after her. They fed her, brushed her hair, treated her burnt hands and talked to her. She just lay there, stiff and clammy, murmuring about the æther. Now she could no longer connect with it, her natural urge was to abandon her body and join with it. It was up to us to quell that urge. To keep her with us.

I swapped two pills for a Sterno, some matches and a tin of beans at Duckett's jerryshop. There were no cards at his stall. They'd all been confiscated by a red-jacket: Kathryn, making sure Liss suffered. She was lucky Warden had prevented her from seeing me.

When I returned to the shack, Julian looked up, his eyes red with exhaustion. His pink tunic was gone, replaced by a ragged shirt and cloth trousers.

'Paige, you've been gone a while?'

'I've been away. Explain later.' I knelt beside Liss. 'Is she eating?'

'I got her to eat a bit of skilly yesterday, but she threw it all back up.'

'And the burns?'

'Bad. We need silvadene.'

'We'll try and feed her again.' I stroked her damp ringlets, pinched her cheek. 'Liss?'

Her eyes were open, but she didn't respond. I lit the Sterno. Cyril drummed his fingers on his knee. 'Come *on*, Rymore,' he said to her, irritated. 'You can't be off the silks for this long.'

'A little sympathy wouldn't go amiss,' Julian said.

'No time for sympathy. Suhail will be after her soon. She's supposed to be performing with me.'

'Haven't they found out yet?'

'Nell's been filling in for her. They look similar in costume, with masks – same height, same hair colour. But Nell isn't as good. She falls.' Cyril gazed at Liss. 'Rymore never falls.'

Julian put the beans on the can. I found a spoon and wrapped an arm around Liss. She shook her head.

'No.'

'You've got to eat something, Liss.' Julian gripped her cold wrist, but she didn't respond.

When the beans were hot, Julian tipped her head back. I spoon-fed her, but she could hardly swallow. Beans ran down her chin. Cyril grabbed the tin and scraped out what remained with his bare hands. I sat back on my heels and watched as Liss sank into her sheets.

'This can't go on.'

'But we can't *do* anything.' Julian clenched a fist. 'Even if we find a deck, there's no guarantee it'll work. It'd be like giving her a new limb. She could reject it.'

'We have to try.' I looked towards Cyril. 'Are there no other cartomancers here?'

'Dead.'

'Even if he's wrong, we can't take someone else's deck,' Julian said, very quietly. 'That's worse than murder.'

'Then we steal from the Rephs,' I said. Crime *was* my forte. 'I'm going to break into the House. They must have supplies in there.'

'You'll die,' Cyril said, with no hint of distress.

'I survived a Buzzer. I'll be fine.'

Julian looked up. 'You saw one?'

'They live in the woods. Warden left me with one of them.'

'Does that mean you passed your tests?' Suspicion crossed his face. 'You're a red-jacket?'

'I don't know. I thought I was, but' – I tugged my tunic – 'this doesn't look red.'

'That's comforting.' He paused. 'What was it like? The Buzzer.'

'Fast. Aggressive. I didn't see much of it.' I looked at his new clothes. 'Didn't you see one?'

His smile was thin. 'Aludra chucked me out just for missing the curfew. Plain old harlie, I'm afraid.'

Cyril was shivering. 'Their bite is death,' he whispered. 'You shouldn't go out there again.'

'I might not have a choice,' I said. Cyril put his head in his arms. 'Jules, pass a sheet.'

He did. I tucked it around Liss. She didn't stop shivering. I rubbed her icy arms, trying to warm them up. Her fingers had blistered.

'Paige,' Julian said, 'do you mean it? About breaking into the House?'

'Warden said they have supplies in there. Secret stores, things we shouldn't see. Maybe silvadene.'

'Has it occurred to you that it might be guarded? Or that the Warden might be lying?'

'I'll risk it.'

He sighed. 'I doubt I can stop you. And if you get in?'

'I'm going to steal as much as I can – anything I can use to defend myself – then I'm going to leave. Whoever wants to join me is welcome. Otherwise I'll go alone. Whatever happens, I'm not going to rot here for the rest of my life.'

'Don't do it,' Cyril said. 'You'll die. Like the ones who died before. The Buzzers ate them too. And they'll eat you.'

'Please, Cyril, enough.' Julian didn't look away from me. 'You go to the House, Paige. I'll try and rally some troops.'

'Troops?'

'Come on.' The flame played in his eyes. 'You're not seriously going to leave without a fight, are you?'

I raised my eyebrows. 'A fight?'

'You're not going to go and pretend this didn't happen. Scion have been doing this for two centuries, Paige. It's not going to end.

What's to stop them dragging you straight back here when you reach SciLo?'

He had a point. 'What do you suggest?'

'A prison break. Everyone gets out. We leave them with no voyants to feed on.'

'There are over two hundred humans here. We can't just walk out. Besides, there are landmines in the woods.' I pulled my knees up to my chin. 'You know what happened during Bone Season XVIII. I won't have all those deaths on my conscience.'

'They won't be on your conscience. People *want* to leave, Paige – they're just not brave enough, not yet. If we can cause a big enough distraction, we can get them through the woods.' He placed a hand over my arm. 'You're from the syndicate. From Ireland. Don't you think it's about time we showed the Rephs they're not in charge? That they can't just keep on taking from us?' When I didn't answer, he squeezed my arm. 'Let's show them. That even after two hundred years, they still have something to fear.'

I wasn't seeing his face any more. I was seeing Finn on that day in Dublin, telling me to fight.

'Maybe you're right,' I said.

'I know I am.' His features lifted in a tired smile. 'How many do you think we need?'

'Start with people who have good reason to hate the Rephaim. The harlies. The yellow-jackets. The amaurotics. Ella and Felix and Ivy. Then work on the white-jackets.'

'What should I tell them?'

'Nothing yet. Just ask some questions. Work out if they'd ever try and escape.'

Julian looked at Cyril.

'No.' Cyril shook his head. Behind his ruined glasses, his eyes were bright and feverish with fear. 'I'm not. No way, brother. They'll kill us. They're immortal.'

'They're not immortal.' I watched the Sterno burn to a low flame. 'They can be hurt. Warden told me.'

'He could be *lying*,' Julian stressed. 'This is Nashira's fiancé we're talking about. The blood-consort. Her right-hand man. Why do you trust a word he says?'

'Because I think he's rebelled against her before. I think he's one of the scarred ones.'

'The what?'

'A group of Rephs that started the rebellion of Bone Season XVIII. They were tortured. Scarred.'

'Where did you hear that?'

'From a bone-grubber. XX-12.'

'You trust a bone-grubber?'

'No, but he showed me the shrine they made for the victims.'

'And you think the Warden is one of these "scarred ones",' he said. I nodded. 'You've seen the scars, I take it?'

'No. I think he hides them.'

'You *think*, Paige. That's not enough.'

Before I could reply, someone swept into the shack. I froze.

The Overseer.

'Well, well, well.' His painted eyebrows jumped up. 'It appears we have an imposter in our midst. Who has been on the silks, if XIX-1 has been in here this entire time?'

I stood. So did Julian. 'She's in spirit shock,' I said. I looked the Overseer dead in the eye. 'She can't perform in this condition.'

The Overseer knelt beside Liss, felt her forehead. She twisted away from his touch. 'Oh dear, oh dear.' He ran his fingers through her hair. 'This is terrible. Terrible tidings. I can't lose 1. My special 1.'

Liss began to shriek. The sounds jolted out of her in heavy, trembling spasms. 'Get away,' she gasped out. 'Get away!' Julian grabbed the Overseer's shoulder and gave him a hard shove.

'Don't touch her.'

I stood beside him. Cyril rocked on his heels. At first the Overseer looked staggered, even aghast; then he started to laugh. He rose to his feet, clapping his hands in delight. One gloved hand reached into his jacket. 'Is this a glimmer of rebellion, children? Have I let two hungry wolves into my flock?'

With a flick of his wrist, he brought out his bullwhip. A tool designed for handling livestock.

'I will not allow you to corrupt 1. Or any of my brood.' He cracked the whip towards me. 'You may not be a performer yet, 40, but you will be. Get back to your keeper.'

'No.'

'Neither of us are going.' A fresh surge of determination crossed Julian's face. 'We're not leaving Liss.'

The Overseer lashed out. Julian staggered. Blood wept from a fresh wound on his cheek. 'You're one of mine now, boy, and you'd better remember it.' I planted my feet shoulder width apart. The grin flashed in my direction. 'There's really no need for this, 40. I will look after 1.'

'You can't make me leave. I'm in the keeping of Arcturus.' I stood my ground. 'I'd pay to see you explain to him why you hit me.'

'I don't intend to hit you, walker. I intend to *herd* you.'

The whip came hissing towards me again. Julian threw a punch at him, sending the blow awry. This was the bone-grubbers all over again. This time we would win.

A wildness rose inside me. I ran at the Overseer. My fist hit his jaw, and his head snapped around. Julian kicked his legs out from under him. His hand loosened around the whip. I tried to grab it, but he held on. His teeth bared at me: half-grin, half-snarl. Julian locked an arm around his neck. I wrested the whip from his hand, raised my hand to strike – only to have the whip snatched away from me. A boot crashed into my stomach, knocking me into the wall.

Suhail. I should have known. Wherever the Overseer went, his superior was never too far behind. Just like on the streets: the muscle and the boss. 'Thought I might find you here, runt.' He grabbed me by the hair. 'Causing trouble again, are we?'

I spat at him. He hit me so hard I saw stars. 'I don't care *who* your keeper is, little mongrel. The concubine doesn't frighten me. The only reason I'm not slitting your throat is because the blood-sovereign has called for you.'

'Bet she'd love to hear you call him "concubine", Suhail,' I forced out. 'Shall I tell her?'

'Tell her what you like. The word of a human means less than the incoherent salivation of a dog.'

He hauled me over his shoulder. I struggled and screamed, but I didn't want to risk using my spirit. The Overseer cut the side of his hand into Julian's head, knocking him to the ground. The last thing I saw was Julian and Liss, both at the mercy of a man I could no longer fight.

The Blossom

The Residence of the Suzerain seemed much colder and darker than it had at the oration. I was alone with Suhail, and I would probably be just as alone with Nashira. Little spasms started to run up and down my legs.

Suhail did not take me to the oration room, nor to the chapel. Instead I was dragged through the corridors and pushed into a high-ceilinged room with round-headed windows. It was lit by an iron chandelier, decked with candles, and a massive fireplace. Its light played across the ceiling, casting shadows on the ribbed plaster vaulting.

At the centre of the room was a long dining table. And at the head of the table, seated in an upholstered red chair, was Nashira Sargas. She wore a black dress with a high collar: sculptural, geometric in design.

'Good evening, 40.'

I didn't speak. She motioned with her hand.

'Suhail, you may leave us.'

'Yes, blood-sovereign.' Suhail shoved me towards her. 'Until next time,' he breathed in my ear, 'mongrel.'

He stalked back through the doorway. I was left in the gloomy room, facing the woman that wanted to kill me.

'Sit,' she said.

I thought about taking the chair at the furthest end of the table – a good twelve feet away – but she indicated the one nearest to hers, on her left side, the side farthest from the fireplace. I walked around and lowered myself into the chair, my head pounding with every movement. Suhail hadn't held back one bit on that last punch.

Nashira didn't take her eyes off me. Green, like absinthe. I wondered whom she'd fed on tonight.

'You are bleeding.'

A serviette lay by the cutlery, clasped by a heavy gold ring. I dabbed my swollen lip with it, spotting the ivory linen with blood. I folded it, hiding the stain, and placed it on my lap.

'I suppose you must be frightened,' Nashira said.

'No.'

I should be. I was. This woman controlled everything. It was her name that was whispered in the shadows, her command that ended lives. Her fallen angels drifted nearby, never too far from her aura.

The silence grew. I didn't know whether or not to look at her. In the corner of my eye, something caught the firelight – a bell jar. It stood in the very centre of the table. Beneath the glass was a wilted flower, the petals brown and shrivelled, propped up by a delicate wire stand. Whatever kind of flower it had been in life, it was unrecognisable in death. I couldn't think why she would have a dead flower in the middle of her dinner table – but then, this *was* Nashira. She kept a lot of dead things hanging around.

She noticed my interest.

'Some things are better off dead,' she said. 'Don't you agree?'

I couldn't take my eyes off the flower. And I wasn't sure, but I thought my sixth sense trembled.

'Yes,' I said.

Nashira looked up. There were lines of plaster faces above the windows, at least fifty of them on each of the longest walls. I studied the nearest one a little more closely, drawn to it. It was a relaxed, feminine face with a soft smile. The woman looked as peaceful as if she was asleep.

A heavy sickening swelled in my gut. It was *L'Inconnue de la Seine*, the famous French death mask. Jax had a replica in the den. He said the woman was beautiful, that she'd been a bohemian obsession in the late nineteenth century. Eliza had made him cover it with a sheet, much to his distaste. She said it gave her the creeps.

I looked slowly around the room. All of the faces – the people – they were *death masks*. I only just stopped myself gagging. Nashira didn't just collect voyant spirits; she collected their faces, too.

Seb. What if Seb was up there? I forced myself to look down but my stomach roiled.

'You seem unwell,' Nashira said.

'I'm fine.'

'I am pleased to hear it. I would hate for you to fall ill at this crucial stage of your time in Sheol I.' She traced her dinner knife with a gloved finger, still looking at me. 'My red-jackets will join us in a few minutes, but I wished to speak to you first. A little "heart-to-heart".'

It fascinated me that she thought she had a heart.

'The blood-consort has kept me informed of your development. He tells me he has tried his utmost to bring out your gift,' she said, 'but you have failed to achieve full possession of a dreamscape – even an animal dreamscape. Is this true?'

She didn't know. 'It's true,' I said.

'A pity. Yet you faced one of the Emim and survived – even

267

wounded the creature. For that reason, Arcturus believes you should be made a red-jacket.'

I didn't know what to say. For whatever reason, Warden hadn't told her about the butterfly. Or the deer. That meant he didn't want her to know about my abilities – but he *did* want me to be a red-jacket. What was he playing at this time?

'How quiet you are,' Nashira observed. Her eyes were glacial. 'You were not quite so timid at the oration.'

'I was told I should only speak when required.'

'You are required now.'

I wanted to tell her where to stick her requirements. I'd been insolent with Warden; I shouldn't think twice about doing the same to her – but her hand still lay on the knife, and her fixed gaze held no qualms. Finally, trying to sound suitably abased, I said: 'I'm happy the blood-consort thinks me worthy of a red tunic. I've tried my best in my tests.'

'No doubt. But let us not be complacent.' She sat back in her chair. 'I have some questions for you. Before your inaugural feast.'

'Inaugural?'

'Yes. Congratulations, 40. You are a red-jacket now. You must be introduced to your new associates, all of whom are loyal to me. Even above their own keepers.'

Blood pounded in my ears. Red-jacket. Bone-grubber. I'd reached the highest echelons of Sheol I, the inner circle of Nashira Sargas.

'I wish to speak to you about Arcturus.' Nashira looked into the fire. 'You have been keeping quarters with him.'

'I have my own room. On the upper floor.'

'Does he ever ask you to come out of it?'

'Only for training.'

'Nothing else at all? Perhaps some light conversation?'

'He has no interest in talking to me,' I said. 'What could I say that would be of any concern to the blood-consort?'

'An excellent point.'

I bit my tongue. She had no idea how much I interested him, how much he'd taught me under her nose.

'I imagine you have explored his quarters. Is there anything in the Founder's Tower that troubles you? Anything out of the ordinary?'

'He has some plant extracts I don't recognise.'

'Flowers.'

When I nodded, she took something from the table. A brooch, badly tarnished by the years, shaped just like the flower on his snuff box. 'Have you ever seen this symbol in the Founder's Tower?'

'No.'

'You seem very sure.'

'I am sure. I've never seen it.'

She looked straight at me, into my eyes. I tried to hold her gaze.

A door closed in the distance. A line of red-jackets walked into the room, escorted by a male Reph I didn't recognise. 'Welcome, my friends.' Nashira beckoned them. 'Please, sit.'

The Reph pressed a fist to his chest and left the room. I scanned the human faces. Twenty bone-grubbers, each well-fed and clean as a whistle. They must come in groups. The veterans from Bone Season XIX were at the front. Kathryn was there, as were 16 and 17. At the back of the line was Carl, clad in a red tunic, his hair combed and parted. He stared at me with wide, reproachful eyes. He must never have seen a pink-jacket at the blood-sovereign's table.

They all took their seats. Carl was forced to sit in the only available chair – the one opposite me. David sat down a few places away. There was a fresh cut on his head, sealed with a row of steri-strips. He looked up at the death masks with raised eyebrows.

'I am pleased you could all join me tonight. Thanks to your continued efforts, there have been no notable Emite attacks this week.' Nashira looked at each of them in turn. 'Having said that, we must not forget the constant threat of the creatures. There is no cure for their brutality, and – thanks to the broken threshold – no way in which to imprison them in the Netherworld. You are all that stands between the hunters and their prey.'

They nodded. They all believed it. Well, maybe not David. He was looking at one mask with a slight smile.

I caught Kathryn's eye across the table. A massive bruise wept down one side of her face. 16 and 17 didn't even glance at me. Good. If they looked at me I might not be able to stop myself chucking a dinner knife at them. Liss was still outside, dying, all because of them.

'22' – Nashira turned to the grubber on her right – 'how is 11? I understand he is still at Oriel.'

The young man cleared his throat. 'He's a little better, blood-sovereign. No sign of infection.'

'His bravery has not gone unnoticed.'

'He'll be honoured to hear it, blood-sovereign.'

Yes, blood-sovereign. No, blood-sovereign. Rephs did love a good ego-stroke.

Nashira clapped her hands again. Four amaurotics came through a small door, each carrying a platter and the overpowering smell of herbs. Michael was among them, but he didn't meet my eye. Working quickly, they laid a magnificent spread on the table, all around the bell jar. One poured chilled white wine into our glasses. A lump blocked my throat. The platters were laden with food. Beautifully cut chicken, tender and succulent, with crispy golden skin; stuffing with sage and onion; thick, sweet-smelling gravy; cranberry sauce; steamed vegetables and roast potatoes and plump sausages wrapped in bacon – a feast fit for the Inquisitor. When Nashira nodded, the bone-grubbers tucked straight in. They ate quickly, but without the feral urgency of starvation.

My gut ached. I wanted to eat. But then I thought of the harlies, living on grease and hard bread in their hovels. So much food in here, and so little out there. Nashira noticed my reservation.

'Eat.'

It was an order. I put a few slices of chicken and some vegetables on my plate. Carl gulped down his wine like it was water. 'Watch it, 1,' said one of the girls. 'You don't want to be sick again.'

The rest of them laughed. Carl grinned. 'Come on, that was just once. I was still a pink.'

'Yeah, come on, leave off 1. He deserves the wine.' 22 gave him a friendly punch on the arm. 'He's still a rookie. Besides, we all had a tough time with our first Buzzer.'

There were murmurs of assent. 'I passed out,' the same girl admitted. A selfless display of solidarity. 'The first time I saw one, I mean.'

Carl smiled. 'But you're great with spirits, 6.'

'Thanks.'

I watched their camaraderie in silence. It was nauseating, but they weren't acting. Carl didn't just like being a red-jacket; it was more than that – he belonged in this strange new world. I could empathise, in a way. It was how I'd felt when I first started working for Jaxon. Maybe Carl had never found a place in the syndicate.

Nashira watched them. She must take pleasure in this weekly charade. Stupid, indoctrinated humans, laughing about the trials she'd put them through – all under her thumb, eating her food. How powerful she must feel. How self-satisfied.

'You're still a pink.' A high-pitched voice came to my attention. 'Have *you* fought a Buzzer?'

I glanced up. They were all looking at me.

'Yesterday night,' I said.

'I haven't seen you before.' 22 raised his dense eyebrows. 'Whose battalion do you fight in?'

'I'm not part of a battalion.' I was enjoying this.

'You must be,' another boy said. 'You're a pink. Which other humans are in your residence? Who's your keeper?'

'My keeper only has one human.' I gave 22 a quick smile. 'You might have seen him around. He's the blood-consort.'

The silence stretched on for what seemed like hours. I took a sip of wine. The unfamiliar alcohol felt sharp my tongue.

'It is well that the blood-consort has chosen such a worthy human tenant as 40,' Nashira said, with a faint laugh. Her laugh was disconcerting, like hearing a bell that had struck the wrong note. 'She was able to fight the Buzzer alone, without her keeper.'

More silence. I guessed none of them had ever been into the woods without a Reph escort, let alone tried to fight a Buzzer single-handed. 30 took the opportunity to voice exactly what I was thinking: 'You mean *he* doesn't fight the Emim, blood-sovereign?'

'The blood-consort is forbidden from engaging with the Emim. As my future mate, it would be inappropriate for him to do the work of red-jackets.'

'Of course, blood-sovereign.'

Nashira was looking at me, I could sense it. I carried on eating my potatoes.

Warden *did* fight the Emim. I'd cleaned his wounds myself. He'd gone against Nashira, and she had no idea – or if she did, it was just suspicion.

For several minutes, only the clink of cutlery disturbed the silence. I ate my vegetables and gravy, still thinking of Warden's secret dealings with the Emim. He'd never had to risk his life, yet he'd *chosen* to go out and fight them. There must be a reason.

The red-jackets talked in low voices. They asked each other about their residences, marvelling at the beauty of the old buildings. Sometimes they slighted the harlies ('Cowards, really, even the nice ones'). Kathryn toyed with her food, flinching if the Rookery was mentioned. 30 was still pink-faced, while Carl chewed with excessive force, alternating mouthfuls with his second glass of wine. Only when all the plates were clean did the amaurotics return to clear the table, leaving us with three dessert platters. Nashira waited for the red-jackets to serve themselves before she spoke again.

'Now you are fed and watered, my friends, let us have a little entertainment.'

Carl wiped the treacle from his mouth with his serviette. A troupe of harlies filed into the room. Among them was a whisperer. When Nashira nodded, he raised his violin to his shoulder and played a soft, lively tune. The others began to perform graceful acrobatics.

'To business, then,' Nashira said. She didn't even look at the performance. 'If any of you have ever conversed with the Overseer, you may know what he does to earn his keep. He is my procurer for the Bone Seasons. For the last few decades, I have been attempting to procure valuable clairvoyants from the crime syndicate of Scion London. No doubt many of you are aware of it; some of you may even have been part of it.'

30 and 18 both shifted in their seats. I didn't recognise either of them from the syndicate, but my work had been limited to I-4 and occasionally, I-1 and I-5. There were thirty-three other sections they could have come from. Carl was open-mouthed.

Nobody looked at the performers. They had their art honed to perfection, and not one person cared.

'Sheol I seeks *quality*, not merely quantity.' Nashira ignored the lowered gazes of half her audience. 'For the last few decades I have noticed a steady drop in diversity among the clairvoyants we capture. All of your skills are respected and valued by the Rephaim, but there are many talents we still require to enrich this colony. We must all learn from each other. It would not do to simply take in card-readers and palmists.

'XX-59-40 is the kind of clairvoyant we now seek. She is our very first dreamwalker. We also require sibyls and berserkers, binders and summoners, and one or two more oracles – any breeds of clairvoyant that might bring fresh insight to our ranks.'

Kathryn looked at me with her bruised eyes. Now she knew for certain that I wasn't a fury.

'I think we could all learn a lot from 40,' David said, raising his glass. 'I'm willing.'

'An excellent attitude, 12. And we do intend to learn a great deal from 40,' Nashira said, turning her gaze on me. 'Which is why I will be sending her on an external assignment tomorrow.'

The veterans exchanged glances. Carl turned red as the strawberry charlotte. 'I will also be sending XX-59-1. And you, 12,' Nashira continued. Now Carl looked elated. David smiled into his glass. 'You will go with one of your seniors from Bone Season XIX, who will keep an eye on your performance. 30, I presume I can count on you to do this.'

30 nodded. 'I'd be honoured, blood-sovereign.'

'Good.'

Carl was on the edge of his seat. 'What will the assignment involve, blood-sovereign?'

'We have a delicate situation to resolve. As 1 and 12 are aware, I have been asking most of the white-jackets to scry for the whereabouts of a group called the Seven Seals. They are part of the clairvoyant crime syndicate.'

I didn't dare look up.

'The Seven Seals are known to be in possession of several rare clairvoyant types, including an oracle and a binder. In fact, the so-called "White Binder" is the key player of the group. From recent scrying attempts, we have deduced that they will be meeting in London the day after tomorrow. The place is called Trafalgar Square, within I Cohort, and the meeting will be at one o'clock in the morning.'

The detail they'd accumulated was incredible. But with that many voyants being used to scry at once, focusing all their energies on one section of the æther, I shouldn't have been surprised. It would produce a similar effect to a séance.

'Do any of you know anything about the Seven Seals?' When no one replied, Nashira looked at me. '40. You must have been involved in the syndicate. If you were not, you would not have remained hidden in London for as long as you did.' Her eyes played no games. 'Tell me what you know.'

I cleared my throat.

'The gangs are very secretive,' I said. 'There's gossip, but—'

'Gossip,' she repeated.

'Rumours,' I clarified. 'Hearsay.'

'Elaborate.'

'We all know their false names.'

'And what might those be?'

'The White Binder, the Red Vision, the Black Diamond, the Pale Dreamer, the Martyred Muse, the Chained Fury and the Silent Bell.'

'I knew most of those names. Not the Pale Dreamer.' Great. 'That suggests to me that there is another dreamwalker. Isn't that a coincidence?' Her fingers tapped the table. 'Do you know where they are based?'

I couldn't deny it. She'd seen my ID card.

'Yes,' I said. 'In I-4. I work there.'

'Is it not unusual for two dreamwalkers to live so close to one another? Surely they would have employed you, too.'

'They didn't know. I kept my head down,' I said. 'The Dreamer is the mollisher of I-4, the Binder's protégée. She would have had me killed if she thought she had a rival. The dominant gangs don't like competition.'

She was toying with me, I was sure of it. Nashira wasn't stupid. She must have put it all together: the pamphlet, the Pale Dreamer, the Seven Seals working in I-4. She knew exactly who I was.

'If the Pale Dreamer *is* a dreamwalker, then the White Binder may well be hiding some of the most coveted clairvoyants in the citadel,' she said. 'It is rare that we have an opportunity to add such precious jewels to our crown. Your competence on this mission is vital, 40. If anyone is going to recognise the dreamwalker from the Seven Seals, it is another dreamwalker.'

'Yes, blood-sovereign,' I said, my throat tight, 'but – why are the Seven Seals meeting at that time?'

'As I said, 40, this is a delicate situation. It seems that a handful of clairvoyants in Ireland are attempting to make contact with the London syndicate. An Irish fugitive named Antoinette Carter is their leader. The Seven Seals will be meeting her.'

So Jax had pulled it out of the bag. I wondered how Antoinette had wormed her way into the citadel. It was nigh-on impossible to cross the Irish Sea. Voyants had tried to leave the country before, mostly heading for America, but few made it. You couldn't cross the ocean in a dinghy. Even if anyone *had* succeeded, Scion would never have let us hear of it.

'It is imperative that an analogous crime syndicate does not form in Dublin. Consequently, this meeting must be stopped. Your aim is to capture Antoinette Carter. I believe she, too, may be a rare type of clairvoyant, and I intend to find out exactly what power she hides. The second aim is to apprehend the Seven Seals. The White Binder is a critical target.'

Jaxon. My mime-lord.

'You will be supervised by the blood-consort and his cousin. I expect results. I will hold you all responsible if Carter is allowed to return to Ireland.' Nashira looked at each of us: 30, David, Carl and I. 'Is that understood?'

'Yes, blood-sovereign,' 30 and Carl said. David swilled his wine around the glass.

I said nothing.

'Your life here is about to change, 40. You will be able to use your gift, and to use it well, on this assignment. I expect you to show gratitude for the long hours Arcturus has poured into your training.' Nashira looked away from the fire, into my eyes. 'You have great potential. If you do not attempt to reach that potential, I shall see to it that you never walk the sheltered halls of Magdalen again. You can rot outside with the rest of the fools.'

There was no emotion in her gaze, but there was hunger. Nashira Sargas was losing her patience.

A Little World

The fifth and six members of our group were found in early 2057, the year after I joined.

It was during a particularly vicious heatwave that they arrived. One of Jaxon's couriers reported two new clairvoyants in I-4. The pair had arrived as part of a tourist party for the annual summer conference at the University, which was always a great success. Eager young tourists were brought in by the hundreds from non-Scion countries, ready to be sent back as advocates for anti-clairvoyant policies. Such programmes had already found support in some parts of America, where opinions over Scion had been divided for decades. The well-meaning courier had spied two auras and run straight to his mime-lord, only to find out that the newcomers weren't permanent residents of I-4. They had no idea that the syndicate existed. They might not even know they were voyant.

The courier had reported that one of the two tourists – a young woman – was almost certainly a whisperer. Jax was unimpressed. Whisperers, he told me, were a kind of sensor – privy to the workings of the æther, the smells and sounds and rhythms of spirits.

They could hear their voices and vibrations, even use them to play instruments. 'A pretty gift,' he said, 'but by no means groundbreaking.' Sensors were rarer than mediums, but not by much. The fourth order of clairvoyance. Still, there weren't many of them in the citadel, and Jaxon did like oddities.

It was the other half of the pair that interested him. The courier had reported an unusual aura, caught between orange and red. The aura of a fury.

Jax had been scouring the streets for a fury for years, but this was his first hopeful case. He couldn't believe his luck. He had a vision, a project. Jaxon Hall didn't just want a gang – oh, no. He wanted a box of jewels, the *crème de la crème* of voyant society. He wanted the Unnatural Assembly to envy him above all other mime-lords.

'I'll convince them to stay,' he'd said, pointing his cane at me. 'Just you wait, my mollisher.'

'They have lives in their country, Jax. Families.' I wasn't convinced. 'Don't you think they'll need time to consider it?'

'No time for that, my dear. Once they leave, I'll never get them back again. They *must* stay.'

'In your dreams.'

'I don't dream. But shall we have a wager?' He extended a hand. 'If you lose, you do two assignments with no pay. And polish my antique mirror.'

'And if I win?'

'I'll pay you double for the same assignments. And you won't have to polish my antique mirror.'

I shook his hand.

Jaxon had the gift of the gab. I knew exactly what my father would have said about him: 'Now there's a man who's kissed the Blarney Stone.' There was something about Jaxon that made you want to please him, to see that wild gleam leap to his eye. He knew he'd get the pair to stay. Having located their hotel and paid a busker to get their names, he sent them an invitation to a 'special event' at a fashionable coffeehouse in Covent Garden. I delivered it to the concierge myself, in an envelope addressed to Miss Nadine L. Arnett and Mr Ezekiel Sáenz.

They sent their details back to us. Half-siblings. Both residents of Boston, the gleaming capital of Massachusetts. On the day of the interview, Jaxon kept us updated by email.

Fabulous. Oh, this is fabulous.

She is most definitely a hisser. Very eloquent. Fantastically rude, too.

The brother intrigues me. Can't put a finger on his aura. Annoying.

Nick, Eliza and I waited for another hour before the golden words came in.

They're staying. Paige, the mirror requires elbow grease.

That was the last time I bet against Jaxon Hall.

Two days passed. While Eliza made room in the den for the newcomers, I walked with Nick to Gower Street to collect them. The idea was that they would just disappear off the radar, as if they'd been abducted and killed. We would leave clues: some blood-ied clothes, a hair or two. Scion would love it. They could use it to advertise more unnatural crimes – but most importantly, they wouldn't come after the missing siblings.

'You really think Jax convinced them to stay?' I said as we walked.

'You know what he's like. Jax could convince you to jump off a cliff if you listened to him long enough.'

'But they must have families. And Nadine is a student.'

'They might not have done well over there, *sötnos*. At least voyants

280

can learn what they are in Scion. Over there, they must just think they're crazy.' He put on his sunglasses. 'In that way, Scion is a blessing.'

He was right, in a sense. There was no official policy on clairvoyants outside Scion; they had no legal recognition, no minority status – they only appeared in fiction. Still, that had to be better than being systematically hunted and killed, like we were. I couldn't work out why they'd stay.

They were waiting outside the University. Nick raised a hand to the nearest of the two.

'Hi. Zeke?' The stranger nodded. 'I'm Nick.'

'Paige,' I said.

Zeke's eyes were like black tea, set in a thin, restive face. He must have been in his twenties, slim for his height, with brittle wrists and skin used to the sun.

'You're with Jaxon Hall, right?' His voice carried an unfamiliar accent. He used his free hand to wipe the sweat from his brow, giving me a glimpse of a vertical scar.

'Yes, but don't say his name again. The SVD could be anywhere.' Nick smiled. 'And you must be Nadine.'

He was looking at the whisperer. She had her brother's eyes and restless features, but that was where the similarities ended. Her hair was dyed red, cut as if with a ruler. Scion citadels tended to use the fashion and slang of the decade they were established; everyone in SciLo wore neutral threads, Victorian style – but Nadine's yellow shirt, jeans and stilettos screamed 'tourist' and 'different'. 'Last I checked,' she said.

Nick narrowed his eyes a little at Zeke. I was struggling to classify his aura, too. Seeing it, Nadine moved closer to her brother.

'What?'

'Nothing. Sorry,' Nick said. He glanced over their heads, watching the University, before he looked at each of them in turn. 'We have to be quick. I take it you've both thought about this, because once you walk away from this building, there's no going back.'

Zeke looked at his sister. She looked at her shoes, arms crossed. 'We're sure,' he said. 'We've made our choice.'

'Then let's go.'

At the end of the street, the four of us piled into a buck cab. Nadine dug around in her bag and took out a pair of headphones. Without another word, she snapped them on and closed her eyes. Her lips seemed to be trembling.

'Monmouth Street, please,' Nick said to the driver.

The cab trundled off. Fortunately for us, buck cabs were unlicensed. They made plenty of push off the backs of their clairvoyant clientele.

The place in Monmouth Street was where Jax lived: a three-storey maisonette above a small boutique. I often stayed overnight, telling my father I was staying with friends. It wasn't exactly a lie. For months I'd learned the ropes of clairvoyant society: the structure of the gangs, the names of their leaders, the etiquette and enmity between the sections. Now Jaxon was testing my gift, teaching me how to be one of them.

A few weeks after starting my new job, I'd been able to consciously crack my spirit out of place. I'd immediately stopped breathing. That was when Jax and Eliza had panicked, thinking they'd killed me. Nick, always the medic, had revived me with a syringe of adrenalin to the heart, and even though my chest had hurt for a week, I was proud as anything. The four of us had gone to Chateline's to celebrate, and Jax had ordered life support for next time.

I fitted with these people. They understood the strangeness of my world, a world I was only just beginning to discover. We'd created a little world in Seven Dials, a world of crime and colour. Now there was a stranger in our midst. Possibly two, if Nadine ended up being interesting.

I felt for their dreamscapes. Nadine's was nothing unusual, but

Zeke's – well, his *was* interesting. A dark, heavy presence in the æther.

'So, Zeke,' Nick said, 'where are you from?'

Zeke looked up.

'I was born in Mexico,' he said, 'but I live with Nadine now.'

He gave no further explanation. I glanced over my shoulder. 'Have you been to a Scion citadel before?'

'No. I wasn't sure if it was a good idea.'

'But you came.'

'We just wanted to get away for a while. Nadine's college was offering places on the conference. I was curious about Scion.' He looked down at his hands. 'I'm glad we decided to come. We've felt different for years, but – well, Mr Hall told us why.'

Nick looked intrigued. 'What's the official stance on clairvoyance in the States?'

'They're calling it ESP – extrasensory perception. All they say is that it's a recognised illness under Scion law, and that the CDC is investigating it. They don't want to commit to any stance on it. I don't think they ever will.'

I wanted to ask about their families, but something told me to save it for later. 'Jaxon's so pleased you're joining us.' Nick offered a smile. 'I hope you'll like it here.'

'You'll get used to it,' I said. 'I hated it when I arrived. It got better when Jaxon hired me. The syndicate will take care of you.'

Zeke looked up. 'You're not English?'

'Irish.'

'I didn't think many Irish people escaped the Molly Riots.'

'I managed.'

'It was such a tragedy. Irish music is beautiful,' he added. 'Do you know the rioters' song?'

'The one about Molly?'

'No, the other one. The one they sang at the end of the riots, when they mourned the dead.'

'You mean "An Ember Morning".'

'Yes, that's it.' He paused, then said: 'Would you sing some of it?'

Nick and I laughed at the same time. Zeke went red to the tips of his ears. 'Sorry – that was weird,' he said. 'I'd just love to hear it sung properly. If it doesn't bother you too much. I used to like listening to Nadine, but – well, she doesn't play any more.'

Nick caught my eye. A whisperer that didn't play music. Jaxon would not be happy. 'Paige,' he said gently. I realised Zeke was still looking at me, waiting for an answer.

I didn't know if I could sing the song. Irish music was forbidden in Scion, especially Irish rebel music. I'd had a strong Irish lilt as a child, but out of fear of the spreading hibernophobia in Scion, I'd dropped it when we moved away. Even at eight years old, I could sense the strange looks people gave me when I pronounced something too oddly for their liking. I used to stand in front of the mirror for hours, copying newsreaders, until I'd cultivated a crisp English public-school accent. I was still fairly unpopular – I was called 'Molly Mahoney' for years – but eventually a small group of girls took me in, probably because my father sponsored the school dance.

Perhaps I owed it to my cousin to remember. I looked out of the window and heard myself recite the song.

> *My love, it was an ember morning*
> *When October was a-dawning.*
> *Fire cried on the honey meadow.*
> *Come, ghost of the vale,*
> *I am standing in the ashes, where you roam.*
> *Erin waits to bring you home.*
>
> *My heart, I saw a flame upon the sky*
> *When October's bitter morn was nigh.*

Smoke choked the honey meadow.
Hark, spirit of the south,
I am waiting near the cloven tree,
Now Ireland's heart is broken by the sea.

There were more verses, but I stopped abruptly. I remembered my grandmother singing it for Finn during the memorial service, the one we'd held in secret in the Vale. Just six of us. No body to bury. That was when my father announced his conscription, leaving my grandparents to face Scion's military occupation of the south. Zeke looked grave. After a moment, Nick squeezed my hand.

By the time we reached Monmouth Street the cab was too hot to bear. I pressed some notes into the driver's hand. He handed one back to me.

'For the pretty song,' he said. 'Bless you, love.'

'Thanks.'

But I left it on the seat. I wouldn't accept money for a memory.

I helped Nick unload the suitcases. Nadine stepped out of the cab and pulled off her headphones. She gave the building a withering look. Her bag caught my eye, from a New York designer. That would have to go. American items sold like hotcakes in the Garden. I'd expected her to have an instrument case, but there was nothing. Maybe she wasn't a whisperer. There were at least three other strains of sensor she could be.

I used my keys to open the red door, which bore a gold plaque reading THE LENORMAND AGENCY. To the outside world, we were a respectable arts agency. Inside, we were not so honest.

At the top of the stairs was Jax, dressed to impress: silk waistcoat, stiff white collar, shiny pocket watch and glowing cigar. He had a small glass cup of coffee in his hand. I tried and failed to work out how cigar and coffee could make a compatible pair.

'Zeke, Nadine. Good to see you again.'

Zeke shook his hand. 'And you, Mr Hall.'

'Welcome to Seven Dials. I am, as you know, mime-lord of this territory. And you are now members of my elite coterie.' Jax was looking at Zeke's face, but I knew his focus was on reading his aura. 'I presume you left Gower Street in a surreptitious fashion.'

'No one saw us.' Zeke tensed. 'Is that a – spirit, over there?'

Jax glanced behind him. 'Yes, that's Pieter Claesz, Dutch vanitas painter. One of our more prolific muses. Died in 1660. Pieter, come and meet our new friends.'

'Zeke can do the honours. I'm tired.' Nadine wasn't looking at Pieter, who'd ignored the order. She wasn't sighted. 'I want my own room. I don't share my space,' she said, looking hard at Jax. 'Just so that's settled.'

I waited to see how Jax would react. He didn't have the most expressive face, but his nostrils flared. Not a good sign.

'You will have what you are given,' he said.

Nadine bristled. Sensing a confrontation, Nick put an arm around her shoulders. 'Of course you'll have your own room,' he said, giving me a weary look over her head. We'd have to put Zeke on a couch. 'Eliza's just sorting it. Can I get you something to drink?'

'Yes, you can.' She raised her eyebrows at Jax. 'I see *some* Europeans know how to treat a lady.'

Jaxon looked as if she'd slapped him. Nick led her off to the kitchenette.

'I am not', he said, with gritted teeth, '*European.*'

I couldn't help but smile. 'I'll make sure nobody disturbs you.'

'Thank you, Paige.' He drew himself up. 'Come through to my office, Zeke. We'll talk.'

Zeke went up the next flight of stairs, still staring at Pieter, who was drifting opposite his newest painting. Before I could speak, Jaxon took me by the arm.

'His dreamscape,' he said softly. 'What does it feel like?'

'Dark,' I said, 'and—'

'Excellent. Say no more.'

He almost ran up the stairs, his cigar lodged in the corner of his mouth. I was left with three suitcases and a dead artist for company, and as much as I liked Pieter, he wasn't a man of many words.

I checked the clock. Half eleven. Eliza would be back in a few minutes. I made some fresh coffee and went to sit in the living room, where a John William Waterhouse canvas took pride of place: a dark-haired woman in a flowing red dress, gazing into a crystal ball. Jax had paid a lot of money to a trader for three blacklisted Waterhouse paintings. There was a painting of Edward VII, too, decked in his regalia. I opened the window and settled down to read the new pamphlet Jaxon was working on, *On the Machinations of the Itinerant Dead*. So far it had told me about four kinds of spirit: guardian angel, ghost, muse and psychopomp. I had yet to read about poltergeists.

Eliza wandered in at twelve, away with the spirits as usual. She handed me a carton of noodles from Lisle Street. 'Hey. Don't suppose you persuaded Pieter to paint *Violin and Glass Ball* again?'

Eliza Renton was Jax's trance medium, four years my senior. Her area of expertise was mime-art. Born within striking distance of Bow Bells, she'd worked in an underground theatre in the Cut until she was nineteen, when she responded to Jaxon's pamphlet and got hired. She'd been his main source of income ever since. She had clear olive skin and apple-green eyes, and she kept her golden hair in sugar curls. She was never short of admirers – even spirits loved her – but Jax had a 'no commitment' policy, and she stuck to it.

'Not yet. I think he's got artist's block.' I put the pamphlet to one side. 'Met the newcomers?'

'Just met Nadine. Barely got a "hello".' Eliza flopped down next to me. 'Are we *sure* she's a hisser?'

I cracked open the steaming noodles. 'I didn't see any instruments, but maybe. Have you seen Zeke?'

'I peeked into the office. His aura's a kind of dark orange.'

'So he's a fury.'

'He doesn't *look* like a fury. Doesn't seem like he'd say boo to a ghost.' She balanced her prawn crackers on her knee. 'Well, if Pieter's being pig-headed I officially have a window in my schedule. You want to try and drift again?'

'Not until Jax gets the life support.'

'Sure. I think the ventilator is supposed to arrive on Tuesday. We'll take it easy until then.' She handed me a sketchbook and a pencil. 'I meant to ask – could you draw your dreamscape?'

I took them. 'Draw it?'

'Yeah. Not the flowers or anything – just the basic shape from a bird's-eye view. We're trying to work out the layout of the human dreamscape, but it's tough when none of us can leave our sunlit zones. We think there are at least three zones, but we need you to split up the picture so we can see if our theories work on it. Can you do that?'

A sense of purpose filled me to the brim. I was proving to be really useful within the group. 'Of course,' I said.

Eliza switched on the TV. I set to work on my sketch, drawing a circumpunct surrounded by three rings.

The background music for ScionEye floated from the TV set. Scarlett Burnish was reading the midday news. Eliza pointed at the screen, chewing her crackers. 'Do you think she's actually older than Weaver, but she's had so much surgery she physically can't develop wrinkles?'

'She smiles too much for that.' I continued to sketch. Now I had something that looked more like a bull's eye, with five sections. 'So we've established that this' – I tapped the centre of the circle – 'is the sunlit zone.'

'Right. The sunlit zone is where spirits have to remain for a healthy mind. The silver cord is like a safety net. It stops most voyants from leaving that zone.'

288

'But not me.'

'Exactly. That's your personal quirk. Say the majority of us have an inch of string between our body and our spirit,' she said, measuring with her fingers. 'You have a mile. You can walk to the outer ring of your dreamscape, which means you can sense the æther for much farther than we can. You can also sense other dreamscapes. We only sense spirits and aura, and not from very far away. I can't sense Jaxon and the others now.'

I could. 'But I have a limit.'

'That's why we have to be careful. We don't know your limits yet. You might be able to leave your body, or you might not. We'll have to see.'

I nodded. Jaxon had talked me through his dreamwalker theory several times, but Eliza was a much better teacher. 'What would happen if you tried to leave your sunlit zone? Theoretically.'

'Well, we think that the second zone is where amaurotic "nightmares" take place. The cord sometimes lets you get that far if you're stressed or nervous. Beyond that, you start feeling a massive pull back to the centre. If you walked beyond the twilight zone, you'd start to go insane.'

I raised an eyebrow. 'I really am a freak, aren't I?'

'No, no, Paige. Don't you dare think like that. None of us are freaks. You're a miracle. A jumper.' She took the sketchbook from my hands. 'I'll have Jax check this out once he's finished. He'll love it. Are you staying with your dad tonight? Weren't you going to stay with him on Fridays?'

'I've got to work. Didion thinks he's found William Terriss.'

'Oh, fuck. Say no more.' She turned to face me. 'Hey, you know what they say about the syndicate. Once you get in, you never get out. Sure you're still happy with that?'

'Never been happier.'

Eliza gave me a smile. It was a strange smile, almost wistful.

'Okay,' she said. 'I'll be upstairs. Need to pacify Pieter.' With a jangle of bracelets, she sidled from the room. I started to shade the rings on my sketch, making each one darker than the last.

I was still working a few hours later, when Jax came down from the second floor. It was getting close to sunset. I'd have to head out and meet Didion soon, but I wanted to transfer my sketch to the computer. Jax looked almost feverish.

'Jax?'

'Unreadable,' he breathed. 'O, my lovely, lovely Paige. Our dear Mr Sáenz is an *unreadable*.'

21

A Burnt Ship

I will never forget Warden's face when he saw me in the red tunic. It was the first time I ever saw fear in his eyes.

It only lasted a split second. But I did see it, just for a moment: a trace of insecurity, softer than a candle flame. He watched me as I headed for my room.

'Paige.'

I stopped.

'How was your inaugural feast?'

'Enlightening.' I traced the red anchor on the gilet. 'You were right. She did ask me some questions about you.'

There was a brief, tense silence. Every muscle in his face was rigid. 'And you answered them.' His voice was cold now, colder than I'd ever heard it before. 'What did you tell her? I must know.'

He wouldn't beg. Warden was proud. His jaw was clenched tight, his lips pressed together in a hard line. I wondered what was racing through his mind. Who to warn, where to run. What to do next.

How long could I make him suffer?

'She did say something that caught my attention.' I sat down on the daybed. 'That the blood-consort is forbidden from engaging with the Emim.'

'He is. Strictly forbidden.' His fingers drummed the arm of the chair. 'You told her about the wounds.'

'I didn't tell her anything.'

His expression changed. After a moment, he poured his amaranth from the decanter into a glass. 'Then I owe you my life,' he said.

'You drink a lot of amaranth,' I said. 'Is it for the scars?'

His gaze flicked up. 'Scars.'

'Yes, the scars.'

'I drink amaranth for my own reasons.'

'What reasons?'

'Health reasons. I told you. Old wounds.' He put the glass back on the table. 'You chose not to tell Nashira that I have been disobedient. I am intrigued as to why.'

'Betraying people isn't really my style.' I didn't miss his evasion. Scars and old wounds were the same thing.

'I see.' Warden looked into the empty hearth. 'So you withheld information from Nashira, but you have been given a red tunic.'

'You recommended it.'

'I did, but I did not know if she would agree. I suspect she has ulterior motives.'

'I have an external assignment tomorrow.'

'The citadel,' he conjectured. 'That is surprising.'

'Why?'

'After all the effort she expended to procure you from the citadel, it seems strange that she should send you back.'

'She wants me to lure out one of the London gangs, the Seven Seals. She thinks they have a dreamwalker, that I can recognise one of my own.' I waited, but he didn't react. Did he suspect me? 'We leave tomorrow night with three red-jackets and one other Rephaite.'

'Who?'

'Your cousin.'

'Ah, yes.' He pressed his fingertips together. 'Situla Mesarthim is Nashira's most trusted mercenary. You and I must be cautious around her.'

'So you're going to treat me like your slave again.'

'A necessary, but temporary situation. Situla is no friend of mine. She will have been assigned to keep an eye on me.'

'Why?'

'Past transgressions.' He caught my look. 'It is better that you know nothing about it. All you should know is that I do not kill unless it is absolutely necessary.'

Past transgressions. Old wounds. That could only mean one thing, and we both knew it – but it still didn't guarantee he could be trusted now. Even if he *was* a scarred one.

'I need to get some sleep,' I said. 'We meet at her residence tomorrow at dusk.'

Warden nodded, not looking at me. I picked up my boots and went to my room, leaving him to drink his remedy.

For most of the day, while I should have been asleep, I thought of every possible scenario that could occur when we reached London. The plan, according to the post-dinner briefing, was to wait until Carter reached the base of Nelson's Column, where she would meet with a representative from the Seals. We would surround them, then strike with everything we had. She seemed to think we'd just walk in there, shoot Carter, grab some prisoners and waltz back to Sheol I in time for the day-bell.

I knew better. I knew Jax. He protected his investments. He would never send a lone representative to meet Antoinette – the whole gang would be there. Vigiles staked out the streets during the night, and they knew how to use basic spirit combat. We would also have the public to contend with, and with voyants on the street, we could end up with a very big fight on our hands. A fight in which I would be dressed for one side, but rooting for the other.

I turned over, restless. This was my chance to escape, or at least to get word out. Somehow I had to reach Nick, if he didn't kill me first. Or blind me with his visions. It was my one and only window of opportunity.

I gave up on sleep in the end. I went to the bathroom, splashed my face, and pulled my hair into a psyche knot. It had grown a few inches, down to my shoulders. Rain pounded at the windows. I dressed in the same uniform, the red traitor's tunic, and went down to the chamber. The grandfather clock told me it was close to seven. I took a seat by the fire. When the hour struck, Warden appeared at the door, his hair and clothes drenched with rain.

'It is time.'

I nodded. He let me through the door, locked it, and walked with me down the stone steps.

'I never thanked you,' he said as we went through the cloisters. 'For your silence.'

'Don't thank me yet.'

The streets were silent. Melting hailstones crunched beneath my boots. When we reached the residence, two Rephs escorted us to the library where Nashira was waiting. She and Warden re-enacted their ritual greeting: his hand on her stomach, her lips to his forehead. This time I noticed things. The rigidity of his movements, how he never met her eyes, how she ran her fingers through his hair, not looking at him. It put me in mind of a dog and its mistress.

'I am pleased you could both join us tonight,' she said. Like we had a choice. '40, this is Situla Mesarthim.'

Situla was almost as tall as Warden. You could see the family resemblance: same ash-brown hair, same honey skin, same strong features and deep-set eyes. She nodded to Warden, who was still kneeling.

'Cousin.' Warden inclined his head. Situla turned her eyes on me. Blue. 'XX-59-40, you will treat me as your second keeper this evening. I hope that is understood.'

I nodded. Warden stood and looked down at his fiancée. 'Where are the other humans?'

'Getting ready, of course.' She turned her back on him. 'You ought to do the same, my faithful one.'

His aura clouded over, like a storm was brewing in his dreamscape. He turned and walked towards a heavy set of crimson drapes. An amaurotic girl hurried after him, carrying a bundle of clothes.

'You will be paired with 1,' Nashira said to me. 'The two of you will go with Arcturus. Situla will take 30 and 12.'

David emerged from behind the drapes, wearing black trousers, boots and a lightweight vest of body armour. The sight of him made me start. He looked exactly like the Overseer on the night he shot me.

'Evening, 40,' he said.

I kept my mouth shut. David smiled and shook his head, as if I were an amusing child. An amaurotic approached me. 'Your clothes.'

'Thank you.'

Without looking at David, I took my bundle to the drapes. Behind them was a tent, a dressing room of sorts. I shucked my uniform and donned the new one: first a long-sleeved red shirt, then the armour – marked with the red anchor, like the gilet – and a black jacket with a red band on one sleeve. Next came glovelettes and trousers, both made of a flexible black fabric and sturdy leather boots. I could run, climb, fight in this attire. There was a syringe of adrenalin in the jacket – and a flux gun. For hunting voyants.

Once I was kitted out, I returned to where the other three humans had gathered. Carl gave me a smile.

'Hello, 40.'

'Carl,' I said.

'How are you finding your new tunic?'

'It fits, if that's what you mean.'

'No, I mean, how are you finding being a red-jacket?'

All three of them were staring at me now. 'Great,' I said, after a pause.

Carl nodded. 'It is great. Maybe they were right to give you so many privileges.'

'Or maybe they were wrong,' 30 said, pulling her thick hair from her collar. She was taller than me, wide in the hips and shoulders. 'We'll find out on the streets.'

I took another look at 30. From her aura, I guessed she was probably a soothsayer – but a less common one, maybe a type of cleromancer. Not particularly rare. She must have clawed her way up the ranks.

'Yes,' I said. 'We will.'

She sniffed.

Warden's return had a stunning effect on 30's demeanour. She bobbed a delicate little curtsey, murmuring 'blood-consort'. At her side, Carl swept into a bow. I just stood there with my arms crossed. Warden glanced at his fan club, but didn't acknowledge either of their tributes. Instead he looked across the room – at me. 30 looked chagrined. Poor old 30.

New clothes had transformed my keeper. In place of the old-fashioned Rephaite regalia, he wore the clothes of a wealthy Scion denizen, the sort no clever thief would try to fine-wire.

'You will be taken to I Cohort in two collection vehicles,' Nashira said. 'Traffic will be cleared for you. You are expected to return here before the day-bell rings.'

We four humans nodded. Warden shrugged on his coat and turned towards the door. 'XX-40, XX-1,' he called.

Carl looked like Novembertide had come early. He ran after Warden, shoving his flux gun into his jacket as he went. I was about to follow him when Nashira caught my arm in her gloved hand. I held very still, resisting the urge to pull away.

'I know who you are,' she said, close to my face. 'I know where you come from. If you do not bring back a dreamwalker, I will assume that I am correct, and that *you* are the Pale Dreamer. That realisation will have consequences for us all.' With a look that made me cold, she turned her back on me and walked towards the doors. 'Have a safe journey, XX-59-40.'

Two blacked-out vehicles were waiting on the bridge. They blindfolded all four of us before they locked us in. I sat in the darkness with Carl, listening to the engine. They must have a nagging fear that we'd learn the route out of the colony.

A team of Vigiles had been dispatched to escort us through the borders, but the procedure for letting people out of Sheol I was complicated. The city was a penal colony, and it was just as much hassle as if prisoners were out on parole. We had tracking chips shot under our skin at one of Scion's outer city sub-stations, just in case we tried to make a run for it, and our fingerprints and auras were examined. They took a tube of my blood, leaving a smudge of bruise at the crease of my elbow. Finally we crossed the last border, and we were back in Scion London. Back in the real world.

'You may remove your blindfolds,' Warden said.

I couldn't get rid of mine fast enough.

Oh, my citadel. I traced the glass, the blue lights glowing into my eyes. The car was rolling through White City in II-3, past the mammoth shopping complex. I never thought I'd miss the dirty gunmetal streets, but I did. I missed bidding on spirits and playing tarocchi and climbing up buildings with Nick to watch the sun sink. I wanted to get out of the car and throw myself into London's poisoned heart.

Carl had been jittery for the journey, bouncing his knee and fiddling with his flux gun, but he'd dropped off to sleep on the motorway. He'd told me that 30 used to be called Amelia, and that her keeper was one Elnath Sarin. As I'd guessed, she was a cleromancer, with a particular gift for dice. It took me a while to remember the exact word: *astragalomancer*. I was getting rusty. Jax had once examined me daily on the seven orders of clairvoyance.

I looked again at Carl. His hair needed a wash. From the circles etched under his eyes, I knew he was as tired as I was – but there were no bruises. More betrayals must have earned his safety. As if he sensed me looking, he opened his eyes.

'Don't try and escape.'

He whispered it. When I didn't answer, he shifted up to me.

'They won't let you go. He won't.' He glanced at Warden through the glass screen. 'Sheol is safe for us. Why would you *want* to leave?'

'Because we don't belong there.'

'It's the one place we *do* belong. We can be clairvoyant there. We don't have to hide.'

'You're not an idiot, Carl. You know it's a prison.'

'And the citadel isn't?'

'No. It isn't.'

Carl looked back at his gun. I looked back at the window.

Part of me knew what he meant. Of course the citadel was a prison – Scion kept us locked in there like animals – but we didn't stand by in the citadel and watch other people get beaten up, or let people die on the streets.

I pressed my head against the glass. That wasn't true. Hector did. Jaxon did. Every mime-lord and mime-queen in the citadel did. They only rewarded those who were useful. The rest were thrown out to rot.

But the gang were like my family. I didn't have to bow to anyone in the citadel. I was mollisher of I-4. I had a name.

Soon we were in Marylebone. As Warden looked out at the unfamiliar territory of the citadel, I wondered if he'd been to London before. He must have, if he'd met previous Inquisitors. It chilled me that Rephs had been on the streets at the same time I was. They'd been in the Archon. Even in I-4.

The driver was a silent, robust man in wire-framed spectacles and a suit, with a red silk pocket square and tie. He wore a Ductaphone on his left ear, which beeped every so often. It was morbidly fascinating to see how organised it was. Scion had all its bases covered: nobody could find out about Sheol I. It was a city under lock and key.

Warden motioned for the driver to stop on a street corner. The man nodded and ducked out of the car. When he returned, he was carrying a large paper bag. Warden passed it to me through the hatch. 'Wake him.' He nodded to Carl, who was asleep again.

Inside the bag were two hot cartons from Brekkabox, the citadel's favourite fast food joint. I prodded Carl. 'Rise and shine.'

Carl came round with a jolt. I opened my box and found a breakfast wrap, a serviette and a pot of porridge. I caught Warden's eye in the rear-view mirror, and he gave me the barest nod of acknowledgement. I looked away.

The car passed into Section 4. My section. My scalp prickled with sweat. My father lived only twenty minutes from here, and we were getting close to Seven Dials – too close. I half-expected to receive something from Nick, but there was total silence in the æther. Several hundred dreamscapes pressed against mine, distracting me from meatspace. When I focused on the nearest few, I sensed nothing unusual, no fresh waves of emotion. These people had no inkling of the Rephaim or the penal colony. They didn't care where unnaturals went, just as long as they were out of sight.

Our car stopped in the Strand, where a Vigile was waiting for us. The ones they put on duty all looked pretty much the same: tall, broad-shouldered, typically mediums. I avoided the man's eyes as I stepped from the car, leaving the empty breakfast cartons under the seat.

Warden, being huge and formidable, was not in the least bit nervous. 'Good evening, Vigile.'

'Warden.' The Vigile touched three fingers to his forehead, one at the centre and one above each eye, then raised his hand in a salute. It was an official sign of his clairvoyance, of his third eye. 'Can I confirm you have Carl Dempsey-Brown and Paige Mahoney in your custody?'

'Confirmed.'

'Identification numbers?'

'XX-59-1 and 40 respectively.'

The Gilly made a note of it. I wondered what had made him turn his back on his own kind. A cruel mime-lord, perhaps.

'You two should remember that you are in custody. You are here to assist the Rephaim. You will be sent straight back to Sheol I when your assignment is complete. If either of you attempts to broadcast Sheol I's location, you will be shot. If either of you attempts to make contact with the general public, or with any member of the syndicate, you will be shot. If either of you attempts to harm your keeper, or a Vigile, you will be shot. Do I make myself clear?'

Well, he'd made it pretty damn clear that whatever we did, we were going to be shot. 'We understand,' I said.

But the Vigile wasn't quite finished. He unpacked a silver tube and a pair of latex gloves from his supply belt. Not another needle. 'You first.' He grabbed me by the wrist. 'Open your mouth.'

'What?'

'Open. Your. Mouth.'

I wanted to look at Warden, but I knew from his silence that he had no objections to this procedure. Before I could comply, the

Gilly prised my mouth open. I wanted to bite the bastard. He scraped the plastic nib over my lips, coating them in something cold and bitter.

'Shut it.'

With no other choice, I closed my mouth. When I tried to open it again, I couldn't. My eyes widened. *Shit!*

'Just a spot of dermal adhesive.' The Gilly pulled Carl towards him. 'Wears off after two or three hours. We're not taking any chances, seeing as all you syndies know each other.'

'But I'm not—' Carl started.

'Shut up.'

And at last, Carl was forced to shut up.

'XIX-49-30 isn't glued. Look at her for orders,' the Gilly said. 'Otherwise, stick to your objectives.'

I pushed my tongue against my lips, but they wouldn't budge. This Gilly must love having one over on ex-syndicate members.

Having sealed our mouths, the Gilly saluted Warden before he returned to the stern grey building he'd emerged from. There was a plaque outside: THE SCION CITADEL OF LONDON – NVD COMMAND POST – I COHORT SECTION 4, with a map of the area covered by that post. I could make out a marker for the shopping centre in Covent Garden, the pot under which the black market bubbled. If only I could get there. Maybe I still could.

Carl swallowed. Even though we had been seeing these plaques for years, they were still daunting. I looked up at Warden. 'Situla and her humans will approach the square from the western side,' he said. 'Are you ready?'

I don't know how he expected us to answer. Carl nodded. Warden reached into his jacket and procured two masks.

'Here,' he said, handing one to each of us. 'These will disguise your identities.'

These were no ordinary masks. They had blank, uniform features, with small eyeholes and slots for air below the nose. When I fitted mine to my face, it bonded to my skin. It wouldn't earn a second glance from busy Scion denizens, but it would also stop the gang from recognising me, and with my lips sealed, I couldn't call for help.

How *clever* it all was.

Warden looked at me for a moment before he put his own mask on. Eerie light burned in the eyeholes. For the first time, I was glad I was fighting on his side.

We walked towards Nelson's Column. Like the Dials, the Monument and most other columns, it turned red or green depending on the security situation. Currently it was green, as were the fountains. A team of Gillies was on patrol, stationed at regular intervals down the Strand, probably having been ordered to back us up if necessary. They shot us guarded looks as we passed, but none of them moved. They all carried M4 carbines. The NVD didn't broadcast their true purpose in the city, but everyone knew they were more than police. You didn't approach a night Gilly with a complaint, not like you might an SVD officer. You approached only in dire circumstances, and never if you were voyant. Even amaurotics didn't like to go near them. After all, they were unnaturals.

Carl kept flexing his fingers in his pockets. How could I get out of this without killing any of my gang? There must be some way I could show them who I was. I had to warn them, or they'd join me in the penal colony. I couldn't let Nashira get them.

Trafalgar Square was artificially lit, but it was dark enough for us to remain inconspicuous. Situla, Amelia and David were approaching from the other side. The three of them disappeared behind one of the four bronze lion statues that guarded Nelson's Column. Warden leaned down to my level.

'Carter will arrive soon,' he said, keeping his voice low. 'We must bide our time until she makes contact with the Seal. Do not allow yourselves to be captured under any circumstances.' Carl nodded.

'Once the area is clear, the NVD will escort us back to the vehicle. You will cease and desist if the Seals leave the boundaries of I Cohort.'

I was starting to sweat. Seven Dials was well within I Cohort. If the gang tried to make it back to base, they could find themselves being tailed there.

Big Ben was two minutes from striking. Warden sent Carl to sit on the steps of the column – as a soothsayer, he was the least conspicuous. Once he was settled, Warden led me past the fountain to one of the statue plinths. There were seven of them, one for each of the people who had facilitated the establishment and continuation of Scion: Palmerston, Salisbury, Asquith, MacDonald, Zettler, Mayfield, Weaver. The seventh plinth always bore the likeness of the ruling Inquisitor, along with his or her motto.

Warden stopped behind a statue. He studied my masked face. 'Forgive me,' he said. 'I did not know you would be silenced.'

I gave no sign that I'd heard him. I had to concentrate on breathing through my nose.

'Do not look yet. Carter is waiting at the base of the column, as planned.'

I didn't want to do this. I wanted Antoinette to get out of here. I wanted to burst into her dreamscape, to make her run away.

And then I sensed them.

It was them, no doubt about it. They were approaching from all different directions. Jax must have mobilised the entire gang, all six of the remaining Seals. Would he recognise my aura straight away, or would he presume there was just another dreamwalker – a tiny chance – in the vicinity?

'I sense a medium,' Warden said. 'And a whisperer.'

Eliza and Nadine. I looked out at the base of Nelson's Column. And yes, there was Antoinette.

She wore a frock coat and a wide-brimmed black hat. Strands of greying red hair fell past her ears. What little of her face I could see bore crevices that had been airbrushed out of the TV show. Between her fingers was a silver cigarette holder, fitted to a roll of what looked like purple aster. She had some gall. No one smoked ethereal drugs in public.

The idea of doing battle with Toni Carter was enough to make me sick with nerves. On her show, she would often have a violent seizure prior to making a prediction, a perk that had blown the ratings through the roof. I could only imagine how she might fight. Nick denounced the idea that she was an oracle; oracles never lost control like that.

Nadine came first. She wore a pinstriped blazer, loosely buttoned. No doubt it hid a set of irons. The others all appeared, one by one, though they gave no hint that they knew one another. Only their auras linked them. When I caught sight of Nick, I thought I would burst: into tears, into laughter, into song. He was heavily disguised. Had to be, given his glittering Scion career. His hair was covered by a dark wig and a hat, and he wore tinted glasses. A few feet away, Jax was tapping his cane. At my side, Warden remained silent. His eyes darkened when one of his targets edged closer to Antoinette. Eliza had been chosen to go forward. Close behind her was Dani, her mouth set in a grim line. She was disguised, too.

Had it been me, I would have made initial contact with Antoinette with one of my 'nudges' to check the coast was clear, but Eliza had no such power. The æther screwed with her, not the other way around. She lifted four fingers of her right hand, three of her left, and ran them through her hair, as if she was checking for knots. Antoinette understood. She stepped towards Eliza and extended a hand. Eliza took it.

Situla struck first. Faster than I could register, she was on top of Antoinette, strangling her. Warden made towards Zeke, just as Carl sent a nearby spirit hurtling towards Eliza. It must have been Nelson, the most powerful spirit in the square: Eliza crumpled against one of the lions, clutching her chest, and cried out in a strangled voice: 'I cannot command winds and weather, nor can I command myself in death!' Amelia flew out next, only to be tackled by an enraged Nick, who had seen Eliza's pain before anything else. David took Jax; or *tried* to take Jax – Dani swung her fist at him, knocking a spurt of blood from his mouth. In less than ten seconds, I was the only one who had not yet come out to fight.

That suited me. It did not suit Jaxon.

He saw me at once, another masked enemy. He drew up a spool of six and hurled it in my direction. I had to move, and fast – the spirits of Trafalgar could pose a serious threat. I sent a flux dart at him, but aimed well above his head. Jax still ducked, sending the spool scattering all over the place. *Give it up*, I thought. *Don't make me attack you.*

But Jaxon never gave up. He was livid. We'd spoiled his plans. He lunged at me, wielding his cane. I tried to land a kick to his stomach, to push him back, but I didn't do it hard enough. He grabbed my ankle, and with a flex of his arms, he flipped me over. Pain. *Move, move.*

Not fast enough. Jax drove his steel-capped boot into my side, kicking me onto my back. His knee crashed down on my chest. His fist flew – a blur – then something solid struck the unprotected part of my face. Knuckleduster. And again, in the ribs. Something cracked, and it hurt. And again. I swung up my arm to block a fourth punch. His eyes were gleaming, hot with bloodlust. Jax was going to kill me.

I had no choice. With my body pinned, I used my spirit.

He wasn't expecting that. He wasn't concentrating on my aura. The thump against his dreamscape made him fall. His cane clattered to the ground. I clawed myself to my feet. My face was pounding, my ribs seared, and my right eye wasn't working as it should be. I grasped my knees, dragging air through my nose. I'd never known Jax could be so brutal.

A screech caught my attention. Near one of the fountains, Nadine had abandoned spirit combat and pinned Amelia to the ground. I pulled out the syringe in my jacket, opened it with bloody fingers, and pushed the needle into my wrist. After a few seconds, the pain dulled to an ache. My vision wouldn't settle, but it wasn't incapacitating. I could still see well out of my left eye.

The red sight of a gun hovered on my chest. They must have snipers in the buildings.

There had to be some way out of this.

With renewed strength, I ran towards the fountain, where Amelia was kicking helplessly. As much as I wanted Nadine to win, I couldn't just watch another human die. I tackled her, taking her down by the waist, straight into the fountain. The water turned red as the security lights changed. Nadine surfaced a half-second after I did. Her teeth were gritted, and the muscles in her neck were straining. I backed away.

'Take that mask off, bitch,' she shouted at me.

I pointed my flux gun at her.

Nadine began to circle me. She opened her coat and took out a knife. She'd always preferred steel to spirits.

I felt my heartbeat everywhere, right down to my fingertips. Nadine rarely missed with a knife, and my body armour would only provide so much protection: if she hit me above the chest, I was dead. David chose that moment to appear. Just as Nadine was about to throw her blade, he hit her dead between the shoulders with a flux dart. Her eyes widened. She tottered, swayed, and folded over the edge of the fountain. David dragged her out of the water and took her head between his hands. We'd been told not to kill, but in the heat of the moment, he seemed to have forgotten. How important could a hisser be?

I didn't pause to think: I threw out my spirit. Zeke would never forgive me if I let his sister die. Time for a quick-fire jump.

I went too far. For the second I was in David's head, I pulled his hands away from Nadine. Another second and I was back in my body, running towards him. I threw my full weight against his side and we both smashed to the ground.

My vision turned black. I'd just possessed David. Only for a heartbeat, but I'd moved his arm.

I had finally possessed a human.

David put his hands to his head. I hadn't been gentle. I struggled to my feet, blinking away a flurry of white stars. Both Antoinette and Situla had vanished.

Leaving Nadine next to David, I ran from the fountain, my clothes drenched. I climbed up onto a lion and surveyed the scene. Both groups had fanned out across the square. Zeke was no fighter, and he'd wisely abandoned ship – *bloody sailor spirits* – when he'd seen Warden coming at him. Having pulled on his balaclava, he was exchanging blows with Amelia. Elsewhere, Warden turned his attention to Nick, who had stunned Carl with a spool. I thought my heart would stop as I watched them. My keeper and my best friend. I dropped back to ground level, gripped by fear. I had to help Nick. Warden could kill him . . .

Then Eliza was there, and she was incensed. Spirits flew at me from every direction. They always sided with mediums. Three French sailors burst into my dreamscape. I stumbled, blinded by their memories: the towering waves, the blast of muskets, fires raging on the deck of the *Achille* – screaming, chaos – then Eliza gave me a shove, and I fell. I thrust up all my mental defences, trying to push out the invaders.

For a moment I was incapacitated. Eliza tried to pin me with her knees. 'Stay in there, guys!'

My dreamscape was flooding. Cannonballs ripped through it.

Burning wood fell past my eyes. Eliza's hands came up to unmask me.

No, no! She couldn't see me. The NVD would shoot her. With a huge effort, I forced out the spirits and kicked her backwards, catching her jaw with my boot. She let out a cry of pain. Guilt flinched in my stomach. I spun around just in time to meet Jax's cane with my flux gun.

'Well, well. A walker in uniform,' he said softly. 'Where did they find you? Where were you hiding?' He leaned close to me, staring into the eyeholes of the mask. 'You can't possibly be my Paige.' The cane forced my arm back. My muscles strained. 'So who are you?'

Before I could do anything, Jax was thrown back by a massive spool, bigger than any a human could make. Warden. I got up, reaching for the gun, but Jax swung blindly with his cane. Instinct jerked my head to the left. Too slow. My ear scalded: a sharp, clean heat. *Blade.* I got a grip on the gun, but a second blow from Jax knocked it out of my hand. The cane blade flashed across my arm, cutting through my jacket and deep into the flesh. A muted scream ripped through my throat. Pain exploded down my arm.

'Come, walker, use your spirit!' Jaxon pointed the blade at me, laughing. 'Use the pain. Leave your wounds behind.'

Amelia threw another spool at Jax. I'd saved her; now she was saving me. Nick returned fire, and Amelia crouched behind a lion. Zeke lay still on the ground. *Don't be dead,* I thought. *Don't let them have got you.*

A flash of red hair. Antoinette was back. Her hat had flown off, and no wonder: she was in a kind of battle trance. Her eyes were wild, her nostrils flared wide, her spirit was a raw blaze. It mocked the blue streetlights of the citadel, the ones designed to soothe the fevered mind. Fists, legs and spirits flew in a volley at Situla, not letting her get a blade in edgeways. Situla hurled a ghost at her. Antoinette danced out of its reach.

And then, with no warning, she took off. Warden spotted her as she parted the screaming people.

'Stop her,' he shouted.

At me. I sprinted after Antoinette. This was my chance to escape.

A Vigile let me past when he saw my uniform, but tackled an amaurotic woman. A man grabbed my jacket – whisperer – but I was running too fast, and he let go. My mind was a streak of pure light. Antoinette was headed straight for the Westminster Archon. She was off the cot to head in that direction, but I didn't care about her motives: she was giving me a priceless opportunity. There was a tube station opposite the Archon. It was always packed out with Underguards, but also with commuters. If I took off my mask and jacket, I could slip past the barriers and disappear into the crowd. The pillars outside would give me shelter from the NVD, and I'd only have to stay on a train for one stop to reach Green Park. I could get to Dials from there. If that didn't work, I'd go for the Thames. I'd swim. I'd do whatever I had to do to escape.

I could do it. I *could* do it.

My legs pumped. The pain in my arm was ferocious, but I couldn't stop. Antoinette's trance seemed to have fuelled her speed. No human being could run like that, not unless she was guided by spirits. I tried to keep their auras in range as I weaved my way through droves of people and cars.

A taxi braked in front of Antoinette. She and Situla split around it, straight into a horde of pedestrians. I took the straightest course: kept running, right up the front of the car and onto the roof, and slid down the other side. Antoinette was through in a flash. Seconds behind her, Situla cut through the human obstacles. They screamed. One of them died. I couldn't stop. If I let up for a moment, Antoinette and Situla would be out of range. Finally, when I thought my lungs would burst, we reached the end of Whitehall.

This was the centre of the citadel, according to the map: I

Cohort, Section 1. Voyants avoided this area like the plague. I looked up at the Westminster Archon, my fingers dripping blood. The clock face burned red, the hands and digits black against the light. This was where Frank Weaver's puppets danced. Had I been in a less life-threatening situation, I would have liked to leave some choice graffiti on the walls.

I ran towards the Starch. Situla was just ahead of me. When she reached the bridge, Antoinette turned to face her foe. Her skin seemed stretched across her bones, like a thin layer of paint, and her lips were pursed and white.

'You are surrounded, oracle.' Situla stepped towards her. 'Surrender yourself.'

'Do not call me "oracle", creature.' Antoinette raised her hand. 'Stay and find out what I am.'

The air iced over.

Situla was indifferent to the threat; she had nothing to fear from a mere human. She made towards Antoinette. Before she could try anything, she was lifted off her feet and thrown backwards, almost off the bridge. I started. Spirit. A breacher. I reached for the æther, trying to identify it. It was something like a guardian angel, a very old and powerful one.

Archangel. An angel that remained with one family for generations, even after the person they saved had died. They were notoriously difficult to exorcise. The threnody wouldn't banish it for long.

Situla regained her footing. 'Hold still.' She took another step. 'Let us find out what you are.'

She reached for a passing spirit – then another, and another, until she had a trembling spool. Antoinette kept her hand outstretched, but her face contorted when Situla began to feed on her. Her eyes turned a terrible vermilion, almost red. For a moment, I thought Antoinette would fall. A bead of blood slipped from her left eye. Then she cut her arm towards Situla, and the archangel

shot towards her. The spool surged together to meet it. As the
æther burst open, I ran.

Most Gillies were sighted. They'd be distracted by the collision
between the spirits. They wouldn't see me. They couldn't. I *had* to
get back to Dials. I sprinted towards Station I-1A.

Beneath my boots, the bridge shuddered with energy. I didn't
stop. I could see the sign above the station on the other side of the
street. I shed my jacket and my body armour. It would make me
faster, and once I got this damned mask off, I wouldn't look like a
red-jacket. Just a girl in a red shirt. I scanned the buildings, searching
for footholds. If I couldn't get into the station, I'd have to climb my
way out of this. If I could just get onto the rooftops, I'd be safe.

Then I was aware of something else.

Pain.

I didn't stop, but it was suddenly harder to run. It couldn't be a
bad injury. The archangel hadn't come anywhere near me. Its
concern was with Situla, the threat. I must have pulled a muscle.

Then a sticky warmth bloomed below my ribs. When I looked
down, my red shirt was turning a different shade of red, and there
was a small, round hole above my hip.

They'd shot me. Shot me like they'd shot the Irish students.

I had to keep running. I lurched onwards, heading for the street,
where traffic was still racing up from the Embankment. *Come on,
Paige, come on. Run.* Nick could fix me up. I just had to reach Dials. I
could see the station now. Another shot came, but they missed. I
had to get out of range. I forced myself to keep moving, but the
pain was growing and I couldn't put weight on my right side. My
staggering run had turned into a limp. There were pillars outside the
station. If I could just get to them, I could staunch the blood and
disappear.

I ran behind a bus, using it for cover, and caught the first pillar on
the other side of the street. All the strength drained from my bones.

I tried to keep moving, but a sharp pain erupted above my hip. My knees buckled.

How quickly death crept up on me. Like it had been waiting for years. The physical world softened to a haze. Lights flashed past. The sounds of the fight were still close, but they were in the æther, not on the street.

So much for the dreamwalker.

I didn't have much time. They might shoot me again. I dragged myself behind one of the pillars, out of sight of the station entrance, where commuters were trying to work out where all the noise was coming from. I curled against the wall. Blood pumped from the little wound. I clamped my trembling hands over it. My lips strained against their binding.

I wouldn't get to Dials. Even if I got on a train, I'd be arrested on the other side. They wouldn't miss the blood on my hands.

At least I hadn't died in Sheol I. That would have been more than I could bear. Here, at least, Nashira couldn't reach me.

Then there was someone at my side, grabbing my arm. I smelled him first. Camphor.

Nick.

He didn't recognise me. He couldn't. He shoved my chin back, exposing my throat to his penknife. 'You damn traitor.'

Nick. The wound burned. My sleeve was soaked with blood.

'Let's see your face,' Nick said. He was quieter now, regretful. 'Whatever you are, you're a voyant. A jumper. Maybe you'll remember that, when you see the last light.'

He peeled the mask from my face. When he saw me, something broke inside him. 'Paige,' he choked out. 'Paige, oh no – *förlåt mig*—' His hands pressed over my ribcage, trying to stop the blood. 'I'm sorry, I'm so sorry, I thought – Jaxon asked—' Of course. Jaxon had wanted the dreamwalker. Nick had shot me, not Scion. 'What have they done to you?' His voice shook. It broke my heart to see him so devastated. 'You'll be fine, I promise. Paige, look at me. Look at me!'

I was finding it difficult to look at anything. My eyelids were so heavy. I raised my fingers to his shirt. He cupped my head against his chest. 'It's okay, sweetheart. Where did they take you?'

I shook my head. Nick stroked my sweaty hair. It was soothing. I wanted to stay. I didn't want them to take me back to that place.

'Paige, don't you dare close your eyes. Tell me where those bastards took you.'

I shook my head again. There was no way I could tell him, not without my voice.

'Come on, *sötnos*. You have to tell me where it is. So I can find you again, like I did before. Remember?'

I had to tell him. He had to know. I couldn't die without telling him where it was. I had to save the others, the other voyants in the lost city. But now I could see a silhouette, an outline of a man. Not a man.

Rephaite.

My fingers were covered in blood. I reached for the wall and traced the first three letters. Nick looked at it.

'Oxford,' he said. 'They took you to *Oxford*?'

I let my hand fall. The faceless man was moving through the darkness. Nick looked up.

'No.' His muscles tightened. 'I'm taking you home,' he said, starting to lift me. 'I won't let them take you there again.'

He pulled a pistol from his jacket. I wrapped my arm around his neck. I wanted him to try and run, to save me from another poppy field – but he'd die if I let him. We would both die. The shadow would dog our footsteps to the Dials. I tugged at his shirt, shaking my head, but he didn't understand. The shadow fell across our path. Nick gripped the gun tighter, his knuckles white, and he pulled the trigger. Once, twice. I screamed behind sealed lips. *Nick, run!* He couldn't hear, he couldn't know. The gun fell from his hand, and all the blood was drawn from his face. A giant, gloved hand gripped his throat. With the last of my strength, I tried to force it away.

'She comes with me.' It was Warden, and he looked demonic. 'Run, oracle.'

My grip on life was slipping. I heard Nick's heart against my ear, felt his fingers lock across my back. The light ebbed. Death had come.

The Triple Fool

Time became a series of moments, interspersed with blank spots. Sometimes there were lights. Sometimes there were voices. I had the sense that I was in a car for a while, a kind of swaying motion.

I became aware of someone cutting my shirt. I tried to push away the intrusive hands, but my body mutinied. I recognised the thick mist of drugs. Next thing I knew, I was tucked up in Warden's bed, tilted on my left side. My hair was wet. Every single part of my body felt broken.

'Paige?'

The voice came as if from underwater. I made a weak sound: half sob, half rattle. My chest was on fire. So was my arm. *Nick*. I reached out blindly.

'Michael, quickly.' A hand grasped mine. 'Hold on, Paige.'

I must have passed out again. When I woke up, I felt as heavy, woolly and shapeless as a duvet. Most of my right arm was numb. It hurt to breathe, but I could open my mouth. My chest heaved.

I supported myself on my elbow, pulling my body to the left, and ran my tongue over my teeth. All present and correct.

Warden was in his armchair, looking at the gramophone. I wanted to smash the thing. Those voices had no right to be so high-spirited. When Warden saw me move, he stood.

'Paige.'

The sight of him set off a heavy pounding in my chest. I pushed myself against the headboard, remembering his terrible eyes in the dark. 'Did you kill him?' I wiped the sweat from my upper lip. 'Did you – did you kill the oracle?'

'No. He is still alive.'

Slowly, watching my face, he eased me into a sitting position. The movement pulled at an IV in my hand. 'I can't see properly.' My voice was hoarse, but at least I could speak.

'You have a periorbital haematoma.'

'What?'

'Black eye.'

I traced the soft skin at the top of my cheek. Jax really had done me down. The whole right side of my face was swollen.

'So,' I said, 'we're back.'

'You tried to escape.'

'Of course I tried to escape.' I couldn't keep the bitterness from my voice. 'You think I *want* to die here and haunt Nashira for the rest of eternity?' Warden just looked at me. A lump rose in my throat. 'Why didn't you let me go home?'

A faint green stain was fading from his eyes. He must have fed on Eliza. 'There are reasons,' he said.

'Excuses.'

For a long time, he didn't speak. When he did, it wasn't to tell me why he'd dragged me back to this cesspit of a city. 'You have an impressive collection of injuries.' He propped me up with pillows. 'Jaxon Hall is far more ruthless than we had anticipated.'

'Give me the list.'

'Black eye, two cracked ribs, split lip, torn ear, bruising, laceration on the right arm, bullet wound to the torso. I find it incredible that you were able to run to the bridge after the first round of injuries.'

'Adrenalin.' I focused on his face. 'Did you get hit?'

'A graze.'

'Just me that got used as a punchbag, then.'

'You encountered a group of extremely powerful clairvoyants and survived, Paige. There is no shame in being strong.'

But there was shame. I'd been overpowered by Eliza, shot by Nick and beaten to a pulp by Jax. That wasn't strong. Warden brought a glass of water to my lips. Reluctantly, I sipped. 'Does Nashira know I tried to escape?'

'Oh, yes.'

'What will she do to me?'

'Your red tunic has been rescinded.' He placed the glass on the nightstand. 'You are a yellow-jacket now.'

The coward's colour. I managed an acrid laugh, but it hurt my ribs. 'I couldn't care less what tunic she puts me in. She still wants to kill me, red-jacket or not.' My shoulders shook. 'Just take me to her. Get it over with.'

'You are tired and wounded, Paige. Things may not look so bleak when you are well.'

'When will that be?'

'You will be able to get out of bed by tomorrow, if you wish.'

I frowned, but stopped when every muscle in my face protested. 'Tomorrow?'

'I asked the driver to collect scimorphine and anti-inflammatory drugs from the SciSORS facility before we left London. You will be fully recovered within two days.'

Scimorphine. The stuff was exorbitant. 'Did you see my father at SciSORS?'

'I did not enter the facility myself. Only a handful of Archon politicians know of our existence.'

He turned his attention to the IV in my hand. His fingers, always sheathed in leather, made sure the tape was still fastened.

'Why do you wear those gloves?' A spark of anger burned inside me. 'Are humans too filthy to touch?'

'It is her ruling.'

My cheeks grew warm under the bruises. However much I disliked him, he must have spent hours patching me up. 'What happened to the others?' I said.

'1 and 12 were unharmed. Situla was made latent, but she has recovered.' He paused. '30 is dead.'

'Dead? How?'

'Drowned. We found her in the fountain.'

The news sank in, chilling me. I hadn't particularly liked Amelia, but she hadn't deserved to die. I wondered which of the gang had done it. 'What about Carter?'

'She escaped. A vehicle took her from the bridge before she could be apprehended.'

At least Carter had got away. Whatever power she had, I didn't want Nashira getting it. 'And the Seals?'

'They escaped. I have never seen Nashira so furious.'

The relief was overwhelming. They were all right. The gang knew I-4 very well, all its secret nooks and boltholes; it would have been easy for them all to disappear, even with Nadine and Zeke wounded. Every voyant in that section answered to Jax. They would both have been carried off by his couriers. I looked back at Warden.

'You saved me.'

His eyes flicked over my face. 'Yes.'

'If you laid a *finger* on the oracle—'

'I did not hurt him. I let him go.'

'Why?'

'Because I knew he was your friend.' He sat on the edge of the bed. 'I know, Paige. I know you are the missing Seal. Only a fool could not have worked it out.'

I held his gaze. 'Are you going to tell Nashira?'

He looked at me for a long, long time. Those were the longest seconds of my life.

'No,' he said, 'but she is not a fool. She has long since suspected who you are. She will know.'

My stomach writhed with nerves. Warden stood and paced towards the fireplace.

'There has been a complication.' He gazed into the flames. 'You and I have saved each other from the first death. We are beholden to one another, bound by a life debt. Such a debt carries consequences.'

'Life debt?' I thought back, working through the remnants of the morphine. 'When did I save *your* life?'

'Three times. You cleaned my wounds, which bought me time to seek aid on the first night. You gave me your blood, preventing me from contracting the half-urge. And when Nashira summoned you to her table, you protected me. If you had told the truth, I would have been executed. I have committed many flesh-crimes, the penalty for which is death.'

I didn't know what *flesh-crime* meant, and I didn't ask. 'And you saved mine just now.'

'I have saved your life on several occasions.'

'When?'

'I would prefer not to divulge that information. But trust me: you owe me your life more than three times over. It means that you and I are no longer merely keeper and student, or master and slave.'

I found myself shaking my head. 'What?'

He rested an arm on the mantelpiece, staring into the flames. 'The æther has made its mark on both of us. It has recognised our tendency to protect one another, and now we are sworn to protect each other always. We are bound together by a golden cord.'

I wanted to laugh at his grave tone, but I got the feeling he wasn't joking. Rephs didn't make jokes. 'Golden cord.'

'Yes.'

'Has it got anything to do with the silver cord?'

'Of course. It slipped my mind. I suppose it has some link, yes – but a silver cord is personal, unique to the individual. A *golden* cord is formed between two spirits.'

'What the hell is it?'

'I hardly know myself.' He poured the dark contents of a vial into his glass. 'From what I understand, the golden cord is a kind of seventh sense, formed when two spirits save each other at least three times from the first death.' He raised the glass and sipped. 'You and I will always have knowledge of each other now. Wherever you are in the world, I will be able to find you. Through the æther.' He paused. 'Always.'

It only took a few seconds for his words to sink in. 'No,' I said. 'No, that's – that's not possible.' When he sipped his amaranth, I raised my voice. 'Prove it. Prove this "golden cord" is there.'

'If you insist.' Warden set his glass on the mantelpiece. 'Let us imagine, for a moment, that we are back in London. It is night, and we are on the bridge. But this time, I am the one that has been shot. I will call you for help.'

I waited. 'This is just—' I started, only to stop when I felt something. A soft hum through my bones, just the tiniest of vibrations. It sent goose bumps rolling all over my skin. Two words materialised in my mind: *bridge, help*.

'Bridge, help,' I repeated, faintly. 'No.'

This was too much. I turned to look at the fire. Now he had his own spiritual bell-pull to summon me. After a minute, the shock turned to anger. I wanted to smash all his vials, punch him in the face – *anything* but share a link with him. If he could track me in the æther, I'd never get rid of him.

And it was my fault. My fault for saving him.

'I do not know what other effects it may have on us both,' Warden said. 'You might be able to draw power from me.'

'I don't want your power. Just get rid of it. Break it.'

'It takes more than a word to break the æther's ties.'

'You knew how to call me with it.' My voice held a tremor. 'You must know how to break it.'

'The cord is an enigma, Paige. I have no idea.'

'You did this on purpose.' I pushed myself away from him, sickened. 'You saved my life to form this cord. Didn't you?'

'How could I possibly have engineered such a thing, when I had no idea whether or not you would ever dream of saving my life in return? You despise the Rephaim. Why would you try to save one?'

It was a good question. 'You can't exactly blame me for being paranoid,' I said.

I sank back, my head in my hands. He came to sit beside me again. He had the good sense not to touch me. 'Paige,' he said, 'you do not fear me. I believe you hate me, but you are not afraid of me. Yet you fear the cord.'

'You're a Rephaite.'

'And you judge me for that. For being Nashira's betrothed.'

'She's bloodthirsty and evil. You still chose her.'

'Did I?'

'You consented, then.'

'The Sargas choose their own mates. The rest of us do not have that privilege.' His voice fell into a soft growl. 'If you must know, I despise her. Every breath she takes is repulsive to me.'

I looked at him, assessing his face. His brow was dark, as if with regret. He caught my gaze and dropped it.

'I see,' I said.

'You do not see. You have never seen.'

He turned his face away. I waited. When he didn't move, I broke the silence.

'I'd like to.'

'I do not know if I can trust you.' The light receded from his eyes. 'I believe you are trustworthy. You are clearly loyal to the people you care most deeply about. It would be regrettable to share a golden cord with someone whom I cannot trust, and who does not trust me.'

So he wanted to trust me. And he was asking me to trust him. An exchange. A truce. I could ask him anything now, anything at all, and he would do it.

'Let me into your dreamscape,' I said.

To his credit, he didn't look surprised. 'You wish to see my dreamscape.'

'Not just see it. Walk in it. If I know what's in your mind, I might be able to trust you. I can see you.' And I wanted to see inside a Rephaite dreamscape. There must be something worth seeing behind all that armour.

'That would require equal trust on my part. I would have to trust you not to damage my sanity.'

'Exactly.'

He seemed to mull it over. 'Very well,' he concluded.

'Really?'

'If you feel strong enough, yes.' He turned to face me. 'Will the morphine affect your gift?'

'No.' I shifted into a sitting position. 'I might hurt you.'

'I will cope.'

'I've killed people by dreamwalking.'

'I know.'

'So how do you know I won't kill you?'

'I do not know. I must take a chance.'

I kept my features carefully blank. This was my chance to break him, to smash his dreamscape like a fly against a wall.

And yet I was curious, more than curious. I'd never really seen another dreamscape – only in flashes, glimpses through the æther. But the iridescent garden in the butterfly – I wanted that again. I wanted to be *immersed*. And here was Warden, offering his mind.

It would be fascinating to see a dreamscape that had been given thousands of years to develop. And after his sudden confession about Nashira, I wanted to know more about his past. I wanted to know what Arcturus Mesarthim looked like on the inside.

'Okay,' I said.

He sat down beside me. His aura touched mine, jarring my sixth sense.

I looked at his eyes. Yellow. This close, I could see that he had no colobomata. He couldn't be unsighted, surely. 'How long can you stay?' he asked.

The question caught me off-guard. 'Not long,' I said. 'Not unless you've got a self-automated BVM handy.' He narrowed his eyes. 'It's like an oxygen mask. It provides artificial respiration when my body stops.'

'I see. And if you have this device, you can remain "adrift" for an extended period?'

'In theory. I've never tried it in a dreamscape. Just the æther.'

'Why do they make you do it?'

It was clear to both of us who *they* were. My instinct was to say nothing, but he knew I worked for Jaxon Hall. 'Because that's the way of the syndicate,' I said. 'Mime-lords expect payment for protection.'

His aura was changing. 'I see.' He was dropping his defences for me, opening his gates. 'I am ready.'

I used the pillows to prop myself up. Then I closed my eyes, took a deep breath and went into my dreamscape.

The poppy field was a blurred painting. Everything was melting, softened by the morphine in my blood. I cut through the flowers, heading for the æther. When I reached the final boundary I pushed my hands through it, watching the illusion of my body fade away before my eyes. You only resemble yourself in your dreamscape if your mind perceives you that way. The instant I left, I took on my spirit form. Fluid, amorphous. A faceless glimmer.

I had seen Warden's dreamscape from the outside before, and it still chilled me. It looked like a black marble, barely perceptible in the silent darkness of the æther. As I approached it, a ripple crossed its surface. He was lowering all those layers of armour he'd accumulated over the centuries. I slid past the walls, into his hadal zone. I'd reached this point during our training sessions, but only in sharp bursts. Now I could go beyond it. I moved through the dwindling darkness, heading for the centre of his mind.

Ash drifted past my face. As I ventured into unfamiliar territory, my make-believe skin crawled. There was absolute silence in Warden's mind. Usually the outer rings would be full of mirages, hallucinations of a person's fears or regrets, but there was nothing. Just a hush.

Warden was waiting for me in his sunlit zone, if you could call it sunlit – more like moonlit. He was covered in scars, and his skin was sapped of colour. This was how he saw himself. I wondered what I looked like. I was in his dreamscape now, playing by his rules. I could see that my hands were the same, albeit with a soft glow. My new dream-form. But was he seeing my true face? I could look like anything: submissive, insane, naïve, cruel . . . I had no idea what he thought of me, and I would never find out. There were no mirrors in a dreamscape. I would never see the Paige he had created.

I stepped onto the barren patch of sand. I didn't know what I'd expected, but this wasn't it. Warden inclined his head. 'Welcome to my dreamscape. Excuse the lack of décor,' he said, pacing without direction. 'I don't often have guests.'

'There's nothing.' My breath steamed in the cold. 'Nothing at all.'

It was no exaggeration.

'Our dreamscapes are where we feel safest,' Warden said. 'Perhaps I feel safest when I think of nothing.'

'But there's nothing in the dark parts, either.'

He didn't reply. I walked a little further into the fog.

'There's nothing for me to see. That suggests to me that there's nothing inside you. No thoughts, no conscience. No fear.' I turned to face him. 'Do all Rephaim have empty dreamscapes?'

'I am not a dreamwalker, Paige. I can only guess at what other dreamscapes look like.'

'What are you?'

'I can make people dream their memories. I can weave them together, create a delusion. I see the æther through the lens of the dreamscape, and through the dreaming herb.'

'Oneiromancer.' I couldn't take my eyes off him. 'You're a sleep-dealer.'

Jax had always said they must exist. Oneiromancers. He'd categorised them several years ago, long after *On the Merits*, but never found one to prove his theory: a type of voyant that could traverse the dreamscape, pick out memories, and lace them into what amaurotics called dreams. 'You've been making me dream.' I took a deep breath. 'I've been going through memories since I've come here. How I became a dreamwalker, how Jaxon found me. It was *you*. You made me dream them. That's how you knew, isn't it?'

He met my gaze.

'That was the third pill,' he said. 'It contained a herb called salvia, which made you dream your memories. The herb that helps me touch the æther. My numen, flowing in your blood. After several pills, I was able to access your memories at will.'

'You kept me drugged' – I could hardly get the words out – 'to get into my mind.'

'Yes. Just as you watched dreamscapes for Jaxon Hall.'

'That's different. I didn't sit there by my fireplace and *watch* memories like – like some kind of film.' I stepped slowly away from him. 'Those memories are mine. They're private. You even looked at – you must have seen everything! Even the way I felt about – about—'

'Nick. You loved him.'

'Shut up. Just shut the fuck up.'

He did.

My dream-form was falling apart. Before I could get out of there myself, I was tossed from his dreamscape like a leaf in a high wind. When I woke in my own body, I put my palms against his chest and shoved him.

'Get away from me.'

My head pounded. I couldn't look at him, let alone be near him. When I tried to get up, the drip pulled at my hand.

'I am sorry,' he said.

An angry blaze flayed at my cheeks. I'd given him an *inch* of trust, less than an inch, and he'd taken me for all I had. He'd taken seven years of memory. He'd taken Finn. He'd taken Nick.

He stayed there for a minute. Perhaps he expected me to say more. I wanted to shout myself hoarse at him, but I couldn't do it. I just wanted him gone. When I didn't move, he closed the heavy drapes around the bed, sealing me off in a dark little cage.

Antiquary

I didn't sleep for hours. I could hear him at his desk, writing away, hidden from me only by the drapes.

My eyes and nose were raw, my throat tight as a fist. For the first time in years, I wanted everything to vanish. I wanted everything to be back to normal, like it was when I was little, before I'd been ripped open by the æther.

I looked up at the canopy. No matter how much I sometimes wanted it, there was no *normal*. There never had been. 'Normal' and 'natural' were the biggest lies we'd ever created. We humans with our little minds. And maybe being normal wouldn't suit me.

It was only when he turned on his gramophone that I started to get drowsy. I hadn't been in his dreamscape long, but I'd done it without life support. I drifted into a doze. The crackling voices blurred together.

I must have slept for a while. When I woke, the drip was gone. In its place was a small plaster.

The day-bell tolled. Sheol I slept during the day, but it seemed I wasn't going to sleep. There was nothing to do but get up and face him.

I hated him so much it hurt. I wanted to smash the mirror, to feel the glass break under my knuckles. I should never have taken those pills.

Maybe it *was* the same as what I did. I spied on people too – but I didn't look into their pasts. I only saw what they imagined themselves to be, not what they were. I saw flashes of people: the edges and the corners, the faint glow of a distant dreamscapes. Not like him. Now he knew everything about me, every little bit of me I'd tried to keep concealed. He'd always known I was one of the Seven Seals. He'd known from the very first night.

But he hadn't told Nashira. Just as he'd kept the butterfly and the deer from her, so he'd kept my true identity. She might have guessed that I was part of the syndicate, but she hadn't got it from him.

I pulled the drapes apart. Golden sunlight poured into the tower, glinting on the instruments and books. Near the window, Michael – the amaurotic – was setting out a breakfast spread on a small table. He looked up and smiled.

'Hi, Michael.'

He nodded.

'Where's Warden?'

Michael pointed at the door.

'Cat got your tongue?'

He shrugged. I sat down. He pushed a stack of pancakes across the table. 'I'm not hungry,' I said. 'I don't want his guilt breakfast.' Michael sighed, wrapped my hand around a fork and stabbed it into the pancakes. 'Fine, but I blame you if I throw it all back up.'

Michael grimaced. Just to please him, I sprinkled the pancakes with brown sugar.

Michael kept a sharp eye on me as he pottered around the room, tidying the bedclothes and the drapes. The pancakes awakened a punishing hunger. I ended up eating my way through the whole stack, along with two croissants with strawberry jam, a bowl of cornflakes, four slices of hot buttered toast, a plate of scrambled eggs, a red apple with crisp white innards, three cups of coffee and an ice-cold pint of orange juice. It was only when I could eat no more that Michael handed me a sealed manila envelope.

'Trust him.'

It was the first time I'd ever heard him speak. His voice was barely more than a whisper.

'Do *you* trust him?'

He nodded, cleared the breakfast table and was gone. And even though it was daytime, he left the door unlocked. I split the wax seal on the envelope and unfolded the sheet of thick paper inside. It was bordered with swirling gold. *Paige*, it began:

> *I apologise for upsetting you. But even if you resent me, know that I sought only to understand you. You can hardly blame me for your refusal to be understood.*

Some apology this was. Still, I continued to read:

> *It is still day. Go to the House. You will find things there that I cannot supply.*
> *Be swift. If you are stopped, tell the guards you are collecting a fresh batch of aster for me.*
>
> *Do not judge too quickly, little dreamer.*

I scrunched the letter into my hand and threw it into the hearth. Just by writing it, Warden was flaunting his newfound trust in me. I could easily take it straight to Nashira. She would recognise his handwriting, I was sure. But I didn't want to help Nashira in any way whatsoever. I hated Warden for keeping me in this place, but I needed to get into the House.

I went to the upper floor and dressed in my new uniform: yellow tunic, yellow anchor on the gilet. A bright, sunshine yellow, visible from a mile off. 40 the coward. 40 the quitter. In a way I liked it. It showed I'd gone against Nashira's orders. I'd never wanted to be red.

I went back to his chamber – slowly, thinking. I still didn't know if I wanted to organise a prison break, but I did want to leave. I would need supplies for the journey home. Food, water. Weapons. Hadn't he said the red flower could hurt them?

The snuff box was on the table, the lid propped open. Inside were samples from several plants: sprigs of laurel, sycamore and oak leaves, mistletoe berries, blue and white aster, and a packet of dry leaves labelled SALVIA DIVINORUM. His numen. Below it, a sealed vial of soft, blue-black powder was tucked into the corner of the snuff box. The tag read ANEMONE CORONARIA. I pulled off the cork, releasing a pungent smell. Pollen of the red flower. These sweet little grains might just keep me safe. I closed the vial and tucked it into my gilet.

There must be guards stationed outside during the day, but I could slip past them. I had my ways. And no matter how Nashira Sargas had classified me, I was no yellow-jacket. I was the Pale Dreamer.

It was time to show her.

I spun a line about collecting aster for my keeper, and to take it up with him if there were any problems. The new day porter wasn't too hot on that idea: he almost threw me onto the street when he read in the ledger who my keeper was. He didn't even mention the backpack on my shoulders. Nobody wanted to piss off Arcturus Mesarthim.

It was strange to see the city in daylight. I sensed the Broad would be empty – there were none of the usual sounds and smells – but I needed to do something before I reached the house. I walked through the passages of the Rookery. Water drizzled through every crack and seam, the aftermath of a passing storm. I found the right shack and moved the tattered drape aside. Julian was asleep, his arm around Liss, keeping her warm. Her aura was burning down, like a candle at the end of its wick. I crouched beside them and emptied my backpack. I tucked a package of breakfast food into the crook of Julian's free arm, where no passing guard could see it, and covered them both with clean white blankets. I left a box of matches in the chest.

Seeing their squalor made me sure I was doing the right thing. They needed more than what I'd scoured from the Founder's Tower. They needed what was in the House.

Spirit shock was a slow process. You had to fight your way through it, fight with every inch of yourself. Only the strong survived it. Save for a few, fleeting moments of lucidity, Liss hadn't regained consciousness since her cards had been destroyed. If she didn't recover soon, she'd lose her aura and succumb to amaurosis. Her only hope was to reunite with a pack of cards, and even then, there was no guarantee that she'd connect with them. I would scour the House until I found some for her.

There were no guards visible on the street, but I knew they would have lookouts. Just to be safe, I climbed up one of the buildings and found a path across the rooftops, using ledges and pilasters to slink across the city. I watched my footing as best I could, but it was slow going: my right arm was mannequin-stiff, and most of my body still throbbed with bruises.

The House was visible from a mile off. Its two spires rose through the mist. I dropped into an alley when I was close; the distance to the next wall was too great to jump. Over that wall was the one residence where only Rephaim were permitted.

I looked at the wall for a long time. Warden was in too deep to betray me now. For some reason he was helping me – and for Liss's sake, I had to accept it. Besides, if I got into trouble, I could always send him a message through the golden cord. If I could work out how. If I could bear it. I climbed the wall, swung my leg over the top, and dropped down onto overgrown grass.

Like many of the residences, this facility had been built around a series of quadrangles. As I crossed into the first one, I compiled a mental list of things I needed to cross No Man's Land. Weapons were crucial, given what lurked in the trees, but medical supplies would be an extra asset. If I put a foot wrong on the minefield, I would need a tourniquet. And antiseptic. It was a horrific thought, but I had to face it. Adrenalin was valuable: not only could I use it to get my energy up and dull pain, but it could also be used to revive me if I had to leave my body. More anemone pollen might be helpful, and any other substances I could find: flux, aster, salt – maybe even ectoplasm.

I went past a few buildings, but none of them were suitable to search. Too many rooms. It was only when I wandered away from the central courtyards, to the very edge of the residence, that a better target caught my eye: a building with large windows and plenty of footholds. I walked through an archway and viewed it from the other side. Red ivy grew in swathes across its façade. I walked around the building, trying to find an open window. There were none. I'd have to break in. Wait – there was one – a small window, open just a crack, on the first floor. I hauled myself onto a low wall, and from there I took the drainpipe. The window was stuck fast, but I forced it open with one arm. I lowered myself into a tiny room, probably a broom cupboard, thick with dust. I cracked open the door.

I found myself in a stone corridor. Empty. This excursion to the House couldn't have gone any better. As I examined the doors, looking for some sign of what might be behind them, I tensed. My sixth sense shivered: two auras. They were behind a door directly to my right. I stopped dead. '. . . *know* anything! Please—'

There was a muffled noise. I pressed my ear to the door.

'The blood-sovereign will not hear your pleas.' The voice was male. 'We know you saw them together.'

'I saw them once, *once* in the meadow! They were just training. I didn't see anything else, I swear!' This voice was high-pitched with terror. I recognised it: Ivy, the palmist. She was almost choking the words. 'Please, not again, not again, I can't stand it—'

An awful scream.

'There will be no more pain when you give us the truth.' Ivy was sobbing. 'Come now, 24. You must have *something* for me. Just a little information. Did he touch her?'

'He – he carried her out of the m-meadow. She was tired. But he was wearing gloves—'

'You're sure?'

Her breathing quickened. 'I – I don't remember. I'm sorry. Please – no more—' Footsteps. 'No, *no!*'

Her pitiful cries twisted my stomach. I wanted to flush out the spirit of her torturer, but the risk of being caught was too great. If I didn't get these supplies, I couldn't save anyone. I clenched my jaw, listening, shaking with anger. What was he doing to her?

Ivy's screams went on and on. My stomach heaved when she stopped.

'No more, *please.*' Ivy was choking on her sobs. 'It's the truth!' Her tormentor was silent. 'But – but he feeds her. I know he feeds her, and she – she always looks clean. And – people say she can possess voyants, and he must be – must be keeping it from the b-blood-sovereign. Otherwise she would have been d-dead by now.'

The silence was damning. After that was a soft, heavy thump, then footsteps and a closing door.

For a long time I was paralysed. After a minute I pushed the heavy door open. There was a single wooden chair inside. Its seat was stained with blood, as was the floor.

My skin grew slick and cold. I ran my sleeve across my upper lip. For a while I crouched against the wall, my head in my hands. Ivy had been talking about me.

I couldn't think about it now. Her torturer might still be in this building. Slowly, I stood and faced the nearest room. The key was in the door. I looked inside. Weapons lined the walls: swords, hunting knives, a crossbow, a slingshot with steel ammunition. This must be where they stored arms to distribute to the red-jackets. I grabbed a knife. An anchor gleamed near the hilt. Scion-made. Weaver was sending weapons here while he and his ministers sat in the Archon, far from the ethereal beacon.

Julian was right. I couldn't just leave. I wanted to make Frank Weaver afraid. I wanted him to know the fear of every voyant prisoner he'd ever transported.

I closed the door and locked it. When I looked up, I found myself facing a large, yellowed map. THE PENAL COLONY OF SHEOL I, it read. OFFICIAL TERRITORY OF THE SUZERAIN. I scanned it. Sheol I was built around the large central residences, tapering off to the meadow and the trees. All the familiar landmarks were there: Magdalen, Amaurotic House, the Residence of the Suzerain, the Hawksmoor – and Port Meadow. I peeled the map from the wall and studied it. The printed letters next to it were mangled, but I made them out.

Train.

My fingers tightened on the edges of the map. The train. It hadn't even crossed my mind. We'd all been brought here by a train – why couldn't we leave on it?

My brain was in overdrive. How, *how* had I not thought of it? I didn't need to cross No Man's Land. I didn't need to walk for miles, or pass the Emim, to reach the citadel. All I had to do was find the train. I could take people with me – Liss, Julian, everyone. The average Scion train could hold nearly four hundred people, more if they were standing. I could get every single prisoner out of this city and still have room for more.

We would still need weapons. Even if we all snuck to the meadow by daylight, moving in small groups, the Rephaim would come after us. Besides, the entrance might be guarded. I reached for a sheathed knife and stowed it away in my backpack. Next I found a few guns.

The palm pistol, a similar model to mine, would come in handy: it was small, easy to conceal, and I knew how to use it. I shifted some illegible paperwork from the top of a metal case. Nick had tried to shoot Warden in the citadel, to no avail. Bullets would work on loyal red-jackets, but we'd need more than guns to take down Rephs. I was reaching for a box of bullets when the sound of footsteps drifted to my ears.

Without pausing, I made for a set of shelves and slotted myself behind them. Just in time: the key fell from the lock, and two Rephs walked in.

I should have expected this. My exit was blocked. If I crawled to the window, I would have to expose myself, and everybody knew my face. I looked between the shelves.

Thuban.

He said something in Gloss. I leaned closer to my peephole, trying to identify his companion. That was when Terebell Sheratan stepped into my line of vision.

Neither of us moved. I couldn't feel my heart. I waited for her to call Thuban, or to drive a blade into my gut. My fingers twitched towards the pollen, hidden in my gilet, but I thought better of it. Even if I took Terebell down, Thuban would disembowel me.

But Terebell surprised me. Instead of acknowledging me, she shifted her gaze towards the guns. 'Amaurotic weaponry *is* intriguing,' she said. 'No wonder they destroy each other so often.'

'Are we speaking the fell tongue now?'

'Gomeisa has told us to maintain our fluency in English. I see no harm in a little practice.'

Thuban snatched the crossbow from the wall. 'If you wish to foul our tongues with it, very well. We can pay homage to the days when you had power over me. What a long, long time ago that was.' He ran his gloved fingers over the lathe. 'The dreamer should have killed Jaxon Hall while she had the chance. It would have been kinder than the death he will have now.'

My throat closed. 'I doubt he will be killed,' Terebell said. 'Besides, Nashira's interest is in Carter.'

'She will have to hold Situla back.'

'No doubt.' She ran her fingers over a blade. 'Remind me: what was in this room before the armaments?'

'With your blasphemous interest in the fell world, I would have thought you would know exactly where all the resources were kept.'

'I think "blasphemous" is a little melodramatic.'

'I do not.' He picked up a handful of throwing stars. 'What was in here before, you ask? Medical supplies. Plant extracts. Salvia, aster. Other stinking leaves.'

'Where were they moved?'

'Have you forgotten *everything* in the last few minutes, miscreant? You're as stupid as the concubine.'

You had to hand it to Terebell: she was either immune to his attitude, or very good at hiding her emotions. If she had any.

'Forgive my curiosity,' she said.

'My family does not forgive. The scars on your back should remind you of that on a daily basis.' His eyes were full of Ivy's aura. 'That's why you want to know. You're trying to steal amaranth — *aren't* you, Sheratan?'

Scars.

Terebell's face was hard. 'Where were the resources moved?'

'I don't like your interest. I suspect it. Are you plotting with the concubine again?'

'That was almost twenty years ago, Thuban. A long time by human standards, wouldn't you say?'

'I do not care for human standards.'

'If you hold the past against me, that is one thing, but I do not think the blood-sovereign would appreciate your attitude towards her consort. Or your questionable descriptions of his role.'

Her voice was harder now. Thuban took a blade from the wall and swung it towards her. It stopped an inch from her neck. She didn't flinch. 'One more word out of you,' he said, his voice a whisper, 'and I will summon *him*. And this time he will not be so temperate.'

Terebell fell silent for a moment. I thought I saw something in her face: pain, fear. They must be talking about one of the Sargas. Gomeisa, perhaps.

'Yes. I believe I remember where the supplies are.' Her voice was low. 'How could I forget Tom Tower?'

Thuban barked a laugh. I absorbed the information, like blood absorbing flux. 'No one could forget it.' He breathed the words against her ear. 'Nor the sound of its bell. Does it ring in your memories, Sheratan? Do you remember how you screamed for mercy?'

My limbs were beginning to ache, but I didn't dare move. Thuban was inadvertently helping me. Tom Tower must be the one that stood above the entrance; the bell tower.

'I did not cry for mercy,' Terebell said, 'but for justice.'

A harsh snarl escaped his throat. 'Fool.' He raised a hand to strike her – then stopped dead. He sniffed.

'I sense an aura.' He sniffed again. 'Search the room, Sheratan. It smells human.'

'I don't sense anything.' Terebell stayed where she was. 'The room was locked when we arrived.'

'There are other ways to enter a room.'

'Now you sound paranoid.'

But Thuban didn't seem convinced. He was walking towards my hiding place, nostrils flared wide, his lips pulled back to bare his teeth. A sickening thought occurred to me: that he was a sniffer, able to smell spiritual activity. If he sniffed me out, I was worse than dead.

His fingers moved towards the box that hid me. In the distance, in another room, something exploded.

In an instant, Thuban took off down the corridor. Terebell followed, but she turned at the door.

'Run,' she said to me. 'Get to the tower.'

And she was gone.

Not waiting to question my good fortune, I pulled on my backpack and vaulted up onto the windowsill. I almost fell down the ivy, scraping my arms and hands.

Blood thumped through my veins. Every shadow looked like Thuban. As I ran through a set of cloisters, heading for the main quadrangle, I tried to pluck some rational thoughts from my mind. Terebell had been helping me. She'd concealed me. It even looked like someone had caused a distraction for me. She'd known I was coming, known what I was after, and she'd only started to speak English after seeing me. She was one of them. The scarred ones. I needed to find out more about their history, to work out what was happening – but first I had to break into Tom Tower, grab the goods and get back to Warden.

The explosion had brought a group of bone-grubbers running from the entrance, away from the bell tower. I halted in a dark archway. Just in time – they came running into the cloisters, exactly where I'd been about to run out. '28, 14, secure the Meadow Building,' one of them called. '6, you're with me. The rest of you, cover the quads. Get Kraz and Mirzam.'

I didn't have much time. I got to my feet and sprinted towards the main quad.

The House was vast, linked together by a series of closed and open-air passages. *Rat in a maze.* I didn't dare stop. I secured the straps of the backpack around my torso. There had to be a way to get inside

338

Tom Tower. Was there a door by the main entrance? I had to be quick: Kraz and Mirzam were Reph names, and the last thing I needed was four Rephs, at least three of whom were hostile, in the House and on my tail. I doubted Warden had many friends like Terebell.

I stopped at the edge of the quadrangle. It was vast, with an ornamental pond in the centre. A statue stood in the middle of the pond. I had no choice but to expose myself. Speed would have to come above stealth.

I broke into a sprint across the grass. My ribs twinged. When I reached the pond, I ran through the shallow water and crouched behind the fountain. I hunkered down low, so the water came up to my waist. When I looked up, I recoiled. Nashira was staring back at me. Nashira, cast in stone.

There was no one on the quadrangle. I could sense an aura, but it was too far away to be a threat. I jumped out of the fountain and ran towards the bell tower. I spotted the narrow archway at once. This must lead to the bell. I shot up the steps, praying that no Rephs would appear – the passageway was so narrow, I'd have no chance. When I got to the top, I gazed up at the sight.

It was a treasure trove. Glass jars sparkled from hundreds of shelves, dappled in sunlight. I was reminded of hard-boiled sweets: bright, glassy colours, glistening like stars. There were iridescent liquids, brilliantly coloured powers, exotic plants wrapped in liquid – all beautiful and alien. The room was full of smells: some sharp, some bad, some sweet and fragrant. I scoured the shelves for medical supplies. Most bottles were labelled with the Scion symbol, written in English, but some bore strange glyphs. There were numa, too, probably confiscated. I caught sight of a shew stone, various *sortes* – and a single pack of cards. Those were for Liss. I flipped through them quickly, assessing the illustrations. It was a Thoth deck – a different design to the one Liss had before – but it could still be used for cartomancy.

I stuffed the deck into my bag. I took silvadene and paraffin and antiseptic. There was another door, probably leading to the bell, but I didn't go through it. This would be my last contraband: the bag was almost too heavy to lift. I hauled the straps over my shoulders and turned towards the steps – only to lock gazes with a Reph.

All my life functions seemed to stop. Two yellow eyes smoked at me from underneath a hood.

'Well, well,' he said. 'A traitor in the tower.'

He made towards me. I dropped the bag and climbed the nearest shelves in a heartbeat.

'You must be the dreamwalker. I am Kraz Sargas, blood-heir of the Rephaim.' He gave me a mock bow. I could see Nashira in his features; in his thick, brassy hair and hooded eyelids. 'Did Arcturus send you?'

I didn't say a word.

'So he lets his tribute to the blood-sovereign go wandering off by itself. She will not be pleased.' He held out a gloved hand. 'Come down, dreamwalker. I will escort you back to Magdalen.'

'And we'll just pretend this never happened?' I stayed where I was. 'You'll take me to Nashira.'

His patience vanished. 'Don't make me crush you, yellow-jacket.'

'Nashira doesn't want me dead.'

'I am not Nashira.'

Now I was in for it. If he didn't kill me, he'd drag me straight to the Residence of the Suzerain. My gaze settled on a jar of white aster. I could wipe his memory.

No such luck. With a single flex of his arm, Kraz brought the whole bookshelf crashing to the ground. Bottles and vials smashed against the floor. I rolled to avoid being crushed, slicing my cheek on a shard of glass. A cry leapt from my lips. My cracked ribs seared.

I wasn't on my feet fast enough. My injuries slowed me down. There were no spirits in here; nothing I could use to repel him. Kraz picked me up by my gilet and smashed me into the wall. I almost blacked out. My ribs were tearing from my chest. Kraz gripped my hair in his hand, pulled my head back, and inhaled – deeply, like he was trying to breathe more than air. I realised what was happening when blood filled my eyes. I kicked and clawed and twisted, gasping for the æther. It was already slipping out of reach.

Kraz was famished. He was going to snuff out my glow.

My right arm was pinned, but my left was free. In the grip of adrenalin, I did what my father had always taught me to do: stabbed Kraz in the eye with my finger. As soon as he let go of my hair, I pulled out the vial in my pocket. Red flower.

Kraz clamped his hand across my throat, his teeth bared. If I tried to attack his mind, my body would be damaged beyond repair. I had no choice. I smashed the vial against his face.

The smell was atrocious. Rot. Sweet, burning rot. Kraz let out an inhuman scream. The pollen had gone straight into his eyes. They were blackened and dripping, and his face was turning an ugly, mottled grey. 'No,' he said. 'No, you – *not*—'

His next words were in Gloss. My vision lurched. Was this an allergic reaction? Bile jerked into my throat. I groped in my backpack, took out the revolver and raised it to his head. Kraz fell to his knees.

Kill him.

My palms were slick. Even after what I'd done to the Underguard on the train, the very crime that had landed me here, I had no idea if I could do this. If I could take another life. But then Kraz pulled his hands away from his face, and I knew he was beyond saving. I didn't even flinch.

I pulled the trigger.

The Dream

The journey back to safety was a blur. I ran over the roofs, past the old church and down the long road towards Magdalen. As I reached the residence an arm swung out from a window and snatched me inside.

Warden. He'd waited for me. Without a word, he pulled me through a door. Back towards the east courtyard. Into the empty passages. Through the cloisters, up the steps. I didn't dare speak. As soon as we were in the tower, I slid to the floor by the fireplace. My fingers left black pollen on the rug. It looked like soot.

Without stopping, Warden locked the door, turned off the gramophone and drew the drapes on both sides of the chamber. He watched through a gap at the east window for a few minutes, keeping an eye on the street. I let the backpack drop to the floor. The straps had cut into my shoulders.

'I killed him.'

He glanced at me. 'Who?'

'Kraz. I shot him.' I was shaking all over. 'I've killed a Sargas – she's going to kill me. *You're* going to kill me—'

'No.'

'Why the hell not?'

'A Sargas is no loss to me.' He looked back at the window. 'You are quite sure he is dead.'

'Of course he's dead. I shot him in the face.'

'Bullets cannot kill us. You must have used the pollen.'

'Yes.' I tried to slow my breathing. 'Yes, I did.'

He didn't speak for a long time. I sat there in the evidence, my lungs fit to burst. 'If a Sargas has been killed by a human,' he finally said, 'the last thing Nashira will want is for word of it to get out into the city. Our immortality must not be questioned.'

'You're really not immortal?'

'We are not indestructible.' He crouched in front of me, looked me in the eye. 'Did anyone see you?'

'No. Wait, yes – Terebell.'

'Terebell will keep your secret. If she was the only one, we have nothing to fear.'

'Thuban was there, too. There was an explosion.' I looked up at him. 'Do you know anything about that?'

'I sensed you were in danger. I had someone standing by in the House. They caused a distraction. All Nashira will hear is that a candle was left too close to a gas leak.'

The news did little to comfort me. That was three lives I'd taken now, not counting the ones I'd failed to save.

'You are bleeding.'

I glanced into the bathroom mirror, visible through the open door. A long, shallow cut crossed my cheek. Just deep enough to bring blood welling to the surface. 'Yes,' I said.

'He hurt you.'

'It was just some glass.' I touched the smarting cut. 'Will you find out what happened?'

He nodded, still looking at my cheek. There was something in his eyes that struck me: a darkness, a tension. He was thinking of something else. He wouldn't meet my gaze; the wound transfixed him.

'This will scar if it is not treated.' His gloved fingers held my jaw. 'I will bring something to clean it.'

'And you'll find out about Kraz.'

'Yes.'

Our gazes met for the briefest instant. My brow creased, and my lips formed a question.

In the end I didn't ask it.

'I will return as soon as I can.' He stood. 'I recommend you clean yourself. There are clothes in there.'

He indicated the armoire. I glanced down at my uniform. The gilet was covered in pollen: damning evidence of my transgressions. 'Right,' I said.

'And keep that wound clean.'

He was gone before I could respond.

I got to my feet and approached the mirror. The laceration was a livid shock against my skin. Did it bother him to see me like this, even after what Jax had done? Did he see my face and think of his own scars – the ones on his back, the ones he kept hidden?

A cloying smell sifted from my hair. The pollen. I locked the bathroom door, kicked off my clothes and ran a steaming bath. My legs shook. I'd skinned my knee while climbing. I sank into the hot water and washed my hair. Old bruises throbbed under my skin, while new ones formed on top of them. I took a few minutes to soak the warmth into my rigid muscles, then picked up a fresh cake of soap and scrubbed away the sweat and blood and pollen. My sallow, battered frame looked no better for the attention. Only once the water had drained did I start to feel calm.

Should I talk to him about the train? He might try and stop me. He'd brought me back when he could have let me go. On the other hand, I needed to know whether or not the train was guarded, and whereabouts on the meadow I would find the entrance. I didn't remember anything from the training session – no hatch, no door. It must be hidden.

When I returned to the chamber I found the clean yellow uniform in the armoire. The pollen had been swept off the carpet. I sank onto the daybed. I'd dispatched Kraz Sargas, blood-heir of the Rephaim, with a single shot between the eyes. Until that moment I'd thought they were too strong to kill. It must have been the pollen – the bullet had just finished him off. By the time I'd left the tower, the corpse had been rotting before my eyes. A few grains of pollen had putrefied him.

When the door opened, I started. Warden was back. His face held all the shadows in the room.

He came to sit beside me. He took a swab, dipped it in a jar of amber liquid, and dabbed the blood from my cheek. I looked at him in silence, waiting for his judgement. 'Kraz is dead,' he said, betraying no emotion. My cheek gave a hot twinge. 'He was heir apparent to the blood-sovereignty. You would be publically tortured if they found out. They know about the missing supplies, but you were not seen. The day porter has been whitewashed.'

'Does anyone suspect me?'

'Privately, perhaps, but they have no proof. Fortunately you did not use your spirit to kill him, or your identity would be obvious.'

My shivering intensified. Classic me, killing someone that important without even knowing who he was. I'd end up as a death mask if Nashira got wind of this. I looked up at him.

'What did the pollen do to Kraz? His eyes – his *face*—'

'We are not what we seem, Paige.' He held my gaze. 'How long was there between the application of the pollen and the shooting?'

The shooting. Not *the murder.* He'd said *the shooting*, as if I'd been a bystander. 'Maybe ten seconds.'

'What did you see in those ten seconds?'

I tried to think. The room had been thick with vapours, and I'd hit my head. 'It was like – like his face was – rotting. And his eyes were white. Like they'd lost all their colour. Dead eyes.'

'There you have it.'

I couldn't think what he meant. *Dead eyes.*

The fire crackled, warming the room. Too warm. Warden lifted my chin, exposing my cut to the light. 'Nashira will see this,' I said. 'She'll know.'

'That can be remedied.'

'How?'

No reply. Every time I asked *how*, or *why*, he would seem to get bored of the conversation. He went to his desk and took out a metal cylinder, small enough to fit into a pocket. The word SCIONAID was printed in red across the side. He unwrapped three adhesive steri-strips. I stayed still as he applied them.

'Does it hurt?'

'No.'

He took his hand from my face. I touched the strips. 'I saw a map in the House,' I said. 'I know there's a train on Port Meadow. I need to know where the entrance to the tunnel is.'

'And why would you need to know that?'

'Because I want to leave. Before Nashira kills me.'

'I see.' Warden returned to his armchair. 'And you assume I will let you go.'

'Yes, I do assume.' I held up his snuff box. 'Or you can safely *assume* that this will find its way to Nashira.'

The symbol caught the light. His fingers drummed on the chair. He didn't try to bargain; he just looked at me, his eyes burning softly. 'You cannot take the train,' he said.

'Watch me.'

'You misunderstand me. The train can only be activated by the

346

Westminster Archon. It is programmed to come and go on particular dates, at particular times. Those times cannot be changed.'

'It must bring food.'

'The train is used only for human transportation. The food is delivered by couriers.'

'So it won't come again until' – I closed my eyes – 'the next Bone Season.' In 2069. My dream of an easy escape unravelled. I'd have to cross the minefield after all.

'I urge you not to attempt a crossing on foot,' he said, as if he'd read my thoughts. 'The Emim use the woods as a hunting ground. Even with your gift, you will not last long. Not against a pack of them.'

'I can't wait.' I gripped the arm of the chair until my knuckles blanched. 'I *have* to leave. You know she's going to kill me.'

'Of course she is. Now your gift has matured, she hungers for it. It will not be long before she strikes.'

I tensed. 'Matured?'

'You possessed 12 in the citadel. I saw you. She has been waiting for you to reach your full potential.'

'Did you tell her?'

'She will find out, but not from me. What is said in this room will not go beyond it.'

'Why?'

'An overture to mutual trust.'

'You went through my memories. Why should I trust you?'

'Did I not show you my dreamscape?'

'Yes,' I said. 'Your cold, empty dreamscape. You're nothing but a hollow shell, aren't you?'

Abruptly, he got to his feet, went to the bookshelf and took out an enormous old tome. My muscles drew into taut bars. Before I could say another word, he removed a thin booklet from inside and tossed it onto the table. I couldn't take my eyes off it. *On the Merits of Unnaturalness*. My copy, plastered in evidence of the syndicate. He'd had it all along.

'My dreamscape may be starved of its old life, but I do not see people in ranks, as the author of that pamphlet does. There is no oneiromancer in there. No Rephaim. I do not see things in that light.' He looked straight at me. 'I have lived with you for several months now. I know your history, even if I have learned it against your will. I did not intend to invade your privacy, but I wished to see what you were like. I wished to *know* you. I did not wish to treat you as a mere human – lower, unworthy.'

That was unexpected. 'Why not?' I said, not taking my eyes off him. 'Why do you care?'

'That is my concern.'

I picked up *On the Merits* and pressed it to my chest, like a child might hold a toy. It felt as if I'd saved Jaxon's life. Warden watched me.

'You truly care about your mime-lord,' he said. 'You want to return to that life. To the syndicate.'

'There's more to Jaxon than this pamphlet.'

'I imagine there is.'

He came to sit beside me on the daybed. There was silence for a few minutes. A human and a Rephaite, as different as night and day – trapped in our own bell jar, like the withered flower. He picked up the snuff box and removed a small vial of amaranth. 'You feel alone.' He emptied it into a chalice. 'I feel it. Your solitude.'

'I am alone.'

'You miss Nick.'

'He's my best friend. Of course I miss him.'

'He was more than that. Your memories of him are extraordinarily detailed – full of colour, full of life. You adored him.'

'I was young.' My tone was clipped. He seemed determined to keep prodding my most sensitive spot.

'You are still young.' He wasn't letting this go. 'I have not seen all your memories. Something is missing.'

'There's no point dwelling on things.'

'I disagree.'

'Everyone has bad memories. Why are you interested in mine?'

'Memory is my lifeline. My route to the æther, just as dreamscapes are yours.' He touched a gloved finger to my forehead. 'You asked to know me through my dreamscape. In return, I ask for your memories.'

His touch chilled me. I drew back. Warden looked at me for a while, assessing my reaction, before he stood and tugged on the bell-pull. 'What are you doing?' I said.

'You need to eat.'

He turned on the gramophone and stared out into the street.

Michael was there before you could say *dumbwaiter*. He listened to the orders Warden gave him. Ten minutes later he was back with a tray, which he set across my lap. There was just enough to boost my strength: a milky cup of tea, a pot of sugar, tomato soup and warm bread. 'Thank you,' I said.

He gave me a quick smile before he made a complicated series of signs at Warden, who nodded. He bowed and left. Warden looked at me, watching to see if I would eat without coercion. I took a sip of tea. I remembered my grandmother giving me tea when I was very little, whenever I fell ill – she was a great believer in tea. I took a few bites of bread. Was he reading me now, reading my emotions? Could he feel the memory calming me down? I tried to focus on him, to use the golden cord, but there was nothing.

When I was finished, he took the tray and deposited it on the coffee table before he came to sit beside me again. I cleared my throat.

'What did Michael say?'

'That Nashira has summoned the remaining Sargas to her

residence. He is quite the eavesdropper,' he added, his tone slightly amused. 'He brings me a great deal of information from her halls. His supposed amaurosis keeps her blind to his comings and goings.'

So Michael was willing to sneak around. I would remember that. 'She's telling them about Kraz.' I framed my temples with my fingers. 'I didn't mean to kill him. I just—'

'He would have killed you. Kraz harboured a terrible hatred for humans. He planned, when the day of our exposure came, to lure human children into our control cities. He had a penchant for their small, fine bones. For cleromancy.'

I felt sick to the deepest pit of my stomach. Cleromancy involved the use of lots, or *sortes*, which spirits arranged into pictures or pushed in a particular direction. All kinds of *sortes* were used: needles, dice, keys. A group called the osteomancers favoured bones, but very old skeletons were usually handled out of respect for the dead. If Kraz had stolen the bones of children to practise cleromancy, I was glad I'd killed him.

'I am thankful that he is dead,' Warden said. 'He was a terrible blight on this world.'

I didn't answer.

'You feel guilty,' he stated.

'Afraid.'

'Afraid of what?'

'What I can do. I keep—' I shook my head, exhausted. 'I keep killing. I don't want to be a weapon.'

'Your gift is volatile, but it keeps you alive. It acts as your shield.'

'It's not a shield. It's like a gun. I live on a hair-trigger.' I looked at the patterns on the carpet. 'I hurt people. That's my gift.'

'Not deliberately. You did not always know what you could do.'

I let out a hollow laugh. 'Oh, I knew I could do it. I didn't know *how*, but I knew who was making people bleed. I knew who was giving people headaches. Whenever people sneered at me

– whenever they brought up the Molly Riots – they'd just *hurt*. All because I'd given them a mental push. I liked it, in a way,' I said. 'Even when I was ten, I liked it. I liked getting my own back. It was my little secret.' He kept his eyes on me. 'I'm not like sensors or mediums. I don't just use spirits for companionship or self-defence. I am one of them. Get it? I can die when I want, become a spirit when I want. It makes people afraid of me. It makes me afraid of them.'

'You are different from them, yes. But that does not mean you should be afraid.'

'Yes, it does. My spirit is dangerous.'

'You are not afraid of danger, Paige. I think you thrive on it. You agreed to work for Jaxon Hall, knowing that it would significantly reduce your lifespan. Knowing the risk of detection.'

'I needed the money.'

'Your father works for Scion. You did not need money. I doubt you have ever touched it. Danger brings you closer to the æther,' he said. 'That is why you take every opportunity to experience it.'

'It wasn't that. I'm not some sort of adrenalin junkie. I wanted to be with other voyants.' Fresh anger seeped into my voice. 'I didn't want to live like a brainwashed Scion schoolgirl. I wanted to be part of something. I wanted to *matter*. Can't you understand that?'

'Those were not the only reasons. You thought about one person in particular.'

'Don't.' My lips shook.

'You thought about Nick.' His gaze held hard. 'You loved him. You would have followed him anywhere.'

'I don't want to talk about that.'

'Why not?'

'Because it's mine. It's private. Do you oneiromancers have *any* concept of privacy?'

'You have kept it secret for far too long.' He didn't touch me, but

351

his look was almost as intimate. 'I cannot take the memory from you while you are awake. But the minute you fall asleep, I will read the pictures from your mind, and you will dream them, as you have before. That is the gift of the oneiromancer. To create a shared dream.'

'Bet you never get bored.' My voice was laced with contempt. 'Seeing people's dirty laundry.'

He ignored the dig.

'You can learn to keep me out, of course, but you would have to know my spirit almost as well as you know your own. And a spirit as old as mine is difficult to know.' He paused. 'Or you could save yourself the trouble and let me see inside you.'

'What good will come of it?'

'This memory is a barrier. I have sensed it inside you, buried deep in your dreamscape.' His eyes never left mine. 'Overcome it, and you will be free of it. Your spirit will be free of it.'

I took a deep breath. The offer shouldn't tempt me. 'Do I just have to sleep?'

'Yes. I can help you with that.' He scooped a handful of crisp brown leaves from the snuff box. 'This was what was in the pills. If I prepare an infusion, will you take it?'

I shrugged. 'What's one more dose?'

Warden regarded me for a few moments.

'Very well,' he said.

He left the chamber. I guessed there was a kitchen down below, where Michael worked.

I rested my head on the cushions. A slow, cold tremor sidled through my chest, filling the space behind my ribs. I had hated Warden with a violent intensity, hated him because of what he was, and because he seemed to understand me. I had thrived on hating him. Now I was about to show him my most private memory. I thought I knew what it was, but I couldn't be sure. I'd have to dream it.

By the time Warden returned, a defiant certainty had surged up inside me. I took the glass cup from his hands. It was filled to the brim with clear ochre liquid, like diluted honey. Three leaves floated on the surface. 'It tastes bitter,' he warned, 'but it will allow me to see the memories more clearly.'

'What did you see before?'

'Fragments. Periods of silence. It depends how you felt at each individual moment, how strongly you felt it. How much that part of the memory still troubles you.'

I looked down at the tea. 'I don't think I'll need this, then.'

'It will make it easier for you.'

He was probably right. The mere thought of confronting such a memory was already making my hands shake. Feeling as if I was about to sign my life away all over again, I lifted the cup to my lips.

'Wait.'

I paused.

'Paige, you do not have to show me this memory. For your sake, I hope you do. I hope you can. But you can say no. I will respect your privacy.'

'I wouldn't be so cruel,' I said. 'Nothing's worse than a story without an end.' Before he could reply, I drank the tea.

Warden had lied: this stuff wasn't just bitter. It was the foulest thing I'd ever tasted, like a mouthful of metal shards. I decided in a heartbeat that I would rather drink bleach than touch salvia tea ever again. I choked on it. Warden took my face in his hands. 'Hold it down, Paige. Hold it!'

I tried. Some of it came back into the cup, but most of it went down. 'What now?' I coughed.

'Wait.'

I didn't have to wait for long. I hunched over, shuddering as waves of nausea rolled over me. The taste was so pervasive I thought it would never leave my mouth.

And then the lights went out. I fell back on the cushions, and I sank.

The Dissolution

We stood in a circle, like we might in a séance. Six out of seven Seals.

Nadine was going to kill someone. I could see it in every inch of her face. In the middle of the circle was Zeke Sáenz, tied with velvet ribbons to a chair, his head between his sister's hands. We'd been attacking his mind for hours, but no matter how much he struggled and groaned, Jax wouldn't relent. If his gift could be learned, it would be an asset to the gang: the ability to resist all external influence, both from spirits and other voyants. So he sat in his chair, smoking a cigar, waiting for one of us to break him.

Jax had studied Zeke for a long time. The rest of us had been forgotten, left to our own criminal devices. Even after rigorous investigation, he hadn't predicted that our unreadable would be in so much pain when we attacked him. His dreamscape was resilient and opaque, impenetrable by spirits. We'd sent spool after spool at him, to no avail. His mind sent them ricocheting all over the room, like water off a marble. Like his new name – Black Diamond.

'Come on, come *on*, you wretched rabble,' Jax barked. His fist hit the desk. 'I want to hear him scream three times as loud as that!'

He'd been playing 'Danse Macabre' and drinking wine all day: never a good sign. Eliza, pink-faced with the effort of controlling so many spirits, gave him a hard look. 'You wake up on the wrong side of the chaise longue, Jaxon?'

'Again.'

'He's in pain,' Nadine said, her cheeks flushed with anger. 'Look at him! He can't take this!'

'*I'm* in pain, Nadine. Agonised by your recalcitrance.' Deadly soft. 'Don't make me get up, children. Do – it – again.'

There was a short silence. Nadine gripped her brother's shoulders, her hair falling across her face. It was dark brown now, and shorter. It attracted less attention, but she hated it. She hated the citadel. Most of all, she hated us.

When nobody moved, Eliza called on one of her spirit aides – JD, a seventeenth-century muse. When it jumped out of her dreamscape, into the æther, the lights flickered. 'I'll try JD.' Her brow was pinched. 'If an old spirit doesn't work, I don't think anything will.'

'A poltergeist, perhaps?' Jax said, perfectly serious.

'We are *not* using a 'geist on him!'

Jax carried on smoking. 'Pity.'

On the other side of the room, Nick pulled the blinds down. He was appalled at what we were doing, but he couldn't stop it.

Zeke couldn't take the suspense. His fevered eyes were on the spirit. 'What are they doing, Dee?'

'I don't know.' Nadine fixed a cold stare on Jaxon. 'He needs rest. You set that spirit on him and I'll—'

'You'll what?' Smoke curled from Jaxon's mouth. 'Play me an angry tune? Please, be my guest. I do enjoy music from the soul.'

Her chin puckered, but she didn't rise to the bait. She knew the punishment for disobeying Jaxon. She had nowhere else to go, nowhere else to take her brother.

Zeke shivered against her. As if he were younger than her, not two years older.

Eliza glanced at Nadine, then at Jaxon. On her silent command, the muse whipped forward. I didn't see it, but I felt it – and from Zeke's cry of agony, so did he. His head slammed back, and the muscles in his neck strained out. Nadine's lips clamped together as she wrapped both arms around him. 'I'm sorry.' She rested her chin on his head. 'I'm so sorry, Zeke.'

Old and determined, JD was naturally obstinate. It had been told that Zeke was going to hurt Eliza, and it fully intended to stop that from happening. Zeke's face shone with sweat and tears. He was almost choking.

'Please,' he said. 'No more—'

'Jaxon, stop it,' I snapped. 'Don't you think he's had enough?'

His eyebrows jumped towards his hairline. 'Are you questioning me, Paige?'

My courage faded. 'No.'

'In the syndicate, you are expected to earn your keep. I am your mime-lord. Your protector. Your employer. The man who keeps you from starving, like the wretched buskers!' He chucked a wad of money into the air, sending Frank Weaver's face fluttering across the carpet. It stared at us from every note. 'Ezekiel has only had "enough" when I say so – when I choose to give him freedom for the day. Do you think Hector would stop? Do you think Jimmy or the Abbess would just *stop*?'

'We don't work for them.' Eliza looked shaken. She motioned to the spirit. 'Come on back, JD. I'm safe.'

The spirit slunk away. Zeke put his head in his shaking hands. 'I'm okay,' he managed. 'I'm fine. I just – just need a minute.'

'You are *not* okay.' Nadine turned back to Jaxon, who was lighting another cigar. 'You preyed on us. You knew about the operation and made out like you were going to make it better. You said you'd fix him. You *promised* you'd fix him!'

'I said I would try.' Jaxon was unmoved. 'That I would experiment.'

'You're a liar. You're just like—'

'If this place is so terrible then go, dear girl. The door is always open.' His voice dropped a few notes. 'The door to the cold, dark streets.' He blew a grey plume in her direction. 'I wonder how long it will take for the NVD to . . . smoke you out?'

Nadine shook with anger. 'I'm going to Chat's.' She snatched her lace jacket. 'No one is welcome to join me.'

She grabbed her headphones and her purse before she stormed out, slamming the door behind her. 'Dee,' Zeke started, but she didn't stop. I heard her kick something on her way down the stairs. Pieter came shooting through the wall, furious at being disturbed, and went to sulk in the corner. 'I think it's home time now, captain,' Eliza said firmly. 'We've been doing this for hours.'

'Wait.' Jax pointed a long finger in my direction. 'We haven't tried our secret weapon yet.' When I frowned, he tilted his head. 'Oh, come now, Paige. Don't play the fool. Break into his dreamscape for me.'

'We've discussed this.' I was starting to get a headache. 'I don't do break-ins.'

'You don't *do* them. I see. I didn't realise you had a job description. Oh! Wait, I remember – I didn't give you one.' He crushed his cigar against the ashtray. 'We are clairvoyants. Unnaturals. Did you think we were going to be like Daddy, sitting in our little Barbican offices from nine to five, sipping *tea* from our little Styrofoam cups?' All of a sudden he looked disgusted, like he couldn't abide how amaurotic people could be. 'Some of us don't want Styrofoam, Paige. Some of us want silver and satin and sordid streets and *spirits*.'

I couldn't help but stare. He took a huge gulp of wine, his eyes fixed on the window. Eliza shook her head. 'Okay, this is getting ridiculous. Maybe we should just—'

'Who pays you?'

She sighed. 'You do, Jaxon.'

'Correct. I pay, you obey. Now, be the saint you are and run upstairs and get Danica for me. I want her to see the magic.'

With lips pursed tight, Eliza left the room. Zeke shot me a look of exhausted desperation. I forced myself to speak again. 'Jax, I'm really not up to it right now. I think we all need some rest.'

'You have a few hours off tomorrow, honeybee.' He sounded absent-minded.

'I can't break into dreamscapes. You know that.'

'Humour me. Try.' Jaxon poured himself some more wine. 'I've been waiting for this for *years*. A dreamwalker versus an unreadable. The ultimate ethereal encounter. Never could I conceive of a more dangerous and daring happenstance.'

'Are you still speaking English?'

'No,' Nick said. Every head turned towards him. 'He's speaking like a madman.'

After a short silence, Jaxon raised his glass. 'An excellent diagnosis, doctor. Cheers.'

He drank. Nick looked away.

It was in the strained aftermath of that moment that Eliza returned with a clean syringe of adrenalin. With her was Danica Panić, the final member of our septet. She'd grown up in the Scion Citadel of Belgrade, but transferred to London to work as an engineer. Nick had been the one to headhunt her, having spied her aura at a drinks event for new recruits. She took great pride in the fact that none of us could pronounce her name. Or her surname. She was solid as a brick, with crimped reddish hair, worn in a low bun, and arms pitted with scars and burns. Her only soft spot was for waistcoats.

'Danica, my dear.' Jaxon beckoned her. 'Come and take a look at this, will you?'

'What am I looking at?' she said.

'My weapon.'

I exchanged a glance with Dani. She'd only been with us for a week, but she already knew what Jax was like.

'Looks like you're having a séance,' she observed.

'Not today.' He waved a hand. 'Begin.'

I had to bite my tongue to stop myself telling him where to stick it. He always buttered up the newcomers. Dani had a bright, hyperactive aura that he hadn't been able to identify – but as usual, he was convinced she would be something valuable.

I sat down. Nick swabbed my arm and punched in the syringe.

'Do it,' Jax said. 'Read the unreadable.'

I gave my blood a minute to absorb the mix of drugs, then closed my eyes and felt for the æther. Zeke braced himself. I couldn't invade him – only caress his dreamscape, feel the faint nuances of its surface – but his mind was so sensitive, even a nudge could hurt him. I'd have to be careful.

My spirit shifted. I registered all five of their dreamscapes, tinkling and shivering like wind chimes. Zeke's was different. He chimed on a darker note, a minor chord. I tried to catch a glimpse of him: a memory, a fear – but there was nothing. Where I'd normally see a shimmer of pictures, like a distorted old film, all I saw was black. His memories were sealed.

I jerked from the æther when a hand grasped my shoulder. Zeke was trembling, his hands over his ears. 'Enough.' Nick was behind me, pulling me to my feet. 'That's enough. She's not doing this. Jaxon, I don't care what you pay me – you're paying me in blood diamonds.' He threw the window open. 'Come on, Paige. You're taking a break.'

I was tired to my bones, but I would never refuse Nick. Jaxon's eyes sent darts into my back. He'd be fine by tomorrow, once he'd finished all the wine. I swung myself out of the window and onto the drainpipe, my vision blurred.

As soon as his feet hit the roof, Nick started to run. Today he was running fast, and running hard. Fortunately there was still adrenalin in my veins, or I would never have kept up.

We'd often do this. Take a *dérive* through the city. In theory, London was everything I hated: huge and grey and stern, raining nine days out of ten. It roared and pumped and pounded like a human heart. But after two years of training with Nick, learning how to navigate the rooftops, the citadel had become my haven. I could fly through traffic and over the heads of the NVD. I could race like blood through the mesh of streets and alleys. I was full to the brim, bursting with life. Out here, if nowhere else, I was free.

Nick dropped down to the street. We jogged along the busy road until we reached the corner of Leicester Square. Without stopping for breath, Nick began to climb the nearest building, right next to the Hippodrome Casino. There were plenty of handholds, window-sills and ledges and the like, but I doubted I could keep up. Even adrenalin couldn't make a dent in my fatigue.

'What are you doing, Nick?'

'I need to clear my head.' He sounded weary.

'In a casino?'

'Above it.' He held out a hand. 'Come on, *sötnos*. You look like you're about to fall asleep.'

'Yeah, well, I didn't know I was going to give my spirit *and* my muscles a thrashing today.' I let him haul me up to the first windowsill, earning a look from a girl with a cigarette. 'How far are we climbing?'

'To the top of this building. If you can handle it,' he added.

'What if I can't handle it?'

'Fine. Jump up.' He pulled my arms around his neck. 'And what's the golden rule?'

'Don't look down.'

'Correct,' he said, imitating Jax. I laughed.

We reached the top without incident or injury. Nick had been climbing buildings since he could toddle; he found footholds where none seemed to exist. Soon we were back on the rooftops, the streets far below us. My feet fell on artificial grass. On my left was a small fountain – no water – and on my right, a bed of shrivelled flowers. 'What is this place?'

'Roof garden. I found it a few weeks ago. I've never seen it used, so I thought I'd make it my new bolthole.' Nick leaned on the railing. 'Sorry to snatch you like that, *sötnos*. Dials can get a little claustrophobic.'

'Just a bit.'

We didn't talk about what had just happened. Nick got too frustrated by Jaxon's tactics. He tossed me a cereal bar. We looked out at the dusky pink horizon, almost as if we were watching for ships.

'Paige,' he said, 'have you ever been in love?'

My hand shook. The mouthful seemed very difficult to swallow: my throat had closed up.

'I think so.' Little cold chills ran up and down my sides. I rested my back on the railing. 'I mean – maybe. Why do you ask?'

'Because I want to ask you what it's like. To try and work out whether or not I'm in love.'

I nodded, trying to create the impression that I was calm. In reality, something slow and unsettling was happening to my body: I was seeing tiny black dots, my head was feather-light, my palms were clammy and my heart was beating hard. 'Tell me,' I said.

His eyes stayed on the sunset. 'When you fall in love with someone,' he said, 'do you feel protective of them?'

This was strange for two reasons. One, because I was in love with Nick. I had known that for a long time, even if I had never done anything about it. And two, because Nick was twenty-seven and I was eighteen. It was as if our natural roles had been reversed. 'Yes.' I looked down. 'At least, I think so. I did – I *do* feel protective of him.'

'Do you ever want to just . . . touch them?'

'All the time,' I admitted, a little shyly. 'Or – more like . . . I want *him* to touch *me*. Even if it's just to—'

'—hold you.'

I nodded, not looking at him.

'Because I feel as if I understand this person, and I want them to be happy. But I don't know *how* to make them happy. In fact, I know that just by loving them, I will make them terribly unhappy.' His brow creased the way book paper does. 'I don't know whether to risk even telling them, because I know how much unhappiness it will cause. Or I *think* I know. Is that important, Paige? To be happy?'

'How can you think it's not important?'

'Because I don't know whether honesty is better than happiness. Do we sacrifice honesty in order to be happy?'

'Sometimes. But it's better to be honest, I think. Otherwise you're living a lie.' I weighed the words, steering him towards telling me, trying to ignore the shattering din in my head.

'Because you have to trust them.'

'Yes.'

My eyes were hot. I tried to breathe slowly, but in my head, a terrible reality was dawning. Nick wasn't talking about me.

Of course, he'd never actually said anything to suggest he felt the same way as I did. Not a word. But what about all the casual touches, all the hours of attention – all the times we'd run together? What about the last two years of my life, when I'd spent nearly every day and night in his company?

Nick was staring at the sky.

'Hey, look,' he said.

'What?'

He motioned to a star. 'Arcturus. I've never seen it that bright.'

The star had an orange tint, and it was huge and brilliant. I felt small enough to disappear. 'So,' I said, trying to sound normal, 'who is it? Who do you think you're in love with?'

Nick brought his hand to his head.

'Zeke.'

At first, I wasn't sure I'd heard him. 'Zeke.' I turned my head to look at him. 'Zeke Sáenz?'

Nick nodded. 'Do you think it's really hopeless?' he asked softly. 'That he could love me?'

My face was losing sensation.

'You never said anything to me,' I began. My chest was locking up. 'I didn't know—'

'You couldn't have known.' He ran a hand over his face. 'I can't help it, Paige. I know I could just find somebody else, but I can't even begin to look. I wouldn't know where to start. I think he's the most beautiful person in the world. I thought it was my imagination at first, but now he's been with us for a year' – he closed his eyes – 'I can't deny it. I really care about him.'

Not me. I just sat there in silence, feeling as if somebody was pumping a numbing agent into my arteries. It wasn't me he loved.

'I think I could help him.' There was real passion in his voice. 'I could help him face the past. I could help him remember things. He used to be a whisperer – I could help him hear the voices again.'

I wished I could hear voices. I wished I could hear spirits, so I could listen to them, and not to this. I had to focus on not crying. No matter what happened tonight, I could not, *would* not cry. I'd be damned if I would cry. Nick had every right to love somebody else. Why shouldn't he? I had never said a word to him about how I felt. I ought to be happy for him. But some small, secret part of me had always hoped that he might feel the same – that he might have been waiting for the right moment to tell me. A moment like this.

'What do you get from his dreamscape?' Nick was looking at me, waiting for a response. 'Anything?'

'Just darkness.'

'Maybe I could try. Maybe I could send him a picture.' He smiled thinly. 'Or just talk to him, like a normal person.'

'He'd listen,' I said. 'If you told him. How do you know he doesn't feel the same way?'

'I think he has enough to deal with. Besides, you know the rules. No commitment. Jaxon would burst a blood vessel if he knew.'

'Stuff Jaxon. It's not fair for you to carry this.'

'I've managed a year, *sötnos*. I can manage longer.'

My throat was tight. He was right, of course. Jaxon didn't let us commit. He didn't like relationships. Even if Nick had loved me, we couldn't have been together. But now the truth was staring me in the face – now the dream had shattered – I could hardly breathe. This man was not mine. He had never been mine. And no matter how much I loved him, he *would* never be mine.

'Why didn't you ever tell me?' I grasped the railing. 'I mean – I know it's none of my business, but—'

'I didn't want to worry you. You've had problems of your own to deal with. I knew Jax would be interested in you, but he's put you through hell and back. He still treats you like a shiny new toy. It makes me sorry I ever brought you into this.'

'No. No, don't think that.' I turned to him and squeezed his hand, too tight. 'You saved me, Nick. Sooner or later I would have lost my mind. I had to know, or I would have always felt like an outsider. You made me feel like I was part of something, part of a lot of things, actually. I'll never be able to repay you for that.'

Shock registered on his face. 'You look like you're going to cry.'

'I'm not.' I let go of his hand. 'Look, I have to go. I'm meeting someone.'

I wasn't.

'Paige, wait. Don't go.' He grasped my wrist, pulled me back. 'I've upset you, haven't I? What is it?'

'I'm not upset.'

'You are. Please, just wait a second.'

'I really have to go, Nick.'

'You've never had to go when I needed you.'

'I'm sorry.' I pulled my blazer close. 'If you want my advice, you should go back to base and tell Zeke how you feel. If he's got even a single bit of sanity left in there, he'll say yes.' I looked up at him with a sad smile. 'I know I would.'

And I saw it. First confusion, then disbelief, then dismay.

He knew.

'Paige,' he started.

'It's late.' I swung myself over the railing, my hands trembling. 'I'll see you on Monday, okay?'

'No. Paige, wait. *Wait*.'

'Nick. Please.'

He closed his mouth, but his eyes were still wide. I climbed back down the building, leaving him to stand beneath the moon. It was only when I reached the bottom that the first and only tears came. I closed my eyes and breathed the night air.

I don't know exactly how I got to I-5. Maybe I took the Underground. Maybe I walked. My father was still at work; he wasn't expecting me. I stood in the empty apartment, gazing at the skylight. For the first time since childhood, I wished for a mother, or a sister, or even a friend – a friend outside the Seals. As it happened, I didn't have any of those things. I had no idea what to do, what to feel. What would an amaurotic girl do in my situation? Spend a week in bed, most probably. But I wasn't an amaurotic girl, and it wasn't as if I'd broken up with someone. Just with a dream. A childish dream.

I thought back to my days at school, when I'd been the sole voyant among amaurotics. Suzette, one of my only friends, had broken up with her boyfriend in our final year. I tried to remember what she'd done. She hadn't spent a week in bed, as I recalled. What had she done? Wait. I remembered. She'd sent me a text, asking me to go with her to a club. *Want to dance my cares away*, she'd said. I'd made an excuse, as I always did.

This would be my night. I would dance my cares away. I would forget that it had ever happened. I would get rid of this pain.

I stripped off my clothes, took a shower, then dried and straightened my hair. I put on lipstick and mascara and kohl. I dabbed a little perfume on my pulse points. I pinched my cheeks to make them pink. When I was done, I slipped a black lace dress on, stepped into a pair of open-toe heels and left the apartment.

The guard looked at me strangely as I passed.

I took a cab. There was a flash house in the East End that Nadine frequented, with cheap mecks (and sometimes real, illegal alcohol) served on weekdays. It was in a rough part of II-6, an area notorious for being one of the few safe places for voyants to hang out: even Gillies didn't like to go there.

A huge bouncer guarded the door, wearing a suit and hat. He waved me through.

It was dark and hot inside. The space was small, cramped, packed with sweating bodies. A bar ran the length of one wall, serving oxygen and mecks from different ends. To the right of the bar was a dance floor. The people were mostly amaurotic, hipster types in tweed trousers, tiny hats and brightly coloured neckties. I had no idea what I was doing here, watching amaurotics jump around to deafening music, but that was what I wanted: to be spontaneous, to forget the real world.

Nine years I had spent adoring Nick. I would make it a clean break. I wouldn't allow myself to stop and feel.

I went to the oxygen bar and perched on a stool. The bartender looked me over, but didn't address me. He was voyant, a seer – he wouldn't want to talk. But it didn't take long for someone else to notice me.

There was a group of young men at the other end of the bar, probably students from USL. They were all amaurotic, of course. Few voyants made it to University level. I was just about to order a shot of Floxy when one of them approached me. Nineteen or twenty, he was clean-shaven and a little sunburned. Must have been to another citadel for his year abroad. Scion Athens, perhaps. He wore a cap over his dark hair.

'Hey,' he said above the music. 'You here by yourself?'

I nodded. He took a seat beside me. 'Reuben,' he said, by way of introduction. 'Can I get you a drink?'

'Mecks,' I said. 'If you don't mind.'

'Not at all.' He motioned to the bartender, who clearly knew him. 'Blood mecks, Gresham.'

The bartender's brow was creased, but he kept his silence as he poured my blood mecks. It was the most expensive of the alcohol substitutes, made with cherries, black grapes and plums. Reuben leaned in close to my ear. 'So,' he said, 'what are you here for?'

'No real reason.'

'You don't have a boyfriend?'

'Maybe.' *No.*

'I just broke up with my girlfriend. And I was thinking, when you walked in – well, I thought stuff I probably shouldn't think when a pretty girl walks into a bar. But then I thought a girl as pretty as you would have a boyfriend with her. Am I right?'

'No,' I said. 'Just me.'

Gresham pushed my mecks across the surface of the bar. 'That'll be two,' he said. Reuben handed him two gold coins. 'Am I to assume you're eighteen, young lady?'

I showed him my ID and he went back to cleaning out the glasses, but he kept an eye on me as I sipped my drink. I wondered what troubled him: my age, my appearance, my aura? Probably all three.

I jerked back to reality when Reuben shifted closer. His breath smelled like apples. 'Are you at the University?' he said.

'No.'

'What do you do?'

'Oxygen bar.'

He nodded, sipped his drink.

I wasn't sure how to do it. To give the sign. Was there a sign? I looked right into his eyes, ran the toe of my shoe along his leg. It seemed to work. He glanced at his friends, who had gone back to their game of shots. 'You want to go somewhere?' His voice was low, hoarse. It was now or never. I nodded.

Reuben linked his fingers through mine and led me through the crowd. Gresham watched me. Probably thinking what a minx I was.

I became aware that Reuben wasn't leading me to my imagined dark corner. He was leading me to the toilets. At least, I thought he was until he guided me through another door, out into the staff car park. It was a tiny rectangular space, only able to hold six cars. Okay, he wanted privacy. That was good. Wasn't it? At least it meant he wasn't just showing off for his friends.

Before I could so much as take a breath, Reuben pushed me up against the dirty brick wall. I smelled sweat and cigarettes. To my shock, he started to unbuckle his belt. 'Wait,' I said. 'I didn't mean—'

'Hey, come on. It's just a little fun. Besides' – he dropped his belt – 'it's not like we're cheating.'

He kissed me. His lips were firm. A wet tongue thrust into my mouth, and I tasted artificial flavouring. I'd never been kissed before. I wasn't sure I liked it.

He was right. Just a little fun. Of course it was. What could go wrong? Normal people did this, didn't they? They drank, they did stupid reckless things, they had sex. This was just what I needed. Jax allowed us to do this – just not to commit. I wasn't going to commit. No strings. Eliza did it.

My head told me to stop. Why was I doing this? How had I ended up here, in the dark, with a stranger? It wouldn't prove anything. It wouldn't stop the pain. It would make it worse. But now Reuben was on his knees, pushing my dress up to my waist. He pressed a kiss to my bare stomach.

'You're so pretty.'

I didn't feel it.

'You never told me your name.' He traced the edge of my underwear. I shivered.

'Eva,' I said.

The thought of sex with him repulsed me. I didn't know him. I didn't want him. But I reasoned it was because I still loved Nick, and I had to make myself stop loving him. I grabbed Reuben's hair and crushed my lips to his. He made a noise and pulled my legs around him.

A little quiver shot through me. I'd never actually done it before. Wasn't it meant to be special, the first time? But I couldn't stop. I had to do this.

The streetlamp shone with a fitful light, blinding me. Reuben placed his hands against the brick wall. I had no idea what to expect. It was exhilarating.

Then pain. Explosive, stunning pain. Like a fist had done a cruel uppercut into my stomach.

Reuben had no idea what had just happened. I waited for it to pass, but it didn't. He noticed my tension.

'You okay?'

'I'm fine,' I whispered.

'This your first time?'

'No, of course not.'

He bent his head to my neck, kissing from my shoulder to my ear. Before he even tried to move, the pain came again, worse this time, a vicious racking pain. Reuben drew back. 'It is,' he said.

'It doesn't matter.'

'Look, I just don't think I should—'

'Fine.' I shoved him away. 'Just – just leave me alone, then. I don't want you. I don't want anyone.'

I pushed off the wall and stumbled back into the flash house, pulling down my dress. I only just made it to the toilet in time to throw up. Pain lashed through my thighs and stomach. I curled myself around the toilet bowl, coughing and sobbing. Never in my life had I felt so stupid.

I thought of Nick. I thought of all the years I had spent thinking about him, wondering if he would ever come back to me. And I thought of him now, pictured his smile, how he looked after me, and it was useless: I just wanted him. I put my head in my arms and cried.

Change

The intensity of the memory knocked me out for a very long time. I had re-lived every detail of that night, down to the faintest tremor. I woke up to total darkness, with no idea what time or day it was. 'It's a Sin to Tell a Lie' strained softly from the gramophone.

There were so many memories I could have shown him. I had lived through the Molly Riots, through my father's bereavement, through years of cruelty at the hands of Scion schoolgirls – yet I'd shown him the night I was turned down by a boy I loved. It seemed so little and so insignificant, but it was my one normal, *human* memory. The one time I had given myself to a stranger. The one and only time my heart had ever been broken.

I didn't believe in hearts. I believed in dreamscapes and spirits. Those were what mattered. Those made money. But my heart had hurt that day. For the first time in my life I'd been forced to acknowledge my heart, and acknowledge its fragility. It could be bruised. It could humiliate me.

I was older now. Maybe I'd changed. Maybe I'd grown up, grown stronger. I wasn't that girl on the brink of maturity, desperate to connect, to find someone to lean on. She was long gone. Now I was a weapon, a puppet to the machinations of others. I couldn't work out which was worse.

A tongue of fire still tantalised the embers in the hearth. It cast light on the figure by the window.

'Welcome back.'

I didn't reply. Warden glanced over his shoulder.

'Go on,' I said. 'You must have something to say.'

'No, Paige.'

A moment passed in silence.

'You think it was stupid. You're right.' I looked at my hands. 'I just – I wanted—'

'To be seen.' He looked into the fire. 'I believe I understand why that memory affects you so deeply. It is at the heart of your greatest fear: that there is nothing to you beyond your gift. Beyond the dreamwalker. That is the part of you you see as truly valuable – your livelihood. You lost your other parts in Ireland. Now you rely on Jaxon Hall, who treats you as his commodity. To him, you are nothing more than quick flesh grafted to a ghost; a priceless gift in human wrapping. But Nick Nygård showed you more than that.'

I was looking at him now.

'That night opened your eyes. When you realised Nick loved another, you faced your greatest fear: that you would never be acknowledged as a human – as the sum of all your parts. Only as a curiosity. You had no choice but to show yourself otherwise. To find the first person who would have you, someone who knew nothing of the dreamwalker. That was all you had left.'

'Don't even think about pitying me,' I said.

'I do not pity you. But I do know what it feels like. To be wanted only for what you are.'

'It won't happen again.'

'But your solitude did not keep you safe. Did it?'

I looked away. I hated that he knew. I hated that I'd let him work me out. Warden came to sit beside me on the bed.

'The mind of an amaurotic is like water. Bland, grey, transparent. Enough to sustain life, but no more. But a clairvoyant mind is more like oil, richer in every way. And like oil and water, they can never truly mix.'

'You're saying that because he was amaurotic—'

'Yes.'

At least there wasn't anything wrong with my body. I had never been brave enough to see a doctor about that night. Scion doctors were cold and unforgiving on such matters.

Something occurred to me. 'If voyant minds are like oil' – I weighed my words – 'what are your minds like?'

For a moment, I wasn't sure he was going to reply. Finally, in a thick, velvet undertone, he said one word.

'Fire.'

That single word sent a tremor through my skin. I thought of what oil and fire did together: exploded.

No. I couldn't think about him like that. He wasn't human. Whether or not he understood me was irrelevant. He was still my keeper. He was still a Rephaite. He was everything he'd been at the beginning.

Warden turned to face me. 'Paige,' he said, 'there was another memory. Before you passed out.'

'What memory?'

'Blood. A great deal of it.'

I shook my head, too tired to think about it. 'Probably when my clairvoyance came out. The poltergeist had a lot of blood in her memories.'

'No. I have seen that memory. There was far more blood in this one. All around you, choking you.'

'I have no idea what you're talking about.' And I didn't. I really didn't.

Warden regarded me for a while.

'Sleep a little longer,' he finally said. 'When you wake up tomorrow, put your mind to better things.'

'Like what?'

'Like escaping from this city. When the time comes, you must be ready.'

'So you're going to help me.' When he didn't answer, I lost my patience. 'I've shown you everything of mine – my life, my memories. I still have no idea what your motives are. What do you want?'

'While Nashira has us both under her thumb, it is best that you know as little as possible. That way, if she interrogates you again, you can safely say that you have no knowledge of the matter.'

'What "matter"?'

'You are very persistent.'

'Why do you think I'm still alive?'

'Because you are inured to danger.' He clasped his hands on his knees. 'I cannot tell you about my motives, but I will tell you a little about the red flower, if you wish.'

The offer took me by surprise. 'Go on.'

'Do you know the story of Adonis?'

'They don't teach the classics in Scion schools.'

'Of course. Forgive me.'

'Wait.' I thought of Jax's stolen books. Jax loved mythology. He called it *deliciously illicit.* 'Was he a god?'

'The beloved of Aphrodite. He was a youthful, beautiful, mortal hunter. Aphrodite was so taken with his beauty, she preferred his company even to that of the other gods. Legend tells that her paramour, the war god Ares, grew so jealous of the pair that he turned himself into a boar and slaughtered Adonis. He died in Aphrodite's arms, and his blood stained the earth.

'As she cradled the body of her beloved, Aphrodite sprinkled nectar over his blood. And from the blood of Adonis sprang the anemone: a short-lived, perennial flower, stained as red as the blood itself – and the spirit of Adonis was sent, like all spirits, to languish in the underworld. Zeus heard Aphrodite crying for her love, and out of pity for the goddess, he agreed to let Adonis spend half the year in life, and half in death.' Warden looked at me. 'Consider it, Paige. There may not be any such thing as monsters, but there are still some pockets of truth in the shrouds of your mythology.'

'Don't tell me you're *gods*. I don't think I could stand the thought of Nashira being holy.'

'We are many things, but "holy" is not one of them.' He paused. 'I have said too much. You need rest.'

'I'm not tired.'

'Even so, you need to sleep. I have something to show you tomorrow night.'

I leaned back against the pillows. I did feel tired.

'This doesn't mean I trust you,' I said. 'It just means I'm trying.'

'Then I can ask no more of you.' He patted the sheets. 'Sleep well, little dreamer.'

I couldn't hold out any longer. I turned over and closed my eyes, still thinking of red flowers and gods.

I woke to the sound of a knock. The sky outside was rosy, bloodshot. Warden stood by the fire, his hand on the mantelpiece. His gaze slashed towards the door.

'Paige,' he said, 'hide. Quickly.'

I got out of the bed and went straight to the door behind the drapes. I left it slightly ajar, pulling the red velvet over the gap, and listened. I could still see the fireplace.

The chamber door unlocked and opened. Nashira stepped into the light of the fire. She must have a key to his tower. Warden knelt, but did not complete the ritual. She ran her fingers over the bed.

'Where is she?'

'Sleeping,' Warden said.

'In her own room?'

'Yes.'

'Liar. She sleeps here. The sheets smell of her.' Her bare fingers grasped his chin. 'Do you really want to go down that road?'

'I do not understand your meaning. I think of nothing and no one but you.'

'Perhaps.' Her fingers tightened. 'The chains still hang. Do not think for a moment that I will hesitate to send you back to the House. Do not think for a moment that there will be a repeat of Bone Season XVIII. If there is, I will not spare a single life. Not even yours. Not this time. Do you understand me?' When he didn't reply, she struck him across the face, hard. I flinched. 'Answer me.'

'I have had twenty years to reflect on my folly. You were right. Humans cannot be trusted.'

There was a brief silence. 'I am pleased to hear it.' Her voice was softer. 'All will be well. We will have this tower all to ourselves soon. You can make good on your vow to me.'

She was insane. How could she go from hitting him to making that kind of overture?

'Am I to understand,' Warden said, 'that 40's time has run out?'

I stayed absolutely still, listening.

'She is ready. I know she took possession of 12 in the citadel. Your cousin told me.' She ran her finger under his chin. 'You have nurtured her gift well.'

'For you, my sovereign.' He looked up at her. 'Will you claim her in the shadows? Or will you show all of Scion your great power?'

'Either will suffice. At *last* I will have the ability to dreamwalk. At last I will have the power to invade, to possess. All thanks to you, my beloved Arcturus.' She placed a small vial on the mantelpiece, and her voice grew cold again. 'This will be your last dose of amaranth until the Bicentenary. I believe you need time to reflect on your scars. To remember why you should look to the future. Not to the past.'

'I will suffer whatever you ask of me.'

'You will not have to suffer for long. Soon we will have our bliss.' She turned towards the door. 'Take care of her, Arcturus.'

The door closed.

Warden stood. For a moment I wasn't sure what he would do. Then he threw out a fist and smashed the glass urn on the mantelpiece. I went to my bed and listened to the silence.

He wasn't my enemy. Not the enemy I'd thought he was.

She'd said she would send him back to the House. Proof that he was involved in Bone Season XVIII. Proof of his betrayal. That was what Thuban had meant when he'd threatened Terebell. They'd tried to help us and been punished for it. They'd chosen the wrong side. The losing side.

I tossed and turned for hours. I couldn't stop thinking about their conversation. How she hit him. How she brought him to his knees. And how soon, very soon, she intended to get rid of me. I kicked the sheets off and lay in the dark with my eyes open. The realisation had taken a long time, but now I understood. Warden was on my side.

I thought of the scars on Terebell's back, the ones Thuban Sargas had mentioned with that hint of cruelty. He and his family had scarred her. She and Warden were the scarred ones. Something terrible had happened in the House after that day, Novembertide of 2039. I didn't know Terebell, but she had saved my life; I owed her. And I owed Warden for taking care of me.

If there was one thing I couldn't bear, it was being beholden to someone. But when he spoke to me next, I would listen. I would hear him out. I sat up. No, *not* when he spoke to me next – now. I had to talk to him. Trusting him was my only chance. I would not die here. I had to know, once and for all, what Arcturus Mesarthim wanted. I had to know if he would help me.

I got out of bed and went into the chamber. Empty. Outside, the rain thundered from black clouds. The grandfather clock chimed four in the morning. I picked up the note on the writing table.

I have gone to the chapel. I will be back before dawn.

To hell with sleep. I'd had enough of games, of crossing wires with him. I pulled on my boots and left the tower.

The wind howled outside. There was a guard in the cloisters. I waited until she passed before I ran. The thunder and the darkness gave me cover, letting me slip past unnoticed. But above the rain, there swelled a new sound: music. I followed it into another passage, where a vast door stood ajar. Beyond it was a small chapel, set apart from the rest of the building by an elaborate stone screen. Candlelight flickered in the darkness. There was someone up there, playing the organ. The sound rang in my ears, through my chest.

A small door stood open in the screen. I went through it, up the steps. At the top was the organ. Warden sat at the bench with his back to me. The music resonated through the ranks of pipes, up to the ceiling: a sound that rose through the chapel, above it. A sound that surged with terrible regret. Nobody could play this without some degree of feeling.

The music stopped. He turned his head. When he didn't say anything, I sat on the bench beside him. We sat in the dark, with only the light from his eyes and the candle.

'You should be sleeping.'

'I've slept enough.' I touched my fingers to the keys. 'I didn't know Rephaim could play.'

'We have mastered the art of mimicry over the years.'

'That wasn't mimicry. That was you.'

There was a long silence.

'You have come to ask about your freedom,' he said. 'That is what you want.'

'Yes.'

'Of course it is. You may not believe it, but it is what I desire most in the world. This place has afflicted me with a terrible wander-lust. I long for your fire, for the sights that you have seen. Yet here I am, two hundred years after I arrived. Still a prisoner, though I masquerade as a king.'

I could empathise with his wanderlust, if nothing else.

'I was betrayed once. On the eve of Novembertide, when the uprising of Bone Season XVIII was to begin, one human chose to betray us all. In exchange for freedom, the traitor sacrificed every-one in this city.' He looked at me. 'You see why Nashira is not threatened by the prospect of a second rebellion. She believes you are all too self-seeking to come together.'

I did see. To have planned so much for human freedom, only to have us bite the hand that fought for us – no wonder he hadn't trusted me. No wonder he'd been so cold.

'But you, Paige – you threaten her. She knows you are one of the Seven Seals, that you are the Pale Dreamer. You have the power to bring the spirit of the syndicate into this city. She fears that spirit.'

'There's nothing to fear from it. It's full of petty criminals and backstabbers.'

'That is dependent on its leaders. It has the potential to become something much greater.'

'The syndicate exists because of Scion. Scion exists because of the Rephaim,' I said. 'You made your own enemy.'

'I recognise the irony. So does Nashira.' He turned to face me. 'Bone Season XVIII rebelled because the prisoners were accus-tomed to being organised. There was strength and solidarity among them. We must resurrect that strength. And this time, we must not fail.' He looked at the window. 'I must not fail.'

I didn't speak. I thought about reaching for his hand, inches from mine on the keys.

In the end, I didn't take the risk.

'I want to leave,' I said. 'That's all I want. To go back to the citadel with as many people as possible.'

'Then our aims are different. If we are to help one another, we must reconcile that difference.'

'What do *you* want?'

'To strike against the Sargas. To show them what it means to be afraid.'

I thought of Julian. I thought of Finn. And I thought of Liss, slipping away into amaurosis. 'How do you propose to do that?'

'I have one idea.' His gaze flicked down to mine. 'I would like to show you something, if you are willing.'

I meant to reply, but I didn't. His chartreuse eyes grew warmer as he looked at me. I was close enough to feel his heat. 'I desire to trust you,' he said.

'You can.'

'Then you will come with me.'

'Where?'

'To see Michael.' He stood. 'There is a disused building to the north of the Great Quad. The guards must not see us.'

Now he had my attention. I nodded.

I followed him from the chapel. He looked through the arches, searching for the guards. None appeared.

He motioned with his hand. A nearby ghost wheeled towards him and raced down the passage, extinguishing the torches. As the darkness closed in, he took my hand. I had to half-run to keep up with his strides. He led me through an archway and out onto a gravel path.

The disused building was as daunting as the others. By the dim flush of dawn I could see a series of arches, rectangular barred windows and a tympanum with a ring carved into it. Warden led me through the arches, took a key from his sleeve and opened a rotten door. 'What is this place?' I said.

'A safe house.'

He went inside. I followed, pulling the door closed behind me. Warden bolted it.

It was pitch black in the safe house. His eyes cast a soft light over the walls. 'These were wine cellars once,' he said as we walked. 'I spent years clearing them. As the highest-ranking Rephaite at this residence, I was able to forbid entry to whichever buildings I chose. This safe house is accessible by only a small group of individuals. Michael included.'

'Who else?'

'You know who else.'

The scarred ones. I shivered. This was their safe house, their meeting place. He opened a gate in the wall. Beyond it was an opening, not much more than a crawl space. 'Go through.'

'What's in there?'

'Someone who can help you.'

'I thought *you* were going to help me.'

'The humans in this city would never trust a Rephaite to organise them. They would think it was a trick, as you have always believed. It must be you.'

'You led us before.'

Warden looked away.

'Go,' he said. 'Michael is waiting.'

His brow was dark. I wondered how many years of work had come crashing down around him.

'It can be different this time,' I said.

He didn't reply. His eyes were dim, and his skin had a soft sheen. The lack of amaranth was already taking its toll.

Not having much of a choice, I crawled into a cool, dark tunnel. Warden closed the gate behind us. 'Keep going.'

I did. When I reached the end, a slim hand grasped mine. I looked up to see Michael, his face lit by a candle. Warden emerged from the tunnel.

'Show her, Michael. It is your work.'

Michael nodded again, beckoning me. I followed him into the darkness. He flicked a switch and a light came on, revealing a large underground room. I looked at the light for a moment, trying to work out why it seemed so strange. Then it hit me.

'Electricity.' I couldn't take my eyes off it. 'There's no power here. How did you—?' Michael was smiling.

'Officially, the power can be restored in only one of the residences: Balliol. That is where the red-jackets coordinate with the Westminster Archon during the Bone Seasons,' Warden said. 'That building has modern electrical wiring. Fortunately, so has Magdalen.'

Michael led me to the corner, where a velvet drape covered a wide, rectangular object. When he whipped the drape away, I stared. His pride and joy was a computer. Horribly outdated, probably from around 2030 – but a *computer*. A link to the world outside.

'He stole it from Balliol,' Warden said. The shadow of a smile touched his lips. 'He was able to restore electricity in this building and establish a connection with Scion's satellite constellation.'

'Sounds like you're a bit of a whiz kid, Michael.' I sat in front of the computer. Michael allowed himself a shy smile. 'What do you use it for?'

'We do not often risk restoring the electricity, but we did use it to monitor the progress of Bone Season XX.'

'Can I see?'

Michael leaned over my shoulder. He accessed a file marked MAHONEY, PAIGE EVA, 07-MAR-59. Video footage from a helicopter.

The camera zoomed in on my face. I sprinted across the rooftops and took a running leap off the edge of the building. The gap looked impossible – I found myself holding my breath – but the girl on the screen made it. There was a shout from the pilot: 'Flux her!' I fell fifty feet, and the line caught between my body and the back-pack. My unconscious form hung like a stiff. The NVD cameraman laughed, breathless. 'Weaver's whiskers,' he said. 'That has got to be the luckiest little bitch I've ever seen.'

And that was it.

'Charming,' I said.

Michael patted me on the shoulder.

'We were disappointed when you did not evade them,' Warden said, 'though relieved that you survived.'

I raised an eyebrow. 'Did you invite your friends over to watch the show?'

'In a manner of speaking.'

He stood and paced the basement. 'What do you want me to do?' I said.

'I am giving you the option to call for help.' When I looked at him, he said, 'Call the Seven Seals.'

'No. Nashira will get them,' I said. 'She wants Jaxon. I'm not bringing him anywhere near this place.'

Michael's face fell. 'At least let them know where you are,' Warden said. 'In case it all goes awry.'

'In case *what* goes awry?'

'Your prison break.'

'My prison break.'

'Yes.' Warden turned to face me. 'You asked me about the train. On the night of the Bicentenary, it will bring a large group of Scion emissaries from the citadel. It will also take them back to London.'

His words sank in. 'We can go home,' I said. The thought was hard to process. 'When?'

'The eve of the first of September.' Warden sat on one of the kegs. 'If you will not contact the Seven Seals, you can use this room to make your plans. They have to be better than mine, Paige. You must remember the lessons of the syndicate.' He looked straight into my eyes. 'I made an error last time. We planned to move against the Sargas in the day, when most of the city would be dormant. Thanks to the traitor, they were ready for us – but even if we had not been betrayed, they would have sensed our movements from the æther. We must strike when there is already a great deal of activity, when the Sargas are distracted. When their ability to retaliate will be limited by their need to uphold their façade of control. What better time than the Bicentenary?'

I found myself nodding. 'We could scare a few Scion officials while we're at it.'

'Precisely.' He held my eye contact. 'This is your safe house now. The computer contains detailed maps of Sheol I for you to plan your route out of the city centre. If you can reach the meadow in time, you can take the train to London.'

'What time will it leave?'

'I do not yet know. I cannot ask too many questions, but Michael has been eavesdropping. We will find out.'

I looked up at him. 'You said our aims differed. You want something else.'

'Scion believes we are too powerful to destroy. That we have no weaknesses. I want you to prove them wrong.'

'How?'

'I have long since suspected that Nashira will try to kill you at the Bicentenary. To claim your gift. There is one, simple way to humiliate her.' He placed his fingers under my chin, lifting it. 'Stop her.'

I searched his face. His eyes were dim, soft. 'If I do,' I said, 'I want to claim my favour.'

'I am listening.'

'Liss. I can't reach her. I have the cards, but she might not accept them. I need—' A spasm closed my throat. I had to force the next words out: 'I need your help.'

'Your friend has been in spirit shock for a long time. She will need amaranth to recover.'

'I know.'

'You are aware that Nashira has stopped my supply.'

I didn't look away. 'You have the last dose.'

Warden sat beside me. I knew what I was asking. He depended on amaranth.

'I wonder, Paige.' His fingers drummed on his knee. 'You do not wish to bring your friends here. But if I were to offer you your freedom, now – would you take it, if it meant leaving Liss?'

'Is that an offer?'

'Perhaps.'

I knew why he was asking me. He was testing me, seeing if I was selfish enough to leave someone so vulnerable behind.

'The risk to me is great,' he said. 'If any of the humans inform the Sargas, I will be severely punished for helping a human. But if you are willing to stay a little longer – to take a risk for me, and for your kind – I will do the same for her. That is the bargain I offer you.'

I did think about it. For one appalling moment, I thought about abandoning Liss, about seizing my freedom. About returning to London and leaving this place behind me, never to look back. Then shame rose inside me, hot and swift. I closed my eyes.

'No,' I said. 'I want you to help Liss.'

I could feel his gaze.

'Then I will help her,' he said.

A small group of harlies had gathered in the shack. Five of them huddled together in the cold, their heads bowed and their fingers clasped. Cyril and Julian were among them. The rain dripped through the cloth they'd stuffed into the gaps between the boards.

Liss had been in spirit shock for too long to recover. All they could do was hold a silent vigil at her bedside. If she lived, she would be an amaurotic husk of her former self. If she died, one of them would speak the threnody. Banish her beyond the reach of her captors. Either way, they would lose their most beloved performer – Liss Rymore, the girl who never fell.

When Warden arrived, with Michael and I at his side, they backed away. Whispers of fright passed between them. Cyril pushed himself into the corner, wild-eyed. The others just looked. Why was the blood-consort here, the right hand of Nashira? Why should he disturb the deathwatch?

Only Julian didn't move.

'Paige?'

I put a finger over my lips.

Liss lay on her blankets, covered in filthy sheets. Bits of silk were twisted into her hair, tokens for good luck and hope. Julian gripped her hand, not taking his eyes off the intruder.

Warden knelt beside Liss. His jaw was clenched, but he didn't mention his pain.

'Paige,' he said, 'the amaranth.'

I passed him the vial. The last vial. His last dose.

'The cards,' Warden said. He was completely focused on his work now. I passed them to him. 'And the blade.'

Michael handed me a knife with a black handle. I pulled it from its sheath and passed it to Warden. More whispers. Julian held Liss's hand on his lap, his eyes fixed on me. 'Trust me,' I said quietly.

He swallowed.

Warden uncorked the amaranth. He shook a few drops onto his gloved fingers, then dabbed the oil onto Liss's lips and philtrum. Julian kept a firm grip on her hand, though her cold fingers gave no response. Warden touched a little amaranth to each of her temples, then corked the vial and handed it to me. He took the knife by the blade and held it out to Julian.

'Prick her fingers.'

'What?'

'I require her blood.'

Julian looked at me. I nodded. With steady hands, he grasped the handle. 'Sorry, Liss,' he said.

He pressed the tip into each of her fingertips. Tiny beads of blood swelled where it touched. Warden nodded.

'Paige, Michael — spread the cards.'

Together, we did. We arranged the new deck into a semicircle. Warden took hold of Liss's hand and wiped her fingers across them, smearing the images with blood.

Warden wiped the blade clean with a cloth. He removed his left glove and clenched his fist around it. There was a gasp. Rephs never removed their gloves. Did they even have hands? Yes, they did. His hand was large, the knuckles scarred. Another gasp came when he drew the sharp edge of the knife through his skin, opening his palm.

His blood seeped from the cut, blurring my perception. He held out his arm and let a few drops of ectoplasm spot each card. Just as Aphrodite sprinkled her nectar on the blood of Adonis. I could feel spirits gathering in the room: drawn to the cards, to Liss, to Warden. They formed a triangle, a rift in the æther. He was opening the door.

Warden pulled on his glove, picked up the cards and sorted them back into a pile. He placed them on Liss's bare décolletage, so they touched her skin, and folded her hands over them.

'And from the blood of Adonis,' he said, 'came life.'

Liss opened her eyes.

The Anniversary

September the first, 2059. Two hundred years since a storm of strange lights crossed the sky. Two hundred years since Lord Palmerston sealed his deal with the Rephaim. Two hundred years since the inquisition into clairvoyance began. And, most importantly, two hundred years since the establishment of Sheol I, and the great tradition of the Bone Season.

A girl stood in front of me, watching me from the gilded mirror. Her cheeks were hollow, her jaw set tight. It still took me by surprise that this hard, cold face was mine.

My body was sheathed in a white dress, with elbow-length sleeves and a square neckline. The elasticated fabric cleaved to what little figure I had left. Though Warden had fed me as much as he could, there wasn't always food to give, and he risked raising suspicions if he gave it. The rest of the time, I'd been on skilly and toke with the harlies.

Nashira had not invited me to another feast.

I smoothed down my dress. I'd been given a special reprieve from yellow in order to attend the ceremony. Nashira had said it was a mark of goodwill. I knew better. I was going prepared. Tucked under the neckline was the pendant Warden had given me. It had lain untouched for weeks, but it might come in useful tonight. There was a small knife concealed in one of my white ankle boots. I could hardly walk in the things, but the Rephaim wanted us to look strong – not beaten and weak. We were expected to stand tall tonight.

The chamber was silent, lit by a candle. Warden had gone with the other Rephaim to welcome the emissaries. He'd left me a note, propped on the gramophone. I sat at his desk and ran my fingers over the ink.

The time is set. Find me in the Guildhall.

I threw it into the embers of the fire. In the gloom, I wound the gramophone and moved the needle over the record. This would be the last time I ever heard it play. No matter what happened tonight, I would never return to the Founder's Tower.

Soft, echoing voices filled the chamber. I checked the name of the record. 'I'll Be Home'. Yes, I would. If everything went to plan, I would be home by morning. I'd had enough of seeing the harlies in poverty, and of having to call them 'harlies'. I'd had enough of watching Liss eat grease and stale bread because she had nothing else to live on. I'd had enough of the red-jackets and the Emim. I'd had enough of being called 40. I'd had enough of the whole damn place, and everybody in it. I couldn't last another night.

Paper hissed on the rug. I knelt by the door and picked up the note that had been pushed under it.

Warden's notes had given me an idea. I'd encouraged Julian to organise a group of couriers, like the one Jax had in the citadel, and keep people in the residences in the loop by sending notes with the amaurotics.

Orpheus did it. All ready.

Lucky

I allowed myself a smile. Felix. I'd made him use a false name for his deliveries. Orpheus was Michael.

It hadn't been difficult to persuade Duckett to lend us his particular expertise. Having threatened to expose his little drug den to Nashira ('Oh no, please, have a heart for a poor old man!'), Julian and I had forced him to make up a surprise for the red-jackets. Something that would make them slow to react when we acted against the Rephaim. With some foot-dragging, he'd made it ('You'll never get away with this, you'll be chopped up like the first lot!'). Powdered purple aster cut with sleeping pills. Perfect.

I'd used a handful of his own white aster to erase his memory as soon as it was done. I didn't like cowards.

We'd slipped the concoction to Michael. He'd been happy to spike the wine the red-jackets had been given during their pre-Bicentenary feast. If all went well, none of them would be fit to defend themselves.

I looked out of the window. The emissaries had arrived at eight, dressed in their best, escorted by armed Vigiles. These Scion men and women had come to bear witness to a new agreement, the Great Territorial Act. It permitted the Rephaim to establish a control city in Paris, the first one outside England. Sheol II.

Scion would no longer be an empire in embryo. It would be born. It would live.

This was just the beginning. If the Rephaim had all the voyants locked up in penal colonies, there would be no way for the rest of mankind to fight them off. The æther was our only weapon. If nobody could use it, we were sitting ducks. All of us.

But I didn't care about that tonight. I cared about getting back to

Seven Dials. To the corrupt syndicate. To my gang. To Nick. At that moment, it was all I wanted in the world.

The gramophone played on. I sat down at the writing table, looking through the window at the moon. It wasn't full, but halved. There were no stars.

Liss, Julian and I had spent the last few weeks spreading seeds of discord through the city, using the safe house as our den. Suhail and the Overseer couldn't hear us there. Liss was fully recovered from her trauma and, with a new determination to survive, she'd been active in rallying the harlies. She'd still been nervous, but one night she'd cracked. 'I can't live like this any more,' she'd said. 'And I can't stop you rebelling. Let's just do it.'

So we did.

Most of the jackets and performers had agreed to help us. Those that had seen Warden heal Liss were more confident, certain of some Reph support. Over the weeks we'd pooled our supplies and hidden them at designated checkpoints. A few harlies had pickpocketed the whitewashed Duckett, depriving him of matches and Sterno cans. A pair of brave white-jackets had tried to venture into the House, but security had tightened since Kraz had been found dead. No one could get close. Instead we'd had to scavenge. We didn't have many guns between us, but we didn't need guns to kill.

Only Julian, Liss and I knew where the train was. We hadn't mentioned it to anyone else. Too risky. All the others knew was that there would be a way out. A flare would be used to mark the spot.

I swung my legs off the bed. Through the bathroom door I could see the mirror. I looked like a bisque doll, but I could have looked worse. I could have looked like Ivy. Last time I'd seen her, she was walking behind Thuban with another human, so dirty and thin I'd barely recognised her. But she hadn't been crying. Just walking. Silent. I'd been surprised she was alive after what had happened in the House.

Warden hadn't let me get that way. He'd grown more and more reticent as September approached. I supposed it was fear. Fear that this rebellion would fail, like the last one. Sometimes it was more than fear. It occurred to me that he was angry. Angry that he was going to lose me. Lose the fight against Nashira.

I shook the thought away. Warden just wanted to protect my gift, like everybody else.

There was no point in prolonging it. I had to face the Guildhall. I stood and wound the gramophone again. It comforted me, somehow, that the music was still playing – that whatever happened outside, a song would fill the empty chamber for a while. I closed the door of the tower behind me.

The night porter had just started her shift. Her hair was threaded into a shining chignon, and she wore rosy lipstick. 'XX-40,' she said. 'You're expected at the Guildhall in ten minutes.'

'Yes, thank you. I know.' Like I hadn't been told time and time again by the Overseer.

'I've been asked to remind you of your instructions this evening. You're not permitted to speak with the ambassadors or the Scion sponsors, unless you're accompanied by a Rephaite chaperone. The entertainment begins at eleven. You'll be on the stage after the play.'

'On the stage?'

'Oh, um—' She looked back at her ledger. 'Nothing. Sorry. That message was for someone else.'

I tried to look, but she shielded it. 'Really?'

'Evening.'

I looked up. David. He wore a suit and a red tie, and he was clean-shaven. My stomach clenched. David did not look drugged. Michael must have done it, he *must* have done.

'I've been sent to take you to the Guildhall.' He extended an arm. 'The blood-sovereign wants you there now.'

'I don't need an escort.'

'They think you do.'

He didn't slur his words. He hadn't so much as touched Duckett's mixture. I brushed past him, ignoring his proffered arm, and headed down the street. This was not a good start.

A path of lanterns had been lit through the city. The Guildhall was situated close to the House, named after the NVD's headquarters in London. The voyants invited to the Bicentenary were those that had reached their pink or red tunics, or particularly talented harlies. Nashira had advertised it as a reward for their good behaviour. They would be allowed to eat and dance with other humans. In return, they had to make it clear not only that they liked spending time with their keepers, but also that they were very grateful for their 'rehabilitation'. That they liked being hidden away from society in a filthy penal colony. That they liked having limbs ripped off by the Emim.

Most of them wouldn't have to pretend. Carl was happy. All the red-jackets were happy. They'd found a place in this colony, but I never would. I was getting the hell out of here.

'Good trick,' David said. 'With the wine.'

I didn't dare look at him.

'Your boy put in a bit too much. I know regal when I smell it. But don't worry – it worked on most of them. Far be it from me to spoil the surprise.'

Two harlies came rushing down the street. Both looked out of breath. They carried rolls of fabric. They slipped into the street between the old church and the Residence of the Suzerain. That was the route they'd take to burn the Room. They must be putting matches there. Matches and paraffin.

Julian had suggested setting fire to the buildings in the centre of the city. Turned out he was a damn good tactician. The harlies would cause the distraction, leaving other streets free for us to go north, to the meadow. They would do it in the early hours, when the emissaries would be growing tired. 'They won't go home much later than two,' he'd said. 'If we do it at midnight, we'll have a solid time to get the ball rolling. We'll be in control. And better early than late.' I'd had no complaints. Everything was going to plan, but the clever redjacket beside me had the power to destroy it all.

'Who have you told?' I asked David.

'Let me give you some food for thought,' he said, ignoring the question. 'Do you think Scion *likes* being ordered around by the Rephaim?'

'Of course not.'

'But you believe Nashira when she says they're under her control. Do you not think one person in the history of Scion would have thought about fighting them?'

'What are you getting at?'

'Just answer the question.'

'They wouldn't. They're too afraid of the Emim.'

'Maybe you're right. Or maybe there's still a grain of sense left in the Archon.'

'What does that mean?' When he didn't answer, I stopped in front of him. 'What the hell does the Archon have to do with anything?'

'Everything.' He pushed past me. 'You get on with your prison break, street princess. Don't worry your head about me.'

He was out of sight before I could answer, past the Victorian entrance hall and into the crowd. My spine tingled. I didn't need a rogue red-jacket around, especially not someone as cryptic as David. He might claim to hate the Rephaim, but he didn't seem to like me, either. He could tell Nashira about the wine. She'd smell a rat at once. Lots and lots of rats.

Thousands of candles had been lit inside the Guildhall. As soon as I crossed the threshold, Michael and a white-jacket hurried me up a flight of stairs, leaving David to seek out the other bone-grubbers.

Michael's assignment from the Rephs was to make sure nobody looked bruised or scruffy – a perfect pretext for one last gathering. When we reached the gallery, I turned to face them.

'Ready?'

'And waiting,' the white-jacket said. Charles, a cryomancer owned by Terebell. He nodded down at the hall, where the Rephaim mingled with the emissaries. 'The bone-grubbers are starting to bite the dust. The Rephs won't notice until it's too late.'

'Good.' I took a deep, steadying breath. 'Well done, Michael.'

Michael wore a simple grey suit. He smiled.

'You got my bag?'

He pointed. My backpack, packed with medicine, sat under the gallery benches. I couldn't take it now, but the harlies knew it was here if they needed it. It was one of many stashes of supplies.

'Paige,' Charles said, 'what time will the flare go up?'

'I'm still waiting to hear. I'll set one off as soon as we find a path.'

Charles nodded. I looked down at the hall again.

So many people were about to risk their lives. Liss, who'd been so afraid. Julian, who'd done so much to help me. The harlies. The white-jackets.

And Warden. I understood now what it meant for him to trust me. If I betrayed him, like the last human, he wouldn't just be scarred – he'd be slaughtered. This was his last chance.

But we had to act now, while there was still a flicker of compassion among the Rephaim. If the scarred ones perished, that hope would be lost.

The door to the gallery crashed open. Suhail loomed in the doorway. He grabbed Charles by the tunic and hauled him back to the stairs. 'The blood-sovereign does not like to be kept waiting, runt,' he said to me. 'You are forbidden from the gallery. Get downstairs.'

As quickly as he'd come, he left. Michael glanced at the door. 'It's time,' I said. I squeezed his hand. 'Good luck. Remember, keep low and look for the flare.'

Michael nodded.

'Live,' was all he said.

I kept my head down as I crossed the ground floor of the Guildhall. Nobody noticed me come in.

The Scion system was used by nine European countries, including England. Unlike England, however, the rest of them had nowhere to send their clairvoyants. Still, all nine governments had sent emissaries. Even Dublin, the youngest and most controversial Scion city, had sent a delegate: Cathal Bell, an old friend of my father. He was a nervous, indecisive man, crumpled by the duties of his role. A thrill shot through my chest when I first saw him – maybe he could help us – but then I remembered: he hadn't seen me since I was five or six years old. He wouldn't recognise me, and I had no name here. Besides, Bell was weak. His party had lost Dublin.

The Guildhall looked spectacular. It had an ornate plasterwork ceiling, hung with chandeliers, and a vast stretch of open floor. The dark flickered with candlelight and Chopin. The delegates were afforded every courtesy. They were free to gorge themselves on all manner of delicious foods, or talk to one another over mecks. Their amaurosis was a privilege, a right. They were served food by the amaurotic slaves, including Michael, who had been made to look like willing participants in the rehabilitation programme. The other amaurotics must have all been too undernourished to appear.

High above some dancers was Liss, hanging from the silks, striking poses like an airborne ballerina. She was relying solely upon her own strength to keep from falling to her death.

I cast my eye around the room, trying to locate Weaver. He was nowhere in sight. Maybe he was late. Other countries would be excused for not sending their Inquisitors, but not England. I could see a few other recognisable Scion officials, including the Commander of Vigilance, Bernard Hock. He was a huge man with a bald head and overdeveloped neck muscles; very good at sniffing out voyants – in fact, I'd always suspected he was a sniffer. Even now, his nostrils were flared. I made a note to kill him if I could.

An amaurotic offered me a glass of white mecks. I refused it. I'd just spotted Cathal Bell.

Bell had a glass in his hand, and he kept straightening his tie. He was trying to make conversation with Radmilo Arežina, Deputy Minister of Migration for Serbia. I smiled to myself. Arežina had authorised Dani's transfer to London, foolishly. I walked towards them.

'Mr Bell?'

Bell jerked, spilling his wine. 'Yes?'

I looked at Arežina. 'I'm sorry to interrupt, Minister, but may I speak with Mr Bell for a moment?'

Arežina looked me up and down. His upper lip arched.

'Excuse me, Mr Bell,' he said. 'I should return to my party.'

He moved off to the safety of his party. I was left facing Bell, who was dabbing the red stain from his jacket. 'What do you want, unnatural?' He was stammering. 'I was having a very important conversation.'

'Well, now you can have another one.' I took his glass and sipped from it. 'Do you remember the Incursion, Mr Bell?'

Bell stopped dead. 'If you mean the Incursion of 2046, then yes. Of course I do.' His fingers shook. The knuckles were purpled, swollen with arthritis. 'Why are you asking? Who are you?'

'My cousin was arrested that day. I want to know if he's still alive.'

'You're Irish?'

'Yes.'

He peered at me. 'What's your name?'

'My name doesn't matter. My cousin's does. Finn McCarthy. He was at Trinity College. Know him?'

'Yes.' The reply was immediate. 'McCarthy was at Carrickfergus with the other student leaders. He was sentenced to hang.'

'And did he?'

'I – I wasn't privy to the details, but—'

Something dark and violent rose inside me. I leaned close to him and breathed into his ear: 'If my cousin was executed, Mr Bell, I will hold you personally responsible. It was *your* government that lost Ireland. Your government that gave up.'

'Not me,' Bell gasped out. His nose was beginning to bleed. 'Don't hurt me—'

'Not you, Mr Bell. Just your kind.'

'Unnatural,' he bit out. 'Get away.' I melted into the crowd, leaving him to staunch his bloody nose.

I felt myself shaking. I snatched another glass of mecks and threw it back in one gulp. I had always thought Finn must be dead, but some small part of me had clung to his memory, to the idea that he might still be alive. Maybe he was, but I wouldn't find out from Cathal Bell.

I caught sight of Nashira, standing below a podium. Beside her was Warden, engaged in conversation with a Greek emissary. After the night-bell he'd received his first amaranth for months; a few drops had transformed him. He wore black and gold, with jacinth at his throat, and his eyes were bright as lamps. I recognised the people closest to Nashira: her elite guard. One of them spotted me – Amelia's replacement – and from the movement of her lips, I guessed she'd informed her boss.

Nashira looked over the heads of her guard. A soft laugh escaped her. Hearing it, Warden turned around. His eyes grew very hot, very fast.

Nashira beckoned me. I approached, handing my empty glass to an amaurotic.

'Ladies, gentlemen,' she said to those assembled around her, 'I would like to introduce XX-59-40. She is one of our most gifted clairvoyants.'

There was a murmur from the delegates: intrigued, repulsed.

'This is Aloys Mynatt, Grand Raconteur of France. And Birgitta Tjäder, Chief of Vigilance in the Scion Citadel of Stockholm.'

Mynatt was a small man, stiff in posture, with no distinguishing features. He nodded.

Tjäder just stared at me. She was in her mid-thirties, with thick blonde hair and eyes like olive oil. Nick had always called this woman the Magpie – her reign of hell in Stockholm was notorious. I could tell she couldn't stand to be near me: her pale lips were pulled tight over her teeth, as if she was about to bite. I wasn't exactly relishing her presence, either.

'I don't want her near me,' Tjäder said, confirming my suspicions.

'But would you not rather they were here, with us, than on your streets?' Nashira said. 'They can do no harm here, Birgitta. We do not let them. Once Sheol III is established, you will never have to look at a clairvoyant again.'

A *third* penal colony? Did they have plans for Stockholm, too? I didn't want to think about a Sheol III with the Magpie as its procurer.

Tjäder didn't take her eyes off me. She had no aura, but I could read the loathing in every inch of her face.

'I can't wait,' she said.

The pianist stopped playing, prompting a round of applause. The dancing couples separated. Nashira glanced up towards a large clock. 'The hour draws near.'

Her voice was very soft. 'Excuse me,' Tjäder said. She turned and marched back to the Swedes, leaving an open space between Warden and me. I didn't dare meet his eyes.

'I must address the emissaries.' Nashira looked at the stage. 'Arcturus, stay with 40. I will need her in due course.'

So she did plan to kill me in public. I looked between the two of them. Warden inclined his head. 'Yes, my sovereign.' He took me roughly by the arm. 'Come, 40.'

Before he could lead me away, Nashira's head whipped around. She grabbed my wrist, pulling me back towards her.

'Did you hurt yourself, 40?'

The steri-strips on my cheek were long gone, but there was still a hairline scar from the broken glass. 'I struck her.' Warden kept a tight grip on my arm. 'She disobeyed me. I punished her.'

I stood like a rag doll, one arm in each of their hands. They looked at each other over my head. 'Good,' Nashira said. 'After all these years, you are learning what it means to be my consort.'

She turned her back on him and walked into the crowd, parting the emissaries.

The musician, whoever it was, began to play some well-chosen piano chords, accompanied by ghostly vocals. I was sure I recognised the voice, but I couldn't place it. Warden led me to the side of the hall, to the long space underneath the gallery, and leaned down to look at me. 'Is everything ready?'

I nodded.

The musician really did have a beautiful voice, a kind of wispy falsetto. It brought on another vague surge of recognition. 'My companions and I performed a séance last night,' Warden said, his voice barely audible. 'There will be spirits to command. Human spirits, the victims of Bone Season XVIII. They will side with you before the Rephaim.'

'What about the NVD? Are they here?'

'They are not permitted in the Guildhall unless they are called. They are stationed by the bridge.'

'How many?'

'Thirty.'

I nodded again. The emissaries all had at least one bodyguard, but they were SVD. They didn't want unnaturals protecting them. Fortunately for us, the SVD couldn't use spirit combat.

Warden looked up to the ceiling, where Liss was climbing the silks. 'Liss seems to have recovered.'

'Yes.'

'Then we are even. All is settled.'

'All debts are paid,' I said. The threnody. It made me think of what was still to come. What if Nashira succeeded in killing me?

'All will go to plan, Paige. You should not give up hope.' He looked at the stage. 'Hope is the one thing that might still save us all.'

I followed his gaze. The bell jar and the lifeless flower stood on a covered plinth. 'Hope for what?'

'Change.'

The music drifted to a close, and applause rang out from the edges of the dance floor. I wanted to look, to find out who had been playing, but I couldn't see over the heads of the emissaries.

A red-jacket stepped onto the stage. 22. His lopsided gait said just how much of Duckett's mix he'd had. 'Ladies and gentlemen,' he said, 'the – the great Suzerain, Nashira Sargas, blood-sovereign of – the Race of Rephaim.'

He staggered down. I bit back a smile. That was at least one less red-jacket less to deal with.

Nashira stepped up to the podium, to continued applause from her audience. She looked at us. Warden looked back at her.

'Ladies and gentlemen,' she said, never breaking his gaze, 'welcome to the Scion capital of Sheol I. I would like to extend our thanks for your attendance at our celebration tonight.

'It has been two hundred years since our arrival to Britain. We have come a long, long way since 1859. As you can see, we have done our utmost to make our first control city into a place of beauty, respect, and above all, *compassion*. Our rehabilitation system allows young clairvoyants to enter our city and receive the best possible quality of life.' Like animals in a menagerie. 'Clairvoyance, as we know, is not the fault of its victims. Like a disease, it preys on the innocent. It afflicts them with unnaturalness.

'Sheol I celebrates two hundred years of good work today. As you can see, it has been a successful venture, the first of many seeds we wish to plant. In exchange for your understanding, we have not only provided a humane means of removing clairvoyants from ordinary society, but prevented hundreds of Emite attacks on the citadel. We are a beacon to which they are drawn – like moths to a flame, as the saying goes.' Her eyes were their own beacons in the gloom. 'But the Emim's number grows greater every day. This colony will no longer be a sufficient means of protection. Emim have been sighted in France, Ireland and, more recently, Sweden.'

Ireland. That was why Cathal Bell was here. That was why he looked so nervous, so frightened.

'It is paramount that we establish Sheol II, that we light another flame,' Nashira said. 'Our method has been tried and tested. With your help, and your cities, we hope that the flower of our alliance can finally bloom.'

Applause. Warden's jaw was set. His expression was terrible to see. Angry. Brutal. Murderous.

I'd never seen him look that way.

'There are a few minutes left until the play, written by our human Overseer. In the meantime, I would like to introduce my partner, the second blood-sovereign, who wishes to make a brief announcement. Ladies and gentlemen – Gomeisa Sargas.'

She extended a hand. Before I could even register that anyone else was there, it was taken by a larger one.

My breath caught.

He was dressed in black robes, with a collar that reached the tops of his ears. He was tall and lean, golden-haired, with gaunt features. His lips pulled downward, as if weighed down by the rows of eye-sized gems around his neck. He seemed older than the other Rephaim – something about his bearing, and the sheer mass of his dreamscape. I could feel that dreamscape like a wall against my skull. It was the most ancient and terrible thing I'd ever felt in the æther.

'Good evening.'

Gomeisa looked at us with the neutral Rephaite expression: that of the impassive observer. His aura was like a hand across the sun. No wonder Liss was so afraid of him. She was wrapped in her ribbons, silent and still. After a moment, she dropped down to the gallery.

'To those humans who reside in Sheol I, I apologise for my long periods of absence. I am the Rephaim's primary emissary to the Westminster Archon. As such, I spend much of my time in the capital city with the Inquisitor, discussing how best to increase the efficacy of this penal colony.

'As Nashira has said, it is a new beginning that we celebrate today. A new age is dawning: an age of perfect collaboration between human and Rephaim, two races that have been estranged for far too long. We celebrate the end of an old world, where ignorance and darkness reigned. We vow to share our wisdom with you, as you have shared your world with us. We vow to protect you, as you have sheltered us. And I promise you, friends: we will not allow our arrangement to falter. Here purity rules with an iron rod. And the flower of transgression will forever remain withered.'

I glanced at the withered flower in the bell jar. He looked at it like he might look at a slug.

'Now,' he said, 'enough probity. Let the play begin.'

The Prohibition

The Overseer swept out, dressed to dazzle. He wore a long red cloak, done up to the neck, that covered his entire body. He bowed.

'Salutations, ladies and gentlemen, and a warm welcome to Sheol I! I am the Overseer, Beltrame. I look after the human population of the city. A particularly heartfelt welcome to those of you who have come from unconverted parts of the Continent. Fear not! After the show, you shall have the chance to alter your cities into Scion citadels, as many other cities have. Our programme enables governments to root out and segregate clairvoyants while they are still young, without the expensive necessity of mass execution.'

I tried not to listen. Not all countries used NiteKind to execute clairvoyants. Many used the lethal injection, or a firing squad, or worse.

'We have already made plans for Sheol II to be established in association with Scion Citadels of Paris and Marseilles, which will become the first French satellite citadels.' Applause. Mynatt smiled. 'Tonight, we hope to pin down potential locations of at least two more control cities on the Continent. But before all that, we have a little play to show you, to prove that many of our clairvoyants use their abilities to do good. Our play will remind us of the dark days before the Rephaim arrived, when the Bloody King still held power. The king who built his house on blood.'

The clock chimed. I watched as the performers walked out in a line, twenty of them. They were going to perform the life story of Edward VII, from his purchase of a séance table and the five murders to the knife in his quarters and his flight from England with the rest of his family. The beginning of the so-called epidemic, and a testimony to why Scion needed to exist. Liss was up there, standing in the background. On either side of her were Nell – the girl who'd been her substitute when she was in spirit shock – and a seer who I thought was called Lotte. All three were dressed up as some of the Bloody King's victims.

In the centre of the stage, the Overseer threw off his cloak to reveal a monarch's regalia. The crowd jeered. He was playing Edward in his days as heir apparent to Queen Victoria, decked in furs and jewels.

The first scene seemed to take place in his bedchamber, where a garish calliope piped out 'Daisy Bell'. The harlie actor nearest the audience introduced himself as Frederick Ponsonby, 1st Baron Sysonby – Edward's private secretary. It was through his eyes that the play would be seen. 'Your Highness,' he said to the Overseer, 'shall we take a turn outside?'

'Do you have your short jacket, Ponsonby?'

'Only a tailcoat, Your Highness.'

'I thought *everyone* must know,' the Overseer boomed, with a risibly aristocratic English accent, 'that a short jacket is always worn with a silk hat at a private view in the morning. And those trousers are quite the ugliest pair I have ever seen in my life!'

Jeering. Hissing. That licentious beast had dared to call himself Victoria's heir. Ponsonby turned back to the audience. 'It was after a long awakening of afflictions – for example, with my tail-coat, and my poor trousers' – laughs – 'that the prince grew tired of his finery. On that very afternoon, he asked me to accompany him on an excursion. Oh, my friends! Human suffering has never surpassed that of the queen, watching her son tread the path towards evil.' I glanced over my shoulder to see Warden's reaction, but he wasn't there.

The repartee between Edward and Ponsonby went on for a while. Each scene was engineered to show Edward as a cruel, lustful idiot and a failure to his mother. I found myself watching, fascinated. They exaggerated his role in Prince Albert's death to a ridiculous degree, even introducing a duel. The widowed Queen Victoria made an appearance, wearing her small diamond crown and veil. 'I never can, or shall, look at him without a shudder,' she admitted to the audience. 'He is as unnatural to me as a changeling.' They cheered. She was a bastion of goodness, the last unsullied monarch before the plague. As the emissaries were charmed by the actress, I kept a sharp eye on the clock. Nearly half an hour had elapsed, and I still didn't know what time the train left.

Next was the crux of the play. The séance. Red lanterns were brought onto the set. When I looked back at the stage, I had to stifle a laugh. The Overseer was really getting into his role. 'Earthly power is not enough,' he said, almost panting with the sheer evil of his character. The séance table was out, and he was waving his arms in circles above it. 'The Victorian era, they say? But what will Edward's era be? What king can truly rise, encumbered by the shackles of mortality?' He leaned over the table, rocking it with his hands. 'Yes, rise. Rise from the shadows. Rise through the gateway, spirits of the dead. Come into me, and into my followers! Breed in the very blood of England!'

As he spoke, the red lanterns moved from the stage, carried by actors dressed in black. They represented the unnatural spirits. They scattered across the room, grabbing at people, making them shriek. They were the plague of unnaturalness.

The music and the laughter of the actors was too loud. My head was spinning. The Overseer roared his incantations. In the darkness and confusion, Warden took my arm. 'Quickly.' His voice was a thrum against my ear. 'Come with me.'

He led me to the trap room: the small, dark space below the stage, piled high with storage crates. The only light was what filtered through the boards. Red, like the lanterns. Dense velvet drapes hung down the length of one side of the room, hiding us from the hall above. It wasn't easy, in this darkened space, to think of what I might soon face upstairs.

It was quieter here. The actors danced above us, but the sound was muffled by the boards. Warden turned to face me.

'You will be the play's last scene. The final act.' His eyes were hot. 'I heard her with Gomeisa.'

My skin prickled. 'We knew it was coming.'

'Yes.'

I'd known from the beginning that Nashira was going to kill me, but hearing it from him made it all the more real. A part of me had hoped she might wait – wait a few days, giving me a chance to get away with the others on the train – but Nashira was cruel. Of course she wanted to do it in public, before Scion. She wouldn't risk keeping me alive.

The light from his eyes made the shadows deeper. There was something different about them: something raw, something volatile.

Cold tremors seized my legs and abdomen. I sank onto a crate. 'I can't fight her,' I said, 'her angels—'

'No, Paige. Think. For months she has waited, biding her time until you could possess another body. If you did not exhibit that skill, there was a danger that she might not gain it from you. She made you a yellow-jacket to ensure your life was never again endangered by the Emim. She placed you under the protection of her own consort. Why would she do so much to preserve you if you did not have a gift she not only wanted, but feared?'

'You taught me how to do it all. All that training on the meadow. The butterfly and the deer. Exercising my spirit. You led me to my death.'

'I was assigned by her to prepare you. That was why she allowed me to take you into Magdalen,' he said, 'but I do not intend for her to have you. I have committed myself to developing your gift – but for *you*, Paige. Not for her.'

I didn't answer. There was nothing to say.

Warden tore one of the drapes. With a soft touch, he started to remove my make-up. I let him. My lips were numb, my skin like ice. I could be dead in the next few minutes, drifting around Nashira in a state of mindless servitude. When he was finished, Warden stroked my hair back from my face. I let him do it. I couldn't focus.

'Don't you dare,' he said. 'Don't you dare let her see it. You are more than that. You are more than what she wants to do to you.'

'I'm not afraid.'

His gaze ran across my face. 'You should be,' he said. 'But do not show it. Not for anything.'

'I'll show her what I like. You're in no position to give me orders.' I disengaged my head from his hands. 'You should have just let me go. You should have let Nick take me back to Dials. That was all you had to do. I could have been home by now.'

He leaned down so our faces were level. 'I brought you back,' he said, 'because I could not find the strength to fight her without you. But for that same reason, I will do everything in my power to see you safely to the citadel.'

Silence fell. I didn't break his gaze.

'Your hair must be tied.' His voice was different, quieter. He pressed an ornamental comb into my hand.

The comb was cold. My fingers shook. 'I don't think I can.' I took a deep, slow breath. 'Will you do it?'

He said nothing. But he did take the comb. As if he was handling the very finest gossamer, he swept my hair to one side of my neck, then gathered it into a knot. Not a psyche knot, like I usually did: an elaborate, braided coiffure that drew together at my nape. His calloused fingers ran over my scalp, arranging the comb. The softest tremor ran down my spine. Warden released my hair, and it held.

His touch had felt strange. Warmer. It was only when I saw his hands that I realised.

He wasn't wearing gloves.

I reached up to my hair, traced the intricate design. Hands as large as his should never have achieved such complexity. 'The train will leave at one o'clock precisely,' he said against my ear. 'The entrance is under the training ground. Exactly where we stood.'

I'd waited so long for those words.

'If she kills me, you have to let the others know.' A thickness rose in my throat. 'You have to lead them.'

His fingers brushed the back of my arm. 'I will not need to lead them.'

My body ran with shivers – but not the kind I expected. When I turned my head to look at him, he tucked a stray curl behind my ear. His other hand came to rest on my abdomen, pressing my back to his chest. The warmth of him was comforting.

And I could feel his hunger. Not for my aura, but for me.

He nuzzled his head against my cheek. His fingers traced my collarbone. His dreamscape was close, his aura intertwined with mine. My sixth sense heightened, taking him in. 'Your skin is cold,' he said throatily. 'I never—' He stopped. My fingers pushed between his naked knuckles. I kept my eyes open.

His lips moved to my jaw. I guided his hand to my waist. The lure of his touch was excruciating; I couldn't flinch. I couldn't refuse him. I wanted this, before the end. I wanted to be touched, to be seen – here in this dark room, in this red silence. I lifted my chin, and his lips closed over mine.

I had always known there was no heaven. Jax had told me so, many times. Even Warden had said so. There was only white light, the last light: a final rest on the edge of consciousness, the place where all things meet an end. Beyond that, who knew. But if there was a heaven, this was what it would have felt like. Touching the æther with my bare hands. I could never have anticipated this, not from him. Not from anyone. I clutched his back, pulling him up against me. He caught the nape of my neck in his hand. I could feel each callus on his palms.

His breath was hot. The kiss was slow. *Don't stop, don't stop.* I couldn't think of anything but those words: *don't stop.* His hands ran up my sides, my back, and clasped me. He lifted me onto a crate. I placed my hand against his neck. I felt the thick beat of him. His rhythm. My rhythm.

My skin burned. I couldn't stop. I'd never felt anything like this in my life – this rising in my chest, this need to touch. His lips nudged mine apart. My eyes opened. *Stop. Stop, Paige.* I started to pull my head away. A word escaped me: maybe 'no', maybe 'yes'. Maybe his name. He framed my face in his hands, traced my lips. His thumbs ran over my cheeks. Our foreheads touched. My dreamscape scorched. He set fire to the poppies. *Don't stop, don't stop.*

Only a moment passed. I looked at him, and he looked at me. A moment. A choice. My choice. His choice. Then he kissed me again, roughly this time. I let him. His arms came around me, lifting me. And I wanted it. I did. Too much. So much. My hands were in his hair, gripping his neck. *Don't stop.* His lips were on my mouth, my eyes, my shoulders and the hollow of my throat. *Don't stop.* He ran his palms over my thighs. Firm, bold strokes, full of surety. Awakening.

I opened his shirt. My fingers slid over his chest. I kissed his surging neck, and he grasped a thick handful of my hair. *Don't stop.* I'd never touched his skin. It was hot and smooth, and it made me want the rest of him. My hands went under his shirt, found his back. Scars under my fingers. Long, cruel welts. I'd always known they were there. The scars of a traitor. He tensed under my touch. 'Paige,' he said softly, but I didn't stop. He made a low sound in his throat, and his lips came back to mine.

I wouldn't betray him. Bone Season XVIII was history, and it would not repeat itself.

Two hundred years was more than enough.

My sixth sense shook me from the haze. I pulled back from Warden. He kept his hands on my waist, locking me against him.

Nashira was there, half-hidden in the shadows. My heart squeezed out a sickening thump.

Run, my numb brain said, but I couldn't run. She'd seen everything. She could see everything *now.* My skin, glossed with sweat; my puffy lips, my wild dishevelled hair. His hands still clasping my hips. His open shirt. My fingers still trespassing on his skin.

I couldn't move them. I couldn't even shift my gaze.

Warden drew me behind him. 'I forced it on her,' he said, his voice thick and rough.

Nashira said nothing.

She stepped into the dim light that filtered through the drapes. And there was something in her hands – the bell jar. I looked into it, my ears ringing. Inside was a flower. A flower in full bloom, strange and beautiful, its eight petals wet with nectar. The flower that had once been dead. 'There can be no mercy,' she said, 'for *this.*'

For a moment Warden looked at the flower, his eyes aglow. His gaze moved to meet hers.

Nashira dropped the bell jar. The glass crashed against the floor, startling me from my paralysis.

I'd just destroyed everything.

'Arcturus Mesarthim, you are my blood-consort. You are Warden of the Mesarthim. But this cannot happen again.' Nashira stepped towards us. 'There is only one way to stop treachery, and that is to make an example of traitors. I will hang your flesh from the walls of this city.'

Warden didn't move. 'Better there than used for your pleasures.'

'Always so fearless. Or foolhardy.' She touched her fingers to his face. 'I will see to it that all your old companions are destroyed.'

'No.' I stepped out from behind him. 'You can't—'

I didn't have time to move. The blow she gave me knocked me off my feet. The corner of a crate glanced across my head, opening a cut above my eye. My hands went straight into the broken glass. I heard Warden say my name, his voice shot with rage – but then Thuban and Situla were there, her trusted servants, the ones that wouldn't let him go. Thuban took the end of his knife and smashed it into Warden's head. But he didn't fall. He wouldn't kneel before the Sargas this time.

'I will deal with your offences later, Arcturus. I divest you of your position as blood-consort.' Nashira stepped away from him. 'Thuban, Situla – take him to the gallery.'

'Yes, my sovereign,' Thuban said. He grasped Warden by the throat. 'Time to pay your dues, flesh-traitor.'

Situla dug her fingers into his shoulder. Ashamed of her traitor cousin. He didn't say a word.

No, no. It couldn't end like this, not like Bone Season XVIII. He was no longer blood-consort. He was ruined. I'd put out the last ray of light. I sought Warden's gaze, desperate for something to hope for, to salvage – but his eyes were still and dark, and all I could feel was his silence. Between them, Thuban and Situla dragged him away.

Nashira walked through the broken glass. I stayed where I was, on the floor, in the wreckage. Bitter heat rose to my eyes. I was such a fool. What was I thinking? What was I *doing*?

'Your time has come, dreamwalker.'

'At last.' Blood seeped from my head wound. 'You waited long enough.'

'You ought to rejoice. From what I understand, dreamwalkers crave the æther. Tonight you can join with it.'

'You'll never have this world.' Now I looked up, and my body was shaking – with anger, not with fear. 'You can kill me. You can claim me. But you can't claim *us*. The Seven Seals are waiting. Jaxon Hall is waiting. The entire syndicate is waiting for you.' I raised my chin and stared her in the face. 'Good luck.'

Nashira pulled me to my feet by my hair. Her face came close to mine. 'You could have been more,' she said. 'So much more. As it happens, you will soon be nothing. Everything that you were will be mine.' With a push of her arm, she flung me into a Rephaite's iron grip. 'Alsafi, take this bag of bones to the stage. It is time for her to surrender her spirit.'

I didn't stop to think as Alsafi walked me up the steps. A bag was over my head. My lips were sore, my cheeks were hot. I couldn't breathe or think straight.

Warden was gone. I'd lost him. My only Reph ally, and I'd let him get caught. Nashira wouldn't just kill him, not when he'd stooped so low as to touch a human with his bare hands. It was more than betrayal. By kissing me, holding me, the blood-consort had debased his entire family. He was no longer a worthy candidate. He was nothing.

Alsafi kept a firm grip on my arm. I was about to die. In less than ten minutes, I would join with the æther, like all the other spirits. My silver cord would break. I would never be able to return to my own body, the body I'd inhabited for nineteen years. From then on, I would have to serve Nashira.

The bag came off my head. I was at the side of the stage, watching the end of the play. Two Rephs – Alsafi and Terebell – stood on either side of me. Terebell leaned down to my level. 'Where is Arcturus?'

'They took him to the gallery. Thuban and Situla.'

'We will deal with them.' Alsafi released my arm. 'You must delay the blood-sovereign, dreamwalker.'

I'd known Terebell was one of Warden's collaborators, but not Alsafi. He didn't look like a sympathiser, but neither did Warden.

The Overseer fled the stage, his costume drenched in artificial blood, leaving his knife behind him. His screams for mercy echoed through the Guildhall. The emissaries cheered as a group of actors chased him out onto the street, all wearing Scion uniforms. The applause was deafening. It continued as Nashira walked up the steps, back onto the stage.

'Thank you, ladies and gentlemen, for your kindness. I am pleased you enjoyed the production.' She didn't look pleased. 'I am also pleased, to end the evening, to give you a brief demonstration of our justice system here in Sheol I. One of our clairvoyants has displayed such disobedience that she cannot be allowed to live. Like the Bloody King, she must be banished beyond the reach of the amaurotic population, where she can do no more harm.

'XX-59-40 has a history of treachery. She hails from the dairy county of Tipperary, deep in the south of Ireland – a region long since associated with sedition.' Cathal Bell shifted his weight uncomfortably. A few of the emissaries murmured. 'After coming to England, she immediately became embroiled in the crime syndicate of London. On the night of March the seventh, she murdered two of her fellow clairvoyants, both Underguards in the service of Scion. It was a cold-blooded, cruel affair. Neither of 40's victims died quickly. On that same night, she was brought to Sheol I.' Nashira paced across the stage. 'We hoped we could educate her, teach her to control her gift. It pains us to lose young clairvoyants. It also pains me to admit that our endeavour to reform 40 has failed. She has repaid our compassion with insolence and brutality. There is no option left for her but to face the judgement of the Inquisitor.'

I looked past her. There was no scaffold on the stage; no gurney, no block. But there was a sword.

My blood stopped in my veins. That was no ordinary sword. Gold blade, black hilt. That was the Wrath of the Inquisitor, the sword that beheaded political traitors. It was only used when clairvoyant spies were discovered within the Westminster Archon. I was the daughter of a prominent Scion scientist. A traitor in the ranks of the naturals.

Alsafi and Terebell disappeared beneath the stage. I was left facing Nashira. She turned her head.

'Come forward, 40.'

I didn't hesitate.

There was a hush as I emerged from behind the drapes. 'Traitor,' Cathal Bell called, followed by some booing from the emissaries. I still didn't look at them. It was rich of Bell to call *me* a traitor.

I walked with my head held high, forcing myself to focus only on Nashira. I didn't look at the emissaries. I didn't look at the gallery, where Warden had been taken. I stopped a few feet away. Nashira circled me, slowly. When she wasn't in my line of vision, I looked straight ahead.

'You may wonder how we deal out justice here. With the noose, perhaps, or the fire of ancient days. Here is the Inquisitor's sword, delivered from the citadel.' She indicated the Wrath. 'But before I swing it, I wish to exhibit something else: the great gift of the Rephaim.'

There was a murmur.

'Edward VII was a curious man. We know all too well that he meddled in things that should not be meddled with. He tried to control a power beyond human knowledge. A power we Rephaim know very well.'

Birgitta Tjäder was staring at the stage, her brow furrowed. Several of the emissaries looked at their SVD bodyguards, Bell among them.

'Imagine the most powerful kind of energy on Earth.' Nashira held out a hand towards a nearby lantern. 'Electricity. It powers your lifestyles. It lights your cities and your homes. It allows you to communicate. The æther, the Source – the life force of the Rephaim – is rather like electricity. It can bring light to the darkness, knowledge to ignorance.' The lantern glowed with a sudden light. 'But when used incorrectly, it can destroy. It can kill.' The light went out.

'I have a gift that has proved very useful over the past two centuries. Some clairvoyant humans display particularly erratic abilities. They channel the æther – the realm of the dead – in ways that can result in madness and violence. The Bloody King had such an ability, resulting in his tragic killing spree. I am able to take those dangerous mutations of the gift away.' She motioned towards me. 'Clairvoyance, like energy, cannot be destroyed – only transferred. When 40 dies, another clairvoyant will eventually develop her gift. But by holding it inside me, I will ensure it is never used again.'

'You like making things up, don't you, Nashira?'

I said it before I'd registered the thought. She turned to look at me. Her eyes flared.

'You will not speak again.'

Her voice was soft.

I risked a glance at the gallery. Empty. Below me, Michael slipped a hand into his jacket. He had one of the guns.

At the back of the Guildhall, a door opened. Terebell, Alsafi and Warden. I met his eyes over the heads of the emissaries. The golden cord trembled. I saw a picture of the knife, the one on the floor, the one the Overseer had left behind. It lay a few feet away from Nashira.

As she turned back towards the audience, my spirit shot across the space between us. With every ounce of strength I could muster, I broke into her hadal zone. She hadn't been expecting the attack. I pictured myself with a massive dream-form, a behemoth, big enough to break down every barrier.

The æther reverberated. Spirits flew across the Guildhall, coming at Nashira from all angles. They joined me at the edges of her dreamscape, breaking down her ancient armour. The five angels were trying to defend her, but now twenty, now fifty, now two hundred spirits had descended on her, and the walls were starting to give. I wasted no time. I hauled my way through the shadows and threw myself into the very heart of her dreamscape.

I could see through her eyes. The room was a whirling blur of colour and darkness, light and fire, a spectrum of things I'd never seen. Was this how Rephs saw? There were auras everywhere. I was sighted – but now I was blind, and her eyes were refusing to see. They didn't want me to see. These weren't my eyes. I forced them open, looked down at my hand. Too large, gloved. My vision clenched. She was fighting me. *Hurry, Paige.*

The knife. The knife was there. *Hurry.* I reached for it. Just moving my hand was like trying to lift a barbell. *Kill her.* My ears rang with screams and strange new sounds, voices, thousands of voices. *Kill her.* My new fingers curled around the handle.

The knife. It was there. I drew back my arm, and with a single stab, drove the blade into my chest. The emissaries shouted. My vision tunnelled again. Everything flickered. I twisted the knife with my new hand, grinding it into whatever hell it was that made up Nashira's body. No pain. She was numb to the bites of an amaurotic blade. I stabbed again, this time on the left, aiming for where the heart would be on a human. Still no pain. But when I raised my arm a third time, I was thrown out of her body.

Spirits scattered across the room, extinguishing every candle. The

Guildhall descended into chaos. When my vision returned, I couldn't see a thing. My ears were full of screaming.

The candles came back to life. Nashira lay across the boards. She didn't move. The knife was embedded in her chest, right up to the handle. 'Blood-sovereign,' a Reph shouted.

The emissaries had fallen silent. My hands shook as I dragged myself across the boards to Nashira. I looked at her face, the eyes devoid of light. The spirits of Bone Season XVIII still hovered around her, as if waiting for her to join them in the æther.

Then a dim glow filled into her eyes. Slowly, her head turned. I felt myself shivering uncontrollably as she rose to her full height.

'Very clever,' she said. 'Very, very *clever.*'

I kept moving, my fingers scraping on the boards. As I watched, she pulled the knife from her chest. There were gasps from the audience. 'Show us more.' Drops of light fell like tears. 'I have no objections.'

With a flick of her hand, the knife was in the air. It hung there for a moment, as if on an invisible thread – then it came flying towards me. It caught my cheek, leaving a glancing wound. The candles guttered.

One of her angels was a poltergeist. It was rare that they could actually lift physical matter, but I'd seen it happen before. Apport, Jaxon called it. Spirits moving objects. A film of cold sweat coated my skin. I shouldn't be afraid. I'd faced a poltergeist once. Now my spirit was mature, I could defend myself.

'If you insist,' I said.

This time I couldn't catch her unawares. She threw up every layer of armour she had on her dreamscape. As if two giant doors had slammed in front of me, I was launched straight back into my own body. My heart stirred. The helmet-like pressure on my head intensified. I heard a familiar voice, but it was lost to a long, high-pitched sound in my ears.

Move. I had to move. She wouldn't stop. She would never stop hunting my spirit. I pushed myself back on my elbows, trying to find the knife. Her outline came into focus, moving towards me.

'You look tired, Paige. Give into it. The æther calls you.'

'Must have missed that call,' I forced out.

I wasn't prepared for what happened next. All five of her angels spooled together and flew at me.

Like a black wave they smashed through my defences. Outside my dreamscape, my head smacked into the floorboards. Inside it, the spirits tore a path through everything, scattering red petals. Images flashed past my eyes. Every thought, every memory was broken. Blood, fire, blood. A moribund field. A giant hand seemed to press down on my chest, pinning me in one place. In a box, in a coffin. I couldn't move or breathe or think. The five spirits cut through me like a sword, snatching pieces of my mind, my soul. I rolled onto my side, twitching like a crushed insect.

Small muscles spasmed in my arms and legs. I opened my eyes. The light burned them. All I could see was Nashira, her hand outstretched, the blade bright under the candles. Then she was gone.

With an effort that forced moisture from my eyes, I raised my head from the boards. Michael had thrown himself onto her back, distracting her. There was a knife in his hand. He stabbed at her neck, missing by inches. With a flick of her arm, Nashira threw him off the stage. He landed on a harlie, sending them both crashing to the ground.

She would turn back in a moment. This time she would finish me off. Her face appeared above me, and her eyes turned red. Her features softened to a haze. She was weakening me, making sure I couldn't use my spirit again. Disrupting my link to the æther. I was dead. She knelt beside me and lifted my head into the crook of her arm.

'Thank you, Paige Mahoney.' The tip of the knife pressed into my throat. 'I will not waste this gift.'

This was it. I didn't even have a final thought. I managed, with my last scrap of energy, to look into her eyes.

Then Warden was there. He was driving her back, using immense spools, whirling them into shields, like a fire-eater with torches. If I were sighted, I thought vaguely, it would probably look magnificent. Terebell and Alsafi were with him; and others, too – was that Pleione? Their outlines ran together. My dreamscape sent strange mirages across my line of sight. Then someone was scooping me into their arms, taking me from the stage.

The world came in flashes. There was a storm in my dreamscape: memories pouring through lightning-like cracks, flowers torn apart by a high wind. My mind had been pillaged.

I was only half-aware of the outside world. Warden was there. I recognised his dreamscape, a familiar presence against mine. He was carrying me up to the gallery, away from whatever had happened in the few minutes I'd been unconscious. As he lowered me to the floor, I could feel the blood drying on my face. I could barely remember where I was.

'Paige, fight it. You *must* fight it.'

His hand stroked over my hair. I watched his face, trying to make the lines stop blurring.

Another pair of eyes appeared. I thought it was Terebell again. I checked out for a while, only to wake with a hollow roaring in my ears. The noise pressed at my temples. When the pain forced me back to meatspace, Warden was looking down at me. We were in the gallery, above the clamour in the hall. 'Paige,' he said. 'Can you hear me?'

It sounded like a question. I nodded.

'Nashira.' I couldn't raise my voice above a whisper.

'She lives. But so do you.'

Still alive. Nashira was still here. I felt the faint stirrings of panic, but my body was too weak to respond. This wasn't over yet.

The sound of a gunshot rang out from below. Save his eyes, everything was dark. 'There was—' Warden leaned closer to my lips to hear me. 'There was a poltergeist. She has a . . . poltergeist.'

'Yes. But you came prepared.' His finger traced my neckline. 'Did I not say this could save your life?'

The pendant caught the light from his eyes; the sublimed object, designed to repel poltergeists. The one he'd given me. The one I'd tried to refuse, and might not have worn. Warden lifted me against his chest, keeping one hand at the back of my head. 'Help is coming,' he said, very softly. 'They came for you, Paige. The Seals came for you.'

There was another blind spot, during which the noise intensified. My dreamscape struggled to heal. The damage had been severe; it wouldn't start to repair itself for days. It might not start at all. Either way, I couldn't move, and time was running out – I had to reach the meadow, to find the exit. I was going home. I *had* to go home.

When I opened my eyes again, a vicious light scalded them. Not candlelight. I tried to block it, my chest heaving. 'Paige.' Someone took my outstretched hand. Not Warden. Someone else. 'Paige, sweetheart.'

I knew that voice.

He couldn't be here. It must be an apparition, an image from my damaged dreamscape. But when he took my hand, I knew he was real. My head still lay on Warden's lap. 'Nick,' I managed to say. He was dressed in his black suit and red tie.

'Yes, *sötnos*, it's me.'

I looked at my fingers. They were turning grey. My nails sat in beds of dark, bluish purple.

'Paige,' Nick said, his voice low and urgent, 'keep your eyes open. Stay with us, sweetheart. Come on.'

'Y-you have to go.' I rasped it.

'I am going. So are you.'

'Get a move on, Vision. No time to lose.' Another voice. 'We'll treat our little lost Dreamer when we reach the citadel.'

Jaxon.

No, no. Why had they come? Nashira would see. 'It'll be too late by then.' The same harsh light gleamed into my eyes. 'No pupil response. Cerebral hypoxia. She'll die if we don't do this.' A hand moved my hair back from my clammy face. 'Where the hell is Danica?'

I couldn't work out why Warden wasn't speaking. He was there, I could feel it.

Another blackout. When my vision returned, there was something clamped over my nose and mouth. I recognised the plastic smell of it – PVS^2, a portable cousin of Dani's life support system. There were more dreamscapes nearby, clustered around me. Nick cradled me in the crook of his arm, keeping the mask cupped over my mouth. I drank in the extra oxygen, heavy-eyed. I had never felt so completely spent in my life.

'It's not working. Her dreamscape's fractured.'

'That train will not wait for us, Vision.' Jaxon's voice had an edge. 'Carry her. We're leaving.'

The words crawled into my brain. For the first time in several minutes, Warden spoke: 'I can help her.'

'Don't come near her.' Nick said.

'There is no time to waste. The NVD will be on their way from the bridge. They will see your aura immediately, Dr Nygård. Your reputation in Scion will be lost.' Warden looked at them. 'Paige will die if you do nothing. Her damaged dreamscape can be repaired, but only if we are quick. Do you want to lose your dreamwalker, White Binder?'

'How do you know my name?' Jaxon flipped like a coin. I couldn't see him in the dark, but I sensed the sudden change in his dreamscape, the rising of defences.

'We have our ways.'

Their words were like a sequence of patterns, impossible to unravel. I couldn't make sense of them. Nick leaned down, exhaling warm air across my cheek. 'Paige,' he said into my ear, 'this man says he can heal you. Can I trust him?'

Trust. I recognised that word. A sun-drenched flower on the edge of perception, beckoning me into a different world. A different life, before the poppy field.

'Yes.'

As soon as I said it, Warden moved towards me. Over his shoulder I could see Pleione. 'Paige, I need you to drop all the mental defences you can,' he said. 'Can you do that?'

Like I had a shred of defence left.

Warden took a vial from Pleione's gloved hand. A vial of amaranth, almost empty. *Scarred one.* They must have been stockpiling them, saving every drop they could. He put a little under my nose, and a little more onto my lips. Heat seeped under my skin. It seemed as if the æther was calling to me, asking me to open my mind. A surge of warmth came in, stitching the rips in my dreamscape. Warden stroked his thumb across my cheek.

'Paige?'

I blinked.

'Are you all right?'

'Yes,' I said. 'I think so.'

I sat up, then tried to stand. Nick helped me back to my feet. No pain. I rubbed my eyes and blinked, trying to adjust to the darkness. 'How the hell did you get here?' I said, gripping his arms. I couldn't take my eyes off him. He was real, he was here.

'With the Scion party. I'll explain later.' He wrapped his arms around me, crushing me to his chest. 'Come on. We're getting out of here.'

Jaxon stood a few feet away, his cane grasped in both hands. On either side of him were Danica and Zeke. They were all dressed in Scion colours. On the other side of the gallery, Nadine was taking pot shots at the emissaries with her pistol. The two Rephaim watched me.

'Warden, how much—' I took in a deep breath, 'how much time do we have?'

'Fifty minutes. You must go.'

Less than an hour. The faster we reached the train, the faster I could send a flare up for the other voyants.

'I trust you still know where your loyalties lie, Paige,' Jaxon said. He looked me up and down. 'You almost made me doubt you, my mollisher, with that little act in London.'

'Jaxon, there are people dying, *voyants* dying in this place. Can we just put that incident aside and concentrate on getting the hell out of here?'

He never had a chance to reply. A group of Rephs burst into the gallery, wielding great spools. Warden and Pleione stepped in front of us.

'Go,' Warden said.

I was torn. Jaxon was already heading down the stairs, followed by the others. 'Paige, come *on*,' Nick urged.

Pleione blocked a spool. Warden turned to face me.

'Run. Get to Port Meadow,' he said. 'I will meet you there.'

I had no choice; I couldn't force him to come with me – I could only do as he said, and hope I was doing the right thing. Nick grabbed my arm, and we ran down the stairs, out into the foyer of the Guildhall. There was no time left to stop.

The harlies and the Rephs had spilled onto the streets. Panicked emissaries and their NVD guards ran through the foyer. Nick was following them. I stopped when the æther trembled.

I turned to face the hall. Something was wrong, I was sure of it. Before I knew what I was doing, I was running back to the flat stone steps. Jaxon called after me: 'And you are going *where?*'

'Just get to the train, Jaxon.'

I didn't hear his reply. Nick came after me, reached for my arm. 'Where are you going?'

'Just go with Jaxon.'

'We *have* to leave. If the NVD see my aura—'

He stopped talking when we reached the deserted hall.

The darkness filled every corner of the room. Most of the candles had gone out, but three red lanterns still shone where they'd fallen. The drapes where Liss had been performing had fallen into two folded heaps. I stepped towards them, sensing the dim flicker of a dreamscape. I ran across the marble floor and threw myself on my knees.

'Liss.' I grabbed her hand. 'Liss, come on.'

What had brought her back to the silks? Her hair was matted with blood. She couldn't be dead, not after we'd saved her life. Not after all we'd worked for together. She couldn't die. Seb had died; why did Liss need to follow?

Liss cracked her eyes open, just a little. Still dressed as a victim of the king. Her lips formed a tiny smile when she saw me.

'Hey.' Her breath rattled. 'Sorry I was – late.'

'No. Don't you dare die, Liss. Come on.' I squeezed her hand. 'Please. We thought we'd lost you before. Don't make us lose you again.'

'Glad somebody cares.' There were tears in my eyes: cold, trembling tears that didn't fall. Blood ran from her mouth. I couldn't tell where the stage blood ended and hers began. 'G-get out,' she said, her voice faint. 'Do what I c-couldn't – I just couldn't. Just wanted to – to see home.'

Her head rolled to the side. Her fingers loosened in mine, and her spirit slipped away into the æther.

For a minute I sat there, looking at the body. Nick bowed his head, and pulled a drape over her face. *Liss is gone.* I made myself think it. *Liss is gone, just like Seb. You didn't save them. They're gone.*

'You should say the threnody,' Nick murmured. 'I don't know her name, *sötnos*.'

He was right. Liss wouldn't want to stay here, in her prison.

'Liss Rymore' – I hoped it was her full name – 'be gone into the æther. All is settled. All debts are paid. You need not dwell among the living now.'

Her spirit disappeared.

I couldn't look at the body. Not Liss – the body, the shell, the shadow on the world she'd left behind.

The flare gun lay under the cold hand. It had been her job to fire it. I gently pulled it from her grasp. 'She wouldn't want you to give up.' Nick watched me check the gun for flares. 'She wouldn't have wanted you to die for her.'

'Oh, I think she would.'

I knew that voice. I couldn't see Gomeisa Sargas, but his voice echoed all through the room. 'Did you kill her, Gomeisa?' I stood. 'Is she good enough for you, now she's dead?'

The silence was damning.

A low voice came from behind me. 'You should not hide in the shadow, Gomeisa.'

I looked. Warden had entered the hall, and his eyes were fixed on the gallery. 'Unless you fear Paige,' he continued. 'The city burns outside. Your façade of power is already dissolved.'

Laughter. I tensed.

'I do not fear Scion. They handed their world over on a silver platter, Arcturus. Now we will dine.'

'Go to hell,' I said.

'I do not fear you either, 40. What have we to fear from death, when we *are* death? Besides, to be displaced from this decaying world – your little world of flower and flesh – well, that would almost be a blessing. If only there was not so much more to be done with it.' Footsteps. 'You cannot kill death. What fire can scald the sun? Who can drown the ocean?'

'I'm sure we can work something out,' I said.

My voice was steady, but I was shaking. Whether it was anger or fear, I could no longer tell. Behind Warden, another male Reph had appeared. At his side was Terebell.

'I would like you both to picture something. Especially you, Arcturus. Given what you have to lose.'

Warden said nothing. I tried to pin down where the voice was coming from. Somewhere above me. The gallery.

'I would like you to imagine a butterfly. Picture it: its coloured, iridescent wings. It is beautiful. Beloved. And then look at the moth. It takes the same shape – but look at the differences! The moth is pale and weak and ugly. A pitiful, self-destructive thing. It cannot command itself, for when it sees a fire, it desires the heat. And as it finds the flame, it burns.' His voice echoed everywhere. In my ears, in my head. 'That is how we see your world, Paige Mahoney. A box of moths, just waiting to be burned.'

His dreamscape was so close. I readied my spirit. I didn't care how much damage I did. He'd killed Liss; now I would kill him. Warden grasped my wrist. 'Don't,' he said. 'We will deal with him.'

'I want to deal with him.'

'You cannot avenge her, dreamwalker.' Pleione didn't take her eyes off the enemy. 'Go to the meadow. Time is short.'

'Yes, go to the meadow, 40. Take *our* train to *our* citadel.' Gomeisa emerged from behind the pillars. His eyes were fresh with aura – the last he'd ever take from Liss Rymore. 'Was it so terrible here, 40? We offered you our sanctuary, our wisdom – a new home. You were not unnatural here; lower, yes, but you had a place. To Scion you are a symptom of the plague. A rash upon their shallow skin.' He held out his gloved hand. 'You have no home there, dreamwalker. Stay with us. See what lies beneath.'

My muscles were stretched to breaking point. He looked straight at me – into my eyes, into my dreamscape, into the darkest parts of me. He knew his words made sense. He knew his twisted logic well; he'd relied on it for two centuries, using it to tempt the weak. Before I could answer him, Warden swept me back with his arm, right off my feet. A curved blade came singing over his shoulder, over my head. I hadn't seen it in the darkness. As I hit the floor, he ran towards Gomeisa. Terebell and the male went after him, both gathering spools, chiming out horrific sounds. Nick pulled me back to my feet, but I couldn't feel his hands. All I could feel was the æther, where the Rephaim were dancing.

The air around me thinned to a silver gauze. I couldn't see the four Rephs, but I felt their movements. Each flex of muscle, each turn and step sent a shockwave through the æther. They were dancing on the edge of life. A dance of giants, the *danse macabre*.

The spirits of the Bone Season still lingered in the hall. Terebell's spool flew through the pillars: thirty spirits, all weaving and rising together, converging on his dreamscape. No voyant could survive being hit by so many at once. I waited for the blow to fall.

Gomeisa's laugh rose to the ceiling. With a wave of his hand, he shattered the spool. Like glass shards from a mirror, the spirits burst all over the hall. Terebell's limp body was thrown into a pillar. The sound of bone on marble snapped through the chilled air. When the other Reph charged at him, Gomeisa simply cut his hand upward. The motion flung his attacker onto the stage. The boards splintered under his weight, sending him into the trap room.

I pushed myself back, my boots sliding on blood. Was Gomeisa some kind of *poltergeist*? He could use apport – move things without touching them. The realisation made my heart pound thick and fast against my ribs. He could smash me into the ceiling on a whim.

Only Warden was left. He turned to face his enemy, terrible in the half-light. 'Come, then, Arcturus,' Gomeisa said, spreading his arms wide. 'Pay for your bounty.'

That was when the stage exploded.

His Parting from Her

The gust of heat blew me back across the room, deafening me. I landed hard on my right side, cracking my hip. I felt Nick grabbing my wrist, hauling me to my feet, pulling me out of the way, into the foyer. We barely reached the door before the flames caught up. I threw myself at the ground, covered my head with my arms. Fire burst from the Guildhall, shattering the windows. I kept low, moving as fast as I could. The flare gun was still in my hand.

None of the harlies had the kind of ordnance to cause such an explosion. Julian must not have told me something. Where had he found a mine, or the time to plant it? Had he taken it from No Man's Land? And what kind of mine sent roaring fire straight through a building?

In the thick of the smoke, Nick took my elbow and hauled me to my feet. Glass fell from my hair. I coughed from my chest, my eyes burning.

'Wait.' I strained away from Nick's hand. 'Warden—'

He couldn't be dead. Nick was shouting something, but he

sounded distant. I tried to use the golden cord. To see, to feel, to hear. Nothing.

Outside, the sirens were howling and a rampant fire smoked in the next street. The Room belched flame and black cloud. One – no, two of the residences were ablaze. One of them was Balliol, the only building with electricity. The emissaries would have trouble getting word out to the citadel now. *Thank you, Julian*, I thought. *Wherever you are, thank you.*

Nick lifted me into his arms. 'We've got to move,' he said, his voice ragged. He looked at the unfamiliar city, his face drawn with stress. 'Paige, I don't know this place – how do we find the train?'

'Just keep going north.' I tried to get down, but he gripped me too tightly. 'I can run, damn it!'

'You just survived an explosion and a poltergeist,' Nick shouted at me. His face was red with anger. 'I didn't come all the way here for you to go and get yourself killed, Paige. For once in your *life*, just let someone carry you.'

Sheol I was in a state of warfare. Now the Guildhall was broken, the rebels had spread out across the streets, where they were fighting with all they had against the Rephaim. Scion emissaries were fleeing in every direction, trailing their bodyguards, who had opened fire on the voyants. Julian's unit, the ones in charge of arson, had risen to their challenge with murderous enthusiasm – they'd already set fire to most of the Rookery. I wanted to stay, to fight, but I had to set off the flare. I'd save more lives that way.

Nick took the safest route, away from the fighting, through a narrow street. I caught sight of another skirmish. Harlies fighting alongside amaurotics and jackets, teaming up to take out individual Rephs – even Cyril had joined the struggle.

A piercing scream reached my ears. I looked over Nick's shoulder. Nell. Her hands were restrained by two Rephs. 'You're not going anywhere, 9. We need to feed.' One of them pulled her head against him, holding her by the hair.

'No! You get your hands off me! You're not ever feeding on me again, you parasite!'

Her screams were cut short when her keeper clapped a hand over her mouth. 'Nick,' I shouted.

He heard the frantic edge to my voice. His arms loosened. I hit the ground running, straight towards Nell. I had no weapons – but I did have my gift. No longer my curse. Tonight it would save a life, not take one.

I threw my spirit at the bigger Reph. I pushed against his dreamscape, forcing my way into his hadal zone, and sprang straight back to my body. I was there in time to throw my hands out, stopping my chin from smacking into the ground. With no idea what had happened, Nell pulled her hands free of the Rephs and knifed the one on her right, stabbing deep into his side. At the same time, she pulled a spirit from nowhere and hurled it into his face. He let out an awful snarl. His companion was still reeling from my attack. Nell grabbed her fallen supplies and sprinted for her life.

The two Rephs were injured, but they were still threats. The one I'd attacked looked up at me, and his eyes – orange – came into focus. He took a blade from a sheath on his arm. 'Go back to the æther, dreamwalker.'

The blade flashed towards my face. I didn't duck fast enough: it caught my arm. Nick let off a round. The bullet hit the Reph in the chest – to no avail. I sent my spirit at his dreamscape. The second attack weakened him. I picked up the blade he'd thrown and drove it into his throat.

My mistake was forgetting about his companion. All the breath was knocked from my lungs as the second Reph crashed into me, pinning me to the ground. His giant fist smashed down, half an inch from my head.

Nick tossed his gun away. As the Reph raised a fist for a second try, Nick snatched three nearby spirits and hurled them in quick succession. I sensed the surge in the æther as he sent a vivid snapshot into the Reph's dreamscape, blinding him. In the second the Reph rolled off me, fighting the spirits and the vision, I was on my feet and running back to Nick.

We hadn't gone far before my sixth sense stung. My head jerked round to face the threat.

'Nick!'

He knew. In one seamless movement, he threw down his backpack and reached for another spool. The target was familiar: Aludra Chertan.

'Dreamer.' She didn't even glance at Nick. 'I believe I still owe you for your little display in the chapel.'

'Stay back,' Nick warned.

'But you look so *refreshing*.'

Her eyes changed colour.

Nick's face contorted. Blood swelled in his tear ducts, and the veins in his neck strained out. 'Almost as refreshing as the walker,' Aludra continued, moving towards us. 'I might just keep you, oracle.'

Nick grasped his knees, trying to hold himself upright. 'I killed your heir apparent,' I said. 'Don't think I won't do the same to you. Just crawl back to the rotten hell you came from.'

'Kraz was an arrogant creature. I am not. I know which of my enemies are worth my precious minutes.'

'And I'm one of them.'

'Oh, yes.'

I grew still. There was something behind her: a shadow. A massive, cumbersome shadow. She was too greedy to see it. The rotten giant. I recognised that blot in the æther. 'How many minutes?'

'Only one.' She raised her hand. 'But a minute is more than enough time to die in.'

Then her expression changed. Shock. She'd felt it, but she didn't turn fast enough. The thing had her in its grip before she could move. White eyes. Dead eyes. I could only see bits of it – the gas lamps had gone out when it appeared – but it was more than enough to scar itself onto my memory, deep into the tissue, grating the delicate fabric of my dreamscape. Aludra stood no chance. Her scream was cut off before it started.

'Yes,' I said. 'More than enough.'

Nick was frozen stiff. His eyes were wide, his mouth clenched. I grabbed his arm and ran.

We sprinted for our lives. The Emim were in the city. Just like Bone Season XVIII. 'How long?' I called to Nick.

'Not long.' He grabbed my hand, pulling me faster. 'What *was* that thing? What's Scion done to this place?'

'A lot.'

We took a side street, one of several that led into the ghost town. A figure came racing down from the opposite side, panting. Nick and I both reacted at the same time: Nick tripped the boy, sending him flying into the pavement, and I pressed my hand against his Adam's apple.

'Going somewhere, Carl?'

'Get off me!' Carl was drenched in sweat. 'They're coming. They've let them into the city.'

'Who?'

'The Buzzers. The Buzzers!' He shoved at my chest, almost in tears. 'You had to ruin it, didn't you? You had to try and change everything! This place is all I've got – you are *not* taking it—'

'You have a whole world. Don't you remember it?'

'A whole world? I'm a freak! We're all freaks, 40! Freaks that talk to dead people. That's why we need *them*,' he said, stabbing a finger in the direction of the city centre. 'Don't you see? This is the only place that's safe for us. They'll start killing us soon – jumping us—'

'Who?'

'The amaurotics. When they realise. When they realise what the Rephaim want. I'm never going out there again. You can keep your precious world. You're welcome to it!'

I released his throat. He scrambled to his feet and bolted. Nick watched him go.

'You've got a long story to tell when we get home.'

I watched Carl disappear around the corner.

It was less than a mile to the meadow, but I wasn't counting on getting there without a fight. Nashira was out there somewhere, and it was possible that not all of the bone-grubbers had taken Duckett's concoction. We kept to the edge of the street, working our way through the ghost town.

There was an explosion in the distance. Nick didn't stop. The windows of the buildings rattled. I couldn't think straight. Were people trying to flee across the minefield? They must be panicking, wondering where the flare was, running through the trees to get away. I had to call them to safety. We ran all the way down the blasted street, then veered off on the path towards Port Meadow. I could see the fences, and the sign. A few voyants and amaurotics had gathered outside. They must have thought they could leave the city this way.

And Warden. He was there. He was filthy, covered in cinders, but alive. He caught me in his arms. 'Where the hell did you go?' The words heaved out of me.

'Forgive me. I was sidetracked.' His gaze shifted towards the city. 'You did not plant that incendiary device under the stage.'

'No.' I grasped my knees, trying to catch my breath. 'Unless—'

'Unless?'

'12. The oracle, the red-jacket. He said something about an alternative plan.'

'Let's just focus on getting out of here.' Nick glanced at Warden, then looked back at me. 'Where's the entrance to the tunnel? It was light when we arrived.' The meadow was pitch black now, too dark to navigate.

'Not far,' Warden said.

'Right.' Nick looked at his old Nixie watch. He wiped his upper lip with a shaking hand. 'Did Binder make it?'

'You can use his real name, Nick.' I could feel sweat running down my neck. 'He knows.'

'Mr Hall and three of your companions are in the meadow, waiting for you,' Warden said. His eyes stayed on the city. 'Paige, I recommend you use one of those flares. You still have time.'

Nick went to the sally port, where Jaxon seemed to be studying the ethereal fence. I went to stand beside Warden.

'I am sorry about Liss,' he said.

'So am I.'

'I will see to it that Gomeisa does not forget her death.'

'You didn't kill him?'

'We were interrupted by the explosion. Gomeisa was much stronger than us, having fed, but we did weaken him. The fire in the Guildhall may have done the rest.'

He was still wearing gloves, even now. Something twinged inside me: hurt, perhaps. Had I thought he would change so easily?

Warden didn't take his eyes off mine. The golden cord shivered, just a little. I didn't know what he was trying to transmit, but I was suddenly more focused, more resolute. I grasped the handle of the flare gun. Warden took a step back. I found a point above the meadow, cocked the hammer and turned my head away.

The flare hung above the meadow, bursting out signal after signal. I watched it scorch and smoke as I stood beside Warden. Red light flickered in his eyes, and at our feet.

I looked past the flare, to the stars. This might be the last time I ever saw the stars like this, in a city without light, without smog. Or perhaps one day the whole world would look like this. The world under Nashira's hand. One great dark prison city.

Warden placed a hand on my back. 'We must go.'

I walked with him to the sally port. When he opened the gate, the voyants and amaurotics – eight of them – moved through into the meadow. When we were on the other side, he pulled the gate wide open and took out another vial. He had more vials than a gallipot.

The contents were pale and crystalline. Salt. He poured a thin line of it across the port. I was about to ask about the Emim when Jax grabbed me by the arms and slammed me against a post. I could feel the power of the fence, so close my hair crackled.

'Idiot.' Jax grabbed the front of my dress. 'You've just shown them exactly where we are, you wretched child.'

'I'm showing *everyone* where we are. I'm not leaving all these people here to die, Jaxon,' I said. 'They're voyants.'

The muscles in his face twitched. His face was contorted with rage. This was the Jaxon I feared – the man that owned my life.

'I agreed to come here to salvage my dreamwalker,' he breathed. 'Not to save a rabble of soothsayers and augurs.'

'Not my problem.'

'It is very much your problem. If you do anything more to compromise this endeavour – the endeavour to rescue *you*, I might add, ungrateful little urchin – I will make sure you work the shallow for the rest of your days. I shall send you to Jacob's Island, and you can busk with the extispicists and the splanchomancers and all the other sacks of *scum* that wash up on the edge of the world. See what they do to you.' His cold hand rested on my throat. 'These people are expendable. We are not. You may have claimed a little independence, O my lovely, but you will do as you are told. And we will go back to how things were before.'

His words stripped layers from my dreamscape. I was back to my sixteen-year-old self, afraid of the world, afraid of everything inside me. Then armour built around me, and I was someone else.

'No,' I said. 'I quit.'

His expression changed.

'You do not *quit* the Seven Seals,' he said.

'I just did.'

'Your life is my property. We made a deal. You signed a contract.'

'I don't give a toss what the other mime-lords say. If I'm your property, Jaxon, then my employment is nothing more than slavery.' I forced him away from me. 'I've had enough of that for a lifetime.'

The words came out, but they didn't seem to come from my head. I was turning numb. 'If I can't have you, no one does.' His fingers tightened. 'I will not surrender a dreamwalker.'

He was serious. After what had happened at Trafalgar Square, I understood his bloodlust. His aura betrayed it. He would kill me if I left his service.

Nick had spotted us. 'Jaxon, what are you doing?'

'I quit,' I said. And again: 'I quit.' I had to hear myself say it. 'When we get back to London, I won't be going to I-4.'

His eyes moved to Jaxon. 'We'll talk about it later,' he said. 'There's no time now. Fifteen minutes.'

The reminder sent a cold dart through my gut. 'We need to get everyone on the train. Now.'

Nadine was back. 'Where's the entrance?' She was sweating. 'We came up from a passage to this meadow. Where is it?'

'We'll find it.' I looked behind her. Only Zeke was there. 'Where's Dani?'

'She's not answering on the transceiver. She could be anywhere.'

'She does work for Scion,' Nick said. 'She might get away with saying she was an emissary. But it's not ideal.'

'Did Eliza come?'

'No, we left her at Dials. We needed one Seal in the citadel.'

Jaxon got to his feet and brushed himself down. 'Let us all be friends for now. We can discuss our differences on our return.' He beckoned. 'Diamond, Bell – cover us, if you please. We have a train to catch.'

'What about Dani?' Zeke looked nervous.

'She'll make it, dear boy. That girl could make it through a minefield.'

Jaxon brushed past me, lighting another cigar as he went. How could he smoke at a time like this? He was putting on a nonchalant act, I was sure. He didn't want to lose me. I wasn't sure I wanted to lose him, either. Why had I said all those things? Jaxon wasn't an oracle or a soothsayer, but his words had sounded prophetic. I couldn't end up busking – or worse, nightwalking – in a voyant slum like Jacob's Island. There were far worse places to be than in Jaxon's employ in the safe area of I-4.

I wanted to apologise. I *had* to apologise. I was a mollisher; he was my mime-lord. But pride stopped me.

I fired another flare. The last one. A last chance for the last survivors. Then I started to run, following Jaxon. Warden shadowed me.

The flare lit our path. A few more humans made it to the sally port. They followed us into the meadow – some in pairs, others alone. Most were voyant. When Michael arrived, he caught my arm. He had a bad cut on his face, running from eyebrow to jaw, but he could walk. He hefted my backpack into my arms.

'Thanks, Michael – you really didn't have to—' He shook his head, his narrow chest heaving. I slung a strap over my shoulder. 'Is anybody else coming?'

He made three quick signs. 'The emissaries,' Warden translated. 'They are coming with their bodyguards. How long?' He held up two fingers. 'Two minutes. We must be well ahead of them when they arrive.'

This was a nightmare. I looked over my shoulder. 'Can't they just let us go?'

'They will have been told to contain every last witness to this event. We may be heading for a fight.'

'We'll give them one.'

A stitch pulled at my side. In our path, a wounded man was sprawled on the grass. His chest rose and fell with shallow breaths. I had half a minute to get this man on his feet or we'd have to leave him here. 'Go ahead,' I said to Warden. 'Let them know I'm coming. Can you open the tunnel?'

'Not without you.' He looked down at the man. I couldn't tell what he was thinking. 'Be quick, Paige.'

He walked ahead with Michael. I knelt beside the man. He was lying on his back, his eyes closed, his hands folded on his chest. He would have looked like an effigy, if not for his Scion uniform – red tie, black suit, all soaked with blood. When I checked his pulse, he opened one eye. With sudden urgency, his ring-laden hand clasped mine.

'You're the girl.'

I kept still. 'Who are you?'

'Wallet. Look.'

After a moment, I pulled the leather wallet from inside his jacket. Inside was an ID card. He was from the Starch. 'You work for Weaver,' I said softly. 'You sick, sick bastard. You did this. All of this. Did he send you to watch me die? To keep an eye on the hell he threw us into?'

He was an obscure person, someone whose name I didn't recognise. 'They will d-destroy – everything.' Blood glinted on his lips.

'Who?'

'The c-creatures.' He drew in a laboured breath, throat rattling. 'Find – find Rackham. Find him.'

With those words, he died. I held his wallet in my hands, shivering in the sudden cold.

'Paige?'

Nick had come back for me. 'He was from Scion.' I shook my head, exhausted. 'I don't understand anything any more.'

'Nor do I. We're being played, *sötnos*. We just don't know what we're playing yet.' He squeezed my hand. 'Come on.'

I let him pull me to my feet. As soon as I was upright, I heard the distant gunshot. My back tensed rigid. *The emissaries.* They must have reached the sally port. At the same time, the æther gave off an odd signal. Four yellow-eyed figures were heading towards us. 'Rephs,' I said. My feet were already moving. 'Run. Nick, *run*!'

He didn't argue. Our boots pounded on the cold earth, but the Rephs were hot on our heels, faster than us. I pulled a knife from my backpack and turned, intending to put it through an eye, but my hand was stopped by Terebell Sheratan. 'Terebell,' I said, my chest heaving. 'What do you want?'

Terebell looked me in the eye. With her were Pleione, Alsafi and a younger female I didn't recognise. And behind them, her shirt torn and bloodied, was Dani. The sight of her took a weight off my shoulders.

'We brought your friend,' Terebell said. Her eyes held little light. 'She will not last long here.'

Ignoring them all, Dani limped past me, heading for the group of stragglers. She looked like death. 'What do you want in return?' I said, wary. 'You don't want to come on the train.'

'If we did wish to come, you would not stand in our way. We have all saved human lives. We have brought your friend to you, and delayed the Night Vigilance Division. You are beholden to us.' Alsafi stared me out. 'Fortunately for you, dreamwalker, we are not bound for the citadel. We have come for Arcturus.'

'He'll come when he's ready.' I still needed Warden.

'Then relay him a message. He is to meet us in the clearing as soon as you are gone. We will be waiting.'

Just as quickly as they'd arrived, they were gone, heading for the fences. They disappeared into the darkness, like dust into shadow, fleeing the inevitable retribution of the Sargas. I turned and made my way towards a training platform, where two lanterns burned in stained glass panes.

Getting here had been the easy part. Now I had to lead these people into the tunnel and onto the train.

The stragglers had gathered on the edges of a concrete platform – but not the right one. This was rectangular. Nick was checking Dani's face. There was a deep gash above her eye, but she shrugged it off. At the back of the rectangle, Jaxon gave the city a cold stare. No sign of Julian. Swallowed by the fire, just like Finn. I hoped it had at least been quick.

'We have to leave,' I said. 'No more waiting.'

'There's no point.' An amaurotic boy gripped his hair with white-knuckled hands. 'The NVD are coming.'

'We got here first.'

A few sets of eyes grew brighter. I pulled a torch out of my back-pack and switched it on. 'Follow me,' I said. 'Move as fast as you can. Carry the injured if possible. We have to reach another marker – an oval. We don't have long.'

'You're with the Rephs,' said an embittered voice. 'I'm not going anywhere with a leech.'

I turned to the man that had spoken and I pointed to the city. 'You want to go back there instead?'

He was silent. I brushed past him, ignoring the twinge in my side, and broke into another painful run.

Once we were past the scrying pool, it was easy to remember the right place. Warden stood where we'd trained all those months ago. 'The entrance is here,' he said when I was close, indicating the concrete oval. 'Nashira rather liked the idea of having the train beneath the training ground.'

'Do you think she's dead?'

'That would be too much to hope.'

I pushed the thought aside. I couldn't think about Nashira now. 'They're waiting for you,' I said. 'In the clearing.'

'I do not intend to go with them yet.'

The words were a relief. I looked down at the oval. 'There's no guard,' I said. 'They didn't just leave it open.'

'They are not that foolish.' Warden pushed back a layer of moss, revealing a silver padlock. A thin bar of white light appeared down the middle, as if a bulb inside it had been activated. 'This padlock contains an ethereal battery. There is a poltergeist inside it. They intended to send a Rephaite guard with the emissaries to unlock it before power is restored to the line – but if *you* can persuade it to leave, the charge will fail, and the lock will spring.'

The marks on my hand stung.

'It cannot hurt you in your dream-form, Paige.' He knew. 'You are best equipped to deal with a breacher.'

'Jaxon is a binder.'

'That will not eliminate the problem. The poltergeist must be persuaded – or compelled – to leave the object, not bound. Until it has been freed from its physical restraints, your friend cannot bind it.'

'What do you expect me to do?'

'You can travel through the æther. You can communicate with the poltergeist without touching the lock, unlike us.'

'There is no "us", Reph.' The voice came from an augur, a little older than me. 'Get away from that lock.'

Warden stood with no argument, but he didn't take his eyes off the augur. There was a heavy pipe in his hands, an improvised weapon from the city. 'What are you doing?' I said.

'There's no such thing as ethereal battery.' His teeth were gritted. 'I'll deal with this. I'm getting out of here.'

He swung the pipe. It crashed down on the padlock.

A shock cut through the æther. The augur was blasted back twenty feet, screaming. 'No, please, don't. I don't want to die. Please! I – I don't *want* to be a slave! No!' He arched his back, shuddered, and was still.

I recognised those words.

'I've changed my mind,' I said. Warden flicked his gaze back to me. 'I can deal with this poltergeist.'

Warden nodded. Perhaps he'd understood.

'Here they come!'

I looked up.

Beneath the moonlight, the NVD charged through the meadow. They were armed with riot shields and batons, escorting a cluster of emissaries. Birgitta Tjäder was among them, as was Cathal Bell. Tjäder spotted us first, and she gave a shout of anger. Nick raised his gun, aiming for her head. No point using spools on amaurotics.

I turned to face the prisoners. For the first time since they'd come here, they needed to be encouraged. They needed to hear a voice telling them that they could do this. That they were worth something.

That voice would be mine.

'Do you see those Gillies?' I pointed at them, raising my voice. 'Those Gillies are going to try and stop us getting out. They're going to kill us, because even now, they don't want us in their capital. They don't want us to share what we've seen. They want us to die – here, now.' My voice was sore, but I pressed on. I had to press on. 'I will open this access hatch, and we will leave this city on time. I promise you that we will be in London by dawn. And there will be no day-bell to send us to our cells!' There were murmurs of assent, of anger. Michael clapped. 'But I need you to defend the meadow. I need you to do this one last thing before we can leave this place for ever. Give me two minutes, and I will give you freedom.'

They didn't say anything. No war cries, no shouts. But in unison, they picked up their improvised weapons, summoned every spirit they could muster, and surged towards the NVD. Nadine and Zeke went after them, straight into the fray. The spirits of the meadow rallied to their cause, flying at the NVD with twice the strength of bullets. Jaxon held still, assessing me.

'An excellent speech,' he said, 'for an amateur.'

It was a compliment. Praise from a mime-lord to his mollisher. But I knew it wasn't really admiration.

I had two minutes. That was my promise.

'Dani,' I said, 'I need the mask.'

She reached into the pocket of her coat. Sweat coated her brow. 'Here.' She threw it at me. 'It's running low on oxygen. Make it count.'

Positioning myself as close as possible to the padlock, I lay down on the grass. Nick looked at Warden. 'I don't know who you are, but I hope you know what you're doing. She's not a toy.'

'I cannot allow you to lead these people through No Man's Land.' Warden cast his eye towards the woods. 'Unless you can think of an alternative, Dr Nygård, this is the only way.'

I strapped PVS^2 over my mouth and nose. It sealed and illuminated, indicating a steady flow of oxygen. 'You haven't got long,' Dani said. 'I'll give you a shake when you have to come back.'

I nodded.

'Warden,' I said, 'what was Seb's middle name?'

'Albert.'

I closed my eyes.

'Timing two minutes,' Nick said, and that was the last thing I heard, at least in meatspace.

I could see the tiny receptacle in the æther. It absorbed me as any dreamscape would, like one small droplet might absorb another. And then I turned to face a lost boy.

I didn't move towards him. I just stood there. But there he was: Sebastian Albert Pearce, the boy I had failed to save. He was hitting the walls, shaking the iron bars of the room. Outside the bars was the endless darkness of the æther. His face was bloody, contorted with rage, and his hair was black with ash.

Last time I'd encountered a poltergeist I'd been in a physical form, but Seb could still do some injury to my spirit. I would have to stop him.

'Seb,' I said, as softly as I could.

It didn't take long for him to see the invasion. He rounded on me, ran at me. I grabbed him by the wrists.

'Seb, it's me!'

'You didn't save me.' He was snarling, rabid. 'You didn't save me and now I'm dead. I'm *dead*, Paige! And I can't' – he hit the wall – 'get out' – again – 'of this room!'

His narrow form shook in my arms. His ribs and bones jutted, like they had before. I forced down my fear and held his filthy face between my hands. The sight of his broken neck made me flinch.

I had to do this. I had to quell the wrath of the spirit he'd become, or he would live in this state for ever. This wasn't Seb. This was Seb's bitterness and pain and hatred. 'Seb, listen to me. I'm so, so sorry. You didn't deserve this.' His eyes were black. 'I can help you. Do you want to see your mother again?'

'Mother hates me.'

'No. Listen, Seb, listen. I didn't free you, and – and I'm sorry.' My

446

voice was about to crack. 'But we can free each other now. If you leave this room, I can leave the city.'

'Nobody leaves. She said "nobody leaves".' He gripped my arm, and his head shook so fast it blurred. 'Not even you. Not even me.'

'I can *make* you leave.'

'I don't want to leave. Why should I leave? She killed me. I should have had longer!'

'You're right. You should have had longer. But do you really want to live in this cage for the rest of forever?'

Seb began to tremble again.

'For ever?'

'Yes, for ever. You don't want that.'

His neck healed.

'Paige,' he whispered, 'do I have to *leave* for ever? I can't come back?'

I was shaking now. Why couldn't I have saved him? Why couldn't I have stopped her?

'For now.' Slowly, carefully, I placed my hands on his shoulders. 'I can't send you all the way to the last light. You know, that white light people say they see at the end. I can't send you there. But I can send you a long way away, to the outer darkness, so nobody can ever trap you again. And then, if you really want, then you can come back.'

'If I want.'

'Yes.'

We stood there for a while, Seb in my arms. He had no pulse, but I knew he must be afraid. My silver cord trembled.

'Don't go after her,' Seb said, grasping at my dream-form. 'Nashira. All they want to do is suck us dry. And there's a secret.'

'What secret?'

'I can't say. I'm sorry.' He took my hands. 'It's too late for me, but not for you. You can still stop this. We'll help you. We all will.'

Seb threaded his arms around my neck. He felt as real as the living boy. That was how I remembered him. I whispered the threnody: 'Sebastian Albert Pearce, be gone into the æther. All is settled. All debts are paid. You need not dwell among the living now.' I closed my eyes. 'Goodbye.'

He smiled.

Then he was gone.

The pocket of æther inside the numen began to collapse. The silver cord jerked, more urgently this time. I took a running jump, and my dreamscape brought me back into its hold.

'Paige. *Paige.*'

My eyes ached in the sudden light. 'She's all right,' Nick said. 'We're out of here. Nadine, round them up.'

'Warden,' I murmured.

A gloved hand squeezed mine, and I knew he was there. I opened my eyes. I could hear gunfire. And his heartbeat.

Warden lifted the access hatch: a heavy door, covered by concrete, which concealed a narrow staircase. The empty padlock clattered away. Warden hitched me over his shoulder, and I wrapped my arms around his neck. The humans spilled down the steps, still firing at the NVD. Tjäder grabbed a dead Gilly's gun. The bullet hit Cyril in the neck, killing him. I caught sight of the city – the light on the sky, the beacon in the dark – before Warden followed the survivors. His warm, solid frame was the only thing I could focus on. My perception returned in painful jolts.

The tunnel was cold. I could smell it: the dry, musty odour of a room that was rarely used. The shouts from above blurred into a senseless cacophony, like the barking of dogs. I clenched my fingers, gripping Warden's shoulder. I needed adrenalin, amaranth, something.

The tunnel wasn't large, barely the size of an Underground

tunnel, but the platform was long and wide enough to accommodate at least a hundred people. Stretchers stood at the far end, piled up on top of one another. I smelled disinfectant. They must have been used to take fluxed voyants from here to the detention facility, or at least to the street. But I was sure I could hear something in the darkness: the vibrant hum of electricity.

Warden shone his torch towards the train. A moment later, the lights came on. I narrowed my eyes.

Power.

The train was a light metro, not designed to carry many passengers. The words SCION AUTOMATED TRANSPORTATION SYSTEM were printed across the back of the train. The carriages were white, with Scion's insignia on the doors. As I looked at them, they opened, and the lights turned on inside. '*Welcome aboard*,' Scarlett Burnish said. '*This train will depart in three minutes. Destination: the Scion Citadel of London.*'

With gasps of relief, the survivors went through into the carriages, leaving their makeshift weapons on the platform. Warden stood still.

'They'll realise.' I sounded tired. 'They'll realise the wrong people are on the train. They'll be waiting for us.'

'And you will face them. As you face all things.'

He let me down, but he didn't release me. His hands cradled my hips. I looked up at him. 'Thank you,' I said.

'You do not need to thank me for your freedom. It is your right.'

'And yours.'

'You have given me my freedom, Paige. It has taken me twenty years to regain the strength to try and claim it back. I have you, and you alone, to thank for that.'

My reply caught in my throat. A few more people boarded the train, Nell and Charles among them. 'We should get on,' I said.

Warden didn't answer. I wasn't sure what had happened over

the last six months – whether any of this was real – but my heart was full and my skin was warm, and I wasn't afraid. Not now. Not of him.

There was a distant sound, like thunder. Another mine. Another pointless death. Zeke, Nadine and Jax staggered into the tunnel, supporting a semi-conscious Dani. 'Paige, are you coming?' Zeke said.

'You get on. I'll be there.'

They went into a carriage near the back. Jaxon looked out of the door at me.

'We'll talk, my dreamer,' he said. 'When we return, we will talk.'

He hit the button inside the carriage, and the doors slid shut. An amaurotic and a soothsayer stumbled into the next carriage, one with a bloody shirt. '*One minute to departure. Please make yourselves comfortable.*' Warden tightened his arms around me.

'How strange,' he said, 'that this should be so difficult.'

I studied his face. His eyes were dim.

'You're not coming,' I said. 'Are you?'

'No.'

The realisation came slowly, like dusk encroaching on a star. I realised I'd never expected him to come – only hoped for it, in the last few hours. When it was too late. And now he was leaving. Or staying. From this point on, I was alone. And in that solitude, I was free.

He touched his nose to mine. A slow, sweet ache rose inside me, and I didn't know what to do. Warden didn't take his eyes off my face, but I looked down. I looked down at our hands, his larger hands on mine: shielded by gloves, hiding the rough skin beneath – and my pale hands, with rivers of blue vein. My nails, still tinged with lilac.

'Come with us,' I said. My throat felt sore, my lips hot. 'Come with – with me. To London.'

He had kissed me. He had wanted me. Maybe he still did.

But anything between us was impossible. And from the look in his eyes, I knew that wanting me wasn't enough.

'I cannot go to the citadel.' He rolled his thumb over my lips. 'But you can. You can go back to your life, Paige. That chance is all I want for you.'

'It's not all I want.'

'What do you want?'

'I don't know. I just want you with me.'

I had never said those words aloud. Now that I could taste my freedom, I wanted him to share it with me.

But he couldn't change his life for me. And I couldn't sacrifice my life to be with him.

'I must hunt Nashira from the shadows now.' He pressed his forehead against mine. 'If I can draw her away from here, the rest may leave. They may give up.' His eyes opened, burning his words into my mind. 'If I never return – if you never see me again – it will mean that everything is all right. That I have ended her. But if I return, it will mean that I have failed. That there is still danger. And then I will find you.'

I held his gaze. I would remember that promise.

'Do you trust me now?' he asked.

'Should I?'

'I cannot tell you that. That *is* trust, Paige. Not knowing whether you should trust at all.'

'Then I trust you.'

As if from miles away, I heard a pounding. Fists on metal, muffled shouting. Nick came running into the tunnel, accompanied by the remaining survivors, who piled onto the train just before the doors snapped closed. 'Paige, get on!' he shouted.

The countdown was over. Out of time. Warden pulled away from me, his eyes hot with remorse.

'Run,' he said. 'Run, little dreamer.'

The train was moving. Nick swung himself over a rail, onto the back, and held out a hand.

'PAIGE!'

I came back to myself. My heart leapt, and all my senses hit me like an iron wall. I turned and ran along the platform. The train picked up speed, almost too fast. I grabbed Nick's outstretched hand, vaulted over the rail, and I was on the train, I was there, I was safe. Sparks flew across the track, and the metal frame shook beneath my feet.

I didn't close my eyes. Warden had vanished into the darkness, like a candle blown out by the wind.

I would never see him again.

But as I watched the tunnel race before my eyes, I was certain of one thing: I did trust him.

Now I had only to trust in myself.

The Pale Dreamer

A Bone Season Novella

The Grisly Case of Anne Naylor

London, 2056

If you were to ask me what I liked most about being an up-and-coming criminal in the year 2056, I'd probably point you to the simple things. Drinking coffee before daybreak in the den, listening to the capital stretch itself awake around me. Sitting beneath the blossom tree in the courtyard and leafing my way through a stack of forbidden novels. Sneaking into Jaxon's room to listen to blacklisted music.

Strange, I know. It wasn't as if I couldn't have done things like that *before* I was employed by Jaxon Hall. Maybe not the blacklisted music and forbidden novels, but I could have found a tree to read by, or made coffee before daybreak, under other circumstances. They were ordinary moments in my newly extraordinary life – and they, in turn, became extraordinary.

As a dreamwalker, I was meant to be a great clairvoyant; a rare one, at least. Jaxon was certain that I was hiding spectacular powers; that I could leave my body, possess other people, and dance them around like mindless puppets if I so desired. But after three months in his employ, I still couldn't do it. Not for want of trying, I should add – I just didn't know how, and nobody agreed on how to teach me.

I first learned of the grisly case of Anne Naylor in October of that year. One Monday afternoon found me in the 'office' in our den, where an old oak desk was piled with paperwork. The den was a three-storey maisonette on Monmouth Street in the small district of Seven Dials. It had three permanent residents – me, Jaxon and Eliza. Nick had his own apartment, but he often stayed with us.

Since I had moved in, I had come to love the den. It was cluttered and dusty and the boiler was useless, but that only made it feel snug and lived-in. Jaxon had gifted me my own room and told me to do as I pleased with it, so I had painted it wine-red and filled it with trinkets from the black market, where I hunted for antiques and curios in the evenings. It was nothing like my room in my father's sterile, ultra-modern apartment, which the government had given him.

Thinking of my father let a butterfly loose in my stomach. After I had left school, I had told him I was living with a friend, looking for a job in the service industry. He was still disappointed that I had decided against applying for a place at the University.

He would be even more disappointed if he knew the truth.

I tapped my pen against the ledger. Jaxon had asked me to find out who in the district hadn't paid their rent, and how much they owed. Mind-numbing work. Not like what Eliza and Nick got to do. Those two were always out hunting spirits or confronting rival clairvoyant gangs – the sort of thing I had envisioned doing when Jaxon had first invited me to join his gang, the Seven Seals. They had worked for him longer than I had, but I still felt impatient – mostly with myself. I longed for an assignment of consequence; something that would really test me.

Not that I would ever ask for it outright. Jaxon Hall could be courteous, even charming, but he was mercurial. Pressing him at the wrong moment could make me look ungrateful for the work, and I couldn't lose this job. I got the feeling that if you were exiled from the voyant underworld, you wouldn't come back.

I couldn't take that gamble. Now I knew this world existed, I would not risk being banished.

My eyelids were heavy. I glanced up from the figures, massaging the sore base of my neck.

The sun was low and copper-gold. Ensconced in here, it was easy to forget that our beloved government could have me hanged if they ever learned what I was – an unnatural. That was what they called clairvoyants.

I sat up straighter and adjusted my jersey when I saw Eliza through the window. She was flushed and bright-eyed, her hair unsettled by the wind.

Eliza Renton was twenty years old and had worked for Jaxon for over a year. From what I had observed about her – I did a lot of observation in between rounds of paperwork – she was both street-smart and absent-minded; a dressmaker, an artist, a voyant. Today she wore a silk dress, the same light green as her eyes, covered by a velvet coat. She had braved the cold to get us lunch, saying she had an errand anyway and I deserved a break from the endless food-and-coffee runs – but her hands were empty.

'No caffeine?' I said as she came up the stairs. But she was already gone, her face set. 'Eliza?'

'Jaxon!'

Her boots clicked on the stairs at speed. I deserted my post and followed her. Any excuse. By the time I reached the second-floor landing, she was knocking on the door to Jaxon's study. She was all nervous energy, tilting her weight from one foot to the other.

The door creaked open. Jaxon Hall stood in his lounging robe, his black hair free of the oil he often used to smooth it back.

'Did you bring that coffee, darling?' he asked. There were greyish circles under his eyes.

'I hate myself for saying this,' Eliza said, 'but we don't have time for coffee.'

She slipped past him. I entered next, giving him a 'no idea' look. He twirled a burning cigarillo between his fingers.

I wasn't sure what to make of Jaxon. I wasn't even sure whether or not I liked him. All that was clear was that my employer was a man with secrets. He was eccentric, to say the least, and intimidating, with a smirk that promised mayhem and milk-blue eyes that saw through everything. Feared and loved in equal measure, he was the most famous mime-lord in the underworld – so Nick said, anyway.

As head of the gang, Jaxon had the best room in the building. It boasted large sash windows, an antique desk, a record player, a stained-glass lamp, bottles of absinthe, and shelf upon shelf of black-market books and ornaments. Nick was already here, lying sprawled on the chaise longue.

Nick Nygård was Jaxon's mollisher, or second-in-command. He was the one who had uprooted me from my old life, introduced me to Jaxon, and welcomed me into this existence.

'Afternoon.' He rubbed his eyes. 'Hey, *sötnos*.'

He had started calling me that a while ago. It meant 'sweet nose' in Swedish. I thought it was lovely. Nick in general was lovely.

'Hey,' I said.

Eliza threw herself down beside him, shunting his legs off to make room.

'Jaxon,' she said, fighting for breath, 'one of our couriers just caught me at the black market – asked me to get word to you straight away. He said Didion Waite—'

'It can't be too dire if it involves Didion Waite, my dear. He's a clown.' Jaxon glanced at me. 'Paige, some tea may be in order.'

Normally I would have asked how many sugars – his preference changed almost every day. Instead, the frustration I had felt for the last three months pooled like lava behind my ribs and bubbled up to my throat, and what came out was:

'I'd like to stay.'

Jaxon's eyebrows jumped towards his hairline.

All the heat inside me froze.

He was going to turf me out. I would have to go back to my father. I would never learn how to use my gift. It would eventually surface, and I would have no idea how to hide or control it. I would end up on the gallows before I turned seventeen. Death by reason of being too proud to make four cups of tea. Death by tea.

'Eliza,' Jaxon said, not taking his eyes off me, 'continue.'

Quietly, I breathed again.

'You know Didion's been looking for valuable spirits to auction? Well, he only went and found *Sarah Metyard*,' Eliza said. Jaxon became very still. 'He hired someone to bind her, but they bungled it and set her off. She's on a rampage.'

Jaxon leaned back in his chair and appeared to fix his full attention on a crack in the ceiling.

'A rogue poltergeist,' he said. 'Oh dear, oh dear. Didion, what *have* you got yourself into?'

We sat in apprehensive silence for a while. Finally, Jaxon breathed in deeply, stood, and took the stairs to the top floor. Nick and Eliza swapped worried glances.

I cleared my throat.

'Sorry,' I said, 'but who's Sarah Metyard?'

Nick chuckled. 'I keep forgetting you've only been here five minutes, Paige. You must have questions upon questions.'

He motioned for me to join them. Eliza nodded her encouragement, though she looked wary. I had always suspected she hadn't wanted there to be any more members of this tight-knit family. I perched on the chaise longue beside Nick, trying not to notice his proximity.

'You know what a poltergeist is, don't you?' Eliza said to me.

'A violent kind of breacher – a spirit that can make contact with the physical world.'

'That's it. Poltergeists are extremely dangerous, as they can cause physical harm – but they're also rare in comparison to other spirits, and hard to catch, so they sell for a lot of money.'

Nick caught my eye. He knew how familiar I was with poltergeists, even if Eliza didn't. He took a file marked M from her, which she had drawn from a bookshelf beside the desk.

'The spirit of Sarah Metyard has been around for a few centuries,' Nick said. 'Metyard was hanged for the murder of a young girl named Anne Naylor – one of her apprentices – in 1758.'

I steeled myself to hear more. 'Why would she murder her own apprentice?'

'Naylor's death was an accident, but it was the result of extreme neglect and cruelty.' With a puckered brow, he opened the file. Inside were witness accounts, yellowed eighteenth-century maps of London, death records, transcripts. I scanned them. 'Metyard and her daughter, who was also called Sarah—'

'But went by Sally,' Eliza chipped in. 'She was also a victim of her mother's brutality. Didn't stop her meting out cruelty on the girls in their care, though. Anyway, Sarah and Sally—'

'—were either milliners or haberdashers, or both. Several girls from local workhouses were apprenticed to their business. One of them was called Anne Naylor, or Nanny.'

I listened closely, trying to remember every detail.

'The girls were all treated badly, but Anne had a weak constitution,' Eliza said. 'She couldn't work as fast as the other apprentices, so she became the focus of the Metyards' contempt. Sarah never fed her enough, worked her to exhaustion, neglected her – the poor girl even had to have a finger removed after an abscess went bad, presumably because they didn't get it treated.' Eliza licked her own finger and turned a page in the folder. 'She escaped twice, but they caught her. As punishment for her second escape, they beat her, tied her to a door, and left her there without anything to eat or drink. After a few days of this, the other apprentices called Sally in a panic.'

My gaze fell to the page, reading exactly what they had said. I could almost hear their frightened voices.

On the fourth day she faltered in speech, and presently afterwards expired. The other girls, seeing the whole weight of her body supported by the strings which confined her to the door, were greatly alarmed, and called out: 'Miss Sally! Miss Sally! Nanny does not move.' The daughter then came upstairs, saying: 'If she does not move, I will make her move'; and then beat the deceased on the head with the heel of a shoe.

'The Metyards tried to revive Anne,' Eliza said, 'but she was dead. She was thirteen.'

I should have been shaken, but I had heard too many stories like this over the past few months. Part of my education had been learning about the more famous spirits of the capital.

'Of course, they tried to conceal Anne's death,' Eliza continued. 'They claimed she'd run away and hid the body in a box in the attic for two months, but they couldn't mask the smell of it for ever. Sarah Metyard removed and burned the hand with the missing finger, in case it could identify Anne, but decided not to risk burning the rest in case the neighbours got suspicious. Eventually, they cut up the body, and Metyard disposed of the pieces in a public sewer – a *gully-hole*, as they called it at the time.'

'Some versions of the story say that they killed Anne's eight-year-old sister Mary, who was also one of their apprentices,' Nick said. 'A watchman discovered the pieces of Anne's corpse, but it was assumed that they had been dumped there by a body-snatcher or a surgeon, so nobody investigated.'

'It seemed like they'd got away with it,' Eliza said – she was clearly enjoying her role as a storyteller, 'but as the years passed, Sarah grew more abusive towards her daughter. Sally finally went to live with a man named Richard Rooker, who had offered her employment. She moved away with him and became his lover, but Sarah wouldn't leave them alone – she was obviously worried that Sally would tell someone about the murder. Eventually, Rooker overheard a confrontation between them, had a bad feeling about what he'd heard, and questioned Sally, who admitted everything. Rooker alerted the authorities, probably thinking Sally would get a lighter sentence, as her mother had done so much to influence her behaviour – but she didn't. Both Metyards were hanged at Tyburn—'

'—in 1768.' Nick snapped the file shut. 'The spirits of murderers often seek out those of their victims. I'll wager that Sarah Metyard, now she's been set off, is after Anne Naylor.'

I wet my lips. And only a few months ago, I thought that the dead stayed dead.

'So,' I said, trying to sound as if I found this all perfectly normal, 'do you know where Anne is?'

Eliza reached for the N folder. 'She became a poltergeist, too, and took up residence in Farringdon tube station. She'll be frantic when she realises her killer is on the loose.'

'She was "on the loose" before, wasn't she?'

'She was around, but poltergeists don't usually become violent unless they're disturbed. If you *do* disturb one, they tend to start visiting places that were important to them in life. Almost like they've been reminded that they're dead.'

Before we could consider the matter any further, Jaxon blazed back down the stairs.

'Paige, get me my pen. On the desk.'

Mild trepidation jolted in my stomach. There were at least eight pens on his desk.

Slowly, I stood. This had to be punishment for my little rebellion. Or was it a test of my clairvoyance? Was I supposed to *know* which pen he wanted? Shit. I made a snap decision and handed him a jewel-encrusted fountain pen, which I had seen him use before.

'No. That,' he said, 'is my writing pen.'

Writing pen. Shit, *shit*. Was there any other use for a pen? Sweating, I offered a slightly cheaper-looking one. He shot me an indecipherable look before he took it.

'First, we must deal with Didion. His incompetence is now a danger to us all,' he said. 'By creating a rogue poltergeist, he has broken syndicate law.'

It still amused me that criminals had laws. The clairvoyant syndicate flouted Scion law merely by existing, yet had its own justice system. Not a very effective one, but it was there.

'Jax,' Eliza said, 'maybe we should just stay out of—'

'No. We will hold Didion accountable for his misdeeds. You will go straight to Cheapside and order him to shut down that *travesty* of a business. And you will tell him to leave – yes, to leave this citadel once and for all, the ham-handed buffoon. He has forfeited his right to a place in this syndicate, and as such—'

'We have no authority to exile Didion, and you know it,' Nick said calmly. 'We'd have to get Hector involved.'

The reminder deflated Jaxon somewhat, but his eyes were still alive with ambition.

'Of course.' He lit another cigarillo. 'Much as I dislike it, you are right. We *would* have to involve Hector.' Slowly, he sank into his chair. 'But . . . there is another option.'

I didn't know enough about the politics of the underworld to intervene, but I listened. If I meant to have a clue what anyone was talking about, I would have to soak up everything I heard.

Jaxon drew an old-fashioned phone across his desk. Scion was thought to listen in to most communication; this had to be a secure line. He dialled and raised the receiver to his ear.

'Get me Didion Waite,' he said, with dangerous delicacy. 'I demand that he speak to me personally.' Pause. 'The White Binder.' His gaze flickered to us. 'I think,' he said, almost to himself, 'that I can see a way to turn this to our advantage. We must get to Metyard before every fool in London tries to catch her.'

He flicked a switch on the phone. There was a rustle before a thick-nosed voice filled the room.

'Jaxon.'

'Didion,' Jaxon said silkily. 'How are you?'

'Well enough.'

Both of their greetings dripped with contempt. I knew Didion Waite was Jaxon's long-standing rival, but Nick had yet to tell me what had started the feud.

'I suppose,' Didion said, 'that you somehow found out about Metyard. Who told you?'

'Oh, I have eyes everywhere, Didion. Even in *your* district.' Jaxon had an unnerving smile on his face. 'I always had my doubts about your little auction house, but I was led to believe that it would be, at the very least, a semi-professional establishment.'

'How dare you imply that I am anything less than professional?' Whoever Didion was, he had a grating voice. 'Metyard was always going to be . . . a tad antagonistic—'

'*A tad antagonistic.* Let me remind you that this woman murdered a thirteen-year-old girl, dismembered her corpse, and interred the pieces in a sewer.'

'I had every assurance that—'

'Assurances mean nothing, you bottle-headed imbecile.' Jaxon's knuckles whitened. 'Was it you who tried to bind Metyard?'

'No. I, ah, referred the task to someone else.'

'That, Didion,' Jaxon purred, 'is because you are a coward. A disgusting, quivering coward.'

'I am most certainly not—'

'A craven. A yellow-belly. A lily-livered curl of besmirchèd slime, unfit for human civilisation.'

'My heart knows no cowardice,' Didion shrilled. 'Damn you. I simply decided to—'

'—palm the work off on an amateur, yes. You disgrace every binder who ever drew breath.' Jaxon kept smiling. 'Now. There are two potential outcomes to this fiasco, Didion. By rights, I should report you to the Underlord for your gross mishandling of a poltergeist. If Hector *is* informed, your establishment will be shut down. Finished. A mere echo of a memory. And you will most likely have your throat cut.'

Probably true. From what I'd heard about the Underlord, he loved a good old-fashioned throat-cutting.

Didion's voice was shrinking: 'And the second potential outcome?'

'You allow my employees to intervene – and in the process, save your neck.' Jaxon swung lazily on his chair, one leg crossed over the other. 'If we bind Sarah Metyard, we claim her. In addition, I have the right to bind Anne Naylor, if the desire seizes me.'

'Are you blackmailing me, sir?'

'Didion, it appears you have finally cultivated a smidgen of intelligence. My heartiest congratulations.'

A strangled noise. 'All right,' Didion choked out, sounding as if he could hardly breathe for rage. 'All right. So long as you say nothing to the Underlord about this . . . situation, I assent to your demands. Send your lackeys to the Juditheon. Promptly, if you please.'

'Excellent. Goodbye, Didion.'

Jaxon settled the phone in its cradle, sat back in his chair, and joined his fingertips.

'So,' Nick said, breaking a long silence, 'we're going to try and bind Metyard.'

'Precisely. Didion has proven that he is unworthy of such a prize. We will take Metyard for ourselves.'

'Didion has no right to promise us Anne Naylor. She's on Ognena Maria's turf.'

I had heard of Ognena Maria, mime-queen of one of the neighbouring sections of the citadel – the one I had lived in for years with my father. 'If you're good to Maria, she'll remember it,' Eliza had told me once. 'If you're not so good to her, she'll make *you* remember it.'

'So long as Didion keeps his mouth shut,' Jaxon said, 'Maria never needs to know.' The corner of his mouth twitched. 'Two of you will go to the Juditheon and obtain as much information as you can about where and when Sarah Metyard was last seen. Relevant details about her life will help you track her – that can be found in the files here. One of you will stay behind to go through those.'

I didn't have to ask to know that I would be the one doing research on Metyard while the others pursued her. I hid my face behind my hair, trying not to let my frustration show. It was true that I'd only been with the gang for three months, and yes, I *was* only sixteen, but being trapped inside was suffocating. I'd signed up to be a criminal, not a clerk.

'We might be back late.' Eliza stood. 'Nick, we can take the Underground to—'

'Stop,' Jaxon said.

She raised an eyebrow. 'Why?'

'I don't want *you* to go, darling. I want Paige to go.'

His words set off a small jolt in my gut. Eliza's lips parted, and she frowned slightly.

468

'Don't give me that look. You'll have your turn again. And it's about time Miss Mahoney had a chance to prove her worth.' Jaxon studied me. 'Would you like that, Paige?'

'Yes,' I said at once. 'Please. If Eliza doesn't mind.'

'No.' She recovered. 'No, not at all. It'll be a nice break, actually. And I hate poltergeists.'

'With good reason.' Heaving a sigh, Nick reached for his trusty cable-knit sweater and pulled it over his head. 'Jaxon, Paige is still so new to this, and Metyard is as hostile as they come. Maybe you should—'

'I want to go,' I cut in.

'Excellent. Then you shall,' Jaxon said, and went on smoothly before Nick could contest the decision. 'Be quick. Once word spreads that Metyard is on the move, others will come for her. Try not to attract any untoward attention from Scion.'

'We'll give Didion your regards.' Nick slung his coat over his shoulder. 'Ready, Paige?'

I was already on my feet.

'When you have her,' Jaxon said, 'I will bind her once and for all.' He extinguished his cigarillo. 'Go.'

As soon as we were out of his office, I dashed into my room and rummaged through the wardrobe. At last, at *last* I could be useful. Jaxon would be asking Nick how I conducted myself on this assignment, and I meant for him to give a good report. If I did well, I might never have to be on desk duty again – the streets of London would be my new workplace.

I wasn't exactly fashionable on the best of days, but now I rootled through my clothes with a critical eye, trying to work out what would achieve the perfect balance between low-key, elegant and intimidating. Eventually I went for a ruffled white blouse, a double-breasted burgundy jacket with a hood, and black trousers. A little on the safe side, but I was a newcomer. Best to be understated. I laced my boots and faced the mirror. A serious, grey-eyed young woman looked back.

I considered my reflection, judging my anonymity. My main fear was that, through some infuriating twist of fate, my father would see me and ask questions. Even from a distance, my hair – white-blonde and curly – would give me away. I covered it with the hood and draped a scarf around my neck, ready to lift it over my face if necessary.

A knock came at the door. Nick was outside, clad in his heavy coat and a scarf that covered his nose and mouth.

'Looking fierce,' he said, eyes shining.

I smoothed the front of my jacket, embarrassed. 'Am I weird to be concerned about this?'

'Not at all. Your image is as integral to your reputation as your actions.' I followed close behind him as he went down the stairs. 'Stay by the phone, Eliza,' he called. 'No coffee runs.'

Her voice floated back from the office: 'You're a cruel man, Nicklas Nygård.'

Jaxon had emerged from his office to see us off. He waited for us in the hallway.

'Paige,' he said, looking me up and down. 'Let us hope that you will dazzle us with your talents this evening.'

'I'll do my best.'

'I expect you will.' A smile hung on his lips, but didn't reach his eyes – they were steely as ever. 'Enjoy your first assignment, but remember: in this citadel, you are an extension of me. You speak with my voice. With that in mind, I expect you always to act in my best interests, and in the best interests of the Seven Seals.'

'I will,' I said, feeling as if I was taking an oath.

'Jaxon, this is Paige's first time on syndicate business,' Nick said. 'What name should she use?'

My palms were clammy.

All of them had aliases. Jaxon was the White Binder, Nick was the Red Vision, and Eliza was the Martyred Muse. I wasn't sure where Jaxon mined the names from; only that I wanted one more than anything. To be a real part of the gang.

Finally, Jaxon spoke. 'Keep out of sight of cameras. You wouldn't want Scion to spy you, darling.'

'Surely all they'd see is me spending time with Nick,' I said. 'My father knows him.'

My voice quaked a little, betraying my disappointment. He hadn't given me a name.

'I shouldn't worry about them seeing *that*. I would, however, prefer them not to catch sight of you on a surveillance camera if you have to do battle with the poltergeist,' Jaxon said. 'That would raise a few eyebrows in Westminster. And lead to you being wanted for immediate questioning, no doubt.'

Good point. The security cameras wouldn't see us using our clairvoyance – they were blind to spiritual activity of any kind, for now – but they would note any suspicious behaviour, and that alone could be enough to condemn us.

'And . . . her name?' Nick prompted softly.

Jaxon considered me. I waited, turning cold under his scrutiny.

'The Pale Dreamer,' he said, with the lingering relish of a man who was tasting a fine wine. 'Yes . . . the Pale Dreamer. A name for all of London to remember.'

Follow the Money

I couldn't stop smiling as we left the den. It was perishing outside, but receiving my alias had sparked a fire inside me.

Jaxon Hall had bestowed his approval of me as his representative. My lips kept forming the words, testing their shape. *The Pale Dreamer.* It sounded dangerous and graceful, like a vengeful spirit. *The Pale Dreamer.* Yes, I could get used to that name. If I meant to keep it, though, I would have to prove myself worthy – and if I meant to prove myself worthy, we had to snare Sarah Metyard.

Over the years, I've classified seven orders of clairvoyance, Jaxon had told me on the day Nick introduced us. *I believe you, my dear girl, are of the very highest order, making you one of the rarest clairvoyants in the modern world.*

It all sounded very impressive. But what if I wasn't?

What if he had been wrong about me?

The warmth guttered out. I wanted badly to impress Jaxon. I wanted to bring a glint into his eyes, the same glint I had seen on that first day – that sparkle of ambition. To know that I had kindled it again would be a victory, and I'd be damned if I didn't do it today. Murder most foul, a spirit on the warpath, and the prospect of a windfall at the end – yes, this was the perfect opportunity to step triumphantly on to the stage of London; to become the Pale Dreamer.

We walked to the nearest Underground station and swiped our travel cards.

'Excited?' Nick asked. He laughed when he saw my face. 'Okay, you're excited.'

'Eliza won't mind me doing this, will she?'

'No. She went through the same thing as you when she first arrived – Jaxon always gave her the paperwork. It's a test of character.' He hurried down the steps. 'Come on. Didion likes punctuality.'

I lowered my voice. 'Seems a strange concern for a criminal.'

'Etiquette is his obsession. Don't tell Jaxon,' he said, 'but I can't blame him.' His gaze darted about, clocking the Underguards around the station. 'The syndicate has been getting more and more corrupt since Haymarket Hector became Underlord. We could use a little etiquette.'

We fell silent when we passed one of the Underguards, who gave us a perfunctory look.

'I don't want to sound as if I'm ordering you around,' Nick murmured as we walked, 'but this is your first time in the field, so it's important that you do everything as I say. First thing to remember: call me Vision, not Nick. And I'll call you Dreamer. No one in the syndicate can know about my day job.'

'You think they'd report you?'

'Possibly,' he said, with a nonchalance that had to be feigned. He hitched up a smile. 'I'll guide you today – you won't have to deal with anything alone. In theory, this is a simple assignment. We find the spirit, let Jaxon know where it is, and he comes to bind it.'

'Couldn't he just … come with us now?'

'He's a mime-lord. He doesn't do search work.' Nick stopped when we reached the right platform. 'I haven't seen a poltergeist in a long time. Only a handful since the day I met you, actually.' His hands sank into his pockets. 'Which feels like a *very* long time ago.'

Not to me. I remembered that day all too well.

I had only just come to England from Ireland, where I had grown up on my grandparents' dairy farm in Tipperary. At the tender age of nine, I had some notion that I was different – but my gift was still buried deep within me, yet to be unlocked.

That year, my father had taken me to a tiny village called Arthyen, near the southern coast, where one of his old friends lived. At the time, I had been lonely and homesick, harbouring more than a little resentment towards him for separating me from my grandparents, who had stayed behind to weather the conflict in Ireland. I was wary of the village and its people, but it was better than going to school, where the other pupils spat at me.

There was a field of poppies at the edge of Arthyen. In that field, I had come face-to-face with my first poltergeist. It had sliced the skin of my left arm to ribbons, then thrown me away to bleed.

Nick had been staying near Arthyen at the time, and had gone for a walk that day which took him through the poppy field. He had found me and recognised my wounds as spirit-made, although he saw nothing in me to give him pause. Nothing that had made me think I was clairvoyant. He had treated me himself, and his kindness had left a lasting impression. Once I was stitched up, he returned me to my father and disappeared from my life as quickly as he had entered it, leaving me even more confused about the world than I had been before.

It would be another seven years before our next meeting. We were reunited at my school, by pure coincidence, only a few months ago. He had come to give a speech to the students about careers in Scion's medical division. I had sought him out after, desperate to ask him what had really happened on that day in the poppy field.

He had remembered me. This time, he had also recognised exactly what I was – a clairvoyant. A dreamwalker. Instead of reporting me for suspected unnaturalness, however, he had asked me to meet him later – and when I had, he had offered me employment with Jaxon to help me control my gift, and to protect me from Scion, who would kill me if they worked out what I was. I had accepted. Once the school year was over, I had gone to live in Seven Dials. It was the best decision I had ever made.

Nick had saved me from ignorance. In doing so, he had saved my life.

All I had left of that encounter with the poltergeist was a trellis of scars on one hand. I traced them now, remembering the white-hot pain as clearly as if it had happened yesterday.

'So,' I said, shaking away the memory, 'what challenges await us today?'

'The main threats are rival gangs and Vigiles. If we see them, we walk away slowly. We don't draw any attention to ourselves.'

'Okay.'

He worked for Scion. His life depended on not drawing attention to himself. A voyant in the employ of an anti-voyant government; they would have him beheaded if they discovered his unnaturalness. I had never understood why he risked the double life. It seemed like something only a mad or desperate man would do, but Nick didn't strike me as either.

We stood on the platform, staying close to one another. It was busy at this time, when Londoners were on their way home from work – lost in their phones and data pads, unable to feel the spirits that wove and danced around them. Once I had been afraid of my clairvoyance, but today I treasured it. I could sense a world they never would. Their lives would always be half-empty.

In silent agreement, neither of us spoke on the train. Too many people. Too quiet. When we stepped off at the right station, we walked to the derelict church that locals called Bow Bells, which stood, pale and tragic, on Cheapside.

A short whip of a man with heavy jowls was waiting for us by a streetlamp outside it. His clothes looked like genuine eighteenth-century garments, complete with hose – he even wore a powdered wig, which was held back from his face with ribbon. His mouth was tightly pursed.

Beside him was an olive-skinned woman in a leather jacket, whose short auburn hair was a notch too bright to be natural. Her face was dominated by dark eyebrows, and she wore gold-framed shades. Nick stopped and drew in his breath when he saw her.

'Who is that?' I asked him.

'Ognena Maria, mime-queen of this section. She must have found out that Didion made a deal with us.'

'Is that bad?'

'Well, it's not good. Her relationship with Didion Waite is … complicated. His auction house – the Juditheon – is in her section, but she gets nothing from it.'

'But all voyant businesses have to give a cut to the local mime-lord or mime-queen.'

'Exactly – the syndicate tax. But the Juditheon was granted immunity from it by the Underlord,' he said. 'It was unheard of, before Didion founded it, for anyone to *auction* spirits – they were just owned by whoever ruled the section they dwelled in, and they could be sold or traded privately at the black market. Didion worked out that organising a bidding could make a lot more money. He's thought to steal spirits from other sections to auction, which is illegal, but Hector does nothing about it – so long as he gets his cut.'

I was beginning to see why Jaxon hated Didion so much. Probably because he was furious that he hadn't come up with the idea of an auction house first.

'That can't have gone down well with Maria,' I said.

'She hates it, naturally. But Didion is still her subject – he's not supposed to bargain away her property without permission, and Anne Naylor is her property.' He sighed and kept walking. 'Jaxon wanted to avoid this. Here's hoping she's not too angry.'

Didion was first to spot us. When Ognena Maria turned to see what he was glaring at, she smiled.

'Well, if it isn't the Red Vision.' Her voice was husky, with an accent I couldn't quite place. 'Haven't seen your face at the market in a few weeks, sunshine. We've missed you.'

'Morning, Maria. It's been too long.' Nick shook her hand with real warmth. 'Hello, Didion.'

'Red Vision.' Didion dealt me a withering look. 'And who is this … person?'

Nick laid a hand on my shoulder. 'This is the Pale Dreamer. Jaxon's newest employee.'

I lifted my chin. Here, I was no longer Paige Mahoney. I was a mystery.

'Ah, finally – Binder found a new addition to the Seven Seals,' Ognena Maria said, chuckling. 'Maybe one day, you'll actually make it to seven.' She tipped down her sunglasses, revealing dark, kohl-rimmed eyes. I held her gaze as she scrutinised me. 'You know, I'm sure I recognise your aura. Do you ever visit Postman's Park?'

I looked her up and down, trying to place her.

'You smoke there,' I finally said.

'I always meant to talk to you. Funny old life.' She cocked an eyebrow at Nick. 'If she's a resident of my section, she ought to be reporting to me, not Binder.'

Nick mirrored her smile. 'Where's that written?'

'Don't test me, Vision. What do you think Binder would say if I sauntered into I-4 and employed a voyant? A rare one, at that.'

'You had every opportunity to ask Dreamer to work for you, if you've seen her. Jaxon got there first.'

'Ah, so it's about *timing* now.'

Maybe I shouldn't have spoken.

'We'll talk about this later,' Nick said. She grunted. 'We have a rogue poltergeist to deal with first.'

'Yes, thanks to *someone*'s attempt to fill his pockets without my knowledge. Yet again,' Ognena Maria said dryly, giving Didion a sidelong glance. He bristled. 'And I understand Binder has decided that you're just the people to capture the aforementioned poltergeist.'

Nick went on calmly: 'We think it might be after someone it killed in life – Anne Naylor.'

'That's why I'm here. Anne resides in this section – *my* section.' The wind knocked a strand of hair into her eyes. 'Anne is … unusual. She's a poltergeist, but she seems harmless. Trust me, I've tested the theory, or I wouldn't have let her stay where she is.'

'What else do you know about her?'

'Only that she's a tortured soul. It's as if her gentle personality is coming into conflict with her anger about her violent death. Consequently, all she does is wail, all day long. Good thing most of us can't hear it.' She folded her arms. 'I have never known Anne to leave Farringdon station. If you're going to net Metyard, I would go there and keep watch. Wait for her to hunt down her victim.'

Nick nodded. 'And we have your permission to do that?'

An arch smile played on her lips. 'I have some conditions.'

'No conditions.' Nick never sounded unfriendly, but his tone invited no argument. 'Didion agreed that Binder would have the right to both spirits in return for—'

Maria cut across him. 'Vision, I've always liked you, but don't try to pretend that your deal with Didion had any legitimacy – I wasn't born yesterday. Hector has strong-armed me into accepting the auction house, and I've embraced it as best I can – I even bid on spirits myself, when it takes my fancy – but I am mime-queen here, and I've never given anyone permission to sell or move Anne Naylor. As both of you are well aware.'

Didion turned up his nose, while Nick dropped his gaze and I tried to look neutral.

'Now,' Maria said, softer, 'I agree that it would be best to keep Hector out of these proceedings. He lives by one rule: follow the money. Sarah Metyard would be worth a significant amount of it, and if he gets involved, none of us will see a penny.'

Nick blew out a breath. 'Okay, we're listening. What are your conditions?'

'This hunt will begin in my territory, so I think it's only fair that I should be one of the parties that benefits. If you can catch Metyard, Binder transfers ownership to me – but you can claim Anne, free of charge. And nobody says a word to Hector.'

'Metyard is more valuable.'

'You have no right to her,' Maria said. 'Anne's a famous spirit. You could sell her for a tidy sum.'

Nick looked frustrated. 'So we'd essentially be catching Metyard *for* you. I don't see how that benefits us. Or what right *you* have to Metyard, given that she wasn't found on your turf.'

Ognena Maria smiled. 'None whatsoever,' she said, 'but *Anne* is on my turf, and she's your best chance of capturing Metyard. If you don't agree to my demands, I'm afraid I'll have to revoke your right to be here. And you'll walk away with nothing.'

I looked at Nick, who looked none too happy. 'I'll need to phone Binder,' he said.

'Go ahead. I'll wait.'

He touched my back before stepping away to make the call, leaving me with the strangers. Voyant strangers.

There was a brief silence.

'So,' Ognena Maria finally said, looking me up and down, 'you're Irish. Interesting.'

'You don't sound English,' I said, a question in my tone.

'Bulgarian. We're both in Scion's bad books.' She tilted her head. 'I'll confess to being intrigued by you, Pale Dreamer. I've never met someone with an aura quite like yours.'

'A curiosity indeed,' Didion said, with disdain. 'Binder is *quite* the hoarder of treasures.'

'Last I checked,' I said, 'I wasn't a collectable.'

His mouth popped open.

'A quick tongue *and* an interesting aura.' Ognena Maria grinned. 'What *are* you, kid?'

My muscles were tensing. Jaxon had told me to hide the fact that I was a dreamwalker. Fortunately, Nick was already back. I moved a little closer to him.

'Binder agrees,' he said heavily. 'He claims the right to bind Anne Naylor at his leisure – but if you sell Metyard, he wants the opportunity to buy her privately. No auction.'

'Agreed. I'll organise the sale myself.' Ognena Maria shook his hand, cutting off Didion's protest with a look. 'You're welcome to stay in my territory for as long as you need. If you want somewhere to gather your thoughts, go to the teahouse on Turnmill Street. The owner will make sure no Vigiles bother you.'

'Thank you,' Nick said. 'I'll send word about our progress. Didion,' he added, 'I have a few questions about how and where you found Metyard. If you don't mind.'

Didion sniffed. 'It seems I have no choice.'

Nick patted him on the back and led him into the derelict church. As I followed, Ognena Maria caught my elbow.

'A little advice for you, Pale Dreamer. From one stranger in this country to another,' she said quietly. 'You seem like a nice enough kid, but you're also from the highest order of clairvoyance, which means some people will put you on a pedestal. Not everyone in this syndicate gets that luxury. There's a hierarchy. An order to things.'

I listened, watching her face. There was no trickery or malice in her expression.

'Being in this syndicate will toughen you up, but don't let it turn you to stone. Don't get too big for your boots. And always question what you're told. Remember what it's like to be an outsider, a nobody. Don't look down on the people who end up at the bottom. Give a bit of coin to the gutterlings. Stay humble. And keep your mind open. You might find it repays you one day.'

She looked almost sorry as she spoke. As if she had seen something pure and new that could only be tainted by the world, no matter how much wool she wrapped around it.

'Thank you,' I said, and smiled a little. 'I'll try not to become a stone-cold killer, at least.'

A short laugh escaped her. 'That's a start.' She grasped my shoulder. 'Remember, if you ever get tired of Binder's bad temper, you can always do some work for me on the quiet. I run the voyant parts of the Old Spitalfields market. Ask for me any time.'

'I'll keep it in mind,' I said, already knowing I wouldn't. Moonlighting was illegal in the syndicate, and I doubted Jaxon would show mercy if he found me doing it.

'Good.' She gave my shoulder a squeeze and strode away. 'See you around, sweet.'

It didn't take long for Nick to wring all he could out of Didion – where Metyard had last been seen, where she had been going. We needed somewhere to plan the next stage of the hunt, so we took a cab to the teahouse in Turnmill Street, which was conveniently close to Farringdon tube station.

'I don't understand,' I said to Nick. 'What's the point in us doing this if you just promised Metyard to Maria?'

He looked grim. 'Jaxon's keen for us to continue. Anne will be worth money, too. And Jaxon would still get Metyard for a good price; Maria will honour that.'

It was warm and sweet-smelling inside the teahouse. When we said we were friends of Ognena Maria, the owner gave us a table by the bay window, where we sat on velveteen stools.

The urge to pinch myself when I looked at Nick remained as strong as ever. When you form an image of someone in your childhood, it inevitably blurs and fades over time, but Nick looked almost exactly the same as he had at our first meeting. A little more careworn; he was clean-shaven now, and wore pomade in his hair in the Swedish style – but otherwise, seven years had hardly touched him.

'Hungry?' Nick said.

I shed my coat. 'Very.'

We took our time perusing the menu, which listed no fewer than forty types of tea. Nick went for ginger and apple, I went for orange blossom, and we ordered a few appetisers to share.

'Let's recap what Didion said.' He took out his notebook. 'He discovered Metyard at the site of Tyburn, where she was hanged. He hired an amateur binder, who failed to capture her.'

'Didion *is* a binder, isn't he?'

'Yes, but Jaxon's right about his cowardice. He never does a hands-on job if someone else can do it for him.'

'And the attempt to capture her is what set Metyard off?' I said. 'She'd never gone on a rampage before?'

'No. Like I said earlier, spirits don't tend to pose a threat if they're left alone – but most poltergeists really don't like to be approached by voyants, let alone bound. It can spark a dangerous reaction. Like startling an animal.' He rubbed the bridge of his nose. 'Only a very skilled binder – like Jaxon – could have snared Metyard. Didion should have known better.'

'Does he always dress like he's fallen out of an eighteenth-century novel?'

Nick laughed, warming me to my bones. 'He's a character, I'll give you that.' He took a phone out of his pocket. 'Let's see what Eliza has turned up in her research.'

He waited until Eliza answered, then leaned in closer to me, so I could press my ear to the back of the phone. I could hear his breath, feel the warmth of his arm pressing on mine.

'I've found two places that were significant to Metyard in her life,' Eliza said. 'The first, of course, is Tyburn, where she and her daughter were hanged.'

'Turns out that's where Didion found Metyard,' Nick said. 'Any others?'

'Shit. Well, we've had a report that she was in Bruton Street earlier, in our section – that's where the Metyards used to live – but she's long gone, apparently. I'll get back to the files.'

His sigh flickered through my hair. 'Okay. Let us know if you find more.'

'Don't have too much fun without me.'

He hung up. I leaned back into my seat.

'So no leads yet,' Nick said. 'Let's hope she finds something useful soon.'

'What if she doesn't?'

He put his notebook away. 'Well, my theory is that Metyard will be searching for Anne. Our best option is to wait for her, as Maria suggested – so, stake out Anne's haunt in Farringdon until Metyard comes. We'll wait for the commute to die down a little first, though.'

As soon as he finished speaking, a voyant waitron brought the food: eggs poached in milk on crisp, butter-gold toast, with wafer-thin lace cookies and cranberry muffins to follow. I tucked in, famished.

While we ate, I checked my watch. The commute would be over in about forty minutes. Forty minutes with Nick to myself. The thought made my palms tingle.

'What happened to Metyard's daughter – Sally?' I said. 'Is her spirit still around?'

Nick looked thoughtful. 'Interesting. I haven't heard of anyone finding Sally, but … she might be drawn to her mother's presence, if she is still in the æther.' He glanced up at me as he sliced into his toast. 'We haven't been able to talk much since you joined the gang. I'm sorry I haven't been around,' he said gently. 'My day job is demanding, and Jaxon works me to the bone when I'm back.'

I tucked a flyaway curl behind my ear. 'Would you ever quit the day job?'

He shrugged. 'Not unless I have to. Jaxon doesn't like me working for Scion, but he does like my salary.'

'You share it with him?'

'Here and there. Jax is an old friend.'

I sipped my tea, savouring its delicate flavour. 'An old friend with expensive tastes.'

'Ah, you noticed.' He smiled. 'Well, he doesn't get it all. I send some to my parents, too.'

'What are their names?'

His smile widened at my curiosity. 'Rune Nygård and Bryndís Ingadóttir – Bryn, to her friends. My mother's from Iceland originally, but she's lived in Sweden for most of her life. They're both voyant.' He dropped his gaze. 'They're good people. I miss them.'

Lightly, I said, 'Anyone special back in Sweden?'

His chuckle was a bit hollow. 'No. No one here, either, in fact. Jax doesn't let us have relationships.'

I had already been made aware of this. Jaxon had taken me aside and been quite clear: no *liaisons* (his word, not mine). I was only allowed to spend one night with another person – no more. I was to be devoted to the Seven Seals and nothing else.

'What about you?' Nick said. 'Nobody special?'

I gave him a wry smile. 'My heritage isn't considered an attractive feature here. Took me a while to learn to mimic an English accent, and my surname was hard to hide.'

His own smile faded. 'I can't imagine.'

'I survived.'

'I'm glad.'

Gooseflesh weaved its way up my arms.

I had to get this under control. Like he said, Jaxon didn't allow relationships. Besides, Nick was kind to everyone, even people he didn't like. I wasn't special.

At school, nobody had looked at me with the same softness he did. Quite the opposite. As the only Irish girl in the place, I had been ostracised at best, harassed at worst. One of the students from the neighbouring boys' school had once asked me out, but I had known it was part of a scheme to humiliate me and told him I was busy that night. And every night following. One of my few victories during my school years had been watching the smug look slide off his face when he realised the Irish girl had rejected him.

I had paid for it later, of course. My sparks of defiance had always come back for me.

'Tell me how you met Jaxon,' I said. Suddenly this conversation was stirring the dust on some very dark memories.

He poured some more tea. 'I came to Britain when I was seventeen. I was due to transfer to London the next year, to start my job officially with Scion; I thought I'd get to know the place first. When I first arrived, I had a vision of Jaxon. It was like the æther was telling me to find him, but I didn't know where to start looking … then one day, I was walking through Trafalgar Square, and there he was. Just like that. He stopped dead when he saw me. It was almost funny, how quickly he stopped – like he'd walked into a brick wall.'

I smiled with him. I couldn't imagine Jaxon losing his composure like that.

'We went to a coffeehouse. He told me he had never seen a clairvoyant with a red aura, not once. I felt I could confide in him about my vision. It was clear that we were meant to meet.' His voice softened a little. 'It turned out that Jaxon had a vision of his own. He wanted six talented voyants to join him to make up the Seven Seals. Preferably rare ones, like me. Like you. I agreed to be his mollisher, to live a double life. The rest is history.'

'It's a good friendship-origin story,' I admitted, 'but not quite as good as ours.'

'No, true.' He winked. 'I hope Jax finds another mollisher soon. It's too much, on top of my job. As you saw with Maria, I'm his voice in the syndicate. He doesn't get his hands dirty.'

'Can't Eliza do it?'

'He wants someone rarer as his protégée.' He scraped up the last of his meal. 'He likes you, you know.'

'He has a strange way of showing it. And I think I'm in his bad books after I refused to make the tea this morning.'

'Oh, I think that was exactly why he let you come out today. You showed your claws. Jax doesn't like outright disobedience,' he said, 'but he does like spark. He would have been disappointed if you'd kept on doing the drudgework.'

I raised my eyebrows. 'You think he was *waiting* for me to speak up?'

'I do,' he said. 'I know him. He wanted you to take control of your place in the gang. Show him you're a fighter. Let him see that you're ambitious, and you'll go far.'

The reassurance took root in my chest and blossomed into pride. I should have known that Jaxon was waiting for me to crack – after all, he hadn't wanted an automaton to order around. He had wanted a criminal, a rebel. Now I felt like a fool for biting my tongue all these months.

A squadron of armed night Vigiles strode past the teahouse, clad in their black-and-red uniforms and helmets. We both tensed, but they didn't look in our direction.

It took us a while to unwind enough to talk again. We started on the lace cookies and oven-warm muffins. He told me about the village of Mölle, where he was born. He had often returned to it with his parents and his little sister, Karolina, before her death. They would spend their summers fishing and swimming. Generally being a family.

It wasn't an image I recognised. It had been years since my father and I had done anything but eat dinner together, and even that formality had been limited to weekends once I had left home.

I hung on to Nick's every word. When he talked about Karolina, his voice strained at the seams. I didn't ask how she had died. I hadn't earned that sort of trust from him.

'Scion killed her,' he said, of his own accord. As if he had seen the question on my face.

An old hatred combusted behind my ribs. It was a latent feeling, a beast I kept restrained most of the time, but it had rankled for a decade, eating at me from within – the knowledge of injustice.

'I'm sorry,' I said. 'Was she voyant?'

'Yes. But … her gift never really got a chance to develop.'

'They killed my cousin, too. He wasn't like us, as far as I remember, but he was hanged for treason.'

He lifted his gaze to mine. 'I didn't know.'

Even now, I found it hard to talk about Finn. My throat tightened.

'If you went out into that street and asked every voyant you saw,' Nick said, 'I think most of them will have lost someone to Scion.'

We fell silent for a while. My tea was cold.

This was too raw a topic. Mentioning Finn led me to tell Nick more about my life in Ireland, where I had been raised by my grandparents before my father was enlisted by Scion's medical division. I told him about how afraid I had been when we landed in England; how I had cried myself to sleep each night; how lonely I had felt. We had come from a war-torn country, straight into the country responsible for the violence.

Nick listened to everything, his expression grave. I felt as though I could talk to him for ever.

I told him about the first time I had given someone at school a nosebleed – without ever raising my hand. I was ten and had no idea I had caused it; I assumed it was coincidence that the girl who had been teasing me suddenly had blood running down to her chin. But as it began to happen more frequently, whenever I felt particularly trapped and powerless, I came to the realisation that I was the source.

'Surely people were suspicious,' Nick said, snapping a lace cookie.

'No one accused me. My father's Irish, but he's also a Scion employee. He gave money to the school. The Schoolmistress put it down to "dryness in the classrooms",' I said darkly, 'which was plausible, given all the hot air that came out of her mouth.'

Nick burst out laughing. My whole body warmed up, as if the sun was on it. It was harder not to fall in love with him when he laughed.

Not that I was falling in love with him.

The conversation became a torrent that neither of us staunched. He told me about the day he had found out he was voyant. At the age of twelve, he had received a vision of his best friend, Lasse Ekström, dying in the family car. Unable to warn Lasse without betraying his gift to Scion, Nick had been forced to stay silent. The

Ekström family had been killed a week later, when their car had hit ice and ploughed into a tree.

'I think about that every day,' Nick said heavily. 'I've never predicted anyone's death since … I didn't see Karolina's. I sometimes wonder if I just … wasn't listening.'

Before I knew what I was doing, I had laid a hand on his arm.

'You still might not have been able to stop it.'

He raised a weary smile. 'Probably not. Lina loved me, but she also loved ignoring my advice.' With a sigh, he opened his wallet. 'Well, I think it's time to find ourselves a poltergeist. We'll start by paying a visit to Anne Naylor. Ready?'

'Ready.'

Exit, Pursued by a Poltergeist

We had talked for a long time, but still not long enough. There was so much I wanted to ask him, to tell him. Everything I said, I thought he understood. I wasn't sure how it was possible for this almost-stranger to unlock parts of my past I had kept hidden for years, but Nick was the sort of person who you wanted to confide in – and I had *missed* being able to talk to someone. I hadn't had that since I had been separated from my grandmother.

I had never spoken with anyone outside of my family about Finn. I had never told anyone else in this country about my life in Ireland.

Some people you meet in life, and they just *click* with you. It doesn't matter how much you have in common; you just work, somehow. That was Nick to me.

Side by side, we walked into Farringdon station, which was quiet. There were people on the platform, but the flow of commuters had dwindled to a trickle. We sat on a bench, and Nick picked up an abandoned copy of the *Daily Descendant* – the only newspaper approved by Scion. Best not read, unless you wanted your brain decocted.

I had learned a lot at the teahouse. It was only now I realised how little we had known about each other.

'Try to sense Anne,' he said to me.

This must be a test of my ability. I concentrated on my sixth sense, the way Jaxon had taught me.

'She's close,' I whispered.

'Yes.'

Slowly, I sat back in my seat and tried to look casual – but something had been bothering me all day, and after our conversation, I found I had the confidence to voice it.

'Why here?' I said. Nick glanced at me. 'Why did Anne come to Farringdon?'

'Nobody knows that. Poltergeists usually return to places that are significant to them, but in Anne's case she might have deliberately chosen somewhere unrelated, so that Metyard would never think to look there. So … it could be random.'

'Right. It could be random,' I said. 'And if it has no connection to her, surely Metyard wouldn't think to come here.'

He turned a page, but I could tell I had his full attention. 'What are you thinking?'

'I'm thinking Metyard might not come here at all. She's been dead for hundreds of years – why would she know Anne was here?'

Nick's brow knitted. 'I see. We all assumed this would be the obvious place, but … maybe not. Say you're right, and given that we have no other leads – what do you propose?'

I mulled it over.

'We could drive Anne from her haunt. Set her off, the way Didion's binder set Metyard off,' I said. 'That might get Metyard's attention – the prospect of a chase.'

'That would be a big risk. Creating another rogue poltergeist to catch the first one.'

'From what Ognena Maria said, Anne isn't dangerous – but Metyard is. We *need* to catch her, today.'

An approving glance slid in my direction. 'You're a quick thinker, Paige.' He nodded slowly. 'It could be worth a try. I'll need to call Maria and okay it with her, though.'

He discarded the newspaper and headed back to the stairs, taking them three at a time. I followed.

We stepped back into the autumn chill and lingered near the entrance to the station as Nick dialled. Twilight had fallen over London; ice-blue streetlamps were pulsing to life. He was lifting the phone to his ear when someone stopped in front of us.

'Hello, Red Vision.'

I tensed.

The owner of the unctuous voice had dark, chin-length hair that hung like strings from beneath a bowler hat. Two small eyes – round and black, like a shark's – sat in a gaunt face. Even his mouth had a whiff of shark about it. A gold pocket watch was in his hand.

A tall woman, who looked to be a couple of years my senior, held his arm with both hands. Her face – sallow and delicate – was framed by hair of deepest rose-red, which came down to her waist. The pair were shadowed by six other voyants, none of whom looked like the sort of people you would want to run into at this time of the evening. Or at any time, really.

'Hector,' Nick said coolly.

The silence went on for eternity, until the woman let out a close-mouthed snicker.

The sound jarred my heart. This must be the Underlord, Haymarket Hector, and his gang, the Underbodies.

'I didn't realise we were on first-name terms,' Hector said. 'Are we on first-name terms, Red Vision?'

Nick looked at the ground.

'Show me. Show me how you will address your leader properly in future.'

'I ask for your pardon, Underlord,' Nick said.

His jaw was tense, but he kept his gaze on the pavement. It nettled me to see him cowed like this.

'You are pardoned, for the time being.' Hector's teeth were lucent and uneven, like chips of blackened seashell. 'I don't think you've met my mollisher, Chelsea.'

Nick nodded stiffly to the redhead. She didn't return the gesture – just looked at him with that little smile.

'And you have company.' Hector moved away from her and paced around me, coming so close I could smell his sweat and the rot on his breath. I just about quelled a shudder. 'My dear friend Binder has been keeping secrets from me. He never informed me of a newcomer.'

'He didn't think you'd be interested,' Nick said.

'Oh, Binder's business *always* interests me. As do his belongings.'

My instinct was to physically recoil from this man, to fold into myself, but gone were the days of shrinking away.

'I'm the Pale Dreamer,' I said, and looked him dead in the eyes. 'Underlord.'

A name for all of London to remember.

'The Pale Dreamer,' Hector echoed. 'Elegant moniker. Curious aura. I can see why the White Binder decided to … harvest you.' Speaking of auras, his was so close to mine that it was making me nauseous. 'We were just on our way to pay a visit to Anne Naylor. What business brings *you* to this part of the citadel, I wonder?' When neither of us replied, he said, 'I see we're playing coy, so let us stop beating around the bush. I know you're here to snare Sarah Metyard, just as we are.'

'We're not here for Metyard,' Nick said too quickly. 'Maria just wanted us to—'

'Shut it,' Chelsea sneered. 'You think we're stupid? You think we didn't know that Metyard would appeal to Binder – that he would send his lapdogs after her?'

I didn't dare say anything. If we were lapdogs, these people were bloodhounds.

Nick had been edging closer to my side. At first I thought the movement was protective – a subtle display of unity – but behind our backs, out of sight of the Underbodies, he passed something to me. I registered a handle against my palm, the rasp of a blade on the pad of my thumb. He had taught me how to use one, but I had never had practical experience.

My heart shouldn't be beating this hard. I had drawn blood for years, but there was something about the cold weight of the knife that I knew would make it harder. When I had used my gift to do it at school, it had been easier to divorce the notion of causing pain from my intention – to balance the scales of justice – but a blade gave that desire a shape.

'Ognena Maria must have struck a deal with you, or you would have been turfed out of this section,' Hector mused. 'You know I should have been informed of a rogue poltergeist.'

'Look, I'll level with you,' Nick said. 'We *are* here for Metyard. We meant to present her to you once—'

'You are not a good liar, Red Vision.' Hector clicked his tongue. 'No, not at all.'

I could tell from Nick's eyes that this run-in with Hector was unexpected. He hadn't reckoned on the Underlord knowing that Metyard was awake, let alone on him having had our idea to stake out Farringdon. And I was willing to bet that we couldn't come to an arrangement with him in the same way we had with Didion and Maria.

'Leave,' Hector said, his voice almost friendly. 'Both of you. All spirits are mine by right.'

'I haven't been in the syndicate long,' I said, 'but I know that's not true.'

Another silence, this one fraught. All the amusement drained out of Hector, turning his face into that of a predator with no understanding of pain, no concept of human empathy. The redhead looked hungrily at the Underlord, wrapping a lock of her hair around one finger.

'Come with us,' Hector said.

Nick stiffened. 'Why?'

'I hope you're not questioning your Underlord,' Chelsea said, staring him out. 'He's given you an order.'

The gang split into two. One half mustered behind us, while the other walked in front.

'Move,' one of them snapped, shoving me in the small of the back. I moved. My knees felt stiff. As they marched us around the corner, Nick leaned down, so his lips were close to my ear.

'We can't fight them in the open,' he breathed. 'I'll get us out of this. Don't worry.'

Easier said than done.

They were leading us into a narrow passage. FAULKNERS ALLEY was displayed in gold lettering about the wrought-iron gate, which Chelsea shouldered open.

I could only think of one reason for them to take us out of sight. Stone-cold dead on my first assignment. Would Hector actually *kill* me for implying he was wrong? I could imagine the gravestone: Paige Eva Mahoney, died because she implied that a greasy-haired criminal was wrong. Nicklas Alvar Nygård, died because he had the misfortune to be with her.

They herded us into the seamy alleyway, which stank of urine. Someone closed the gate. We were surrounded.

Hector turned to me, still wearing that placid smile. There was something underneath it that made me even more uneasy than before – a sort of avarice. It was the look of a man who had seen something he wanted, and whose thirst for it would not be easily slaked.

'Pale Dreamer, I feel that as Underlord, I should welcome you personally into the syndicate.' He snapped his fingers. 'Underhand, Bloatface. Greet the young lady.'

'No.' Nick put himself in front of me. 'Don't. Don't, Hector.'

Two members of Hector's group pared away from the rest. A powder-white, bald man who looked as if someone had squashed him together from modelling clay, and a taller one who was swollen with muscle. Each of his hands were larger than both of mine put together.

'She's sixteen,' Nick said, quieter. 'She's new to the syndicate.' When this failed to soften any faces, he tried a different tack. 'Binder won't be happy if she's hurt.'

My heartbeat had thickened. It drummed in my ears and the hollow of my throat. Stupid, stupid thing to do. Their looks were bloodthirsty – they meant business. And there was a fine line between using my voice and throwing myself headfirst into danger.

'I'm quite sure Binder will find it in his heart to forgive me,' Hector said. 'We're such good friends, he and I. All I want is for the Pale Dreamer to understand where she belongs. It's a lesson all of you have learned, one way or another. Blood now, or blood later, it's all the same.'

Something gleamed in Nick's hand, and then he was pointing a knife at them. Its blade caught the blue glow from a streetlamp.

'Don't be a fool, boy,' Hector said very softly.

'Nick, *no*,' I hissed.

Sweat beaded along my nape. I couldn't let him get beaten or killed for me.

'I ask your forgiveness,' I said to Hector, swallowing my pride. 'I'm sorry. I'm … not used to the ways of the syndicate.'

'Which is why we are here, Pale Dreamer. To remedy your ignorance,' Hector said, almost gently. 'To teach you the rules.'

He nodded to the larger of the two men. A fist sailed, hitting Nick straight in the jaw.

His head snapped to the side. Before I could so much as say his name, a giant hand clapped over my throat and another seized the front of my jacket, lifting me bodily off my feet. Suddenly I was face-to-face with Hector's muscular henchman, who seemed intent on cold-blooded murder. Choking, I kicked at his knees and scratched at the arm that held me up, to no avail. I had been manhandled before, but not like this.

My vision swam as he squeezed my throat. I was sure I was about to black out, that I was dead – then he slammed me into the wall and let me crumple to the ground.

'Before we can fight with spirits,' Hector said, while I heaved and coughed, 'we must learn to fight with our bodies. We must learn to stomach pain. A few bruises, a damaged bone or two … I doubt it will hurt you in the long run.' He paced towards his mollisher and wound an arm around her. 'Bloatface, the Pale Dreamer likes to backtalk. Break her jaw.'

My eyes were watering, my throat on fire. I tried to look defiant, but I couldn't breathe for fear.

I didn't want to die today. I had been lonely and afraid for years – now I wasn't. I had been told by strangers that I should die – I hadn't.

I wouldn't give them the satisfaction now.

The bald man bore down on me. Breathing in rasps, I struggled away from him and held up my knife, which seemed comically small in the shadow of this behemoth. Nick had been too soft on me in training. I tried to remember where to stab, where to avoid.

I am the Pale Dreamer. I am the Pale Dreamer.

'Hector.' Nick was already back on his feet, his lips like wet ruby. 'Don't touch her. She didn't—'

'We all spill blood on London's streets,' the Underlord said. 'Fail to do so, and we have no right to walk them.'

Being thrown against the wall had winded me, and I knew I would be bruised, but I stood, my jaw set in resolve. The bald man closed in on me. This time, I was ready. I watched his fists, ducked his first punch that slammed towards me, and twisted away from the second.

'Look, Hector. This one's got some fight in her,' Chelsea said.

Bloatface turned slowly to face me again. I thrust my knife towards his face.

'Come on, then,' I breathed.

'Oblige her, Bloatface,' Hector drawled.

Bloatface charged. I was conscious of Nick grappling with the Underhand – I was on my own. I lurched out of the way, just in time to avoid being head-butted straight in the ribcage, and slashed at Bloatface with the knife. When his elbow smashed into my cheek-bone, all Nick's training flew out of my head, as if the blow had knocked it loose. I hacked again and again and again – until finally, *finally*, the blade ripped through a hard-wearing jacket. Bloatface jerked his head around and bared a line of little white teeth. Doll teeth, too small for his mouth. He seized my wrist, wrenching me against him, thumping my breath away. I smelled the alcohol on his breath before his skull cracked into mine.

Bells rang in my ears. Blood burst from my lip as blinding pain erupted between my eyes.

Shock had numbed my sixth sense, but now it crashed and broke over the others like a wave. Suddenly I could feel the same pressure I had felt so often at school: the heartbeat in my temples, the quiver at the corners of my vision. I coaxed it out from hiding, playing myself in a mental tug of war, until it ignited and surged outward, into the alley. Being closest, Bloatface caught the brunt of it. Blood slithered from his nostrils, and his eyes watered.

Hector's gang reeled away from me. Their expressions flicked from amused to shocked to wary.

Bloatface rubbed his fingers across his lips, smearing the blood away. He stared me out and slowly licked them clean, using the full length of his tongue. My hand shook as I raised the knife again.

That was when the spirit burst out of the station.

Above the gate, a lantern flickered and went out. Like actors at the end of a play, we froze.

A poltergeist was hovering above us. Anne Naylor. Drawn from her haunt – by the commotion, perhaps – she floated ominously at the end of the alley. I could see nothing, but my sixth sense knew it.

It had been seven years since I had encountered a poltergeist, but I remembered the friction in the æther, the flurry of ice through my blood, the way my lungs had forgotten how to take in air.

The glass panes of the lantern iced over. Hector's lackeys backed away from the presence. Nick was restrained by the Underhand, whose massive arms embraced his throat. Bloatface grabbed me again and dragged me by the hair to the side of the alley, where he pinned me to a wall.

'Nobody move,' Hector breathed. 'Hello, Anne.'

Anne only drifted.

'There, now.' Hector took a careful step towards her. 'No need to be alarmed, sweet Nanny. All we want is for your murderer to get a little whiff of you …'

Anne began to tremble. Nick met my gaze.

Bloatface twisted my hair viciously, but I kept quiet. If we timed this right, we could get Anne on the move, creating enough of a disturbance to attract Metyard – and make our escape at the same time. All we had to do was make her panic and flee, which would distract the Underbodies from us.

There were other spirits nearby. They were always there in London, as thick in the æther as birds in the sky. Nick had taught me how to 'spool' them – to gather them together and wield them against other voyants, disorienting them. If you were in a tight corner, a spool was the simplest way to make someone retreat.

It might also cause a skittish poltergeist to bolt.

I concentrated on my aura. Nick had said that in order to make a spool, I had to send out a kind of signal to spirits that I wanted assistance, usually accompanied by a hand motion. My arm was trapped, but I tried crooking a finger. A ghost swirled towards me.

Sensing what I was trying to do, Nick took over. He had years of experience under his belt. With a sweep of his arm, he whirled all five of the nearby spirits into a spool and flung them at Anne.

Her reaction was explosive. I couldn't hear the æther, but in that moment, I learned that it was possible to *feel* a scream – a shiver in the bones, a twist in the gut. Windows burst into splinters above us, raining down glass from both sides. I shielded my eyes. As Anne rammed into the Underhand, flinging him off his feet and forcing him to let go of Nick, I sank my teeth into Bloatface's wrist and thrust my elbow into his stomach, loosening his grip enough for me to writhe free. I dived towards Nick and grabbed his arm, and together we hightailed it out of the alley.

'Hunt them down,' Hector howled. 'I wouldn't cross me on your first day, Pale Dreamer!'

We crashed through the gate and sprinted up Cowcross Street. My cheek was throbbing.

'Are you okay?'

'Fine.' My voice came out hoarse. 'You?'

His lip was still bleeding. 'I've had worse.'

Boots thumped on the pavement behind us. Three people. My mouth had already turned dry when I realised that Anne was following us, too.

'Do all your assignments go this smoothly?' I called to Nick as we parted around a startled couple.

'Pretty much.' There was a laugh in his voice. 'You sure you're in?'

In answer, I started laughing, too. Breathless, giddy laughs that sparkled through me like a firework. I had never thought that running for my life from criminals and spirits would be this much fun.

Anne veered off to the right; most of the Underbodies pursued her. We took the next left turn into a lane and cut between the buildings, emerging on a busy road.

'Follow me,' I said. I had grown up in this area; I knew it like I knew the lines on my hands, including its tangle of alleyways, which would make for good pockets to lie low in.

It was starting to rain. We barrelled towards a parked car, and had ducked out of sight by the time two of the Underbodies rounded the corner behind us. They argued and swore for a while before they separated. One raced past our hiding spot and inspected several buildings before disappearing beneath the archway at the very end of the road, into the public square beyond.

As soon as he was gone, I tugged Nick's sleeve and pulled him a little farther, towards what looked, to the naked eye, like a shop. The front of the building was white stone, shifting to red brick from the second floor up. You would assume it had two entrances, but I knew that one of them – the narrow one – led to an alley. Hard to make out with a hasty glance; I doubted the Underbody had even seen it. I had often spied people smoking there during the week. Nick followed me inside, under the engraved name, the only thing that gave it away: PASSING ALLEY.

We stopped to catch our breath. The alley was closed, cool and dark, just about wide enough for us to stand opposite one another without touching.

'Damn it … I can't believe Hector showed,' Nick said. 'He must really want Metyard.'

I massaged my aching throat. 'I can't believe he had the same idea we did.'

'He's lazy, but he's also smart. Did you see where she went?'

'Took a right back there.' I motioned to the street. 'The Underbodies went after her.'

'She'll lose them soon enough. But it means we've lost our bait for Metyard.' I could only just make out his face. 'Paige, we have to work out where Metyard will go next, before Hector does.'

'Does he have a binder in his gang?'

'Yes.' He blotted sweat from his brow. 'Personally, I think she'll pick up on Anne's presence and chase her.'

'Then we need to start thinking like Anne,' I said. 'To work out where she'd run.'

'Exactly. Consider it: you're a young girl, an orphan, neglected and abused by the two women you were working for. You come from the workhouse with your sister, but your sister can't protect you. You're vulnerable and afraid, and you have a weak constitution, so you're not physically strong. Nobody helped you. When you died, nobody cared. Where would you go?' He rubbed his forehead. 'Personally, I think we should consider the site of the Metyard house in Bruton Street.'

'The house she died in?' I said, unconvinced. 'That's the last place I'd want to go.'

'It's a strong possibility. Poltergeists often are drawn to the place they died.'

I sifted through other possibilities. Tried to think the way Anne would, to put myself in the shoes of a girl who had died almost three centuries ago. A girl with no parents, whose only family – her sister – was trapped in the same prison. She must have been afraid every time she woke up, every time she fell asleep, knowing that the two people who were meant to care for her had absolute power over her being. They had controlled her food, her freedom, her existence.

'The workhouse, maybe,' Nick murmured, more to himself than to me. 'Where she lived before …'

That option didn't feel right.

Twice Anne Naylor had escaped, and twice she had been brought back to her prison. She had mettle, this girl, to try a second time. Knowing what her employers would do to her if she was caught.

Guilt kicked me in the stomach, fresh and unexpected.

Anne had finally escaped Metyard in death, hidden where she thought she would never be found – and we had just exposed her to her murderer again. Her life and her death had been one long injustice.

Wait.

'I don't think Anne will run from Metyard,' I said quietly. 'Not this time. I think she's going to confront her. It's not a hunt – it's a final showdown. One they both want, now they've been set off.'

'I don't know.' Nick was frowning. 'You really think they'd go to the same place?'

'Anne Naylor was braver than we're giving her credit for. We need to think of somewhere that was important to *both* of them. And I think I know it.' I took a deep breath. 'The gully-hole. The place where Sarah Metyard disposed of Anne's body.'

'Why there?'

'For Sarah, it was where she thought things had ended. She disposed of Anne there, hiding the evidence – it was only her daughter, later, that exposed them. In her mind, it *should* have ended at the gully-hole,' I said. 'As for Anne, the memory of that place must enrage her. Her body was handled with the utmost disrespect – dumped in pieces in human waste, without any way for anyone to identify it. It was also where a chance for justice was missed.' Rain drummed on the pavement. 'You said a watchman found what was left of Anne, but assumed it was the work of body-snatchers. Just another pauper's corpse. Nobody asked questions.'

'The body was decomposed. After all that time—'

'I know, but someone should have realised she was missing. Sarah Metyard should have been arrested then – not ten years later. Those were ten years in which she could have hurt or murdered other girls.'

I could see the set of his mouth, the uncertainty. He took out his phone.

'Muse,' he said, once Eliza was on the line, 'it's us. Listen—'

'Metyard's on the move.' Eliza sounded nervous. 'We've heard reports of windows being broken, streetlamps going out, tables being overturned at the market—'

'Hector's involved. Turns out everyone wants a piece of her.'

She cursed under her breath. 'Where are you now?'

'Passing Alley.'

'Ha. You know it used to be called Pissing Alley, right?'

'Yeah, thanks. Listen – Dreamer wants to know where the sewer was – where Anne Naylor's body was disposed of.'

'I was just about to call you about that, funnily enough. Thought it might be a significant place. But you're going to need to make a choice here.' The line crackled. 'According to the sources we have, the gully-hole where Metyard dumped Anne was in "Chick Lane" – but there's no longer a street by that name in London.'

Nick exchanged a glance with me. 'Does the street still exist under a different name?'

'Yes, but here's the catch: I've found two places that were once called Chick Lane.'

We had no time for error. If we turned the wrong way, I would blow my opportunity to impress Jaxon, and I doubted he was a second-chance man.

'One is very close to you – Charterhouse Street. If it is there, it would explain why Anne haunts Farringdon tube station, which is nearby. She has no other historical connection to Farringdon that I can see.'

'And the other?' I said, leaning closer to the phone.

'West Street.'

Nick's eyebrows shot up. 'The same West Street that's less than a minute from our den?'

'The very same,' Eliza said. 'I'll leave the choice to you. Do you want me to tell Binder that Hector is involved?'

Nick sighed. 'He might as well know. Thanks for the help.'

He pushed his phone back into his inner pocket. I waited for his judgement.

This was one hell of a fork in the road. We wouldn't have time to try both locations, not with Hector on our trail.

'Hector will have researched Metyard's life, too,' Nick said. He sounded as tense as he looked. 'I say Charterhouse Street. We've always wondered why Anne haunts Farringdon – that explains it.'

'Anne didn't go in the direction of Charterhouse Street,' I said. 'Anyway, the gully-hole couldn't have been there – Metyard wouldn't have carried the remains from Bruton Street all the way to this part of London to dump them.' I held his gaze. 'It's West Street.'

Nick let his head fall back against the wall, closed his eyes, and released a long breath.

'This is your day. It's your chance,' he finally said. 'Let's hope you're right.'

No Rest for the Damned

We hailed a cab to get us to West Street. My insides were racked by nerves on the journey back to our district, though I made sure to appear composed. The Pale Dreamer did not show fear. She was confident in her decisions. Her face was a mask.

Nick had said that this was my chance, but it was a chance I could so easily squander. I was trusting my gut, going on what I thought was most logical, but there were so many unknowns, so many *mights*. Anne and Metyard might not both consider the gully-hole the most important part of their story. The gully-hole might have been in the other Chick Lane. Hector might be one step ahead of us. He might know something we didn't about Anne or Metyard. In short, I might be wrong about everything.

I felt ill at the thought of botching this. Nick could be putting too much trust in me.

When we got out of the cab, there was no sign of devastation. No hint that two enraged, three-hundred-year-old poltergeists had torn through the district.

'Tell the others we're here,' Nick said. 'I'll wait.'

'Do you know how we're going to improvise our way to netting Metyard yet?'

'I'm thinking.'

A dull sickness throbbed in the pit of my stomach. If I was wrong about this … I couldn't imagine Jaxon's anger. It would be the end of my career in unnaturalness. Yet again, I envisioned crawling back to my father, stifling my gift as best I could, and counting down the days until Scion apprehended me.

When I knocked on the door of the den, it was a wide-eyed Eliza who answered.

'There you are.' She pulled me into the hallway. 'Where's Nick?'

'Outside. Might be an idea to get Jaxon out here.'

'You chose West Street, then?' When I nodded, she said, 'I'll get him. You stay with Nick. If all goes to plan, you make a spool and work with Nick to keep Metyard in one place – okay?'

Before I could respond, she was already rushing up the stairs, calling for Jaxon. I retraced my steps, letting the door swing shut behind me. I was halfway back to Nick when our quarry arrived.

I felt them in the æther. A creeping darkness, like a spill of crude oil on the surface of water.

They veered around the sundial pillar at the heart of Seven Dials. Anne, weaving and ducking wildly, racing towards me at breakneck speed – and the poltergeist in pursuit of her, Sarah Metyard. Both returning to the gully-hole. I was wary of Anne, knowing she was a poltergeist, but Metyard played havoc with my survival instinct. Her approach made me feel as if the sun had been swallowed.

I had been right.

They had taken me by surprise by coming so soon. I threw myself out of the rogue spirits' path; my back slammed into a doorway. Metyard and Anne slashed past me, striking the side-mirror off a car, and careered around the corner into West Street. A man on the pavement let out a shout. Not a voyant. He wouldn't have experienced the same gust of pressure that I had. All he would have seen with his own eyes was the car mirror flying off.

'Sorry,' I called to him. 'It's been loose for weeks.'

He shot me an uncertain look before walking on. A breath hissed between my teeth. We had to finish this quickly, before someone got suspicious and summoned the Vigiles. I checked that my hood was up before I sprinted after the pair.

I found Nick on his knees, breathing deeply. Light-headed with dread, I crouched beside him, searching his face for the silver slashes that marked the wounds of a poltergeist.

'I'm okay,' he said hoarsely. 'Anne got a little too close for comfort. Where's Jaxon?'

'Eliza's getting him.'

His lips had turned slightly blue. 'We need to get off the street – take Metyard somewhere where Jaxon can bind her without attracting any unwanted attention.' His hand went straight to his scarf, ensuring that his face was covered. 'We'll try to lure her into the courtyard behind the den.'

'How?'

'We get her to chase us instead of Anne.'

I helped him to his feet. 'In other words, we piss her off?'

'Exactly.'

Murderer and victim had stopped a little farther down the street, and now circled each other slowly, gracefully, as if they moved in water. A woman walked right past them, oblivious.

Metyard lunged at Anne, making her flinch – tormenting her, even in death. She couldn't kill the girl again, but she could weaken and hound her. She would never leave her alone, and it was our fault for driving her from her hideaway.

Anne lashed back, driving Metyard away for a moment. I watched as Nick prepared to make a spool.

Movement from down the street. Twelve black-clad voyants, all with the same sort of aura, all wearing necklaces and belts made from what looked like hundreds of sewing needles. When they clapped eyes on us, they started running.

'The Threadbare Company,' Nick muttered. He sounded torn between amusement and frustration.

I had heard of them. A gang from another section of the citadel. 'Gossip spreads fast around here,' I said. 'Let me guess. They're here to claim Metyard, too?'

He grimaced in answer. 'They're from the district where Tyburn once stood. So, technically, Didion *did* steal her from them ...'

'Well,' I said, 'she's on our turf now.'

His face hardened. 'Right. As soon as we're through the gate to the courtyard, lock it behind us.'

The other voyants were sprinting towards us now, towards Metyard and Anne. This was chaos. 'They're ours, Red Vision,' one of them bellowed. Nick gathered his breath.

'Get ready,' he said.

I braced myself. He released the spool.

The knot of spirits careered between Anne and Metyard like a ball through skittles, knocking them away from each other, before it snapped back into his grasp. I could feel their attention turn to us.

'Come on,' he barked, and started to run. I followed, feeling Metyard plunge after us. When we reached the next street, Eliza was stepping out of the den. 'Muse, the courtyard!'

Eliza retreated without protest.

The Threadbare Company were hot on our heels. We crashed through the wrought-iron gate beside the den, into the shaded passageway that led to the courtyard. Nick cleared the steps in one jump, chased by a furious Metyard and an equally angry Anne, while I turned to lock the gate – just as one of the Threadbare Company's members slammed into it, his face contorted with such outrage that my hands shook in panic.

'Let it go,' he snarled, spewing spittle, 'or I'll carve a necklace on your throat.'

'Can't if you can't reach me,' I bit out, shoving the gate closed with my shoulder.

Sarah Metyard rushed between the bars, turning my skin cold. I twisted the key and ran around the corner and after Nick, leaving the Threadbare Company to scream their threats.

This was absurd. Absolute madness. I would have been laughing if not for the danger.

As I rounded the corner, I sensed Anne nearby, but it wasn't Anne that scared me. I reached for the handrail and threw myself after Nick. He was standing at the far end of the courtyard with Eliza at his side, feet planted a shoulder's width apart, both hands outstretched, palms facing Metyard. She had backed them into the doorway on the opposite side to this one, which was blocked by another gate.

Where the *hell* was Jaxon?

Nick gathered another spool to defend himself. I ran towards him. As Metyard rushed him, the spirits formed a shield, but she was stronger than all of them, older and incensed. He clenched his teeth as he tried to hold the spool together. The hangman had slain Sarah Metyard, but her lust for violence had followed her to the æther.

When I got too close, she lashed out at me. I actually felt the sensation of a hand against my chest, a shove driven as if by living muscle, before I went flying. I twisted just in time to land. The impact was so hard that I lost my footing and staggered into the tree. I caught myself and flung a spool of my own, but I was so new to the art that my efforts were little more than a beesting to Metyard. All her attention was fixed on Nick and Eliza, who were trembling with the effort of keeping her at bay. Eliza had also formed a spool, and they were working together to suspend the poltergeist between them, giving her no way out. Anne lingered behind my shoulder, almost as if she was watching the show.

The back door to the den finally opened. Jaxon Hall stepped on to the bone-pale paving stones.

From his leisurely pace, he had to have been testing us with his absence – for the last few minutes, at least. Seeing how long we could hold on to Metyard.

He carried a knife with a white handle. Nothing else. I had never seen Jaxon use his clairvoyance before. He was secretive about the nature of it – with me, at least. I knew he was a binder, someone able to bend a spirit's will to his own, but I didn't know exactly how he did it – only that it involved using a spirit's name to exert control over them. And a knife, apparently. He levelled an amused gaze on his prize before calmly unbuttoning the cuff of his shirt and pushing it up to the elbow.

Metyard had caught wind of danger. She shook off Nick and Eliza and hurtled towards Jaxon. Before I knew what I was doing, I had sidestepped, putting myself in front of him.

I didn't have enough time to make a spool.

What I did have was my gift.

It stirred in me again. It opened like a flower, and it grew, too big for me to grasp. It was a mechanism, designed to respond to danger. Metyard met it with a force that I felt in every nerve-end. A polter-geist could interact with living flesh: rend it, scar it.

Jaxon had to be able to imprison her. I had to give him time.

All at once, I was soaked to the bone in icy sweat. Behind me, Jaxon hissed through his teeth as he began the binding.

My hands pushed out – not because I thought I could shove Metyard away, but to convince myself that I was in control of this *force* inside me. I was a pressure-cooker on the brink of boiling over, brimming with power.

Jaxon muttered under his breath. Agony swelled at the front of my skull and exploded into black and red light. I wasn't strong enough. A copper taste ran over my tongue and licked down the back of my throat. Blood oozed from my nose and dripped down to my chin, soaking into the collar of my blouse.

'Jax,' Eliza shouted. She, too, was trembling under the strain.

'Keep her there' was his only reply.

She clenched her teeth. 'No rush. Really, I'm loving this—'

'Keep. Her. There.'

He went back to his murmuring. Wisps of hair were plastered to my temples. More and more strength was leaving me, pouring away by the moment. Sensing weakness, Metyard pushed closer, making my muscles tremble. Anne shoved at her, to no avail. If Metyard touched my skin, I would be scarred for life, like I had been as a child. Eliza and Nick brought their spools to bear against her, but it was me she was after, me she had to remove if she wanted to incapacitate Jaxon.

'More, Paige,' Jaxon said, low enough that only I could hear. 'Come, now, Pale Dreamer. Let your spirit fly at last.'

A soft, unbroken ring filled my ears. I wanted to answer, but I couldn't breathe.

'Do it. You're a *dreamwalker*, darling. I know you can do more than this …'

I tried. Closing my eyes, I pictured all the moments in my life that had made me afraid. The school corridors, lined with mocking smiles and dagger eyes. The streets of Dublin, where I had seen my cousin for the last time. My father in his armchair, hiding behind his newspaper, avoiding my gaze whenever we spoke, never telling me why.

It wasn't enough. Metyard's rage had festered and boiled for three centuries – it eclipsed mine. The poltergeist shoved closer, buckling my knees. I didn't know what he wanted me to do, or how to do it. Jaxon let out a low curse.

'Someone has made an error,' he said to us. 'The binding has had no effect. The name must be incorrect.'

I was too aware of my heartbeat.

'Try it with another "e",' Eliza called, panting. 'M-E-T-E-Y-A-R-D. Some of the documents spelled it that way—' Her words slid into a groan. 'Hurry.'

Nick reeled another spirit into his spool and pushed back against the poltergeist, releasing the pressure on me for just long enough for me to get back to my feet. I thought of how Anne Naylor had been beaten and terrorised, treated like dirt, and how no one had helped her. How that happened all too often. How it still happened now, three centuries later. I would fight this battle with her, even if it killed me. I would help give her the justice she had been denied in life.

Moisture seeped down my cheek from my hairline and soaked the back of my neck. Finally, Jaxon said, 'No effect.' Almost lazily, he drew up a spool of his own and added its strength to our labours. 'Are we quite sure that this poltergeist *is* Sarah Metyard? It would hardly surprise me if Didion had misidentified it.'

'It must be.' Nick's voice was straining. 'Who else would want to confront Anne?'

It had to be Sarah. The woman who had starved and neglected the girl to death. The woman who had carried her body in pieces to the gully-hole. Who else could it be?

Suddenly I found myself thinking back to the paperwork, remembering what the frightened children had cried when they found Anne senseless in her bindings.

Miss Sally! Miss Sally! Nanny does not move.

It hadn't been the old woman they had called for. It had been Sarah Metyard the younger. The daughter. *If she does not move*, she had answered, *I will make her move*.

Sally.

Sally, who had been brutalised by her mother – who had beaten the girls in the shop, and been beaten herself. Sally, who had eventually run from the house Anne had died in.

Sally, who had condemned them both when she confessed their crime.

As the pieces slotted together, it began to add up.

I will make her move, Sally had said. But even though she had struck Anne's corpse, even though they had shaken and screamed at her, Anne had not moved. That stillness continued to mock Sally.

I will make her move. I will make her move.

Now she was here again, to make Anne move. To keep her moving, so she would never have peace.

'There were t-two Metyards,' I said. My lips were trembling. 'This is the daughter.'

Realisation dawned on Nick's face.

'But she was called Sarah Metyard, too,' Eliza said, her voice cracking with frustration. 'Sally was just a nickname.'

'I seem to remember a middle name,' Jaxon said. 'From the record of the hanging.'

'Oh! Yes, yes – she did have a middle name. Wait.' Sounding frantic, Eliza released her spool and pelted past us, back into the den. 'I need to see the death record. Just hold on for a few more seconds—'

'Hurry, Eliza,' Nick said. Sweat was streaming off him, and he was deathly pale.

All I could taste was metal. I thought I would die of the pain in my temples, but I had crossed a line somewhere. I could hold on. I could survive this.

It must have been seconds, but it felt like hours before the shout came from the window above us:

'Morgan. Sarah *Morgan* Metyard!'

Jaxon set to work at once. In the final moments of the binding, I fell to my knees again, almost retching at the pain. Another sound-less scream went through the æther.

And then, just like that, the poltergeist was calm. She hung between us – passive and still.

The beast had been tamed.

Silence descended in the courtyard. It was as if I had been swimming underwater and my head had finally broken the surface. All the tension in my back and shoulders melted away, and I slumped forward, trembling all over. As I caught my breath, Anne Naylor drifted close to me – as close as she could come without touching my face. Every hair on my arms stood on end.

'She won't hurt you any more.' I couldn't raise my voice above a whisper. 'I promise.'

I thought I felt a small glow in the æther. Anne brushed past my aura, turning my skin to ice, and slipped quietly out of the courtyard.

'Don't try binding her, Jaxon,' Eliza said. 'You're going to lose too much blood.'

'Yes. Thank you, Eliza,' was the curt reply.

Nick crouched beside me and grasped my arms. My eye sockets felt tighter, my jaw too stiff to move, and my vision was furred with black around the edges, but I could still just about see. Spots of ruby dotted the paving stones around Jaxon's shoes and veined one of his arms. I looked up to see him wiping the blade of his knife with a silk handkerchief.

'Done,' he said, his eyes on the docile spirit. 'Not the Metyard we wanted, but I suppose it is *a* Metyard.'

'Maria won't bargain with you now,' I rasped. 'She wanted Sarah, not Sally. So we've lost Anne, too.'

His face was blank. 'Yes.' He beckoned to the spirit. 'Maria and I are old friends – we may be able to come to a new agreement. If not … well. I'm sure we can find some way to make this day something other than an abject waste of time.'

As he walked into the den, Sally followed. I was drained, weighed down by the sense that he was disappointed in me, but relief spread through my chest. Let Anne Naylor return to the resting place she had chosen for herself. Let her be still. Perhaps she wouldn't scream now, knowing that her pursuer was gone. That was a victory, I supposed.

It just wasn't the victory Jaxon Hall had hoped for.

In the den, it was as if nothing had happened. I washed the blood off my face and changed into a new shirt. Jaxon asked me to kindly make him a black coffee and get back to work on the rent, which I did, but no sooner had I sat down than I succumbed to exhaustion. My head dropped on to the desk, and I knew no more.

When I opened my eyes, I was in my own room, and it was dark. In the moonlight, I could make out a moth on the open window.

I jolted upright, only to reel back to my pillow, swallowing a groan. My head was killing me. When had I gone to bed? Had I finished the paperwork? I shifted on to my side, fighting to gather my thoughts. Gooseflesh washed over my skin.

When I remembered what had happened, I pulled a sheet over my head. I had failed. Jaxon would fire me in the morning. I stifled a weak laugh at the prospect of dismissal from my criminal job. First I had failed to impress him with my gift; then I had fallen asleep mid-task. I might as well pack my bags and go now, save myself the humiliation.

A light switched on outside my room. I kept the sheet over my eyes. A weight sank on to the edge of the mattress.

'Paige, are you awake?'

'What time is it?' I murmured.

'One in the morning.' Eliza poked me. 'I made tea. Dealing with 'geists always gives me a chill.'

I emerged, pushing my curls back from my face. Eliza was in her nightclothes and a cardigan, and her face was bare. She offered a steaming mug, which I took.

'Did you fall asleep?' I asked.

'No. I had to finish your paperwork,' she said. When I dropped my gaze, she touched my shoulder. 'Jaxon did, though. Nick and I were using spools – you two were using your gifts. Yourselves. This is part of what it is to be clairvoyant. There's a saying in the syndicate: *the æther takes as often as it gives.*'

Jaxon had been just as burned out by the encounter with Sally, then. It was only a small consolation.

Eliza produced a hand-chased silver pillbox from her pocket. 'Here.' She flicked it open and plucked out a pill. 'Nick said you'd have a headache.'

'Jaxon's going to fire me, isn't he?' I asked quietly.

No reply. I wasn't sure whether she hadn't heard, or was just ignoring me. She busied herself with inspecting my cheek, where Bloatface had caught me with his elbow.

'That'll be a nasty bruise,' she said. 'And your throat – that will hurt for a while.'

'Eliza.'

'We'll talk about Jaxon later. You've been asleep for hours – you need something to eat. I think it's about time we introduced you to Chateline's, the best cookshop in London.'

'Now?'

'It's open all night. Rumour has it that the owner never sleeps – he won't let anyone else cook.' When I went for my clothes, she said, 'No need to dress up. I regularly go in my slippers.'

A lump was swelling in my throat. She and Nick often went for supper in the evenings. They had never invited me before. This must be a final kindness before they cut me loose.

I gave my hair a quick brush and shrugged on a jacket. We went into the night – she really did wear her slippers – and I listened to her talk about how wonderful Chateline's was, and how much she liked the eponymous owner, and how he could turn even the simplest meal into a work of art. She was obsessed with Chat's honey loaf; the recipe was a closely-guarded secret. As she brought it to life with her words, I felt I was glimpsing a world I would never belong in. If I had just worked out what Jaxon had wanted to see from me, this could have been my life.

We passed the sundial pillar, and she led me into the tiny, inconspicuous alleyway that led to Neal's Yard, a hidden nook between the buildings of Seven Dials. Inside was a shop – or what I'd thought was a shop – that I'd passed a few times while I was carrying out errands; I'd never had cause to go in. Eliza pushed open the door.

The interior was beautiful in a moth-eaten way, an ode to lost grandeur. Patrons crowded the tables, which were lit by wax candles. Nick was waiting for us in a booth in the corner.

'Evening, Muse.' A bald, ruddy man was cleaning the bar. 'I see you've finally brought the newcomer.'

'I've decided to let her in on our haven,' Eliza said, and he chuckled. 'Dreamer, this is Chateline.'

'Chat.' He held out a callused hand. The other arm ended in a stump below the elbow. 'Muse and Vision have been telling me all about you.' I blinked. 'Seeing as this is your first time eating here, dinner's on the house. Whatever you want.'

'That's kind of you,' I said, surprised. 'Thank you.'

'Ah, if you're a friend of Binder, you're a friend of mine.'

We joined Nick at the booth. He, too, looked as if he had just rolled out of bed.

'Hi, *sötnos*,' he said, moving a silk cushion to make room for me. 'I took the liberty of ordering our usual. We wanted to give you your official Chateline's initiation.'

'We have a tradition,' Eliza chimed in. 'Breakfast for supper, here, every Friday.' She leaned closer and laid a ring-clad hand over mine. 'And from now on, you're coming, too.'

I tried to smile, with limited success. 'I'm honoured.'

They chattered away for a while, and seemed content to let me nod and smile in the right places. Chat brought us platter after platter of breakfast food, cooked to perfection, along with a brimming coffee press and a silver tureen of cream.

'What made you choose West Street?' Eliza said to me, between mouthfuls of pancake.

I poured coffee. 'I just … thought Metyard would dispose of the body close to home.'

'I should have realised, too. The watchman who found the body – his statement says that he was based in Holborn, round the corner. I was reading in such a rush the first time.' She pulled a face. 'You saved my skin by guessing right. Jax would have been furious if we'd chosen wrong, with the answer right under my nose.'

'It was a guess. A lucky one.'

'Like the lucky guess that Sarah was really Sally,' Nick said, nudging me. 'And the lucky guess that Anne and Metyard would confront each other at the gully-hole.'

'It made the most sense.'

Eliza took the coffee I handed her. 'You sound down, Paige. Aren't you happy?'

'Happy?' I echoed.

'With your success.'

I looked between their smiling faces. Confused, I said, 'But I wasn't successful. Whatever Jaxon wanted to see from me earlier, he didn't see it.' When neither of them replied to this, I put down my cup. 'Look, it's lovely of you both to do this for me, but … I'd rather it was a clean break.' My breath came short. They exchanged quizzical glances. 'Please, just tell me. Is Jaxon going to let me go?'

'Let you go?' Eliza burst out laughing. '*What?*'

'Oh, Paige – no. Of course not,' Nick said gently. 'I've come back from assignments empty-handed more times than I can count. Even Jaxon Hall doesn't always get what he wants.'

'You held Metyard back *on your own*. We can only repel spirits with spools.' Eliza shook her head. 'You're a *dreamwalker*, Paige. Rarest of them all. Jax has always known that, but today, you gave him a taste of what you can do. Maybe you haven't unlocked your gift to its full extent yet, but that's fine. You can learn more, in time.'

My heart thumped. 'Really?'

'Really,' they said in unison.

'You did a great job, as far as he's concerned,' Eliza said. 'You guessed the real identity of the poltergeist. You were the one who suspected the spirits would return to the sewer.' She reached into her knitted bag and produced the file marked M. 'Chick Lane was clearly important to everyone involved in the crime. This is the transcript of the Metyards' trial from the Old Bailey. Take a look at what Richard Rooker – Sally's lover – said when he was testifying.'

I pulled the folder towards me and peered at where her finger rested. In the transcript, Richard Rooker was recounting a conversation he had overheard between Sarah and Sally.

I heard the daughter say to the mother, Mother, you are the Chick-lane ghost; remember the gully-hole.

'The Chick-lane ghost,' I said, and released a long breath. 'So Metyard was known as that even in life.'

Eliza closed the folder. 'Right. Both Metyard and Anne had a clear link to that street. Jaxon had a strong suspicion that if those two spirits wanted to confront each other, that was where they would do it. He told me as much when you and Nick set off.'

I shook my head. 'Why didn't you tell us? Why send us on a wild-goose chase?'

She bit back a smile. 'Jaxon asked me to test you, see if you could work it out yourself. He was *delighted* when I told him you'd asked about the gully-hole.'

'Were you in on this?' I said to Nick. When he held up his hands, I turned to Eliza again. 'Fine. You knew Chick Lane was probably the place – but did you know the *right* Chick Lane was West Street?'

'No. I really didn't,' Eliza said. 'We took a gamble on your intuition. You were right.'

I sat in silence for a long time, stunned.

Jaxon wasn't going to cut me loose. I might not be a full-fledged dreamwalker yet, but I had the ability to hunt and restrain spirits, and I had survived an encounter with the Underlord. Remembering that prompted me to ask: 'What about Hector?'

'You'll have to watch your back for a while,' Nick admitted, 'but Jaxon will smooth everything over in the end. We all keep an eye on each other. That's what the Seven Seals is about.' He wrapped an arm around my shoulders and squeezed gently. My cheeks warmed. 'We're a family, Paige. And you are part of that family now.'

My throat was closing; my eyes prickled. I didn't know what to say.

'To you, Pale Dreamer,' Nick said, and the three of us raised our glasses. 'And your career in unnaturalness.'

'Get ready for it.' Eliza grinned. 'There's no rest for the damned.'

And I started to realise: this might really be my life. Things might just be like this for ever.

Epilogue

For a few weeks, nothing changed in Seven Dials, except that I would now join Nick and Eliza every Friday at Chat's. I still didn't go out much, and the more tedious paperwork inevitably landed on my desk, but I conquered it with new resolve. When Jaxon asked for coffee, it was the best damned coffee in London. The paperwork was the neatest and most detailed it had ever been.

Jaxon displayed no change in his attitude towards me. Courtesy, occasional charm. Solid indifference most of the time. That was all right. Everything was.

The bruise on my cheek faded. According to reports, Anne Naylor was back in Farringdon station, but she didn't scream as often as she had before. Most of the time, she was quiet and sanguine. Jaxon thought it likely that Metyard the elder was lurking somewhere, but for now, Anne seemed to have found a little peace.

On the last day of October, I was permitted to join Eliza while she collected the rent from local voyants, including Chat. It was a modest promotion, but to me, it was another sign of my acceptance into the gang. I was stepping into the skin of the Pale Dreamer, and I planned to stay in it for a very long time.

Eliza took me into hidden shops where seers sold the knowledge in their crystal balls; where card-readers offered to map out my whole life with their images. We stopped for coffee. We avoided Vigiles. We were so preoccupied with our underworld existence that we almost forgot about the anti-unnaturalness messages on the transmission screens, and the voyants being executed, and the omnipresent government that loomed above us all, waiting to catch us. I had never thought I would be able to forget about Scion while I lived in it.

Nick told me that this was how we rebelled against their tyranny. Quietly, in the shadows – but by existing, by thriving, by daring to profit from our gifts, we defied Scion. I knew from experience that defying them through other means would only end in all our deaths. This was the way things were, and we were content with this, with our secret mutiny.

We collected the last of the rent before sunset. Back at the den, we sat and talked with Nick and told each other stories about our lives from before we had joined the Seven Seals. Eliza, who had been in the syndicate since she had been abandoned in Soho as a baby, was full of them. When we finally turned in for the night, my cheeks were aching from laughing so hard.

The first thing I noticed was that another moth had landed on my window. The second was the curl of paper on my pillow. Familiar, elegant writing fanned across it.

Meet me now at the sundial pillar.

The old fear stirred again. I steeled myself and pulled on my jacket.

As soon as I stepped out of the den, I saw him. He was standing before the illuminated pillar that formed the centre of the district, holding one of his antique canes. He didn't move as I approached.

'Good evening, Paige.'

I stopped beside him and pushed my hands into my pockets. 'Hello.'

My spine was taut, my stomach roiling. Even after three weeks, a small part of me asked if he had just been biding his time, and now he would get rid of me. Perhaps Eliza and Nick had been wrong.

'I trust you enjoyed your day.'

'Yes,' I said.

His gaze was on the sundials. Seven Dials was where seven streets came together, converging in a junction around the pillar – but it had only six sundial faces at its summit. Nick had told me that the district had originally been designed with six streets, hence the absence of a seventh face. Locals now thought of the pillar itself as the missing dial. I took in the blue faces and golden engravings.

'I have a matter to discuss with you, Paige. An offer to make.'

The first half of what he said would have frightened me out of my wits, but *offer* was less threatening. Last I'd checked, you didn't *offer* to fire someone.

'As you have no doubt seen,' Jaxon said, 'Dr Nygård has been a great asset to me for the last eight years – but his work in Scion makes it difficult for him to commit as fully as I would like to the lifestyle of the Seven Seals. You've seen it now, darling. You know how demanding our work is. How dangerous.' He tapped his cane against the pavement. 'Eliza is a medium. Talented, yes, and hardworking, but not quite the calibre of voyant to become the heir and protégée of the White Binder.'

A frown pinched my brow.

'After they proved themselves, I gave both Nick and Eliza one of these sundial faces. To mark their places in the Seven Seals.'

He swung his cane up to point at the sundial that faced the den, then traced a path between us, indicating the street we were standing in.

'You see this, O my lovely? This is yours,' he said. 'This street, this path, is yours to walk. If you follow it, it will lead you into the labyrinth of London's underworld, where you truly belong. All you need do is embrace the Pale Dreamer. Let her deep into your soul. Let her take away all the doubt, the solitude, the *fear* you store as Paige Mahoney, and turn it into riches. Let her draw out the gift that lies dormant within you. Do this,' he said, 'and you will make me a fine mollisher.'

Mollisher. Second-in-command. He couldn't be making me this offer, not after so little time.

'Mollisher,' I finally said.

'Correct.'

He was going to choose me over Eliza, who had been with him for almost exactly a year longer than I had. I couldn't help but think of what Ognena Maria had told me.

'It shouldn't be me,' I said quietly. 'Eliza—'

'—will understand, and respect my decision. My mollisher must be someone rare, someone *singular*. When you fought Sally Metyard, you proved yourself to be everything I hoped. I know you can do more, but we have years to perfect your technique. We have the rest of your life, if you make the commitment I ask.'

I hesitated.

I hated the thought of usurping Eliza; and yet he insisted that she would understand, and he knew her far better than I did.

'As my mollisher, you will be heir to my section. Upon my death, you will become mime-queen of I-4 and inherit my home in Seven Dials. You will want for nothing. All I ask for in exchange is your loyalty.' He looked me in the face. 'Do you accept my proposal?'

My heartbeat was racing now, faster than it ever had – not in fear, but in anticipation.

I still didn't know what to make of Jaxon Hall, or what kind of promise I was making. For all I knew, I was striking a deal with the devil – but if it saved me from Scion, so be it.

'Yes,' I said. 'Yes, I'll be your mollisher. And you have my loyalty. Now and always.'

The corner of his mouth lifted.

'Excellent,' he said. 'Until tomorrow, then, Pale Dreamer.'

With that, he walked away.

A cold wind was rising. I stayed where I was for a long while, too shocked to move.

High above London, the stars bore witness to my oath. In that moment, I almost couldn't see the darkness that surrounded them. I almost couldn't hear the sirens in the distance. Taking a deep breath, I turned back to the den and allowed myself the softest of smiles.

Now I was free to be what I pleased.

I am Paige Mahoney. I am the Pale Dreamer.

Glossary

The slang used by clairvoyants in *The Bone Season* is loosely based on words used in the criminal underworld of London in the nineteenth century, with some amendments to meaning or usage. Other words have been taken from modern colloquial English or reinterpreted. Terms specific to the Family – those humans who reside in Sheol I – are indicated with an asterisk*.

Æther: [noun] The spirit realm, accessible by clairvoyants. Also called the Source.

Amaurosis: [noun] The state of non-clairvoyance.

Amaurotic: [noun *or* adjective] Non-clairvoyant.

Barking irons: [noun] Guns. 'To raise one's barking irons' = to prepare for a struggle.

Bleached mort: [noun] A fair-haired woman. Mildly offensive.

Blow: [verb] Tattle; whistle-blow.

Bob: [noun] Slang term for a gold coin; one British pound.

Bone: [adjective] Good or prosperous.

Bone-grubber*: [noun] A derogatory term for a *red-jacket*.

Bones*: [adjective] Dead.

Boon: [noun] Lucky star.

Brain plague: [noun] A slang term for *phantasmagoria*, a debilitating fever caused by Fluxion 14.

Breacher: [noun] A spirit that can cause an impact on the corporeal world due to its age or type. Includes poltergeists and archangels.

Broads: [noun] Cards used for clairvoyance, usually Tarot cards.

Broadsider: [noun] An outdated term for a cartomancer. Still recognised in conversation but rarely used in the citadel.

Buck cab: [noun] A rogue, unlicensed cab, generally frequented by clairvoyants.

Busking: [verb] Cash-in-hand clairvoyance. Most buskers offer to read fortunes for money. Not permitted within the clairvoyant crime syndicate.

Buzzers*: [noun] Emim.

Cokum: [adjective] Shrewd; cunning.

Cold spot: [noun] A small tear between the æther and the corporeal world. Manifests as a permanent patch of ice. Can be used, with ecto-plasm, to open a conduit to the Netherworld. Corporeal matter (e.g. blood and flesh) cannot pass through a cold spot.

Courtier: [noun] Purple aster addict. The name comes from St Anne's Court, Soho, where the purple aster trade began in the early twenty-first century.

Crib: [noun] Place of residence.

Dethroned: [adjective] Being fully recovered from the influence of purple aster.

Dollymop: [noun] An affectionate, if condescending term for a young woman or girl (often shortened to *dolly*).

Donop: [noun] A pound; weight measurement. Used primarily within the ethereal drug community.

Dreamer: [noun] Shorthand for *dreamwalker*, typically used by Rephaim.

Dreamscape: [noun] The interior of the mind, where memories are stored. Split into five zones or 'rings' of sanity: sunlight, twilight, midnight, lower midnight and hadal. Clairvoyants can consciously access their own dreamscapes, while amaurotics may catch glimpses when they sleep.

Drifters: [noun] Spirits in the æther that have not been banished to the outer darkness or last light. They can still be controlled by clairvoyants.

Duckett: [noun] A vendor. Also the alias of Sheol I's pawnbroker.

Ecto: [noun] Ectoplasm, or Rephaite blood. Chartreuse yellow. Luminous and slightly gelatinous. Can be used to open cold spots.

Emim, the: [noun] [singular *Emite*] The purported enemies of the Rephaim; 'the dreaded ones'. Described by Nashira Sargas as carnivorous and bestial, with a taste for human flesh. Their existence is shrouded in mystery.

Family, the*: [noun] All humans that reside in Sheol I, with the exception of *bone-grubbers* and other traitors.

Fine-wire: [verb] To pickpocket skilfully.

Flam: [noun] Lie.

Flash house: [noun] A oxygen bar or other social area. Generally patronised by criminals.

Flatches: [noun] Money; keep. 'To earn one's flatches' = to earn a living.

Flimp: [noun] Pickpocket.

Floxy: [noun] Scented oxygen, inhaled through a cannula. Scion's alternative to alcohol. Served in the vast majority of entertainment venues, including oxygen bars.

Flux: [noun] Fluxion 14, a psychotic drug causing pain and disorientation in clairvoyants.

Gallipot: [noun] A specialist in ethereal drugs and their effects on the dreamscape.

Ghost: [noun] A spirit that has chosen a particular place in which to reside, most likely the place in which he or she died. Moving a ghost from its 'haunt' will annoy it.

Gilet: [noun] A sleeveless jacket.

Gillie: [noun] Vigile.

Glow: [noun] Aura.

Glym jack: [noun] A street bodyguard, rented to protect denizens from unnaturals at night. Identified by a distinctive green light.

Golden cord: [noun] A link between two spirits. Very little is known about it.

Greasepaint: [noun] Make-up.

Harlie*: [noun] Performer.

Hisser: [noun] A condescending term for a whisperer or polyglot.

Irons: [noun] Guns.

Janxed: [adjective *or* verb] Busted; broken.

Jerryshop: [noun] Pawnbroker.

Julker: [noun] Polyglot.

Lamps: [noun] Eyes. See also *shiners*.

Last light: [noun] The centre of the æther, the place from which spirits can never return. It is rumoured that a final afterlife is encountered beyond the last light.

Macer: [noun] A cheat.

Meatspace: [noun] The corporeal world; Earth.

Mecks: [noun] Non-alcoholic substitute for wine. Has a syrupy, sweet consistency. Comes in white, rose and 'blood', or red.

Mime-crime: [noun] Any act involving the use of, or communication with, the spirit world, especially for financial gain. Considered high treason under Scion law.

Mime-lord: [noun] A gang leader in the clairvoyant syndicate; a specialist in mime-crime. Generally has a close group of five to ten followers, but maintains overall command over all clairvoyants in one section within a cohort. Member of the Unnatural Assembly.

Mime-queen: [noun] Title used by some female mime-lords.

Mollisher: [noun] A young clairvoyant associated with a mime-lord or mime-queen, sometimes shortened to 'moll'. Usually presumed to be [a] the mime-lord's lover and [b] heir to his or her section.

Nib: [verb] Arrest.

Nightwalker: [noun] One who sells his or her clairvoyant knowledge as part of a sexual bargain.

Nose: [noun] A spy or informer. 'To turn nose' = to betray a person or organisation.

Numen: [noun] [plural *numa*] Objects used by soothsayers and augurs to connect with the æther, e.g. mirrors, cards, bones.

Ossista: [noun] Attendant in an oxygen bar.

Outer darkness: [noun] A distant part of the æther that lies beyond the reach of clairvoyants.

Paddy wagon: [noun] A vehicle used to transport prisoners.

Penny dreadful: [noun] Cheap, illegal fiction produced in Grub Street, the centre of the voyant writing scene. Serialised horror stories. Distributed among clairvoyants to make up for the lack of fantastical literature produced by Scion. Penny dreadfuls cover a wide range of supernatural subjects. They include *The Vamps of Vauxhall*, *The Fay Fiasco* and *Tea With a Tasser*.

Penny gaff: [noun] Low, sometimes ridiculous entertainment, usually applied to illegal theatre productions.

Performer*: [noun] A human resident of Sheol I who has failed his or her tests and is under the command of the Overseer.

Pink-jacket*: [noun] Second stage of initiation in Sheol I. A pink-jacket must prove themselves against the Emim to become a red-jacket. If this test is failed, the pink-jacket becomes a white-jacket again.

Push: [noun] Money.

Querent: [noun] Any person that seeks knowledge of the æther. They may ask questions or offer part of themselves (e.g. blood, palm) for a reading. Soothsayers and augurs may use a querent to focus on certain areas of the æther, making predictions easier.

Red-jacket*: [noun] The highest rank for humans in Sheol I. Red-jackets are responsible for protecting the city from the Emim. In return for their service, they are given special privileges. Also called *bone-grubbers*.

Reef: [verb] To hit; to strike.

Regal: [noun] Purple aster.

Reigning: [verb] Using purple aster.

Rephaim, the: [noun] [singular *Rephaite*] Biologically immortal, human-oid inhabitants of the Netherworld, known to feed on the aura of clairvoyant humans. Their history and origin are uncertain.

Rookery: [noun] Slum. In Sheol I, the shantytown in which performers are forced to live.

Rottie: [noun] *Amaurotic*.

Screever: [noun] A forger of documents, employed by mime-lords to provide fake travel papers for their employees.

Scrying: [noun] The art of seeing into and gaining insight from the æther through numa. A querent may be used.

Scurf: [noun] A greedy, exploitative employer.

Shiners: [noun] Eyes. See also *lamps*.

Silver cord: [noun] A permanent link between the body and the spirit. It allows a person to dwell for many years in one physical form. Unique to each individual. Particularly important to dreamwalkers, who use the cord to leave their bodies temporarily. The silver cord wears down over the years, and once broken cannot be repaired.

Skilly*: [noun] A thin gruel, usually made of meat juices.

Slate: [verb] To beat.

Sortes: [noun] Lots. A category of numa used by cleromancers. Includes needles, dice, keys, bones and sticks.

Spool: [noun] A group of spirits. Can also be used as a verb, 'to spool' = to gather (a group of spirits).

Stiff: [noun] Dead body.

Subliming: [noun] A process by which an ordinary object is transfigured into a numen.

Syndicate: [noun] A criminal organisation of clairvoyants, based in the Scion Citadel of London. Active since the early 1960s. Governed by the Underlord and the Unnatural Assembly. Members specialise in mime-crime for financial profit.

Syndies: [noun] Members of the clairvoyant crime syndicate. Generally used by Vigiles.

Tasser: [noun] Shorthand for a tasseographer.

Threnody: [noun] A series of words used to banish spirits to the outer darkness.

Tincto: [noun] Laudanum. An illegal narcotic. The slang comes from its trade name, Tincture of Opium.

Toke*: [noun] Stale bread.

Tooler: [noun] [1] A class of pickpocket; [2] A disobedient child.

Underlord: [noun] Head of the Unnatural Assembly and mob boss of the clairvoyant syndicate. Traditionally resides in the Devil's Acre in I Cohort, Section 1.

Voyance: [noun] Clairvoyance.

Voyant: [noun] Clairvoyant.

Waitron: [noun] Gender-neutral term for anyone in Scion's service industry.

Walker: [noun] Shorthand for *dreamwalker*.

White-jacket*: [noun] Initial rank given to all humans in Sheol I. A white-jacket is expected to display a certain degree of proficiency in their particular type of clairvoyance. Passing this test enables them to become a *pink-jacket*; failing means banishment to the Rookery.

Whitewash: [noun] Long-term amnesia caused by white aster or [verb] to use white aster on someone.

Yellow-jacket*: [noun] The lowest rank in Sheol I. Given to humans if they show fear during a test. Can be used as a synonym for *coward*.

Zeitgeist: [noun] German word meaning the 'spirit of the age'. Literally 'time spirit'. Most voyants use the word metaphorically, but some worship the zeitgeist as a deity.

Acknowledgements

I owe a great debt to the Godwin family, most of all to David, for giving me such a warm welcome into the world of publishing. A big hand for Kirsty McLachlan, Caitlin Ingham and Anna Watkins for all their hard work on the film and foreign rights side. I couldn't have asked for a better agency than I've found at DGA.

To the Bloomsbury team: before meeting you, I had no idea just how much passion and teamwork went into creating a book. I'd like to express my gratitude to the inimitable Alexandra Pringle, whose passion for this novel has been the best inspiration I could ask for; to Alexa von Hirschberg, my wonderful editor, who has gone miles beyond the call of duty and been there for me at the drop of a hat; and to Rachel Mannheimer, Justine Taylor and Sarah Barlow, all of whom have helped make *The Bone Season* the absolute best it could be. Heartfelt thanks to Katie Bond, Jude Drake, Amanda Shipp, Ianthe Cox-Willmott, Eleanor Weil and Oliver Holden-Rea in the UK, and to George Gibson, Cristina Gilbert, Nancy Miller, Marie Coolman, Laura Keefe and Sara Mercurio in the US. You've all been fantastic.

Andy Serkis, Jonathan Cavendish, Chloe Sizer, Will Tennant and the rest of the team at Imaginarium: it is a privilege to be working with you. Thank you for your dedication to every aspect of this book, far beyond the visual. On an artistic note, many thanks are owed to András Bereznay for designing the map; David Mann for the beautiful cover – you are the Mann – and Leiana Leatutufu for being my own personal automatiste.

To say this book has been my life for the past two years would be an understatement. There are far too many of you to name in this small space, but thank you so much to the friends that have been there for me over those years – and before them. A particularly big thanks to Neil Dymond and Fran Tracey; to Emma Forward, my inspiring English teacher; and to Rian, Jesica and Richard for inviting me along to Ireland. If not for you, I'd never have met Molly Malone in person.

To my translators around the world, thank you for making this book available in more languages than I could ever master. Many thanks to Flo and Alie for giving me a hand with French and Serbian names, and to Devora at Agam Books for sharing her knowledge of Hebrew.

Thank you to all the people that have followed my blog and Twitter feed on the road to publication, especially Susan Hill. Your support has given me so much confidence. Extra thanks to the staff and students at St Anne's College for being so kind and accommodating over this last chaotic year. Stanner love.

And of course, thank you to my family – most of all to Mum, for giving me constant strength and support, and Mike, my super step-father and the undisputed king of tasseography. The two of you have handled me at my worst, so in the spirit of Marilyn Monroe, you sure as hell deserve me at my best.

JD, thanks for being my muse for this one. You are my number one dead poet. And last but not least, thank you to Ali Smith for giving me the courage to send *The Bone Season* out into the world.

Thank you all for taking a chance on a dreamer.

A fugitive who will not be silenced

THE
MIME ORDER

It is a dark time for clairvoyants. Scion is in league with the Rephaim, an extraordinarily powerful, otherworldly race, who wish to make humans their slaves.

In an unprecedented feat of bravery, Paige Mahoney has succeeded in leading a mass break-out of the brutal camp, Sheol I, where she and other clairvoyants have been systematically imprisoned.

Paige is desperate to reach the safety of the London underworld, but the ruthless leader of the Rephaim, Nashira Sargas, is not likely to let her escape so easily...

'Language as rich as a figgy pudding, the best terminology in the genre and gripping, edge-of-the-seat plotting to boot ... Fabulous'
Daily Mail

'A trailblazer ... The way Shannon's characters shift, backstab and fall are as fascinating as the twists and turns of the plot'
Independent

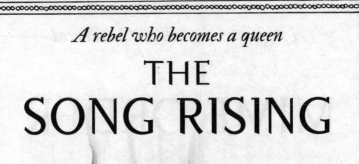

A rebel who becomes a queen

THE
SONG RISING

Following a bloody battle against foes on every side, Paige Mahoney
has risen to the dangerous position of Underqueen, ruling over
London's criminal population.

But, having turned her back on Jaxon Hall and with vengeful enemies
still at large, the task of stabilising the fractured underworld has
never seemed so challenging.

Little does Paige know that her reign may be cut short by the introduction
of Senshield, a deadly technology that spells doom for the clairvoyant
community and the world as they know it...

Be aware, my good Reader, that this Pamphlet, no matter how controversial its content, must never fall into enemy Hands

ON THE MERITS OF

UNNATURALNESS

being an extraordinary treatise upon the

SEVEN ORDERS OF CLAIRVOYANCE

The most important piece of clairvoyant literature written in the twenty-first century, *On the Merits of Unnaturalness* is a pamphlet first published anonymously in 2031 by Jaxon Hall, the voyant who would later become the mime-lord known as the White Binder.

Hall was the first to index both known and supposed forms of Unnaturalness, resulting in the classification of the Seven Orders. This controversial piece of literature spread across the voyant underworld like a plague, revolutionising the syndicate but also creating discord in the form of brutal gang wars between the newly divided categories, the scars of which can still be seen today.

Revelatory and subversive, *On the Merits of Unnaturalness* is a must-read for any reader with a desire to further immerse themselves in the incredible world of Samantha Shannon's *The Bone Season*.

'Dynamic and direct ... There is exciting breadth to Shannon's world'
Evening Standard

'Enough to transport even hardened sceptics of the fantasy genre into its imaginative realm'
Metro

'We are completely sucked into her world'
Huffington Post